ALSO BY DON WINSLOW

*The Winter of Frankie Machine*

*The Power of the Dog*

*California Fire and Life*

*The Death and Life of Bobby Z*

*While Drowning in the Desert*

*A Long Walk up the Water Slide*

*Way Down on the High Lonely*

*The Trail to Buddha's Mirror*

*A Cool Breeze on the Underground*

# The
# Dawn
# Patrol

# The Dawn Patrol

**DON WINSLOW**

Alfred A. Knopf    New York  2008

*This Is a Borzoi Book*
*Published by Alfred A. Knopf*

Copyright © 2008 by Don Winslow

All rights reserved. Published in the United States by Alfred A. Knopf, a division of Random House, Inc., New York, and in Canada by Random House of Canada Limited, Toronto.
www.aaknopf.com

Knopf, Borzoi Books, and the colophon are registered trademarks of Random House, Inc.

Library of Congress Cataloging-in-Publication Data
Winslow, Don, [date]
The dawn patrol / by Don Winslow.    1st ed.
p.   cm.
"This is a Borzoi Book."
ISBN 978-0-307-26620-0 (alk. paper)
1. Surfers—Fiction.    2. Private investigators—Fiction.
3. California—Fiction.    I. Title.
PS3573.I5326D38    2008
813'.54—dc22        2008006531

Manufactured in the United States of America
First Edition

wave (n): a disturbance that travels through a medium from one location to another location.

Let me take you down, cos I'm going to,
Strawberry Fields. . . .

Lennon/McCartney

# The Dawn Patrol

# 1

The marine layer wraps a soft silver blanket over the coast.

The sun is just coming over the hills to the east, and Pacific Beach is still asleep.

The ocean is a color that is not quite blue, not quite green, not quite black, but something somewhere between all three.

Out on the line, Boone Daniels straddles his old longboard like a cowboy on his pony.

He's on The Dawn Patrol.

# 2

The girls look like ghosts.

Coming out of the early-morning mist, their silver forms emerge from a thin line of trees as the girls pad through the wet grass that edges the field. The dampness muffles their footsteps, so they approach silently, and the mist that wraps around their legs makes them look as if they're floating.

Like spirits who died as children.

There are eight of them and they *are* children; the oldest is fourteen, the youngest ten. They walk toward the waiting men in unconscious lockstep.

The men bend over the mist like giants over clouds, peering down into their universe. But the men aren't giants; they're workers, and their universe is the seemingly endless strawberry field that they do not rule, but that rules them. They're glad for the cool mist—it will burn off soon enough and leave them to the sun's indifferent mercy.

The men are stoop laborers, bent at the waist for hours at a time, tending to the plants. They've made the dangerous odyssey up from Mexico to work in these fields, to send money back to their families south of the border.

They live in primitive camps of corrugated tin shacks, jerry-rigged tents, and lean-tos hidden deep in the narrow canyons above the fields. There are no women in the camps, and the men are lonely. Now they look up to sneak guilty glances at the wraithlike girls coming out of the mist. Glances of need, even though many of these men are fathers, with daughters the ages of these girls.

Between the edge of the field and the banks of the river stands a thick bed of reeds, into which the men have hacked little dugouts, almost caves. Now some of the men go into the reeds and pray that the dawn will not come too soon or burn too brightly and expose their shame to the eyes of God.

# 3

It's dawn at the Crest Motel, too.

Sunrise isn't a sight that a lot of the residents see, unless it's from the other side—unless they're just going to bed instead of just getting up.

Only two people are awake now, and neither of them is the desk clerk, who's catching forty in the office, his butt settled into the chair, his feet propped on the counter. Doesn't matter. Even if he were awake, he couldn't see the little balcony of room 342, where the woman is going over the railing.

Her nightgown flutters above her.

An inadequate parachute.

She misses the pool by a couple of feet and her body lands on the concrete with a dull thump.

Not loud enough to wake anyone up.

The guy who tossed her looks down just long enough to make sure she's dead. He sees her neck at the funny angle, like a broken doll. Watches her blood, black in the faint light, spread toward the pool.

Water seeking water.

# 4

"Epic macking crunchy."

That's how Hang Twelve describes the imminent big swell to Boone Daniels, who actually understands what Hang Twelve is saying, because Boone speaks fluent Surfbonics. Indeed, off to Boone's right, just to the south, waves are smacking the pilings beneath Crystal Pier. The ocean feels heavy, swollen, pregnant with promise.

The Dawn Patrol—Boone, Hang Twelve, Dave the Love God, Johnny Banzai, High Tide, and Sunny Day—sits out there on the line, talking while they wait for the next set to come in. They all wear black winter wet suits that cover them from their wrists to their ankles, because the early-morning water is cold, especially now that it's stirred up by the approaching storm.

This morning's interstitial conversation revolves around the big swell, a once-every-twenty-years burgeoning of the surf now rolling toward the San Diego coast like an out-of-control freight train. It's due in two days, and with it the gray winter sky, some rain, and the biggest waves that any of The Dawn Patrol have seen in their adult lives.

It's going to be, as Hang Twelve puts it, "epic macking crunchy."

Which, roughly translated from Surfbonics, is a term of approbation.

It's going to be good, Boone knows. They might even see twenty-foot peaks coming in every thirty seconds or so. Double overheads, tubes like tunnels, real thunder crushers that could easily take you over the falls and dump you into the washing machine.

Only the best surfers need apply.

Boone qualifies.

While it's an exaggeration to say that Boone could surf before he could walk, it's the dead flat truth that he could surf before he could run. Boone is the ultimate "locie"—he was conceived on the beach, born half a mile away, and raised three blocks from where the surf breaks at high tide. His dad surfed; his mom surfed—hence the conceptual session on the sand. In fact, his mom surfed well into the sixth month of her pregnancy, so maybe it isn't an exaggeration to say that Boone could surf before he could walk.

So Boone's been a waterman all his life, and then some.

The ocean is his backyard, his haven, his playground, his refuge, his church. He goes into the ocean to get well, to get clean, to remind himself that life is a ride. Boone believes that a wave is God's tangible message that all the great things in life are free. Boone gets free every day, usually two or three times a day, but always, always, out on The Dawn Patrol.

Boone Daniels lives to surf.

He doesn't want to talk about the big swell right now, because talking about it might jinx it, cause the swell to lie down and die into the deep recesses of the north Pacific. So even though Hang Twelve is looking at him with his usual expression of unabashed hero worship, Boone changes the subject to an old standard out on the Pacific Beach Dawn Patrol line.

The List of Things That Are Good.

They started the List of Things That Are Good about fifteen years ago, back when they were in high school, when Boone and Dave's social studies teacher challenged them to "get their priorities straight."

The list is flexible—items are added or deleted; the rankings change—but the current List of Things That Are Good would read as follows, if, that is, it were written down, which it isn't:

1. Double overheads.
2. Reef break.
3. The tube.
4. Girls who will sit on the beach and watch you ride double overheads, reef break, and the tube. (Inspiring Sunny's remark that "Girls watch—women *ride*.")

5. Free stuff.
6. Longboards.
7. Anything made by O'Neill.
8. All-female outrigger canoe teams.
9. Fish tacos.
10. Big Wednesday.

"I propose," Boone says to the line at large, "moving fish tacos over all-female outrigger canoe teams."

"From ninth to eighth?" Johnny Banzai asks, his broad, generally serious face breaking into a smile. Johnny Banzai's real name isn't Banzai, of course. It's Kodani, but if you're a Japanese-American and a seriously radical, nose-first, balls-out, hard-charging surfer, you're just going to get glossed either "Kamikaze" or "Banzai," you just are. But as Boone and Dave the Love God decided that Johnny is just too rational to be suicidal, they decided on Banzai.

When Johnny Banzai isn't banzaiing, he's a homicide detective with the San Diego Police Department, and Boone knows that he welcomes the opportunity to argue about things that aren't grim. So he's on it. "Basically flip-flopping them?" Johnny Banzai asks. "Based on what?"

"Deep thought and careful consideration," Boone replies.

Hang Twelve is shocked. The young soul surfer stares at Boone with a look of hurt innocence, his wet goatee dropping to the black neoprene of his winter wet suit, his light brown dreadlocks falling on his shoulder as he cocks his head. "But, Boone—all-female outrigger canoe teams?"

Hang Twelve loves the women of the all-female outrigger canoe teams. Whenever they paddle by, he just sits on his board and stares.

"Listen," Boone says, "most of those women play for the other team."

"What other team?" Hang Twelve asks.

"He's so young," Johnny observes, and as usual, his observation is accurate. Hang Twelve is a dozen years younger than the rest of The Dawn Patrol. They tolerate him because he's such an enthusiastic surfer and sort of Boone's puppy; plus, he gives them the locals' discount at the surf shop he works at.

"What other team?" Hang Twelve asks urgently.

Sunny Day leans over her board and whispers to him.

Sunny looks just like her name. Her blond hair glows like sunshine. A force of nature—tall, long-legged—Sunny is exactly what Brian Wilson meant when he wrote that he wished they all could be California girls.

Except that Brian's dream girl usually sat on the beach, whereas Sunny surfs. She's the best surfer on The Dawn Patrol, better than Boone, and the coming big swell could lift her from waitress to full-time professional surfer. One good photo of Sunny shredding a big wave could get her a sponsorship from one of the major surf-clothing companies, and then there'll be no stopping her. Now she takes it upon herself to explain to Hang Twelve that most of the females on the all-female outrigger canoe teams are rigged out for females.

Hang Twelve lets out a devastated groan.

"You just ripped a boy's dreams," Boone tells Sunny.

"Not necessarily," Dave the Love God says with a smug smile.

"Don't even start," Sunny says.

"Is it my bad," Dave asks, "that women love me?"

It's not, really. Dave the Love God has a face and physique that would have caused a run on marble in ancient Greece. But it's not even so much Dave's body that gets him sex as it is his confidence. Dave is confident that he's going to get laid, and he's in a profession that puts him in a perfect position to have a shot at every snow-zone *turista* who comes to San Diego to get tanned. He's a lifeguard, and this is how he got his moniker, because Johnny Banzai, who completes the *New York Times* crossword in ink, said, "You're not a 'life guard'; you're a 'love god.' Get it?"

Yeah, the whole Dawn Patrol got it, because they have all seen Dave the Love Guard crawl up to his lifeguard tower while guzzling handfuls of vitamin E to replace the depletion from the night before and get ready for the night ahead.

"They actually give me binoculars," he marveled to Boone one day, "with the explicit expectation that I will use them to look at scantily clad women. And some people say there's no God."

So if any hominid with a package could get an all-female outrigger canoe team member (or several of them) to issue a gender exemption for a night or two, it would be Dave, and judging by the self-satisfied lascivious smile on his grille right now, he probably has.

Hang Twelve is still not convinced. "Yeah, but, fish tacos?"

"It depends on the kind of fish in the taco," says High Tide, né Josiah Pamavatuu, weighing in on the subject. Literally weighing in, because the

Samoan crashes the scales at well over three and a half bills. Hence the tag "High Tide," because the ocean level rises anytime he gets in the water. So High Tide's opinion on food commands respect, because he obviously knows what he's talking about. The whole crew is aware that your Pacific Island types know their fish. "Are you talking about yellowtail, ono, opah, mahimahi, shark, or what? It makes a difference, ranking-wise."

"Everything," Boone says, "tastes better on a tortilla."

This is an article of faith with Boone. He's lived his life with it and believes it to be true. You take anything—fish, chicken, beef, cheese, eggs, even peanut butter and jelly—and fold them in the motherly embrace of a warm flour tortilla and all those foods respond to the love by upping their game.

Everything does taste better on a tortilla.

"Outside!" High Tide yells.

Boone looks over his shoulder to see the first wave of what looks to be a tasty set coming in.

"Party wave!" hollers Dave the Love God, and he, High Tide, Johnny, and Hang Twelve get on it, sharing the ride into shore. Boone and Sunny hang back for the second wave, which is a little bigger, a little fuller, and has a better shape.

"Your wave!" Boone yells to her.

"Chivalrous or patronizing, you decide!" Sunny yells back, but she paddles in. Boone gets on the wave right behind her and they ride the shoulder in together, a skillful pas de deux on the white water.

Boone and Sunny walk up onto the beach, because the morning session is over and The Dawn Patrol is coming in. This is because, with the exception of Boone, they all have real j-o-b-s.

So Johnny's already stepping out of the outdoor shower and sitting in the front seat of his car putting on his detective clothes—blue shirt, brown tweed jacket, khaki slacks—when his cell phone goes off. Johnny listens to the call, then says, "A woman took a header off a motel balcony. Another day in paradise."

"I don't miss *that*," Boone says.

"And it doesn't miss you," Johnny replies.

This is true. When Boone pulled the pin at SDPD, his lieutenant's only regret was that it hadn't been attached to a grenade. Despite his remark, Johnny disagrees—Boone was a good cop. A very good cop.

It was a shame what happened.

But now Boone is following High Tide's eyes back out to the ocean, at which the big man is gazing with an almost reverential intensity.

"It's coming," High Tide says. "The swell."

"Big?" Boone asks.

"Not big," says High Tide. "Huge."

A real thunder crusher.

Like, ka-*boom*.

# 5

What is a wave anyway?

We know one when we see one, but what *is* it?

The physicists call it an "energy-transport phenomenon."

The dictionary says it's "a disturbance that travels through a medium from one location to another location."

A disturbance.

It's certainly that.

Something gets disturbed. That is, something strikes something else and sets off a vibration. Clap your hands right now and you'll hear a sound. What you're actually hearing is a sound *wave*. Something struck something else and it set off a vibration that strikes your eardrum.

The vibration is energy. It's transported through the phenomenon of a wave from one location to the other.

The water itself doesn't actually move. What happens is one particle of water bumps into the next, which bumps into the next, and so on and so forth until it hits something. It's like that idiot wave at a sports event—the *people* don't move around the stadium, but the *wave* does. The energy flows from one person to another.

So when you're riding a wave, you're not riding water. The water is the medium, but what you're really riding is energy.

Very cool.

Hitching an energy ride.

Billions of $H_2O$ particles work together to transport you from one place to another, which is very generous when you think about it. That last statement is, of course, airy-fairy soul-surfer bullshit—the wave doesn't care whether you're in it or not. Particles of water are inanimate objects that don't know anything, much less "care"; the water is just doing what water does when it gets goosed by energy.

It makes waves.

A wave, any kind of wave, has a specific shape. The particles knocking into one another don't just bump along in a flat line, but move up and down—hence the wave. Prior to the "disturbance," the water particles are at rest, in technical terminology, *equilibrium*. What happens is that the energy disturbs the equilibrium; it "displaces" the particles from their state of rest. When the energy reaches its maximum potential "displacement" ("positive displacement"), the wave "crests." Then it drops, *below* the equilibrium line, to its "negative displacement," aka, the "trough." Simply put, it has highs, lows, and middles, just like life its own self.

Yeah, except it's a little more complicated than that, especially if you're talking about the kind of wave that you can ride, *especially* the kind of giant wave that's right now rolling toward Pacific Beach with bad intent.

Basically, there are two kinds of waves.

Most waves are "surface waves." They're caused by lunar pull and wind, which are sources of the disturbance. These are your average, garden-variety, everyday, Joe Lunchbucket waves. They show up on time, punch the clock, and they range in size from small to medium to, occasionally, large.

Surface waves, of course, give surfing its name, because it appears to the unenlightened eye that surfers are riding the surface of the water. Surfers are, if you will, "surfacing."

Despite this distinction, surface waves are the mules of the surfing world, unheralded beasts of burden not incapable, however, of kicking their traces from time to time when whipped into a frenzy by the wind.

A lot of people think that it's strong winds that make big waves, but this really isn't true. Wind can cause some big surf, blowing an otherwise-average wave into a tall peak, but most of the energy—the disturbance—is on the surface. These waves have height, but they lack depth. All the action is on top—it's mostly show; it's literally superficial.

And wind can ruin surf, and often does. If the wind is blowing across the wave it will ruin its shape, or it can make the surf choppy, or, if it's coming straight in off the ocean, it can drive the crest of the wave down, flattening it out and making it unridable.

What you want is a gentle, steady, offshore wind that blows into the face of the wave and holds it up for you.

The other kind of wave is the *sub*surface wave, which starts, duh, under the water. If surface waves are your middleweight boxers, dancing and shooting jabs, the subsurface wave is your heavyweight, coming in flat-footed, throwing knockout punches from the (ocean) floor. This wave is the superstar, the genuine badass, the take-your-lunch money, walk-off-with-your-girlfriend, give-me-those-fucking-sneakers, *thank you for playing and now what parting gifts do we have for our contestant, Vanna* wave.

If surface waves lack depth, the subsurface wave has more bottom than a Sly and the Family Stone riff. It's deeper than Kierkegaard and Wittgenstein combined. It's *heavy,* my friend; it ain't your brother. It's the hate child of rough sex at the bottom of the sea.

There's a whole world down there. In fact, *most* of the world is down there. You have enormous mountain ranges, vast plains, trenches, and canyons. You have tectonic plates, and when they shift and scrape against each other, you have earthquakes. Gigantic underwater earthquakes, violent as a Mike Tyson off meds, that set off one big honking disturbance.

At its most benign, a big beautiful swell to ride; at its most malevolent, a mass-murdering tsunami.

This is a disturbance, a mass transportation of energy phenom, that will travel thousands of miles either to give you the ride of your life or fuck you up, and it doesn't care which.

This is what's rolling toward Pacific Beach as The Dawn Patrol gets out of the water this particular morning. An undersea earthquake up near the Aleutian Islands is hurtling literally thousands of miles to come crash on Pacific Beach and go—

Ka-boom.

# 6

Ka-boom is good.

If you're Boone Daniels and live for waves that make big noises.

He's always been this way. Since birth and before, if you buy all that stuff about prenatal auditory influences. You know how some mothers hang out listening to Mozart to give their babies a taste for the finer things? Boone's mom, Dee, used to sit on the beach and stroke her belly to the rhythm of the waves.

To the prenatal Boone, the ocean was indistinguishable from his mother's heartbeat. Hang Twelve might *call* the sea "Mother Ocean," but to Boone it really is. And before his son hit the terrible twos, Brett Daniels would put the kid in front of him on a longboard, paddle out, and then lift the boy on his shoulder while they rode in. Casual observers—that is, tourists—would be appalled, all like, "What if you drop him?"

"I'm not *going* to drop him," Boone's dad, Brett, would reply.

Until Boone was about three, and then Brett would *intentionally* drop him into the shallow white water, just to give him the feel of it, to let him know that other than a few bubbles in the nose, nothing bad was going to happen. Young Boone would pop up, giggling like crazy, and ask for his dad to "do it again."

Every once in a while, a disapproving onlooker would threaten to call Child Protective Services, and Dee would reply, "That's what he's doing—he's protecting his child."

Which was the truth.

You raise a kid in PB, and you know that his DNA is going to drive him out there on a board, you'd *better* teach him what the ocean can do. You'd better teach him how to live, not die, in the water, and you'd better teach him young. You teach him about riptides and undertow. You teach him not to panic.

Protect his child?

Listen, when Brett and Dee would have birthday parties at the condo complex pool, and all Boone's little friends would come over, Brett Daniels would set his chair at the edge of the pool and tell the other parents, "No offense, have a good time, have some tacos and some brews, but I'm sitting here and I'm not talking to anybody."

Then he'd sit at the edge of the kid-crowded pool and never take his eyes off the *bottom* of the pool, not for a single second, because Brett knew that nothing too bad was going to happen on the surface of the water, that kids drown at the bottom of the pool when no one is watching.

Brett was watching. He'd sit there for as long as the party lasted, in Zen-like concentration until the last kid came out shivering and was wrapped in a towel and went to wolf down some pizza and soda. Then Brett would go eat and hang out with the other parents, and there were no irredeemable tragedies, no lifelong regrets ("I only turned my back for a few seconds") at those parties.

The first time Brett and Dee let their then seven-year-old boy paddle out alone into some small and close beach break, their collective heart was in their collective throat. They were watching like hawks, even though they knew that every lifeguard on the beach and every surfer in the water also had their eyes on young Boone Daniels, and if anything bad had happened, a mob would have showed up to pull him out of the soup.

It was hard, but Brett and Dee stood there as Boone got up and fell, got up and fell, got up and fell—and paddled back out, and did it again and again until he got up and stayed up and rode that wave in while a whole beach full of people played it casual and pretended not to notice.

It was even harder when Boone got to that age, right about ten, when he wanted to go the beach with his buddies and didn't want Mom or Dad showing up to embarrass him. It was hard to let him go, and sit back and worry, but that was also a part of protecting their child, to protect him from perpetual childhood, to trust that they had done their job and taught him what he needed to know.

So by the time he was eleven, Boone was your classic gremmie.

A gremmie is nature's revenge.

A gremmie, aka "grom," is a longhaired, sun-bleached, overtanned, preadolescent, water-borne, pain-in-the-ass little surfer. A gremmie is karmic payback for every annoying, obnoxious, shitty little thing *you* did when you were that age. A gremmie will hog your wave, ruin your session, jam up the snack bar, and talk like he knows what he's talking about. Worse, your gremmie runs in packs with his little gremmie buddies—in Boone's case, this had been little Johnny Banzai and a young Dave the yet-to-be Love God—all of them equally vile, disgusting, smart-mouthed, obscene, gross little bastards. When they're not surfing, they're skateboarding, and when they're not surfing or skateboarding, they're reading comics, trying to get their filthy little mitts on porn, trying (unsuccessfully) to pull real live girls, scheming to get adults to buy beer for them, or trying to score weed. The reason parents let their kids surf is that it's the *least* sketchy thing that the board monkeys get up to.

As a gremmie, Boone got his fair share of shit from the big guys, but he also got a little bit of a pass because he was Brett and Dee Daniels's kid, glossed "the Spawn of Mr. and Mrs. Satan" by a few of the crankier old guys.

Boone grew out of it. All gremmies do, or they're chased out of the lineup, and besides, it was pretty clear early on that Boone was something special. He was doing scary-good things for his age, then scary-good things for *any* age. It wasn't long before the better surf teams came around, inviting him onto their junior squads, and it was a dead lock that Boone would take home a few armloads of trophies and get himself a sweet sponsorship from one of the surf-gear companies.

Except Boone said no.

Fourteen years old, and he turned away from it.

"How come?" his dad asked.

Boone shrugged. "I just don't do it for that," he said. "I do it for . . ."

He had no words for that, and Brett and Dee totally understood. They got on the horn to their old pals in the surf world and basically said, "Thanks but no thanks. The kid just wants to surf."

The kid did.

# 7

Petra Hall steers her starter BMW west on Garnet Avenue.

She alternately watches the road and looks at a slip of paper in her hand, comparing the address to the building to her right.

The address—111 Garnet Avenue—is the correct listing for "Boone Daniels, Private Investigator," but the building appears to be not an office but a surf shop. At least that's what the sign says, a rather unimaginative yet descriptive PACIFIC SURF inscribed over a rather unimaginative yet descriptive painting of a breaking wave. And, indeed, looking through the window she can see surfboards, body boards, bathing suits, and, being that the building is half a block from the beach, 111 Garnet Avenue would certainly appear to be a surf shop.

Except that it is supposed to be the office of Boone Daniels, private investigator.

Petra grew up in a climate where the sun is more rumor than reality, so her skin is so pale and delicate that it's almost transparent, in stark contrast to her indigo black hair. Her charcoal gray, very professional, I'm-a-serious-career-woman suit hides a figure that is at the same time slim and generous, but what you're really going to look at is her eyes.

Are they blue? Or are they gray?

Like the ocean, it depends on her mood.

She parks the car next door in front of The Sundowner Lounge and goes into Pacific Surf, where a pale young man behind the counter, who would appear to be some sort of white Rastafarian, is playing a video game.

"Sorry," Petra says, "I'm looking for a Mr. Daniels?"

Hang Twelve looks up from his game to see this gorgeous woman standing in front of him. His stares for a second; then he gets it together enough to shout up the stairs, "Cheerful, brah, civilian here looking for Boone!"

A head peers down from the staircase. Ben Carruthers, glossed "Cheerful" by the PB crew, looks to be about sixty years old, has a steel gray crew cut and a scowl as he barks, "Call me 'brah' one more time and I'll rip your tongue out."

"Sorry, I forgot," Hang Twelve says. "Like, the *moana* was epic tasty this sesh and I slid over the ax of this gnarler and just foffed, totally shredded it, and I'm still amped from the ocean hit, so my bad, brah."

Cheerful looks at Petra and says, "Sometimes we have entire fascinating conversations in which I don't understand a word that is said." He turns back to Hang Twelve. "You're what I have instead of a cat. Don't make me get a cat."

He disappears back up the stairs with a single word, "Follow."

Petra goes up the stairs, where Cheerful—a tall man, probably six-six, very thin, wearing a red plaid shirt tucked into khaki trousers—is already hunched over a desk. Well, she takes it on faith that it's a desk because she can't actually see the surface underneath the clutter of papers, coffee cups, ball hats, taco wrappers, newspapers, and magazines. But the saturnine man is punching buttons on an old-fashioned adding machine, so she decides that it is, indeed, a desk.

The "office," if you can grace it with that name, is a mess, a hovel, a bedlam, except for the back wall, which is neat and ordered. Several black wet suits hang neatly from a steel coatrack, and a variety of surfboards lean against the wall, sorted and ordered by size and shape.

"Forty-some years ago," Cheerful says, "a bra was something I tried with trembling fingers and little success to unsnap. Now I find that I *am* a brah. Such are the insults of aging. What can I do for you?"

"Would you be Mr. Daniels?" Petra asks.

"I *would* be Sean Connery," Cheerful replies, "but he's already taken. So is Boone, but I wouldn't be him even if I could."

"Do you know when Mr. Daniels will be in?"

"No. Do you?"

Petra shakes her head. "Which is why I asked."

Cheerful looks up from his calculations. This girl doesn't take any crap. Cheerful likes that, so he says, "Let me explain something to you: Boone doesn't wear a watch; he wears a sundial."

"I take it Mr. Daniels is somewhat laid-back?"

"If Boone was any more laid-back," Cheerful says, "he'd be horizontal."

# 8

Boone walks up Garnet Avenue from the beach in the company of Sunny.

Nothing unusual about that—they've been in and out of each other's company for coming on ten years.

Sunny originally flashed onto The Dawn Patrol like daytime lightning. Paddled out, took her place in the lineup like she'd been born there. Boone was about to launch into a six-foot right break when Sunny jumped in and took it from him. Boone was still poised on the lip when this blond image zipped past him as if he were a buoy.

Dave laughed. "Man, that babe just ripped your heart out and fed it to you."

Boone wasn't so freaking amused. He caught the next wave in and found her coming back out through the white water.

"Yo, Blondie," Boone said. "You jumped my wave."

"My name isn't 'Blondie,'" Sunny said. "And when did you buy the beach?"

"I was lined up."

"You were late."

"My ass I was."

"Your ass was late," Sunny said. "What's the matter, the big man can't take getting beat by a girl?"

"I can take it," Boone said. Even to himself, it sounded lame.

"Apparently not," Sunny said.

Boone took a closer look at her. "Do I know you?"

"I don't know," Sunny said. "Do you?"

She lay out on her board and started to paddle back out. Boone had no choice but to follow. Catching up with her wasn't easy.

"You go to Pac High?" Boone asked when he got alongside.

"Used to," Sunny said. "I'm at SDSU now."

"I went to Pac High," Boone said.

"I know."

"You do?"

"I remember you," Sunny said.

"Uh, I guess I don't remember you."

"I know."

She kicked it up and paddled away from him. Then she spent the rest of the session kicking his ass. She took over the water like she owned it, which she did, that afternoon.

"She's a specimen," Dave said as he and Boone watched her from the lineup.

"Eyes off," Boone said. "She's mine."

"If she'll have you." Dave snorted.

Turned out she would. She outsurfed him until the sun went down, then waited for him on the beach until he dragged his ass in.

"I could get used to this," Boone said to her.

"Get used to what?"

"Getting beat by a girl."

"My name's Sunny Day," she said ruefully.

"I'm not laughing," he said. "Mine's Boone Daniels."

They went to dinner and then they went to bed. It was natural, inevitable—they both knew that neither one of them could swim out of that current. As if either one of them wanted to.

After that, they were inseparable.

"You and Boone should get married and produce offspring," Johnny Banzai told them a few weeks later. "You owe it to the world of surfing."

Like, the child of Boone and Sunny would be some sort of mutant superfreak. But marriage?

Not happening.

"CCBHS" is how Sunny explained herself on this issue. "Classic California broken home syndrome. There ought to be a telethon."

Emily Wendelin's hippie dad had left her hippie mom when Emily was three years old. Her mom never got over it, and neither did Emily, who learned not to give her heart to a man because men don't stay.

Emily's mom retreated into herself, becoming "emotionally unavailable," as the shrinks would say, and it was her grandmother—her mother's mother—who really raised the girl. Eleanor Day imbued Emily with her strength, her grace, and her warmth, and it was Eleanor who gave the girl the nickname "Sunny," because her granddaughter lit up her life. When Sunny turned eighteen, she changed her surname to Day, regardless of how pseudohippie it sounded.

"I'm matrilineal," she explained.

It was her grandmother who persuaded her to go to college, and her grandmother who understood when, after the first year, Sunny decided that higher education, at least in a formal setting, wasn't for her.

"It's my fault," Eleanor had said.

Her house was a block and a half from the beach, and Eleanor had taken her granddaughter there almost every day. When eight-year-old Sunny said that she wanted to surf, it was Eleanor who saw that a board was under the Christmas tree. It was Eleanor who stood on the beach while the girl rode wave after wave, Eleanor who smiled patiently when the sun went down and Emily would wave from the break, holding up one imploring finger, which meant "Please, Grandma, one more wave." It was Eleanor who went to the early tournaments, who sat calmly in the ER with the girl, assuring her that the stitches in her chin wouldn't leave a scar, and that if they did, it would be an interesting one.

So when Sunny came to her and explained that she didn't want to go to college, and tearfully apologized for letting her down, Eleanor said that it was *her* fault for introducing Emily to the ocean.

"So what do you intend to do?" Eleanor asked.

"I want to be a professional surfer."

Eleanor didn't raise an eyebrow. Or laugh, or argue, or scoff. She simply said, "Well, be a great one."

*Be* a great surfer, not *marry* one.

Not like the options were mutually exclusive, but neither Sunny nor Boone was interested in getting married, or even living together. Life was just fine the way it was—surfing, hanging out, making love, and surfing. It was all one and the same thing, one long, unbroken rhythm.

Good days.

Sunny waited tables in PB while she worked on her surfing career; Boone was happy being a cop, a uniformed patrolman with the SDPD.

What busted it up was a girl named Rain Sweeny.

Things changed after Rain Sweeny. After she was gone, Boone never

really came back. It was like there was this distance between Boone and
Sunny now, like a deep, slow current pulling them apart.

And now this big swell is coming, and they both sense that it's bringing
a bigger change.

They stand outside Boone's office.

"So . . . late," Sunny says.

"Late."

Walking away, Sunny wonders if it's *too* late.

Like she's already lost something she didn't even know she wanted.

Boone walks into Pacific Surf.

Hang Twelve looks up from *Grand Theft Auto 3* and says, "There's an
inland betty upstairs looking for you. And Cheerful's way aggro."

"Cheerful's *always* aggravated," Boone replies. "That's what makes
him Cheerful. Who's the woman?"

"Dunno." Hang Twelve shrugs. "But, Boone, she's *smokin'* hot."

Boone goes upstairs. The woman isn't smokin' hot; she's smokin' *cold*.
But she is definitely smokin'.

"Mr. Daniels?" Petra says.

"Guilty."

She offers her hand, and Boone is about to shake it, when he realizes
that she's handing him her card.

"Petra Hall," she says. "From the law firm Burke, Spitz and Culver."

Boone knows the law firm of Burke, Spitz and Culver. They have an
office in one of the glass castles in downtown San Diego and have sent him
a lot of work over the past few years.

And Alan Burke surfs.

Not every day, but a lot of weekends, and sometimes Boone sees him
out on the line during the Gentlemen's Hour. So he knows Alan Burke, but
he doesn't know this small, beautiful woman with the midnight hair and
the blue eyes.

Or are they gray?

"You must be new with the firm," Boone says.

Petra's appalled as she watches Boone reach behind his back and pull the cord that's connected to a zipper. The back of the wet suit opens, and then Boone gently peels the suit off his right arm, then his left, then rolls it down his chest. She starts to turn away as he rolls the suit down over his waist, and then she sees the flower pattern of his North Shore board trunks appear.

She's looking at a man who appears to be in his late twenties or early thirties, but it's hard to tell because he has a somewhat boyish face, made all the more so by his slightly too long, unkempt, sun-streaked brown hair, which is either intentionally unstylishly long or has simply not been cut recently. He's tall, just an inch or two shorter than the saturnine old man still banging away on the adding machine, and he has the wide shoulders and long arm muscles of a swimmer.

Boone's oblivious to her observation.

He's all about the swell.

"There's a swell rolling down from the Aleutians," he says as he finishes rolling the wet suit over his ankles. "It's going to hit sometime in the next two days and High Tide says it's only going to last a few hours. Biggest swell of the last four years and maybe the next four. Humongous waves."

"Real BBM," Hang Twelve says from the staircase.

"Is anyone watching the store?" Cheerful asks.

"There's no one down there," Hang Twelve says.

"'BBM'?" Petra asks.

"Brown boardshorts material," Hang Twelve says helpfully.

"Lovely," Petra says, wishing she hadn't asked. "Thank you."

"Anyway," Boone says as he steps into the small bathroom, turns on the shower, and carefully rinses not himself but the wet suit, "everyone's going out. Johnny Banzai's going to take a mental-health day, High Tide's calling in sick, Dave the Love God's on the beach anyway, and Sunny, well, you know Sunny's going to be out. Everyone is *stoked*."

Petra delivers the bad news.

She has work for him to do.

"Our firm," Petra says, "is defending Coastal Insurance Company in a suit against it by one Daniel Silvieri, aka Dan Silver, owner of a strip club called Silver Dan's."

"Don't know the place," Boone says.

"Yeah you do, Boone," Hang Twelve says. "You and Dave took me there for my birthday."

"We took you to Chuck E. Cheese's," Boone snaps. "Back-paddle."

"Aren't you going to introduce me?"

It's amazing, Boone thinks, how Hang Twelve can suddenly speak actual English when there's an attractive woman involved. He says, "Petra Hall, Hang Twelve."

"Another nom de idiot?" Petra asks.

"He has twelve toes," Boone says.

"He does not," says Petra. Then she looks down at his sandals. "He has twelve toes."

"Six on each foot," says Boone.

"Gives me sick traction on the board," Hang Twelve says.

"The strip club is actually immaterial," Petra says. "Mr. Silver also owns a number of warehouses up in Vista, one of which burned to the ground several months ago. The insurance company investigated and, from the physical evidence, deemed it arson and refused to pay. Mr. Silver is suing for damages and for bad faith. He wants five million dollars."

"I'm not an arson investigator," Boone says. "I can put you in touch with—"

"Mr. Silver was having a relationship with one of his dancers," Petra continues. "One Ms. Tamara Roddick."

"A strip club owner banging one of his dancers," Boone says. "Just when you think you've seen it all . . ."

"Recently," Petra says, "Mr. Silver broke off the relationship and suggested that Ms. Roddick find employment elsewhere."

"Let me finish this for you," Boone says. "The spurned young lady, in a sudden attack of conscience, decided that she couldn't live with the guilt anymore and came forward to the insurance company to confess that she saw Silver burn his building down."

"Something like that, yes."

"And you *bought* this shit?" Boone asks.

Alan Burke is way too smart to put this Tammy babe on the stand,

Boone thinks. The opposing lawyer would shred her, and the rest of Burke's case with her.

"She passed a polygraph with flying colors," Petra says.

"Oh," Boone says. It's the best he can think of.

"So what's the problem?" he asks.

"The problem," Petra says, "is that Ms. Roddick is scheduled to testify tomorrow."

"Does she surf?" Boone asks.

"Not to my knowledge."

"Then there's no problem."

"When I tried to contact her yesterday," Petra says, "to make arrangements for her testimony—and to bring her some court-appropriate clothes I bought for her—she didn't respond."

"A flaky stripper," Boone says. "Again, brave new world."

"We've made repeated attempts to contact her," Petra says. "She neither answers her phone nor returns messages. I rang her current employer, Totally Nude Girls. The manager informed me that she hasn't shown up for work for three days."

"Have you checked the morgue?" Boone asks.

Five million dollars is a lot of money.

"Of course."

"So she's taken off," Boone says.

"You have a keen grasp of the obvious, Mr. Daniels," Petra says. "Therefore, you should have no trouble discerning what it is that we require of you."

"You want me to find her."

"Full marks. Well done."

"I'll get right on it," Boone says. "As soon as the swell is over."

"I'm afraid that won't do."

"Nothing to be afraid of," Boone says. "It's just that this . . ."

"Tamara."

". . . Tammy babe could be anywhere by now," Boone says. "It's at least an even bet that she's at a spa in Cabo with Dan Silver. Wherever she is or isn't, it's going to take a while to find her, so whether I start today, or tomorrow, or the day after, it really doesn't matter."

"It does to me," Petra says. "And to Mr. Burke."

Boone says, "Maybe you didn't understand me when I was talking about the big—"

"I did," Petra says. "Something is in the process of 'swelling,' and certain people with sophomoric sobriquets are, for reasons that evade my comprehension, 'stoked' about it."

Boone stares at her.

Finally he says, as if to a small child, "Well, Pete, let me put it to you in a way you can understand: Some very big waves—the sort of waves that come only about once every other presidential administration—are about to hit that beach out there, for one day only, so all I'm going to be doing for those twenty-four hours is clocking in the green room. Now go back and tell Alan that as soon as the swell passes, I'll find his witness."

"The world," Petra says, "doesn't come to a screeching halt on account of 'big waves'!"

"Yes," Boone says, " it does."

He disappears into the bathroom, shutting the door behind him. The next sound is that of running water. Cheerful looks at Petra and shrugs, as if to say, What are you going to do?

# 10

Petra walks in to the bathroom, reaches into the shower, and turns on the cold water.

"Naked here!" Boone yells.

"Sorry—didn't notice."

He reaches up and turns off the water. "That was a sketchy thing to do."

"Whatever that means."

Boone starts to reach for a towel but then gets stubborn and just stands there, naked and dripping wet, as Petra looks him straight in the eyes and informs him, "Mr. Daniels, I intend to make partner within the next three years, and I am not going to achieve that goal by failing to deliver."

"Petra, huh?" Boone says. He finds a tube of Headhunter and rubs it over his body as he says, "Okay—your dad was Pete and he wanted a boy child, but that didn't work out, so he glossed you Petra. You figured out pretty young that the best way to earn Daddy's affection was to add a little testosterone to the mix by growing up to be a hard-charging lawyer, which sort of accounts for that log on your shoulder but not the anal-retentiveness. No, that would be the fact that it's still the law firm of Burke, Spitz and Culver, not Burke, Spitz, Culver and Hall."

Petra doesn't blink.

Actually, Daniels's shot in the dark isn't far off. She *is* an only child, and her British father, a prominent barrister, had wanted a son. So, growing up in London, she had kicked a football around the garden with her dad, attended Spurs matches, and accompanied him to British Grand Prix at Silverstone.

And perhaps becoming a lawyer was yet more of an effort to earn her father's approval, but doing it in California had been her American mother's idea. "If you pursue your career in England," her mother said, "you will always be Simon Hall's daughter to everybody, including yourself."

So Petra took a first at Somerville College in Oxford, but then had crossed the water to Stanford for law school. Burke's talent spotters had plucked her easily from the crowd and made her an offer to come to San Diego.

"Your off-the-cuff psychoanalysis," she says with a smile, "is all the more amusing coming from a man whose parents named him Daniels, Boone."

"They liked the TV show," Boone says. It's a lie. Actually, it was Dave the Love God who, back in junior high, gave him the "Boone" tag, but Boone is not about to reveal this—or his real first name—to this pain in the butt.

"And what *are* you putting on your body?" she asks.

"Rash guard."

"Oh, dear."

"Ever had wet suit rash?" Boone asks.

"Nor a rash of any other kind."

"Well, you don't want it," Boone says.

"I'm sure. Towel?"

Boone takes the towel, wraps it around his waist, and shuffles out into the office.

# 11

"What's the state of the nation?" Boone asks Cheerful.

Cheerful punches a few more numbers into the adding machine, looks at the result, and says, "You can either eat or pay rent, but not both."

This is not an unusual short list of options for Boone. His perpetually shallow cash flow isn't because Boone is a bad private investigator. The truth is, he's a very *good* private investigator; it's just that he'd rather surf. He's totally up front about the fact that he works just enough to get by.

Or not, because he is now three months late on the rent and would be facing eviction if not for the fact that Cheerful is not only his business manager but also his landlord. Cheerful owns the building, Pacific Surf, and about a dozen other rental properties in Pacific Beach.

Cheerful is, in fact, a millionaire several times over, but it doesn't make him any more cheerful, especially not with tenants like Boone. He's taken on the redemption of Boone's business affairs as a quixotic challenge to his own managerial skills, sort of Edmund Hillary trying to summit a mountain of debt, fiscal irresponsibility, unpaid bills, unfiled taxes, unwritten invoices, and uncashed checks.

For an accountant and businessman, Boone Daniels is Mount Everest.

"As your accountant," he tells Boone now, "I strongly advise you to take the case."

"How about as my landlord?"

"I strongly advise you to take the case."

"Are you going to evict me?"

"You have negative cash flow," Cheerful says. "Do you know what that means?"

"It means I have more money going out than I have coming in."

"No," Cheerful says. "If you were *paying* your bills, you'd have more money going out than coming in."

Boone performs the complicated maneuver of putting on jeans while still keeping the towel wrapped around him as he moans, "Twelve to twenty feet . . . double overheads . . ."

"Oh, stop whinging," Petra says. *Whinge* is one of her favorite Brit words—a combination between a whine and a cringe. "If you're as good as your reputation, you'll find my witness before your swelling goes down."

She proffers a file folder.

Boone pulls a North Shore T-shirt over his head, followed by a hooded Killer Dana sweatshirt, slips into a pair of Reef sandals, takes the file, and walks downstairs.

"Where are you going?" Petra calls after him.

"Breakfast."

*"Now?"*

"It's the most important meal of the day."

# 12

Despite his name, Dan Silver always wears black.

For one thing, he'd look pretty stupid dressed in silver. He knows this for a fact, because back when he was a professional wrestler, he dressed all in silver and he looked pretty stupid. But what the hell else was a wrestler named Dan Silver going to wear? He started off as a good guy, but soon found out that the wrestling fans didn't buy him as a hero. So he traded the silver for black and became a villain by the name of "Vile Danny Silver," which the fans *did* buy.

And, anyway, bad guys made more money than good guys.

A life lesson for Danny.

He did about five years in the WWE, then decided that it was easier dealing with strippers than getting the shit kicked out of you three nights a week, so he cashed out and opened his first club.

Now Dan has five clubs, and he still dresses in black because he thinks the black makes him look sexy and dangerous. And slim, because Dan is starting to get that fifties tire around his waist, some heavy jowls, and a second chin, and he doesn't like it. He also doesn't like that his rust red hair is starting to thin and black clothes can't do a thing about it. But he still wears a black shirt, black jeans, and a thick black belt with a wide silver buckle, as well as black cowboy boots with walking heels.

It's his trademark look.

He looks like a trademark asshole.

Now he goes to meet the guy down on Ocean Beach near the pier.

The sea is kicking up like a nervous Thoroughbred in the starting gate. Dan could give a shit. He's lived by the water all his life, never been in it above his ankles. The ocean is full of nasty stuff like jellyfish, sharks, and waves, so Dan's more of a Jacuzzi man.

"You ever hear of anyone drowning in a hot tub?" he asked Red Eddie when the subject of getting into the ocean came up.

Actually, Red Eddie had, but that's another story.

Now Dan walks up the beach and meets Tweety.

"You take care of it?" Dan asks.

Dan is a big guy, six-four and pushing 275, but he looks small standing face-to-face with Tweety. Fucking guy is built like an industrial-size refrigerator and he's just as cold.

"Yeah," Tweety says.

"Any trouble?" Dan asks.

"Not for *me*."

Dan nods.

He already has the cash, twenty one-hundred-dollar bills, rolled into one of his thick hands.

Two grand to pitch a woman off a motel balcony.

Whoever said life is cheap overpaid.

It's too bad, Dan thinks, because that was one hot chick, and a little freak to boot. But she'd seen something she shouldn't have seen, and if there's one thing Dan's learned about strippers after twenty-plus years of trying to manage them is that they can't keep their legs or their mouths shut.

So the girl had to go.

It's no time for taking chances.

There's another shipment due in, and the merchandise is worth a lot of money, and that kind of money you don't let some dancer jeopardize, even if she is a freak.

Dan slips Tweety the money and keeps walking, making sure to stay far away from the water.

# 13

Boone usually eats breakfast at The Sundowner.

For one thing, it's next door to his office. It also serves the best eggs *machaca* this side of . . . well, nowhere. Warm flour tortillas come on the side, and, as we've already established, everything . . .

Although mobbed with tourists in the afternoon and at night, The Sundowner is usually inhabited by locals in the morning, and it has a congenial decor—wood-paneled walls covered with surfing photos, surfing posters, surfboards, broken surfboards, and a television monitor that runs a continuous loop of surf videos.

Plus, Sunny works the morning shift, and the owner, Chuck Halloran, is a cool guy who comps Boone's breakfast. Not that Boone is a freeloader; it's just that he deals largely in the barter economy. The arrangement with Chuck has never been formalized, negotiated, or even discussed, but Boone provides sort of de facto security for The Sundowner.

See, in the morning it's a restaurant full of locals, so there is never a problem. But at night it's more of a bar and tends to get jammed up with tourists who've come to PB for the raucous nightlife and to provoke the occasional hassle.

Boone is often in The Sundowner at night anyway, and even if he isn't, he lives only two blocks away, and it just sort of evolved that he deals with problems. Boone is a big guy and a former cop and he can take care of business. He also hates to fight, so more often than not he uses his laid-back manner to smooth the rough alcoholic waters, and the hassles rarely escalate to physical confrontations.

Chuck Halloran believes that this is the best kind of problem solving, taking care of a situation before it becomes a problem, before damage is done, before the cops get involved, before the Liquor Licensing Board gets to know your name.

So one night a few years back, Chuck's eyeballing a situation where a crew of guys from somewhere east of the 5 (doesn't matter specifically where—once you're east of Interstate 5, it's all the same) are about to leave with a young *turista* who's about three sips from unconscious. Chuck overhears the word *train*.

So, apparently, does Boone, because he gets up from his seat at the bar and sits down at the booth with the guys. He looks at the one who is clearly the alpha male, smiles, and says, "Dude, it's not cool."

"What isn't?" The guy is big; he puts his time in at the gym, takes his supplements. One of those barrel-chested chuckleheads, his shirt opened to his chest and a chain with a crucifix nestled into his fur. He's got enough brew down him to think it's a good idea to get hostile.

"What you have in mind," Boone says, jutting his chin at the young lady, who is now taking a brief nap with her head on the table. "It's not cool."

"I dunno," Bench Press says, grinning at his crew. "I think it's cool."

Boone nods and smiles. "Bro, I'm tellin' ya, it's not on. We don't do that kind of thing here."

So Bench Press says, "Who are you, like the sheriff here?"

"No," Boone says. "But she's not leaving with you."

Bench Press stands up. "*You* gonna stop me?"

Boone shakes his head, like he can't believe this walking cliché.

"That's what I thought, bitch," Bench Press says, mistaking Boone's gesture. He reaches down and grabs the *turista* by the elbow and shakes her awake. "Come on, babe, we're all gonna party."

Then suddenly he's sitting down again, trying to breathe, because Boone has jammed an open hand into his chest and blown all the air out of it. One of his boys starts to go for Boone, then looks up and changes his mind because a shadow has fallen over the table. High Tide is standing there with his arms crossed in front of his chest, and Dave the Love God is right over his shoulder.

"S'up, Boone?" Dave asks.

"Nuch."

"We thought maybe there was a problem."

"No problem," Boone says.

No there's not, because the sight of a 350-pound Samoan tends to have a tranquilizing effect on even the most hostile drunks. Truly, even if you're more or less totally faced and you're thinking about throwing down, one sight of Boone backed by High Tide and an evilly grinning Dave the Love God (who *does* like to fight and is very, *very* good at it) will usually make you go Mahatma Gandhi. If that crew shows you the door, the other side of that door is going to knock Disneyland off the Happiest Place on Earth throne.

"I gotta pay the check," Bench Press says.

"I got it," says Boone. "Peace."

Bench Press and his crew go out like March lambs. Boone pays their bill; then he, High Tide, and Dave revive the *turista* long enough to find out what motel she's in, take her back, put her in bed, and go back to The Sundowner for an aloha beer.

The next morning, Boone went in for breakfast, and no bill was forthcoming.

"Chuck says no," Sunny explained.

"Listen, I don't expect—"

"Chuck says no."

And that was that. The unspoken deal was in place. Boone's breakfast is on the house, but he always leaves a tip. Lunch or dinner, he pays, and still leaves a tip. And if a situation occurs in or around The Sundowner, Boone settles it before it becomes a problem.

# 14

Now, Boone comes into The Sundowner, slides into a booth, and is annoyed but not surprised when Petra takes a seat across the table.

Dave the Love God, sitting at the counter as he packs down a stack of blueberry panckakes, notices her, too.

"Who's the betty with Boone?" he asks Sunny.

"Dunno."

"Bother you?"

"No," Sunny says. "Why should it?"

Petra may not bother her—which is a lie anyway—but she's sure as shit bothering Boone. "I should have thought," Petra's saying, "given the urgency, that you would want to get right at it."

"There's a limit," Boone says, "to what you can accomplish on an empty stomach."

Actually, Petra thinks that there's a limit to what he can do on a full stomach, too, but she refrains from saying so. There must be something to this oceangoing Neanderthal that I'm missing, she thinks, because with all the reputable detective firms in San Diego, Alan Burke was adamant about hiring him, and Alan Burke may be the best trial lawyer in captivity. So he must have a high opinion of Mr. Daniels, or perhaps it's just that Alan thinks that Mr. Daniels is simply the man to call when you need to locate a stripper.

Chuck E. Cheese's, my aching teeth.

Sunny comes over and asks him, "The usual?"

"Please."

For the inland betty's benefit, Sunny recites Boone's usual order, "Eggs *machaca* with jack cheese, corn *and* flour tortillas, split the black beans and home fries, coffee with two sugars."

Petra stares at Boone. "Have you *no* restraint?"

"And throw in a side of bacon," Boone says.

"And for you?" Sunny asks Petra.

Petra picks up the edge in her voice right away and knows without doubt that Boone Daniels and this woman have slept together. The waitress is drop-dead gorgeous, a stunner with long blond hair, longer legs, a figure to kill for, and a golden suntan. No, Surf Boy is most decidedly not a stranger to this lovely creature's bed.

"Would you like to order?" Sunny asks.

"Sorry, yes," Petra says. "I'd like a small oatmeal, raw brown sugar on the side, dry wheat toast, and a decaffeinated tea, please."

"Decaffeinated *tea*?" Boone asks.

"Is that a problem?" she asks him.

"No problem," Sunny says, giving her a golden smile. She already *hates* this woman.

Sunny fires Boone a look.

"Uh, Sunny," says Boone, "this is Petra. Petra, Sunny."

"Pleasure to meet you," Petra says.

"You, too. What brings you to PB?" Sunny asks.

"I'm attempting to engage Mr. Daniels's services," Petra says, thinking, As if it's any of your business what brings me to Pacific Beach.

"That's not always easy to do," Sunny says, glancing at Boone.

"As I am discovering," says Petra.

"Well, discover away," Sunny says. "I'll get your drinks."

The bitch wants to sleep with him, Sunny thinks as she walks to the kitchen to place the order, if she hasn't already. A "small oatmeal, raw brown sugar on the side," as if the skinny Brit needs to watch her waistline. But why does it bother me? Sunny wonders.

Back at the booth, Petra asks Boone if there's a toilet in the place.

"Go down the bar, take a left."

Boone watches Dave the Love God eyeing her as she walks past him.

"No," Boone says.

"What?" Dave asks with a guilty smile.

"Just no."

Dave smiles, shrugs, turns around, and goes back to reading the tide report in the *San Diego Union-Tribune.* It looks good, very good, for the big swell.

Boone opens the Tammy Roddick file.

"After I've finished eating," he says when Petra gets back, "I'm going over to Tammy's place."

"I was just there," Petra says. "She wasn't."

"But her car might be, and that would tell us—"

"There is no vehicle registered in her name," Petra says. "I checked."

"Look," Boone says, "if you know better how to find your witness, why don't you just go do it, save yourself the money and me the grief?"

"You're easily offended," Petra says.

"I'm not offended."

"I didn't imagine that you'd be so sensitive."

"I'm not sensitive," Boone replies.

"He's speaking the truth," Sunny says as she sets the food on the table.

"Could you make this to go?" Boone asks her.

# 15

Except when he gets out to the street, a tow truck just about has its hook into the Boonemobile.

The Boonemobile is Boone's van, an '89 Dodge that the sun, wind, and salt air have turned to an indiscriminate, motley splatter of colors and lack thereof.

Despite its modest appearance, the Boonemobile is a San Diego icon that Boone has used to carry him to a few thousand epic surfing sessions. Ambitious young chargers have been known to cruise the Pacific Coast Highway, scanning the beach parking lots for the Boonemobile to learn what break its owner is hitting that day. And there is no doubt among the greater San Diego beach community that the van, when it goes to its inevitable and well-deserved rest, will find a home in the surf museum up in Carlsbad.

Boone doesn't care about any of that; he just loves his van. He has lived in it on long road trips and when he didn't have the scratch to rent an apartment. What Fury was to Joey, what Silver was to the Lone Ranger, that's what the Boonemobile is to Boone.

And now a tow truck operator is trying to sink his hook into it.

"Yo, whoa!" Boone yells. "What's up?"

"You missed two payments," Tow Truck Guy says, bending down to fix the hook under the van's front bumper. He wears a red ball cap with a SAN DIEGO WRECK AND TOWING logo, a dirty, grease-stained orange jump-suit, and brown steel-toed work boots.

"I haven't missed any payments," Boone says, placing himself between the hook and the van. "Okay, one."

"Two, dude."

"I'm good for it," Boone says.

Tow Truck Guy shrugs, like, Not so far you ain't good for it. Boone looks like he's going to cry as Tow Truck Guy starts to tighten the chain. You put the hook on the Boonemobile, he thinks, it might not be able to take the strain.

"Stop!"

Petra's voice freezes Tow Truck Guy in his tracks. Then again, Petra's voice could freeze a polar bear in its tracks.

"If," she pronounces, "you damage this rare vintage automobile by as much as a scratch, I'll keep you in litigation until you are no longer capable of recalling exactly why your personal and professional life is in such a shambles."

"'Rare vintage automobile'?" Tow Truck Guy laughs. "It's a piece of shit."

"In which case, it is a rare vintage piece of shit," Petra says, "and unless you are in possession of the appropriate seizure orders, I shall have you arrested for grand theft auto."

"The papers are in my truck."

"Kindly go fetch them?"

Tow Truck Guy kindly goes and fetches them. He hands them to Petra and stands there nervously while she peruses them.

"They seem to be in order," she says. She pulls her checkbook out of her purse and asks, "How much is owed?"

Tow Truck Guy shakes his head. "No checks. *He* writes checks."

"Mine don't bounce," Petra says.

"Says you."

She gives him the full benefit of the withering glare to which Boone has become so quickly accustomed. "Don't get cheeky with me," she says. "Simply enlighten me as to the required amount and we shall all be on our separate ways."

Tow Truck Guy is tough. "My boss told me, 'Don't take a check.'"

Petra sighs. "Credit card?"

*"His?"* This strikes Tow Truck Guy as pretty funny.

"Mine."

"I'll have to call it in."

She hands him her cell phone. Five minutes later, Tow Truck Guy has driven off and the cold sweat of terror has evaporated from Boone's face.

"I must say, I'm shocked," Petra says.

"That I'm behind in the payments?"

"That you have *payments*."

"Thanks for what you did," Boone says.

"It's coming out of your fee."

"I'll write you a receipt," Boone says as he settles himself into the comforting familiarity of the well-worn driver's seat, the upholstery of which is held together by strips of duct tape. "So you think this is a rare vintage automobile?"

"It's a piece of shit," Petra says. "Now may we *please* go and collect Ms. Roddick?"

That would be good, Boone thinks.

"Collecting" Tammy Roddick would be really good.

Epic macking good.

# 16

Two minutes later, Boone's still trying to get the engine to turn over while he balances a Styrofoam go-plate on his lap and tries to eat eggs *machaca* with a plastic fork.

He turns the ignition key again. The engine moans, then grudgingly starts, like a guy with a hangover getting up for work.

Petra sweeps some Rubio's and In-N-Out wrappers off the seat, takes a handkerchief from her purse, wipes the cushion, then delicately sits down as she considers how this might fit into her dry-cleaning schedule.

"Stakeouts," Boone says.

Petra looks behind her. "This is a hovel on wheels."

"Hovel" is a little harsh, Boone thinks. He prefers "randomly ordered."

The van contains North Shore board trunks, a couple of sweatshirts, a dozen or so empty go-cups from various fast-food establishments, a pair of Duck Feet fins, a mask and a snorkel, an assortment of sandals and flip-flops, several plaid wool shirts, a blanket, a lobster pot, a stick of deodorant, several tubes of sunblock, a six-pack of empty beer bottles, a sleeping bag, a tire iron, a sledgehammer, a crowbar, an aluminum baseball bat, a bunch of CDs—Common Sense, Switchfoot, and the Ka'au Crater Boys—numerous empty coffee cups, several containers of board wax, and a torn paperback copy of *Crime and Punishment.*

"Doubtless you thought it was an S and M novel," Petra says.

"I read it in college."

"You went to college?"

"Almost a whole semester."

Which is a lie.

Boone got his B.S. in criminology from San Diego State, but he lets her think what she wants. He doesn't inform her that when he goes home (which doesn't contain a television set) pleasantly tired from a day of surfing, his idea of bliss is to sit with a cup of coffee and read to the accompaniment of the sound of the surf.

But it's the sort of thing you keep to yourself. You don't trot this out for The Dawn Patrol or anyone else in the greater Southern California surfing community who would consider any overt displays of intellectuality to be a serious social faux pas, not that any of them would admit to knowing the term *faux pas,* or anything else in French, for that matter. It's all right to know that stuff; you just aren't supposed to talk about it. In fact, having someone find a skanky porn book in the back of your van would be less embarrassing than a volume of Dostoyevsky. Johnny Banzai or Dave the Love God would give him endless shit about it, even though Boone knows that Johnny is at least as well read as he is, and that Dave has an almost encyclopedic and very sophisticated knowledge of early Western films.

But, Boone thinks, let the Brit chick indulge in stereotypes.

Speaking of which—

"Is this actually your vehicle," Petra asks, "or the primary residence for an entire family of hygienically challenged amphibians?"

"Leave the Boonemobile alone," Boone says. "You may be old, rusty, and need Bondo yourself someday."

Although he doubts it.

"You *named* your car?" Petra asks.

"Well, Johnny Banzai did," Boone says, feeling about as adolescent as he sounds.

"Your development isn't just arrested," Petra says. "It's been arrested, tried, and summarily executed."

"Get out of here."

"No, I'm serious."

"So am I," Boone says. "Get out."

She digs in. "I'm coming with you."

"No, you're not," Boone says.

"Why not?"

He doesn't have a good answer for this. She is the client, after all, and it's not like finding some wayward stripper is exactly dangerous. The best he can come up with is, "Look, just get out, okay?"

"You can't make me," Petra says.

Boone has the feeling that she's uttered these words many times, and that she's usually been right. He glares at her.

"I have pepper spray in my bag," she says.

"You don't need pepper spray, Pete," says Boone. "Some dude attacks you? Just talk at him for a minute and he'll take him*self* out."

"Perhaps we should take *my* car," Petra says.

"Let me ask you something, Pete," says Boone. "Do you have a boyfriend?"

"I don't see how that is—"

"Just answer the question," Boone says.

"I'm seeing someone, yes."

"Is he, like, *miserable*?"

Petra's a little surprised that this remark actually hurts her feelings. Boone sees the little flinch in her eyes and the slight flush of color on her cheeks, and he's as surprised as she is that she's capable of hurt.

He feels a little bad about it.

"I'll try one more time," he says; "then we'll take your car."

He cranks the key again and this time the engine starts. It's not happy—it coughs, gags, and sputters—but it starts.

"You should have your mechanic check the gaskets," Petra says as Boone pulls out onto Garnet Avenue.

"Petra?"

"Yes?"

"*Please* shut up."

"Where are we going?" Petra asks.

"The Triple A cab office."

"Why?"

"Because Roddick now dances at TNG, and that's the cab service the TNG girls always use," Boone replies.

"How do you know?"

Boone says, "It's the sort of specialized local knowledge you're paying the big bucks for."

He doesn't bother to explain to her that most bars—strip clubs included—have arrangements with certain cab companies. When tourists ask a Triple A driver to take them to a strip club, he'll take them to TNG. In exchange, whenever the bartender or bouncer at TNG has to call a cab for a customer who might otherwise be charged with DUI, he returns the courtesy. So if Tammy Roddick called a taxi to pick her up at her place, she probably called Triple A.

"How do you know she didn't have a friend pick her up?" Petra asks. "Or that she didn't just walk?"

"I don't," Boone replies. "It just gives me a place to start."

Even though he doesn't think that Roddick took a cab anywhere. What he thinks is that Silver, or some of his muscle, or all of the above came and took her on a long trip to somewhere.

And that they'll never find Tammy Roddick.

But he has to try.

When you get on a wave, you ride the wave.

All the way to the end, if it lets you.

He drives through Pacific Beach.

# 17

Pacific Beach.

PB.

The old beach town sits just a few miles northwest of downtown San Diego, just across Mission Bay from the airport. The marshlands that used to separate it from the city were drained, and now the old swamp is the site of SeaWorld, where thousands of people come to see Shamu.

On the coastline itself, running south to north, you have the great play-ground stretch of Ocean Beach, Mission Beach, and Pacific Beach—OB, MB, and PB to locals, people too busy to speak in entire words, or to read-ers of windshield decals. Ocean Beach is cut off from the other two by the Mission Bay Channel, but Mission Beach runs seamlessly into Pacific Beach, the only division being the arbitrary border of Pacific Beach Drive at the head of Mission Bay.

Pacific Beach started as a college town.

Back in 1887, the real estate speculators who had bought the barren stretch of dirt, then a long carriage ride from the city, were trying to figure out how to attract people and came up with the idea of higher education, so they built the San Diego College of Letters. This was during the great boom of the late 1880s, when the railroads were offering six-dollar fares from Nebraska, Minnesota, and Wisconsin and midwesterners flocked to San Diego to play real estate hot potato.

Things did boom in Pacific Beach for the first couple of years. The rail-road stretched from downtown, so the city dwellers could come out to the beach to play, and new pilgrims lived in tents on the beach while their gingerbread cottages were being built on lots, some of which doubled in value between morning and noon. A weekly newspaper came into being, largely funded by real estate ads. The American Driving Park was built alongside the beach, where The Sundowner and Boone's office now sit, and Wyatt Earp, on the run from an Arizona murder indictment, came out to race his horses.

It was all good for about a year; then the boom went bust. In a single day, lots that had been worth hundreds were finding no buyers at twenty-five dollars, the San Diego College of Letters shut its doors, and the American Driving Park slowly yielded to the salt air, the hot sun, and sad abandonment.

Wyatt Earp left for Los Angeles.

A few committed hangers-on kept their lots and built cottages, a few of which still cling to life among the hotels and condo complexes that line Ocean Boulevard like fortresses. But for the most part, Pacific Beach slid into decline.

Well, as the trite saying goes, When God hands you lemons . . .

Plant lemon trees.

Left with little but dirt and sun, the developers of Pacific Beach used them both to plant lemon trees, and around the turn of the century, the community proclaimed itself "the Lemon Capital of the World." It worked for a while. The flats now occupied by rows of houses were then rows of citrus trees until cheap steamship rates and relaxed import laws made Sicily the Lemon Capital of the World instead; the lemon trees of Pacific Beach were no longer worth the water it took to irrigate them, and the community was back to a search for an identity.

Earl Taylor gave it one. Earl came out from Kansas in 1923 and started buying up land. He built the old Dunaway Drugstore, now the on the corner of Cass and Garnet, a block east of Boone's current office, and then put up a number of other businesses.

Then he met Earnest Pickering, and the two of them conspired to build Pickering's Pleasure Pier.

Yeah, Pleasure Pier.

Right at the end of present-day Garnet Avenue, the pier jutted out into the ocean, and this wasn't a pier for docking ships; this was a pier for, well, pleasure. It had a midway with all kinds of carnival games and cheap food treats, and a dance hall, replete with a cork-lined dance floor.

It opened for business on the Fourth of July, 1927, to flags, fanfare, and fireworks and was a massive success. And why not. It was a beautifully simple, hedonistic idea—combine the beauty of the ocean and the beach with women in "bathing costumes," junk food, and then the nocturnal Roaring Twenties pleasures of illegal booze, jazz, and dancing, with sex to follow at the beachside hotels that sprang up around the pier.

All good, except that Earl and Earnest forgot to creosote the pilings that supported the pier, and "water-born parasites" started eating the thing. (The uncharitable would have it that water-born parasites—that is, surf bums—still infest Pacific Beach.) Pickering's Pleasure Pier started crumbling into the ocean and, a year after opening, had to be closed for safety purposes. The party was over.

Truly, because with exquisite Pacific Beach timing, the town had reinvigorated itself just in time for the Great Depression.

The tents went up again, but the Depression wasn't as severe in San Diego as it was in a lot of the country, because the navy base in the harbor cushioned the unemployment. And a lot of people loved Pacific Beach in those years for precisely what it didn't have: a lot of people, houses, traffic. They loved it precisely because it was a sleepy, friendly little town with one of the best stretches of beach in these United States, and the beach was free and accessible to everyone, and there were no hotels or condo complexes, no private drives.

What changed Pacific Beach forever was a nose.

Dorothy Fleet's sensitive nose, to be exact.

In 1935, her husband, Reuben, owned a company called Consolidated Aircraft, which had a contract with the U.S. government to design and build seaplanes. The problem was that Consolidated was located in Buffalo, and it was hard to land seaplanes on water that was usually ice. So Reuben decided to move the company to warm and sunny California, and he gave his wife, Dorothy, a choice between San Diego and Long Beach. Dorothy didn't like Long Beach because of the "smelly oil wells" nearby, so she picked San Diego, and Fleet built his factory on a site near the airport, where he and his eight hundred workers came out with the great PBY Catalina.

Airplanes had a lot to do with creating modern Pacific Beach, because Japanese bombers hitting Pearl Harbor launched the Consolidated factory into high gear. Suddenly faced with the job of producing thousands of PBYs plus the new B-24 bomber, Fleet imported thousands of workers— 15,000 by early 1942, 45,000 by the war's end. Working 24/7 they pumped out 33,000 aircraft during the war.

They had to live somewhere, and the nearby empty flats of Pacific Beach made the perfect location to put up quick, cheap housing.

And it wasn't just Consolidated Aircraft, for San Diego became the headquarters of the Pacific Fleet, and between the navy bases around San Diego Harbor and the marine training bases at Elliott and Pendleton, up by Oceanside, the whole area became a military town. The city's population jumped from 200,000 in 1941 to 500,000 by 1943. The government built a number of housing projects in Pacific Beach—Bayview Terrace, Los Altos, Cyanne—and a lot of the men and women who came to live in them temporarily never went home. A lot of the sailors and marines who were stationed in San Diego on their way to and from the Pacific front decided to come back and build lives there.

Much of PB, especially inland from the beach, still has that blue-and-khaki-collar mentality—unlike its tonier neighbor to the north, La Jolla—and a fiercely egalitarian ethic that is a holdover from the close-living, pooled ration card, and backyard party days of the war. Notoriously casual, PB residents aren't at all bothered by the fact that two of their major streets are actually misspelled: Felspar should be Feldspar and Hornblend should be Hornblende, but nobody cares, if they even know. (So much for the San Diego College of Letters.) Nobody seems to know why the major east-west streets were named after precious stones in the first place, except that it seemed to be some kind of lame effort to suggest that PB was the gem of the West Coast. And you know a PB locie by the way he or she pronounces Garnet Avenue. If they say it correctly—"Garnet"— you know right away they're from out of town, because the locals all mispronounce it, saying "Garnette."

Anyway, if you drive west on Garnet, however the hell you say it, you're going to run into Pickering's old Pleasure Pier, renamed Crystal Pier, another PB landmark revived by the PBY and B-24. The midway is gone, and so is the dance hall, replaced by the white cottages with blue shutters that line the north and south edges of the pier, then give way to empty space for fishermen who have been known to hook the occasional surfer trying to shoot the pilings.

But the concept of pleasure remains.

PB is the only beach in California where you can still drink on the sand. Between noon and eight p.m., you can slam booze on the beach, and for that reason PB had become Party Town, USA, Beach Division. The party is always on, at the beach, along the boardwalk, in the bars and clubs that line Garnet between Mission and Ingraham.

You've got Moondoggies, the PB Bar & Grill, the Tavern, the Typhoon Saloon, and of course, The Sundowner. On weekend nights—or *any* nights in the summer, spring, or fall—Garnet is rocking with a young crowd, many of them locals, a lot of them tourists who've heard about the party all the way from Germany, Italy, England, Ireland, Japan, and Australia. You've got a drunk and horny United Nations General Assembly down there, and the bartenders on Garnet have probably done more for world peace than any ambassador ever double-parked outside Tiffany's.

Yeah, except that something different has been creeping up the past few years as gangs from other parts of the city have been drawn to the PB nightlife, and fights have broken out in the clubs and on the street.

It's a shame, Boone thinks as he drives past the strip of nightclubs and bars, that the laid-back surfer atmosphere is giving way to alcohol- and gang-fueled rage, scuffles in bars that turn into fights in the streets outside.

It's weird—where you used to see signs that read NO SHIRT, NO SHOES, NO SERVICE and might just as well have added AND NO ENFORCEMENT, now you see signs in the club doorways banning gang colors, hats, hooded sweatshirts, and any gang-related gear.

PB is getting a seedy, almost dangerous reputation, and the family tourist trade is starting to move to Mission Beach or up to Del Mar, leaving PB to the young and single, to the booze hounds and the gang bangers, and it's all too bad.

Boone has never much liked change anyway, certainly not this change. But PB has changed, even from the time Boone was growing up in it. He saw it explode in the Reagan eighties. A hundred years after its first real estate boom, Pacific Beach hit another one. But this time it wasn't lots of land for little one-story cottages; this time it was condo complexes and big hotels that bulldozed the little cottages into memories and robbed the few survivors of their sunlight and ocean views. And with the condos, the chain stores moved in, so a lot of Pacific Beach looks like a lot of every-where else, and the small businesses that gave the place its charm—like The Sundowner and Koana's Coffee—are now exceptions.

And prices continued to rise, to the point where the average working person, the man or woman who built the town, can't even think about buy-ing a place anywhere near the beach and will soon be priced out of the market entirely—threatening to turn the beachfront area into that weird dichotomy of a rich person's ghetto, where the rich lock themselves inside at night when the streets are taken over by drunk tourists and predatory gangs.

Now Boone drives east on Garnet, past all the clubs and bars and into the area of coffee shops, ethnic restaurants, tattoo parlors, palm-reading joints, used-clothing stores, and fast-food restaurants, then into the mostly residential neighborhood of the flats. He crosses the 5, where Garnet becomes Balboa Avenue, and pulls into the parking lot of Triple A Taxi.

Just around the corner from the old Consolidated Aircraft factory, where Reuben Fleet won the war and Pacific Beach got lost.

# 18

The taxi office is a small, formerly white clapboard building in need of a paint job. A metal security screen is open, revealing the company logo stenciled in fading red on the front window. Off to the left is a garage, where a taxi is up on a rack. Another half a dozen cabs are parked haphazardly around the parking lot.

"Wait in the van, okay?" Boone says as he turns off the engine.

"And flirt with hepatitis C for what reason?" Petra asks.

"Just stay in the van," Boone says, "and try to look aggro."

"'Aggro'?"

"Aggravated," Boone translates. "Angry, annoyed, pissed off."

"That shouldn't be difficult," she says.

"I didn't think so." He takes his watch off and hands it to her. "Take this. Keep it in your lap."

"You want me to *time* you?"

"Just do it. Please?"

She smiles. "Cheerful said you'd have a sundial."

"Yeah, he's a hoot."

Boone walks across the parking lot into the dispatch office. A young Ethiopian guy has the chair tipped back and his feet on the desk. Almost all the cab companies in San Diego are run by East African immigrants. Triple A Taxi is a strictly Ethiopian operation, Boone knows, while United Taxi is Eritrean. Sometimes they get into border skirmishes in the taxi line at the airport, but usually they get along okay.

"Can I help you?" the dispatcher asks as Boone walks in. He's a kid, barely out of his teens. Skinny, dressed in a ratty brown sweater over new 501 jeans that look freshly pressed. He doesn't take his Air Jordans off the desk. Boone isn't dressed so you'd have to take your feet off the desk for him.

"Dude," Boone drawls, so it sounds more like "Duuuuuuude." "I'm in trouble."

"Breakdown?"

"Break*up,*" Boone replies. "See the chick in the van?"

The dispatcher swings his feet off the desk, brings the chair down on its wheels, adjusts his thick glasses on his nose, and looks out the window into the parking lot. He sees Petra sitting in the van's passenger seat.

"She's pissed off," the dispatcher says.

"Way."

"How come?"

Boone holds his left wrist out, showing white skin in the exact shape of a watch and band.

"Your watch is missing," the dispatcher says.

Boone nods in Petra's direction. "She gave it to me for my birthday."

"What happened to it?"

Boone sighs. "You keep a secret?"

"Yes."

I hope not, Boone thinks, then says, "My boys and me partied last night? Some girls dropped in and I got a little friendly with one, maybe a little too friendly, you know what I'm saying, and I wake up and she's gone. Dude, with the watch."

"You're fucked."

"Totally," Boone says. "So I told my girlfriend that it was my roommate Dave who was with the stripper but that he was in *my* room because Johnny was in *his* and I passed out by the pool, you know, but I'd left the watch in my room and the dancer, this Tammy chick, just, like, took it, you know, because she thought it was Dave's and she's pissed he called her a cab. So I was wondering maybe you could tell me where she went?"

"I'm not supposed to do that," the dispatcher says. "Unless you're the police."

"Bro," Boone says, pointing out the window, "I ain't nailing *that* again until I get that watch back. I mean, check her out."

The dispatcher does. "She's hot."

"She's *filthy*."

"You shouldn't have gone with that other girl," the dispatcher says, looking indignantly outraged for the pretty girl in the van.

"I was hammered," Boone says. "But you are right, brother. So you think you can toss a drowning man a rope here? See if you sent a cab to 533 Del Vista Mar, chick named Tammy? Where you took her? I'll do a solid for you sometime."

"Like what?"

Nice to see that the Ethiopians have adapted to the American way of life, Boone thinks. MTV, fast food, capitalism. Cash on the barrelhead. He takes his wallet out of his pants and holds out a twenty. "It's all I have, bro."

Which is pretty much the truth.

The dispatcher takes the twenty, goes into his log, and comes back with "You say her name was Tammy?"

"Yeah, Gilooley . . . Gilbert . . ."

"Roddick?"

"That's it," Boone says.

"One of our drivers took her to the Crest Motel."

Well, I'll be damned, Boone thinks. He says, "Right here in PB."

"Five o'clock this morning."

A stripper on the move at five a.m.? Boone thinks. Strippers aren't up at *five,* unless they're *still* up at five. He says, "Hey, thanks, brah."

"Your girlfriend . . ."

"Yeah?"

"She's beautiful."

Boone looks out the window to where the dispatcher is staring. Petra's sitting erect in the seat, looking into the mirror as she carefully applies fresh lipstick.

Yeah, Boone thinks, she is.

He walks back to the van and gets in.

"Six minutes and thirty-eight seconds," she says, consulting the watch.

"What?"

"You wanted me to time you," she says. "It took rather longer than I would have expected from a professional of your reputation."

"Tammy went to the Crest Motel," Boone says, "right here in Pacific Beach. You owe me twenty bucks."

"I'll need a receipt."

"You want a *bribe* receipt?"

She considers this. "Just get me *any* kind of receipt, Boone."

"Cool." In fact, it's the first cool thing he's heard her say. "Let's go pick up your witness."

Then I can shed you, Boone thinks, get my big-wave gear rigged out, and be in the water in plenty of time for the big swell.

The first thing he sees when he pulls the van into the Crest parking lot is an alarming band of yellow caution tape.

Police tape.

With police behind it.

Including Johnny Banzai of the SDPD Homicide Squad.

This can't be good, Boone thinks.

# 19

That's what Johnny Banzai thinks, too.

When he sees Boone.

Normally, Johnny likes to see Boone. Normally, most people do. But not here, not *now*. Not when there's a dead woman who dived off a third-floor balcony and missed, her body now sprawled a scant two feet from the swimming pool, her red hair splayed on her outstretched arm, her blood forming a shallow, inadequate pool of its own.

A tiny angel is tattooed on her left wrist.

Behind the pool are the four floors of the Crest Motel, built in two angular wings, one of a dozen ugly, indistinct hotels thrown up in the early eighties, catering to budget-minded tourists, economy-priced hookers, and anonymity-seeking adulterers. Each room has a tiny "balcony" over-looking the "pool complex," with its small rectangular swimming pool and requisite Jacuzzi, which Johnny thinks of as basically a swirling, bub-bling mass of potential herpes infections.

Now he ducks under the tape and steps into Boone's way. "Get out of here before the lieutenant sees you," Johnny says.

Boone looks over his shoulder at the body. "Who is she?"

"What are you doing here anyway?"

"Matrimonial."

Johnny sees the woman in Boone's van. "With the wife in tow?"

"Some people have to see for themselves," Boone says. He juts his chin at the crime scene, where the ME is squatting by the body, doing his voodoo. Lieutenant Harrington squats beside him, his back to Boone. "Who's the jumper?"

In his gut he already knows the answer, but being an optimist, he hopes his gut is wrong.

"One Tammy Roddick," Johnny says.

Gut one, optimism zero, Boone thinks.

"She checked in early this morning," Johnny says. "Checked out a little while later."

"You calling it a suicide."

"I'm not calling it anything," Johnny says, "until we get the blood work back."

Sure, Boone thinks, to see what drugs are running through her system. Happens all the time in a party town like San Diego—a girl starts thinking the drugs are Peter Pan and she's Wendy, and Neverland starts looking not only good but reachable. The problem is . . . well, *one* of the problems is that the second she jumps she already knows it's a mistake, and she has those long seconds to regret her impulse and know she can't take it back.

Gravity being gravity.

Every surfer knows the sensation.

That big wave you get in, and get in *wrong,* but then it's too late and you're just up there knowing you're about to go down and there's nothing you can do about it but take the fall. And you just have to hope that the water's deep enough to slow you down before you hit the bottom.

Like maybe Tammy was hoping she'd make it to the pool.

"Now get out of here before Harrington scopes you," Johnny is saying.

Too late.

Harrington straightens up, turns around to look for Johnny Banzai, and sees him talking to Boone Daniels.

A cat and a dog, a Hatfield and a McCoy, Steve Harrington and Boone Daniels. Harrington comes across the tape, looks at Boone, and says, "If you're looking for cans and bottles, sorry, the trash guys already came."

Harrington's got a face like barbed wire—his bones are so sharp, you think you could cut yourself on them. Even his blond hair is sharp, cut short and gelled wiry, and his mouth looks like it was slashed with a knife between his thin lips. He wears a gray herringbone jacket, a white shirt with a brown tie, black trousers, and highly shined black shoes.

Harrington is hard-core.

Always has been.

"What are you doing at my scene, surf bum?" Harrington asks him. "I thought you'd be too busy getting little girls killed."

Boone goes for him.

Johnny Banzai grabs Boone.

"Let him go," Harrington tells him. "Please, John, do me a favor, let him go."

"Do *me* a favor," Johnny says to Boone. "Back-paddle."

Boone backs off.

"Good choice," Harrington says, then adds, "Pussy."

Boone's head clears enough for him to see Petra breezing past all of them, striding right toward the scene.

"Hey!" Harrington yells, but it's too late. Petra is standing over the body. Boone sees her look down, then straighten up and walk real fast back to the van. She lays both hands on the car as if she's being frisked. Her head is down.

Boone walks over to her. "Go ahead and throw up," he says. "Everyone does, the first time."

She shakes her head.

"Go on," he says. "You can be human; it's all right."

But she shakes her head again and says something, although he can't quite make it out.

"What?" he asks.

She speaks a little louder.

"That's not Tammy Roddick," she says.

# 20

Boone hustles Petra into the van.

The thing starts up first try and he drives for two blocks before he pulls over and asks, "What?"

"That's not Tammy Roddick," Petra repeats.

"Are you sure?"

"Yes, I'm sure," she says. "I interviewed her half a dozen times, for God's sake."

"Okay."

"And I didn't have to vomit," she says. "I was just trying to get you away from the police officers so I could tell you."

"Sorry, I didn't mean to imply that you were a flesh-and-blood human being," he says. But she does look paler, if that's possible. "Look, you want my advice?"

"No."

"We should go back right now and tell them they've got a wrong ID," Boone says. "You're an officer of the court, and if you withhold information that's material to the investigation of an unattended death—"

"Hello?" she says, waving her hand. "*I'm* the attorney? Stanford Law? Top of my class?"

"And if *I* withhold information, they could yank my license."

"Then forget I told you," she says. "Look, I'll swear that I didn't tell you, all right?"

"How did you do in ethics class?" Boone asks.

"An *A*," she says. Like, What else?

"What, did you cheat on the final?"

"When did you become such a Goody Two-sandals?" she asks. "I thought you were so laid-back."

"I need my PI license to eke out a meager living," Boone says, realizing as it comes out of his mouth that it makes him sound totally lame. The rules were not made to be broken, but they were made to be bent, and any PI who doesn't bend them into pretzels isn't going to be in business for long.

Besides, Boone thinks, there's a solid reason for not telling the SDPD that the dead woman at the Crest Motel isn't Tammy Roddick. The deceased checked into the motel, pretending for some reason to be Tammy. It's possible that someone bought the act and killed her because of it. So the real Tammy, out there somewhere, is safe until the truth gets out.

The problem is to find her before the killer realizes his mistake.

Petra is saying something about ". . . could put her in danger."

"I'm there already," Boone says.

Which, to his surprise, shuts her up.

Must be the shock, he thinks. Seeing as how he's ahead of her in the wave, he decides to ride it out. "Then the first step is to find out, if the dead woman isn't Tammy—"

"She isn't."

"I got that," Boone says, thinking, Well, it was nice while it lasted. Then: "Who was she?"

"I don't know."

Boone shakes his head to make sure he heard her say that she didn't know something, then he says, "We'd better find out."

"How are we going to do that?"

"*We're* not," Boone says. "*I* am."

Because Boone knows:

You want to find out about physics, you go to Stephen Hawking; you want to learn about basketball, you go to Phil Jackson; you want to know about women who take their clothes off for a living, you go to—

# 21

Dave the Love God sits on his lifeguard tower at Pacific Beach and intently scopes two young women making their way up the beach.

"Visible tan lines, fresh," Dave tells Boone, who's sitting beside him on the tower, in violation of God knows how many rules. The two women, one a slightly overweight blonde with a big rack, the other a taller, skinnier brunette, are walking past now. "Definitely Flatland Barbies. I say Minnesota or Wisconsin, secro-receptionists, sharing a double room. Which makes for a challenge, but not one without its rewards."

"Dave . . ."

"I have needs, Boone. I'm not ashamed of them." He smiles. "Well, I *am* ashamed of them, but—"

"It doesn't stop you."

"No."

Dave is a living legend, both as a lifeguard and a lover. In the latter category, Dave's a tenth-level black belt of the horizontal *kata*. He's been spread over more tourist flesh than Bain de Soleil. Johnny Banzai insists that Dave is actually listed in Chamber of Commerce brochures as an attraction, right alongside SeaWorld.

"No, really," Johnny has said. "They go see the Shamu show, they check out the pandas at the zoo, and they fuck Dave."

"You know what I love about tourist women?" Dave now asks Boone.

The list of possible answers is staggering, so Boone simply says, "What?"

"They leave."

It's the truth. They come for a good time, Dave gives them one, and then they go home, usually thousands of miles away. They go away, but they don't go away mad. They like Dave every bit as much when they go to bed with him as when he doesn't drive them to the airport.

They even give him *references.*

Truly, they go home and tell their girlfriends, "You're going to San Diego? You have to look up Dave."

And they do.

"Doesn't it make you feel cheap and used?" Sunny asked him one morning out in the lineup.

"Yes," Dave said. "But there are drawbacks, too."

Although he couldn't think of any at the moment.

It was Dave the Love God who actually coined the term *betty,* and this is how it happened.

The Dawn Patrol was out one glassy morning, and there were long waits between sets, so there was ample time for a now-infamous and admittedly sick conversation to kick up about which cartoon character they'd most like to have sex with.

Jessica Rabbit got a lot of run, although Johnny Banzai went with Snow White, and Hang Twelve admitted to having a thing for both the girls in *Scooby-Doo.* Sunny was torn between Batman and Superman ("mystery versus stamina"), and while she was trying to make up her mind, Dave made himself an immortal in surf culture by chiming in, "Betty Rubble."

There was a moment of stunned silence.

Then Boone said, "That's sick."

"Why is that sick?" Dave asked.

"Because it is."

"But why?" Johnny Banzai asked Dave. "Why Betty Rubble?"

"She'd be great in the sack," Dave replied calmly, and it was chillingly clear to everyone that he had given this considerable thought. "I'm telling you, those petite sexual hysterics, once they cut loose . . ."

"How do you know she's a sexual hysteric?" Sunny asked, already having forgotten they were discussing a literally one-dimensional character that existed only in the fictional prehistoric town of, uh, Bedrock.

"Barney's not getting the job done," Dave replied with supreme confidence.

Anyway, it was just about a half hour later when a petite black-haired woman came down the beach and Johnny Banzai scoped her, grinned at Dave, and pointed.

Dave nodded.

"A real betty," he said.

It was done.

Dave's specific figment of perverted imagination entered the surfing lexicon and any desirable woman, regardless of hair color or stature, became a "betty."

But Dave is also legendary as a lifeguard, and for good reason.

Kids in San Diego talk about lifeguards the way NYC kids discuss baseball players. They're role models, heroes, guys you look up to and want to be like. A great lifeguard, male or female, is simply the best water-man around, and Dave is one of the greats.

Take the time that riptide hit—on a weekend, like they always seem to do, when there are a lot of people in the water—and swept eleven people out with it. They all made it back in because Dave was out there almost before it happened. He was already running for the water as it started, and he commanded his crew with such cool efficiency that they got a line out beyond the tide and netted the whole eleven in.

Or the time that snorkler got caught up underwater in the kelp bed that had drifted unusually close to shore. Dave read it by the color of the water, got out there with a knife, dived down, and cut the guy loose. Got him back to shore and did CPR, and the snorkler, who would have drowned or at least suffered brain damage if Dave hadn't been such a powerful swim-mer, was just freaked out instead.

Or take the famous tale of Dave's shark.

Dave's out one day showing a young lifeguard some of the finer points. They're on those lifeguard boards, bright red longboards the size of small boats, paddling south, cutting across the long bend of coast from La Jolla Shores to La Jolla Cove, and suddenly the young lifeguard sits upright on his board and looks deathly pale.

Dave looks down and sees blood flowing into the water from his boy's right leg and then he sees why. A great white, cruising the cove for its favorite dish, has mistaken the rookie's black wet-suited leg for a seal and taken a chunk out of it. Now the shark is circling back to finish the meal.

Dave paddles between them—and you get this story from the rookie, not from Dave—sits up, kicks the shark in the snout and says, "Get out of here."

Kicks it again and repeats, "I said get your skanky shark ass out of here."

And the shark does.

It does a dorsal flip and scoots.

Then Dave cuts the leash off his board, ties it off as a tourniquet for the newbie's leg, and tows him to shore. Gets him into an ambulance, announces he's hungry, and walks over to La Playa for a burger at Jeff's Burger.

That's Dave.

("You know what I did after I had that burger?" Dave told Boone privately. "I went to the can by tower thirty-eight and threw it all up. I was that scared, man.")

Lifeguard candidates go to great lengths either to get into Dave's training classes or to dodge them. The ones who aspire to be great want him as their instructor; the ones who just want to get by avoid him like wet-suit rash.

Because Dave is brutal.

He *tries* to wash them out, doing everything this side of legal to expose their weaknesses—physical, mental, or emotional.

"If they're going to fail," he said one day to Boone as they watched one of his classes do underwater sit-ups in the break, "I want it to be *now,* not when some poor kook who's about to drown needs them to succeed."

That's the thing: It doesn't matter if there's twenty people taken out by the undertow or blood in the water and sharks circling; a lifeguard has to arrive in the middle of that chaos as cool as a March morning and ask in a mellow tone if people would like to work their way to shore now, but there's, like, no rush.

Because the thing that kills most people in the water is panic.

They brain-lock and do stupid things—try to fight the tide, or swim in exactly the wrong direction, or start flapping their arms and wearing themselves out. If they'd just chill out and lie back, or tread water, and wait for the cavalry to arrive, ninety-nine times out of a hundred, they'd be okay. But they panic and start to hyperventilate and then it's over—unless that calm, cool lifeguard is out there to bring them back.

This is why Dave keeps trying to recruit Boone.

He knows that BD would make a great lifeguard. Boone's a natural waterman with genius-level ocean smarts, an indefatigable swimmer, his body *ripped* from daily surfing. And as for cool, well, Boone is the walking definition of cool.

The panic gene just skipped Boone.

And it's not just speculation on Dave's part. Boone was out there that day the riptide took all those people. Just happened to be there shooting the shit with Dave and *deliberately* swam out into a riptide and paddled around, calming the terrified tourists, propping up the ones who were about to go under, and smiling and laughing like he was in a warm wading pool.

And Dave will never forget what he heard Boone saying to the people as the lifeguard and his crew were desperately struggling to save lives: "Hey, no worries! We've got the best people in the world out here to bring us in!"

"What brings you to my realm?" Dave asks him now.

"Business."

"Anytime you're ready to sign on the dotted," Dave says, "I have a gig for you. You could be wearing a pair of these way-cool Day-Glo orange trunks inside a month."

It's a joke between them—why lifeguard trunks, life jackets, and even life rafts are manufactured in the exact color that research has shown is most tantalizing to sharks. Day-Glo orange is just catnip to a great white.

"You have an encyclopedic knowledge of local strippers," Boone says.

"And a lot of people think that's easy," Dave says. "They don't realize the long hours, the dedication—"

"The sacrifices you make."

"The sacrifices," Dave agrees.

"But *I* do."

"And I appreciate that, BD," Dave says. "How can I be of service to you?"

Boone's not sure he can, but he's hoping he can, because the dead woman at the pool had that stereotypical teased-out stripper hair, and a stripper body. And it's been Boone's experience that strippers have stripper friends. This is because of the odd hours, and also because women who aren't strippers usually don't want to have friends who are because they're afraid the dancers will steal their boyfriends.

So he's playing the odds that say the Jane Doe is a stripper.

"I need to ID a dancer," Boone says. "Redhead, an off-the-rack rack, an angel tattoo on her left wrist."

"Gimme putt," Dave says. "Angela Hart."

"Angel *Heart*?"

"A nom de strip," Dave says. "What about her?"

"She a . . . uh, *friend* of yours?"

"A gentleman doesn't tell, BD," says Dave. "But that's a serious tone you've adopted. What's underneath it?"

"She's dead."

Dave stares out over the ocean. The waves are starting to get bigger, and choppy, and the color of the water is a dark gray.

"Dead how?" Dave asks.

"Maybe suicide."

Dave shakes his head. "Not Angela. She was a force of nature."

"She ever work at Silver Dan's?"

"Didn't they all?"

"Was she friends with a girl named Tammy?"

"They were tight," Dave says. "What's she got to do with this?"

"I don't know yet."

Dave nods.

He and Boone sit and look at the water together. Boone doesn't rush things. He knows his friend is working through it. And the ocean never gets boring—it's always the same and always different.

Then Dave says, "Angela was pure nectar. You need any help finding out who killed her, you give me a shout."

"No worries."

Dave's back on the 'nocs, scoping the Flatland Barbies back to their hotel room.

Boone knows that he's looking but he *isn't,* you know.

# 22

Boone doesn't get far from the lifeguard tower.

He's on the boardwalk, heading back toward his ride, when who should he see, on a kid's dirt bike with tires thicker than a Kansas prom queen, than—

Red Eddie.

Red Eddie is a Harvard-educated, Hawaiian-Japanese-Chinese-Portuguese-Anglo-Californian with traffic-cone red hair. Yeah, yeah, yeah—traffic cones aren't red, they're orange, and Eddie's first name isn't Eddie, it's Julius. But there isn't a soul on this earth who has the stones to call the dude "Orange Julius."

Not Boone, not Dave the Love God, not Johnny Banzai, not even High Tide, because Red Eddie is usually surrounded by at least a six-pack of super size Hawaiian *moke* guys and Eddie don't think nothing about letting the dogs out.

Red Eddie deals *pakololo*.

His old man, who owned a few dozen grocery stores in Oahu, Kauai, and the Big Island, sent Eddie from the north shore of Oahu to Harvard and then to Wharton Business School, and Eddie returned to the island with a sound business plan. It was Eddie who put the Wowie in Maui, the high in hydro. He brings massive amounts of the stuff in by boat. They drop it offshore in watertight plastic wrap, and Eddie's guys go out at night in Zodiacs, the small double-pontoon motorboats, and bring it in.

"I'm a missionary," Eddie said to Boone one night at The Sundowner. "Remember how missionaries sailed from America to Hawaii to spread the good word and totally fuck up the culture? I'm returning the favor. Except my good news is benevolent and your culture *needs* fucking up."

Benevolence has been good to Red Eddie, giving him an ocean-view mansion in La Jolla, a house on the beach in Waimea, and a 110-foot motor yacht docked in San Diego Harbor.

Red Eddie is totally Pacific Rim, the epitome of the current West Coast economic and cultural scene, which is a mélange of Cali-Asian-Polynesian. Like a good salsa, Boone thinks, with a little mango and pineapple mixed in.

Boone and Eddie go back.

Like a lot of stories in this part of the world, it starts in the water.

Eddie has a kid from a high school indiscretion.

The kid doesn't live with Eddie—he lives with his mother in Oahu—but Keiki Eddie comes for visits. He was about three years old on one of these visits, when a big swell hit the coast and Keiki Eddie's idiot nanny decided it would be a good idea to take her charge for a walk on La Jolla Cove to see the big waves. (Like he had never seen them on the North Shore, right?) One of the big waves smashed into the jetty and took Keiki Eddie back with it, so the kid was really getting a close-up look at the big mackers.

These things usually end badly. Like, the best news is they find the body.

Call it luck, call it God, call it karma—but Boone Daniels, designed by DNA for just this situation, was also there checking out the big waves, using the long view from La Jolla to scope the best break. He heard a scream, saw the nanny pointing, and spotted Keiki Eddie's head bobbing in the surf. Boone jumped into the next wave, grabbed Keiki Eddie, and kept them both from being smashed into the rocks.

It made the *Union-Tribune.*

LOCAL SURFER RESCUES CHILD.

Next day, Boone was hanging at home, chilling out from the big wave session he'd done after hauling the kid out of the water, when the doorbell rang. Boone opened the door to see this diminutive guy with red hair, tattoos on every part of his exposed skin except his face.

"Anything you want," the guy said. "Anything you want in this world."

"I don't want anything," Boone said.

Eddie tried to lay cash on him, dope on him; Eddie wanted to buy him a freaking house, a boat. Boone finally settled for dinner at the Marine Room. Eddie offered to *buy* him the Marine Room.

"I don't see myself in the restaurant business," Boone said.

"What do you see yourself in?" Eddie asked. "You want in my business, brah, speak the word, I'll set you up."

"I play for the other team," Boone said, not meaning that he was a lesbian all-female outrigger canoe paddler, but a freaking police officer.

Not that it got in the way of their friendship. Boone wasn't on the narc squad and he didn't make judgments. He had done a little herb in his grom past, and even though he'd grown out of it, he didn't much care what other people did.

So he and Eddie started hanging out a little bit. Eddie became sort of an adjunct member of The Dawn Patrol, although he didn't turn up too often because dawn for Eddie is about one p.m. But he did come around, got to know Dave and Tide, Hang, Sunny and even Johnny, who kept a little distance, due to the potentially adversarial nature of their professions.

Boone, Dave, and Tide would go over to Eddie's house and watch MMA matches on his flat-screen plasma. Eddie's really big into the mixed martial arts, which sprang up in Hawaii anyway, and sponsors his team of fighters, named, unsurprisingly enough, Team Eddie. So they'd hang and watch the fights, or go in Eddie's entourage to the live shows in Anaheim, and Eddie even got Boone to voyage as far away from the ocean as Las Vegas to catch some fights with him and Dave.

And most of The Dawn Patrol was present at Eddie's notorious house-warming party in La Jolla.

Eddie's sprawling modernist mansion occupies an acre on a bluff overlooking the ocean at Bird Rock. The neighbors were, like, *appalled,* what with the *moke* guys coming and going, and the parties, and the pounding music, the sounds from Eddie's skateboard tube (Eddie has been known to board off the roof of his house into the barrel), his skeet-shooting range, and his racing up and down the street on his mountain bike while screened by a squadron of heavily armed bodyguards. So the pink polo shirt, yellow golf trouser set that live around Eddie was seriously geeked by him, but what were they going to do about it?

Nothing, that's what.

Nada.

They weren't going over there to complain about the noise; they weren't going to call the police; they weren't going to go to the zoning board with questions about whether a skeet-shooting range or private skateboard park were even allowed in their heretofore quiet neighborhood.

They weren't going to do any of these things, because the neighbors were scared shitless of Red Eddie.

Eddie felt bad about this and tried to alleviate their anxieties by inviting the whole neighborhood over for a luau one Sunday afternoon.

Of course, it turned into a shipwreck.

And one of the first people Eddie invited aboard the *Titanic* was Boone.

"You *gotta* come," Eddie said into the phone after he'd explained the purpose behind the invitation. "Moral support. Bring your whole *hui,* the *ohana.*"

By which he meant The Dawn Patrol.

Boone was reluctant, to say the least. It *doesn't* take a weather vane to know which way the wind blows, and it didn't take a Savonarola to predict how this little Sunday afternoon gathering was going to turn out. But misery does love company, so Boone brought the subject up at the very next meeting of The Dawn Patrol and was surprised when most of them actually expressed enthusiasm about going.

"You're kidding, right?" Boone asked.

"I wouldn't miss this circus for the world," Johnny Banzai said.

Yeah, well, circus was about right.

The hula dancers were fine, the ukulele, slack-key guitar, and surf-reggae combo was interesting, if somewhat esoteric, and the sumo wrestlers were, well, sumo wrestlers. High Tide, a late entry, nevertheless took the bronze, while Cheerful wondered aloud just what the hell fat men in diapers were doing bumping bellies in a circle of sand.

So far so good, Boone thought. It could be a lot worse.

But maybe it was when Eddie—blissed-out on a buffet of ecstasy, Maui Wowie, Vicodin, rum colas, and the sheer joy of neighborliness—demonstrated his walking-over-hot-coals meditation technique and insisted that some of his guests share in the transcendental experience that things got seriously weird.

After the EMTs left, Eddie persuaded the surviving guests to lie down side by side between two ramps and then knieveled them on his mountain bike, after which he released his psychotic rottweiler, Dahmer, from its cage and went *mano-a-pawo* with it, the two of them rolling around on the patio—blood, saliva, fur, and flesh flying until Eddie finally pinned the dog in a rear-naked chokehold and made it bark uncle.

As the guests offered some weak, somewhat stunned applause, Eddie—

sweating, bleeding, huffing, but flushed with victory—muttered to Boone, "Jesus, these *haoles* are hard to entertain. I'm busting a hump, *bruddah*."

"I dunno," Boone said, "I guess some people just don't have an appreciation for the finer points of human-canine combat."

Eddie shrugged, like, Go figure. He leaned over and scratched Dahmer's chest. The dog, panting, bleeding, huffing, and embarrassed by defeat, nevertheless looked up at Eddie with unabashed adoration.

"So what should I do now?" Eddie asked Boone.

"Maybe just chill," Sunny suggested. "Dial it down a little, let people enjoy their food. The food is great, Eddie."

Sunny looks great, Boone thought, with her long flower-print sarong, a flower in her hair, and a dot of barbecue sauce on her upper left lip.

"I had it flown in," Eddie said.

Yes, he had, Boone thought. Mounds of poi, huge platters of fresh ono and opah, pulled pork, chili rice, grilled Spam, and several pigs, the baking pits for which had been dug out of Eddie's back lawn with backhoes.

"Maybe it's time for the tattoo artist," Eddie said.

"Maybe not so much," Sunny said.

"Fire-eater?" Eddie asked.

"There you go," Boone said. He looked at Sunny raising her eyebrow. "What? Everyone likes a fire-eater."

Well, maybe not everybody. Maybe not a La Jolla crowd whose usual entertainment tended more toward chamber orchestras playing in museum foyers, cocktail-bar pianists warbling Cole Porter tunes, or investment-fund managers pointing toward every upward-climbing diagonal line.

The La Jollans stared at the performer—who was clad only in ankle-to-neck tattoos and something resembling a loincloth as he shoved rods of fire down his throat with a Lovelacian dexterity that would have sent a porno superstar into a paroxysm of envy—and prayed to a host of Episcopal saints that Eddie was not going to ask for any more volunteers from the audience. They surreptitiously eyed the front gate, with its promise of relative safety and sanity, but none of them wanted to earn Eddie's attention by being the first to leave.

Boone found Eddie a little later out by the saltwater wading pool ("'Bad for the *glass*. Bad for the *glass*,'" Johnny B. delighted in repeating) in a conversation with Dave.

"Eddie and I were just talking about *The Searchers,*'" Dave said. "He has it below *High Noon* but above *Fort Apache*?"

"Above them both, but nowhere near *Butch Cassidy,*" Boone said.

"Ah, *Butch Cassidy,*" Dave said. "Good flick."

Dave had dressed for the party in an expensive-looking silk Hawaiian-print shirt in reds and yellows, featuring parrots and ukuleles, and a pair of white slacks over his best dress sandals. His blond hair was neatly brushed back and he was wearing his "social," as opposed to his "business," shades, a pair of wraparound Nixons.

*"Shane,"* said Eddie.

"Another one," Dave said.

The party was definitely winding down, as was Eddie, whose constant toking had finally soothed his manic drive toward being the perfect host.

The guests—who were much more afraid of Eddie than when they'd arrived—departed in possession of stolen property, their white-knuckled hands clutching gift bags that contained, among other things, boxed sets of Izzy Kamakawiwo'ole CDs, iPods, Rolex watches, little balls of hashish wrapped in festively colored foil, gift certificates for a hot-rock massage at a local spa, Godiva chocolates, ribbed condoms, a selection of Paul Mitchell hair-care products, and ceramic bobblehead dolls of hula dancers with AHOLA (mis)printed on their stomachs.

Dave left in possession of a gift bag and two of the other guests.

Eddie thought the party a great success, and was surprised, disappointed, and even a little hurt when a forest of FOR SALE signs went up on his block and none of the guests ever came back, not even for a cup of coffee or a breakfast blunt. In fact, the neighbors would actually cross the street while walking their dogs, for fear of bumping into Eddie and being invited inside.

Not that living in Eddie's proximity was all negative—it wasn't. The residents had Neighborhood Watch, but they didn't *need* Neighborhood Watch, not with the twenty or so *hui* guys armed like Afghan warlords constantly peering from the walls of Eddie's estate. No B and E guy in his remotely right mind would take a chance on robbing any of the houses, lest he fuck up and break into Red Eddie's. You may, may, *may* break in, but you ain't ever breaking *out,* and the only fate worse than being an invited guest is being an uninvited one, what with Eddie already having trouble finding playmates for Dahmer.

Now Eddie does a couple of 360 wheelies on his bike and throws the bike sideways, squeaking the front tire an inch from Boone's feet.

# 23

"Boone Dawg!"

Red Eddie's retro-Afro orange hair is jammed under a brown Volcom beanie; he has a sleeveless Rusty shirt over a pair of cargo pants that are at least three sizes too big for him. No socks, Cobian sandals, Arnette shades that have to go two bills.

And he reeks of the chronic.

"Eddie," Boone says.

"S'up?"

"Not much."

"That's not what I hear," Eddie says.

"Okay, what do you hear?"

"I hear," Eddie says, flashing Boone forty g of cosmetic dentistry, "that you're dogging some stripper who thinks she saw something she didn't see."

"That didn't take long."

"Time is mo-naaay."

Well, Boone thinks, time is money if you actually *make* money. If you don't, time is just time.

"So, *bruddah,*" Red Eddie says, "can you back out dis wave?"

Which rings some alarm bells in Boone's head. Like, why does Eddie care? Eddie goes to Dan's clubs from time to time, but they're not, like, *boys*. That Boone knows of anyway. So he asks, "What's it to you, Eddie?"

"I come to a *bruddah* with an ask," Red Eddie says. "I have to have a reason?"

"It would help."

"Where's your aloha? Where's da love?" Red Eddie asks with a tone of hurt disappointment. "You can be very *haole* sometimes, Boone."

"I am a *haole,*" Boone says.

"Okay," Red Eddie says. "Talking story now, Dan Silver is a degenerate gambler, *bruddah* Boone, bad at picking basketball games. He got in deep water, I pulled him out; now he can't pay me. He owes the big dog a pile of bones he don't have, which he ain't going to have if he doesn't win his lawsuit against the insurance company. We on the same wave, coz?"

"It's beach break." Straight, simple, easy to read.

"So," Red Eddie says, "you would be showing me your aloha if you would sit out on the shoulder for a while. Now I'm hip that you need to rake lettuce to live, Boone brah, so whatever the *haoles* are paying you to do, I'll double you to don't. You know me, coz—I never come with my hand out, I don't have something in the other."

Yeah, but what? Eddie wonders. It brings up the age-old Christmas shopping conundrum: What do you give to the man who has everything? More precisely, what do you give to the man who wants nothing? That's the problem with trying to bribe the Boone Dawg: He's unique in the fact that his needs are simple, basic, and already met. The man needs cash, but it doesn't mean enough to him to be a swaying factor. So what's the tipping point? What can you offer B-Dog that would move him off his perfectly balanced ball?

Boone looks down at the weathered wood of the boardwalk, then back to Red Eddie. "I wish you'd come to me a couple of hours ago," he says. "Then I could have said yes."

"What happened then and now?"

"A woman was murdered," Boone says. "That puts it over the line."

Red Eddie doesn't look happy.

"So much as I hate to say no to you," Boone says. "I have to ride this one through, bro."

Red Eddie looks out to the ocean.

"Big swell coming," he says. "There's gonna be some real thunder crushers out there. Wave like that can suck you in and take you over the falls. Man's not careful, Boone Dawg, he could get crushed."

"Yeah," Boone says, "I know a little about big waves sucking people in, Eddie."

"I know you do, brah," Eddie says. "I know you do."

Red Eddie does a doughnut and pedals away. Shouts over his shoulder, *"E malama pono!"*

Take care of yourself.

# 24

Johnny Banzai goes back into room 342 at the Crest Motel.

It's your basic Pacific Beach motel room away from the water. Cheap and basic. Two twin beds, a television set bolted to a counter, the remote control bolted to a bedside table beside a clock radio. A couple of sun-faded photographs of beach scenes hang on the walls in cheap frames. A glass slider opens out to the little balcony. It's open, of course, and a light breeze blows the thin curtain back inside the room.

It took Johnny a while to settle Harrington down. You put Boone Daniels in front of Harrington, it's the proverbial red cape before a bull. The lieutenant wanted to know just what the fuck Boone was doing there, and, truth be told, so does Johnny.

For a PI, Boone is a shitty liar, and besides, he does very little matrimonial work. And no PI in his right mind brings the wife along to see live and in color what the husband's been up to. Not to mention the fact that the woman is a real looker who is not likely to be cheated on, and that she wasn't wearing a wedding ring.

So Boone's story is bullshit *totale,* and one of the very next things that Johnny is going to do is track Boone down and find out what he was doing at a motel where a woman played Rocky the Flying Squirrel with tragic results.

Now, Johnny Banzai and Boone Daniels are boys.

They go way back together, all the way to fifth grade, where they would drop their pencils at the same time so they could duck under their desks together, look at Miss Oliveira's legs, and giggle.

That was before Johnny got into the soft-core porn business.

What Johnny would do was buy back issues of *Playboy* from an older cousin, cut out the pictures, and slip them into the lining of his three-ring binder, which he had carefully sliced and covered over for the purpose. Then he'd sell them in the boys' room for fifty cents to a dollar each.

Johnny was doing a brisk trade in the boys' room one day when some ninth graders came in and decided to take him off. Boone came in like "Here I am to save the day," the surfer dude ready to rescue his little yellow brother, except that Johnny didn't exactly need rescuing.

Boone had heard the word *judo* before, but he had never *seen* judo, and now he watched in sheer awe as Johnny literally wiped the floor with one of his attackers, while a second sat against the wall trying to remember his name, and the third just stood there rethinking the whole idea.

Boone punched him in the stomach, just to help the thought process along a little bit.

That was *it*—he and Johnny had been friends before, but now they were *friends*. And when Johnny took his porn money down to Pacific Surf and bought a board with it, they were locked in. They've been buddies ever since, and when all the shit went down with Boone, Johnny was the only cop who stood by him. Johnny would kill for Boone and knows that Boone would do the same for him.

But—

They inhabit roughly the same professional sphere, and there are times when the Venn diagram intersects. Usually when this happens they're on the same side—they cooperate, share information. They've even done stakeouts together. But there are other times when they find themselves on opposite sides of a case.

Which is a problem that could fuck up a friendship. Except, being friends, they work it through what they call "the jump-in rule."

The jump-in rule states the following:

If Johnny and Boone find themselves on the same wave—following the metaphor, it's just like when someone jumps in on your wave—it's on. You do what you have to do and it's nothing personal. Johnny and Boone will go at it like the sheepdog and the coyote in those old cartoons, and, at the end of the day, when they punch out, they'll still meet at the beach, grill some fish together, and watch the sunset.

It's the jump-in rule, and if one guy asks a question the other guy can't answer, or asks the other guy to do something he can't do, all the other guy has to say is "jump-in rule," and enough said.

Game on.

This is what Johnny plans to say when he finds Boone—ask him some very pointed questions, and if Boone doesn't have some very good answers, then Johnny's going to arrest his ass for impeding an investigation. Doesn't want to do it, won't like doing it, but he will do it and Boone will understand. Then Johnny will go in and spring for bail money.

Because Johnny has a thing about loyalty.

Of course he does. If you're Japanese and you grew up anywhere in California, you have a thing about loyalty.

Johnny's too young to remember it—Johnny was a long way from even having been born—when the U.S. government accused his grandparents of disloyalty and hauled them off to a camp in the Arizona desert for the duration of the war.

He's heard the stories, though. He knows the history. Hell, the cop shop that he works out of is just blocks away from what used to be "Little Japan," down on Fifth and Island, on the south edge of the Gaslamp District.

San Diego's Nikkei community had been in the area since the turn of the century, first as immigrant farmworkers, or tuna fishermen down in Point Loma. They'd worked their asses off so that the next generation could buy land in Mission Valley and up in North County near Oceanside, where they became small, independent farmers. Hell, Johnny's maternal grandfather still grows strawberries up east of O'side, stubbornly hanging in there against the dual enemies of age and urban development.

Johnny's paternal grandfather moved into Little Japan and opened up a bath and barber shop, where the Japanese men came in to get their hair cut and then take long hot baths in the steaming *furo* down in the basement.

Johnny's father has walked him through the old neighborhood, pointing out the buildings that still survived, showing him where Hagusi's grocery store was, where the Tobishas had their restaurant, where old Mrs. Kanagawa kept her flower shop.

It was a thriving community, mixed in with the Filipinos and the few Chinese who stayed after the city tore down Chinatown, and the blacks and the whites, and it was a nice place to be and to grow up.

Then Pearl Harbor happened.

Johnny's father heard it on the radio. He was seven years old then, and he ran to the barbershop to tell *his* father. By the next morning, the FBI had rounded up the president of the Japanese Association, the faculty of the

Japanese School, the Buddhist priests, and the judo and kendo instructors and thrown them in a cell with the common criminals.

Within a week, the fishermen, the vegetable growers, and the strawberry farmers had been arrested. Johnny's father still remembers standing on a sidewalk downtown and watching as they were marched—in handcuffs—from one jail to another. He remembers his father telling him not to look, because these men—leaders of their community—were looking down at the ground in their humiliation and their shame.

Two months later, the entire Nikkei community was forced out of its homes and taken by train to the racetrack at Santa Anita, where they stayed for almost a year behind wire before being moved to the internment camp in Poston, Arizona. When they returned to San Diego after the war, they found that many of their homes, businesses, and farms had been taken over by whites. Some of the Nikkei left; others yielded to reality and started over; some—like Johnny's maternal grandfather—began the long and tortuous legal process to recover their property.

But Little Japan was no more, and the once-tight Nikkei community scattered all over the county. Johnny's father went to college, on to medical school, and then set up a successful practice in Pacific Beach.

He always thought his son would join the practice and take it over, but Johnny had other ideas. Young Johnny was always a little different from his siblings—while he dutifully fulfilled the stereotype of the diligent Asian student, Johnny preferred action to academics. He got through the school day to get to the baseball field, where he was an All-City second baseman. When he wasn't on the diamond, he was in the water, a hard-charging grom ripping waves. Or he was in the dojo, learning judo from the older Japanese men, Johnny's one real bow to his heritage.

When it came time for Johnny to choose a career path, he had the grades to go premed but went prelaw instead. When it came time to go to law school, Johnny checked out of that wave. He dreaded more hours at the library, more days behind a desk. What he craved was action, so he took the police exam and shredded it.

When Johnny told his father about his decision to become a cop, his father thought about the police who had led his own father in handcuffs through the streets of downtown San Diego, but he said nothing. Heritage, he thought, should be a foundation, not an anchor. Johnny didn't become a doctor, but he married one, and that helped to ease the sting. The important thing was that Johnny become a success in his chosen field, and Johnny rocketed through the uniformed ranks to became a very good detective indeed.

His connections to the Japanese community, though, are tenuous. He retains enough Japanese to be an annoyance in a sushi bar, he goes to the Buddhist temple with less and less frequency, and he's even missed one or two of the monthly visits to his grandfather at the old farm. It's just the way things are in this modern American, Southern California life. The Kodanis are just busy people—Beth puts in brutal hours at the hospital and Johnny works his files like a machine with no off switch. Then there's all the stuff with the kids—soccer games, Little League, karate, ballet, tutoring sessions—it's small wonder there's little room in the schedule for the old traditions.

Now the good detective opens the cheap, lightweight sliding door, which reveals a narrow closet. No clothes on the wire hangers, no shoes on the floor. A woman's suitcase—more of an overnight bag—is set on a free-standing rack, and now Johnny goes through it. A pair of jeans, a folded blouse, some underwear, the usual assortment of cosmetics.

Either Tammy Roddick wasn't planning on being gone long or she didn't have time to pack. But why would a woman contemplating suicide pack an overnight bag?

Johnny goes into the bathroom.

It hits him right away.

Two toothbrushes on the sink.

One of them is pink, and small.

A child's.

# 25

The girl walks on the trodden dirt path on the side of the road.

Her skin is a rich brown, her hair black as freshly hewn coal. She trips over a brown beer bottle that was thrown out the window of a car the night before, but she keeps walking, and as she does, she fingers a small silver cross held by a thin chain around her neck. It gives her courage; it's her one tangible symbol of love in an unloving world.

In shock, not really sure where she's going, she keeps the ocean to her left because it's something she recognizes, and she knows that if she keeps the water to her left, she will eventually reach the strawberry fields. The fields are bad, but they are the only life she has known for the past two years, and her friends are there.

She needs her friends because she has nobody now. And if she can find the strawberry fields, she will find her friends, maybe even see the *guero* doctor, who was at least nice to her. So she keeps walking north, unnoticed by the drivers who rush past in their cars—just another Mexican girl on the side of the road.

A gust of wind blows dirt and garbage around her ankles.

# 26

Boone stops off at The Sundowner for a jolt of caffeine and a delay in trying to explain the inexplicable to Petra Hall, attorney-at-law and all-around pain in the ass.

High Tide's there, his bulk perched with surprising grace on a stool at the bar, his huge hands clutching a sandwich that should have its own area code. He wears the brown uniform of the San Diego Public Works Department, in which he's a foreman. Tide is basically in charge of the storm drains in this part of the city, and with the oncoming weather, he knows he could be in for a long day.

Boone sits down beside him as Sunny looks up from wiping some glasses, walks over to the coffeepot, pours him a cup, and slides it down the bar.

"Thanks," Boone says.

"Don't mention it." She turns back to wiping the glasses.

What's she torqued about? Boone wonders. He turns to Tide. "I just had a conversation with one of the more interesting members of the greater Oceania community."

"How *is* Eddie?" Tide asks.

"Worked up," Boone says. "I thought you island types were supposed to be all laid-back and chill and stuff."

"We've picked up bad habits from you *haole*," Tide says. "Protestant work ethic, Calvinist predetermination, all that crap. What's got Eddie's balls up his curly orange short hairs?"

"Dan Silver."

Tide takes a bite of his sandwich. Mustard, mayonnaise, and what Boone hopes is tomato juice squirt out the sides of the bread. "Don't make no sense. Eddie don't go to strip clubs. When he wants all that, the strip club comes to Eddie."

"Says Dan owes him a big head of lettuce."

Tide shakes his head. "I ain't ever heard that Eddie puts money on the street. Not to *haoles* anyway. Eddie will front to Pac Islanders, but that's about it."

"Maybe he's expanding his customer base," Boone says.

"Maybe," Tide says, "but I doubt it. Way it works, you owe Eddie money and you don't pay, he don't take it up with you; he takes it up with your family back home. And it's a disgrace, Boone, a big shame, so the family back on the island usually takes care of the debt, one way or the other."

"That's harsh."

"Welcome to *my* world," Tide says. It's hard to explain to a guy, even a friend like Boone, what it's like straddling the Pacific. Boone's literally lived his whole life within a few blocks of where they're sitting right now; there's no way he, or Dave, or even Johnny can understand that Tide, who was born and bred just up the road in Oceanside, is still answerable to a village in Samoa that he's never seen. And the same thing applies to most of the Oceania people living in California—they have living roots back in Samoa, Hawaii, Guam, Fiji, what have you.

So you start making some money, you send some of it "home" to help support relatives back in the *ville*. A cousin comes over, he stays on your couch until he makes enough scratch at the job you got him to maybe get his own place, where he'll have another cousin crash. You do something good, a whole village five thousand miles away celebrates with pride; you do something bad, the same village feels the shame.

All that's a burden, but . . . your kids have grandmas and grandpas, aunties and uncles, who love them like their own kids. Even in O'side, the children go back and forth between houses like they were huts in the village. If your wife gets sick, aunties you never knew you had show up with pots of soup, cooked meat, fish, and rice.

It's *aiga*—family.

And if you ever get in trouble, if someone outside the "community" takes you on, threatens your livelihood or your life, then the whole tribe shows up over your shoulder; you don't even have to ask. Just like The Dawn Patrol—you call the wolf, you get the pack.

Back in the day, Tide was a serious gang banger, a *matai*—chief—in the Samoan Lords. S'way it was, you grew up in Oceanside back then, especially in the Mesa Margarita neighborhood: You played football and you g'd up with your boys. Thank God for football, High Tide thinks now, remembering, because he loved the game and it kept him off the drugs. Tide wasn't your drive-by, gun-toting banger hooked on *ma'a*. No, Tide kept his body in good shape, and when he went to war with the other gangs, he went Polynesian-style—flesh-to-flesh.

High Tide was a legend in those O'side rumbles. He'd place his big body in front of his boys, stare down the other side, then yell *"Fa'aumu!"*—the ancient Samoan call to war. Then it was *on, hamo,* fists flying until it was the last man standing.

That was always High Tide.

Same thing on the football field. When High Tide came out of the womb, the doctor looked at him and said, "Defensive tackle." Samoan men play football, period, and because O'side has more Samoans than anyplace but Samoa, its high school team is practically an NFL feeder squad.

High Tide was where running games went to die.

He'd just eat them up, throw off the pulling guard like a sandwich wrapper, then plow the ball carrier into the turf. Teams that played O'side would just give up on the ground game and start throwing the ball like the old Air Coryell Chargers.

Scouts noticed.

Tide would come home from practice to stacks of letters from colleges, but he was interested only in San Diego State. He wasn't going to go far from home—to some cold state without an ocean to surf in. And he wasn't going far from *aiga,* from family, because for a Samoan, family is everything.

So Tide started for four years at State. When he wasn't slaughtering I-Backs, he was out surfing with his new friends: Boone Daniels, Johnny Banzai, Dave the Love God, and Sunny Day. He gave up the gang banging—it was just old, tired, dead-end shit. He'd still go have a beer with the boys sometimes, but that was about it. He was too busy playing ball and riding waves, and became sort of a *matai* emeritus in the gang— highly respected, listened to and obeyed, but above it all.

He went early third round in the NFL draft.

Played one promising season, second string for the Steelers, until he got locked up with a Bengals center and the pulling guard came around and low-jacked him.

Tide heard the knee pop.

Sounded like a gunshot.

He came home to O'side depressed as hell, his life over. Sat around his parents' house on Arthur Avenue, indulging himself in beer, weed, and self-pity, until Boone swung by and basically told him to knock that shit off. Boone practically dragged him back down to the beach and pushed him out into the break.

First ride in, he decided he was going to live.

Used his SDSU glory days to get a gig with the city. Found himself a Samoan woman, got married, had three kids.

Life is good.

Now he explains to Boone some of the intricacies of Oceania business protocol.

"That's why Eddie only deals with the *ohana,* bro," Tide says. "He knows if he goes to a *haole* family with a debt, they say, 'What's it got to do with us?' Family's a different concept on this side of the pond, Boone."

"Yes, it is."

"Yes, it is."

Boone eyes Sunny, who's very deliberately not eyeing him back.

"What's her problem?" he asks Tide.

Tide has heard all about the British betty from Dave. He slides off his stool, shoves the last bite of the sandwich into his mouth, and pats Boone on the shoulder. "I got work to do. For a smart man, Boone, you're a fuck-ing idiot. You need any more anthropological insights, give me a ring."

He pulls his brown wool beanie onto his head, slips on his gloves, and goes out the door.

Boone looks at Sunny. "Hey."

"Hey."

"What's up?"

"Not much," Sunny says, not looking at him. "What's up with you?"

"Come *on,* Sunny."

She walks over to him. "Okay, are you sleeping with her?"

"Who?"

"Bye, Boone." She turns away.

"No, she's a client, that's all."

"All of a sudden you know who I'm talking about," Sunny says, turning toward him again.

"I guess it's obvious."

"Yeah, I guess."

"She's a client," Boone repeats. Then he starts getting a little pissed that he has to explain. "And, by the way, what's it to you? It's not like we're . . ."

"No, it's not like we're anything," Sunny says.

"You see other guys," Boone says.

"You bet I do," Sunny shot back. And she has, but nobody even close to serious since she and Boone split up.

"So?"

"So nothing," Sunny says. "I just think that, as friends, we should be honest with each other."

"I'm being honest."

"Okay."

"Okay."

"Okay." She walks away and goes back to wiping glasses.

Boone doesn't finish his coffee.

# 27

Dan Silver and Red Eddie are also having an unhappy conversation.

"What did you do, Danny?" Eddie asks.

"Nothing."

"Killing a woman is 'nothing'?"

Well, apparently.

Danny drops his head, which is a mistake because Eddie shoots a wicked slap across his cheek. "Did you think I wouldn't find out? I have to hear this from Boone when I go to him with an ask for *you*? You let me do that, not tell me you went ahead like some kind of cowboy you dress up like?"

"She was going to talk, Eddie." Dan can still feel the burn on his cheek, and for a nanosecond he considers doing something about it—he's about twice Eddie's size and could toss him against the wall like a Ping-Pong ball—then decides against it because Eddie's *hui* boys linger on the edge of the conversation like sharks.

"That's why you were going to take her out of town, wasn't it?" Eddie asks. "Nobody ever said nothin' 'bout killing nobody."

"Things got a little out of hand," Dan says.

Eddie looks at him incredulously. "They hook her to you, they hook you to me, I'm gonna cut you loose like tangled fish line, Danny boy."

Dan's getting a little tired of Eddie's superior shit. So the tattooed little freak went to Harvard, so fucking what? There's a lot of things you can't learn at Harvard. So he decides to educate Eddie a little. "A stripper takes a walk off a motel balcony. How long you think that's going to occupy the cops? An hour? Hour and a half? Nobody gives a crap, Eddie."

"Daniels does."

"Is he going to back off?"

"Probably not," Eddie says. "Backing off ain't Boone's best thing."

Dan shrugs. "Daniels is a low-rent surf bum who couldn't cut it with the real cops. He's fine for a skip trace or throwing a drunk out of The Sundowner, but he's in over his head here. I wouldn't worry about it, I were you."

"Well, you ain't me," Eddie says. "You're you, and you better fucking worry about it. Let me tell you something about that surf bum—"

Dan's cell phone rings.

"What?"

He listens. It's a cop from downtown, a sergeant who drinks free at Silver Dan's and gets a lap dance comped every once in a while. He wants to let Dan know that one of his girls has been positively ID'd, DOA from a jump at a Pacific Beach motel.

Her name is Angela Hart.

Dan thanks the guy and clicks off.

"What was that?" Eddie asks.

"Nothing."

But it's a big freaking nothing. Dan's head is whirling, his stomach doing trampoline routines.

Tweety killed the wrong piece of ass.

# 28

Petra starts to ask something, then changes her mind.

"What?" Cheerful asks.

As pretty as the woman is, Cheerful's getting tired of her sitting around the office waiting for Boone to get back. It's a bad idea, clients involving themselves in the minute-by-minute of a case. They should pay the bill, back off, and wait for results. He mumbles something to that effect.

"Sorry?" Petra asks.

"If you have something on your mind," Cheerful says, "get it off."

"Boone used to be a police officer?" Petra asks.

"You already knew that," Cheerful says. This girl does her homework, Cheerful thinks. She'd have done due diligence on Boone.

"What happened?" Petra asks.

"Why do you think that's any of your business?" Cheerful asks.

"Well . . . I don't. . . ."

Cheerful looks up from the adding machine. It's the first time he's seen this girl nonplussed. "What I mean is," he says, "are you asking as a client, or as a friend?"

Because there's a difference.

"I'm not asking as a client," Petra says.

"Boone pulled his own pin," Cheerful says. "He wasn't thrown out. It wasn't for taking money or anything like that."

"I didn't think that," Petra says. She saw the interaction between Boone and the detective at the motel. She didn't hear what was said, but she saw that Boone had to be restrained. It was rather intense. "Money doesn't seem to be a priority for him."

"Boone's too lazy to steal?" Cheerful says.

"I'm not trying to pick a fight. I was just wondering."

"It had to do with a girl," Cheerful snaps.

Of course, Petra thinks. Of course it did. She looks at Cheerful as if to say, Go on, but Cheerful leaves it at that.

She seems like a good person, but it's early.

Some stories have to be earned.

# 29

Rain Sweeny was six years old when she disappeared from the front yard of her house.

Just like that.

Gone.

Her mother had been out there with her, heard the phone ring, and went in to answer it. She was only gone a minute, she'd say between sobs at the inevitable press conferences later. A beautiful summer day, a little girl playing out in her yard in a nice middle-class neighborhood in Mira Mesa, and then—

Tragedy.

It didn't take long for the cops to get a lead on who did it. Russ Rasmussen, a two-time loser with a "short eyes" sheet, was renting a room in a house just down the street. When the detectives went to interview him, he was gone, and the neighbors said that they hadn't seen his green '86 Corolla parked on the street since the afternoon that Rain went missing.

Coincidence, maybe, but no one believes in that kind of coincidence.

An APB went out on Russ Rasmussen.

Boone had been on the force for three years. He loved his job; he *loved* it. It was just perfect for him—active, physical, something new happening every night. He'd come off his shift and go straight to the beach in time for

The Dawn Patrol, then get some breakfast at The Sundowner and go home to his little apartment to grab some sleep.

Then get up and do it all over again.

It was perfection.

He had his job, he had Sunny, and he had the ocean.

Never turn your back on the ocean.

That's what Boone's dad always taught him: Never get relaxed and turn your back on the ocean, because the second you do, that big wave is going to come out of nowhere and smack you down.

A week after Rain Sweeny was kidnapped, Boone was cruising one night with his partner, Steve Harrington, who had just tested out and was headed to the Detective Division. It had been a quiet night, and they were taking a spin down through the east part of the Gaslamp District, over near the warehouses that the tweekers liked to break into, when they spotted a green '86 Corolla parked in an alley.

"Did you see that?" Boone asked Harrington.

"See what?"

Boone pointed it out.

Harrington pulled over to the entrance to the alley and flashed a lamp on the car's license plate.

"Holy shit," Harrington said.

It was Rasmussen's car.

The man was sound asleep in the front seat.

"I'd have thought he'd be far away by now," Harrington said.

"Should I call it in?" Boone asked.

"Fuck that," Harrington said. He got out of the cruiser, pulled his weapon, and approached the car. Boone got out on the passenger side and walked behind him and to the side, covering him. Harrington holstered his weapon, jerked the Corolla door open, and yanked Rasmussen out of the car. Before Rasmussen could wake up and start screaming, Harrington dropped a knee on his neck, twisted his arm behind his back, and cuffed him.

Boone slipped his revolver back into its holster as Harrington hauled Rasmussen to his feet and pushed him against the car. Rasmussen was a big man, over two and a half bills, but Harrington lifted him like he weighed nothing. The cop's adrenaline was screeching.

So was Boone's as he walked back to the cruiser.

"Stay off that fucking radio," Harrington snapped.

Boone stopped in his tracks.

"Help me get him in the car," Harrington said.

Boone grabbed one of Rasmussen's elbows and helped Harrington drag him to the black-and-white, then held Rasmussen's head down as Harrington pushed him into the seat. Harrington slammed the door shut and looked at Boone.

"What?" Harrington asked.

"Nothing," Boone said. "Let's just get him to the house."

"We're not going to the house."

"The orders are—"

"Yeah, I know what the orders are," Harrington said. "And I know what the orders *mean*. The orders mean under no circumstances do you bring him in until he's told you what he did with the girl."

"I don't know, Steve."

"I do," Harrington said. "Look, Boone, if we take him to the house, he'll lawyer up and we'll never find out where that little girl is."

"So—"

"So we take him down to the water," Harrington said. "We hold his head under until he decides to tell us what he did with the girl. No bruises, no marks, no nothing."

"You can't just torture a man."

"Maybe *you* can't," Harrington said. "I can. Watch me."

"Jesus, Steve."

"Jesus nothing, Boone," Harrington said. "What if the girl is still alive? What if the sick fuck has her buried somewhere and the air is running out? You really want to wait to go through 'the process,' Boone? I don't think the kid has the time for your moral scruples. Now get in the fucking car; we're going to the beach."

Boone got in.

Sat there in silence while Harrington headed the car toward Ocean Beach and started in on Rasmussen. "You want to save yourself some pain, short eyes, you'll tell us right now what you did with that little girl."

"I don't know what you're talking about."

"Keep it up," Harrington said. "Go ahead, make us madder."

"I don't know anything about any little girl," Rasmussen said. Boone turned to look at him. The man was terrified—sweating, his eyes popping out of his head.

"You know what we have in mind for you?" Harrington asked, peeking into the rearview mirror. "You know what it's like to drown? When we pull you out after a couple of minutes breathing water, you'll be begging to tell us. What did you do with her? Is she alive? Did you kill her?"

"I don't know—"

"Okay," Harrington said, pushing down on the gas pedal. "We're going to the submarine races!"

Rasmussen started to shake. His knees knocked together involuntarily.

"You piss your pants in my cruiser," Harrington told him, "I'm going to get really mad, Russ. I'm going to hurt you even worse."

Rasmussen started screaming and kicking his feet against the door.

Harrington laughed. It didn't matter—Rasmussen wasn't going anywhere and nobody was going to hear him. After a couple of minutes, he stopped screaming, sat back in the seat, and just whimpered.

Boone felt like he was going to throw up.

"Easy, surfer boy," Harrington said.

"This isn't right."

"There's a kid involved," Harrington said. "Suck it up."

It didn't take long to get to Ocean Beach. Harrington pulled the car over by the pier, turned around, looked at Rasmussen, and said, "Last chance."

Rasmussen shook his head.

"All right," Harrington said. He opened the car door and started to get out.

Boone reached for the radio. "Unit 9152. We have suspect Russell Rasmussen. We're coming in."

"You cunt," Harrington said. "You weak fucking cunt."

Rasmussen never told what he did with the girl.

The SDPD held him for as long as they could, but without evidence they couldn't do anything and had to kick him. Every cop on the force looked for the girl's body for weeks, but they finally gave up.

Rasmussen, he went off the radar.

And life got bad for Boone.

He became a pariah on the force.

Harrington moved to Detective Division, and it was hard to find another uniform who wanted to ride with Boone Daniels. The ones who would were bottom-of-the-barrel types, cops whom other cops didn't want to ride with—the drunks, the losers, the guys with one foot out the door anyway—and none of the pairings lasted longer than a couple of weeks.

When Boone would call for backup, the other cops would be a little slow in responding; when he went into the locker room, no one spoke to him and backs were turned; when he'd go to leave, he'd pick up mumbled comments—"weak unit," "child killer," "traitor."

He had one friend on the force—Johnny Banzai.

"You shouldn't be seen with me," Boone told him one day. "I'm poison."

"Knock off the self-pity," Johnny told him.

"Seriously," Boone said. "They won't like you being friends with me."

"I don't give a shit what they like," Johnny said. "My friends are my friends."

And that was that.

One day, Boone was leaving the locker room when he heard a cop named Kocera mutter, "Fucking pussy."

Boone came back in, grabbed him, and put his brother cop into a wall. Punches were thrown, and Boone ended up with a month's unpaid suspension and mandatory appointments with a department counselor who talked to him about anger management.

The subject of Rain Sweeny didn't come up.

Boone spent most of the month on Sunny's couch.

He'd get up by eleven in the morning, drain a couple of beers, and lie there watching television, looking out the window, or just sleeping. It drove Sunny nuts. This was a Boone she'd never seen—passive, morose, angry.

One day when she gently suggested that he might want to go out for a surf session, he replied, "Don't *handle* me, okay, Sunny? I don't need *handling*."

"I wasn't handling you."

"Fuck."

He got up off the couch and went back to bed.

She was hoping things would get better when he went back to work.

They didn't. They got worse.

The department took him off the street altogether and put him behind a desk, filing arrest reports. It was a prescription to drive an active, outdoor man crazy, and it did the trick. Eight to five, five days a week, he sat alone in a cubicle, entering data. He'd come home bored, edgy, and angry.

He was miserable.

"Quit," Dave the Love God told him.

"I'm not a quitter," Boone replied.

But three months into this bullshit, he did quit. Pulled his papers, turned in his badge and gun, and walked away. No one tried to talk him out of it. The only word he heard was from Harrington, who literally opened the door for him on the way out.

The word was "Good."

Two hours later, Boone was back on Sunny's couch.

Surfing was out. Boone went AWOL from The Dawn Patrol. He never showed up anymore. He didn't go out at all.

One night, Sunny came home from a long shift at The Sundowner, found him stretched out on the sofa in the sweatpants and T-shirt that he'd had on for a week, and said, "We have to talk about this."

"Which really means *you* have to talk about this."

"You're clinically depressed."

"'Clinically depressed'?" Boone asked. "You're a shrink now?"

"I talked to one."

"Fuck, Sunny."

It got him off the couch anyway. He went out to her little porch and plopped down on one of the folding beach chairs. She followed him out there.

"I know you're angry," she said. "I don't blame you."

"I do."

"What?"

"I do," Boone repeated, staring out toward the ocean. She could see tears running down his face as he said, "I should have done what Harrington said. I should have helped him hold that guy under the water . . . beat him . . . hurt him . . . whatever it took to make him give up what he did with Rain Sweeny. I was wrong, and that girl is dead because of me."

Sunny thought that this was a cathartic moment, that he'd start to heal after this, that things would get better.

She was wrong.

He just sank deeper into his depression, slowly drowning in his guilt and shame.

Johnny Banzai tried to talk to him. Came over one day and said, "You know that girl was almost certainly dead before you picked up Rasmussen. All the data show that—"

"Sunny ask you to come over?"

"What difference—"

"Fuck your 'data,' Johnny. Fuck you."

The whole Dawn Patrol tried to work him out of it. No good. Even Red Eddie came by.

"I have all my people out," Eddie said, "looking for your girl, looking for that sick bastard. If he raises his head anywhere, Boone, I'll have him."

"Thanks, Eddie,"

"Anything for you, *bruddah,*" Eddie said. "Anything in this world."

But it didn't happen. Even Eddie's soldiers couldn't find Russ Rasmussen, couldn't find Rain Sweeny. And Boone sank deeper and deeper into his depression.

A month later, Sunny gave him an ultimatum. "I can't live like this," she said. "I can't live with *you* like this. Either you go get some help or . . ."

"Or what? Come on, say it, Sunny."

"Or find another place to live."

He took the "or."

She knew he would.

You don't give a guy like Boone an ultimatum and expect any other result. The truth was, she was relieved to see him go. She was ashamed of it, but she was glad to be alone in her place. Alone was better.

Better for him, too.

He knew that he was just taking her down with him.

If you're going to sink, he told himself, at least have the decency to sink alone. Go down with your own ship.

Alone.

So he left the police force, he left Sunny, he left his friends, The Dawn Patrol, and he left surfing.

Never turn your back on the ocean.

You may think you can walk away from it, but you can't. The pull of

the tide brings you back; the water in your blood yearns for its home-
coming. And one morning, after two more months of lying around his
apartment, Boone picked up his board and paddled out alone. He didn't
think about it, had no *intention* of going out that morning; he just went.

The ocean healed him—slowly and not completely, but it healed him.
He went out in the roughest, baddest surf he could find; he wandered from
break to break like Odysseus trying to navigate his way home. At Tourma-
line, Rockslide, Black's, D Street, Swami's, Boone sought the pounding
he felt that he deserved, and the ocean gave it to him.

It beat him, battered him, scrubbed his skin with salt and sand. He'd
trudge home exhausted and sleep the sleep of the dead. Get up with the sun
and do it again. And again and again, until one morning he reappeared at
The Dawn Patrol.

It was nothing dramatic—there was no moment of decision—it was
just that he was there in the lineup when the rest of them paddled out.
Johnny, High Tide, Dave, and Sunny. Nobody said anything to him about
it; they just picked up where they'd left off, as if he'd never been gone.

On the beach at the end of that session, Johnny asked him, "What are
you going to do now?"

"You're looking at it."

"Just surf?"

Boone shrugged.

"Did you win the lottery?" Johnny asked. "You need to make a living,
don't you?"

"Yeah."

Dave offered to get Boone on as a lifeguard. He'd need to take a couple
of courses, Dave said, but it should only take about six months. Boone
declined; he figured he wasn't that good at guarding people's lives.

It was Johnny's idea for Boone to get his PI's license.

"All kinds of work for ex-cops," Johnny said. "Insurance investiga-
tions, security, bond jumpers, matrimonial stuff."

Boone went with it.

He wasn't thrilled about it, but that was the point. He didn't want a job
that he loved. You love something, it hurts when you lose it.

Which is what worried Sunny. To the rest of his world, Boone was
back, same as he ever was—laid-back, joking, refining the List of Things

That Are Good, grilling fish on the beach at night, making supper for his friends, wrapping everything in a tortilla. Among The Dawn Patrol, Sunny was the only one who knew that Boone *wasn't* back, not fully. She suspected that he now inhabited a world of diminished expectations, both of himself and of other people, of life itself. That Boone only wanted to work enough to support his surfing jones might have seemed hip, but she understood it as the disappointment that it was.

Disappointment in life.

In himself.

They stayed close; they stayed tight. They even slept together now and then for old times' sake or out of loneliness. But they both knew it wasn't going anywhere and they both knew why—Sunny knew that Boone was still missing a piece of himself, and neither she nor he was willing to settle for anything less than the whole man.

The ironic thing was that it was Boone who pushed her to be everything she could be. Boone who did for her what she couldn't do for herself, and what she couldn't do for him. It was Boone who told her that she couldn't settle for anything less than her dream. When she was discouraged and ready to sell out, get a real job, it was Boone who told her to hang in, keep waiting tables so that she could surf, that success was riding the next wave her way.

Boone wouldn't let her quit.

The way he quit on himself.

What Sunny doesn't know is that Boone's still trying to find Russ Rasmussen. In those soulful hours of the morning, he sits at his computer at home, tracking him down. Trying to find a trail—a Social Security number showing up on a job, a rental application, a gas bill, anything. When he runs into skells, he asks them if they've heard anything about Rasmussen, but none of them have.

When the man disappeared, he disappeared.

Maybe he's dead, taking the truth with him.

But Boone doesn't give up. Boone Daniels, one of the most peaceful creatures in the universe, keeps a .38 in his apartment. He never takes it out, never carries it. He just saves it for the day when he finds Russ Rasmussen. Then he's going to walk the man to a quiet place, make him talk, and then put a bullet in his head.

# 30

Boone walks back to the office.

To the office, not *into* the office.

What he's going to do is just get in his van and take off to Angela Hart's place. If Angela took Tammy's place, there's a good chance that Tammy took Angela's. Anyway, it's the best shot he has. And he needs to hurry, because Johnny Banzai's gonna figure out on the quick that he's got the wrong ID and he'll be *on* it.

So will Danny Silver, Boone thinks. Cops get comped at strip bars, for the same reasons he gets free nosh at The Sundowner, so there's any number of guys who could have given Danny the heads-up.

It doesn't really matter who it is, Boone thinks; it only matters *that* it is, and now we're in a race to get to Tammy Roddick. So if Tammy's lying low in Angela's place, Boone thinks, I'd better get over there first. And I sure as hell don't need Pete coming with me, endlessly busting balls, getting in the way. Better she busts Cheerful's balls. He likes being miserable—they're perfect together.

But when he gets to the Boonemobile, Petra's sitting in the passenger seat like a dog that knows it's going for a ride.

"I've been meaning to get that lock fixed," Boone says as he gets behind the wheel.

"So," Petra asks, "where are we going?"

# 31

Boone heads south through Mission Beach.

"Why do they call this Mission Beach?" she asks. "Is there a mission here?"

"Sure," Boone says. He knows what the mission is, too. Lie on the beach all day, pound beer, and get laid.

"Where is it?" Petra asks.

"Where's what?"

"The mission," Petra says. "I'd like to see it."

Oh, *that* kind of mission.

"They tore it down," Boone tells her, lying. "To build *that*."

He points seaside—to Belmont Amusement Park, where the old wooden roller coaster looms over the landscape like a funky man-made wave. It's been there a long time and is one of the last of the old-style wooden coasters. There used to be a lot of them, all up and down the coast. Seemed like the first thing people did when they settled a beach town was to build a wooden roller coaster.

Of course, that was before the Hawaiians taught us to surf, Boone thinks. Speaking of missionaries . . . We sent people over there with Bibles, and they sent guys back with boards.

The Hawaiians sure got the shitty end of that stick.

Anyway, thank you, *mahalo*.

Boone heads to Ocean Beach.

Ocean Beach is not a place that time actually forgot. It's more like time got up to about 1975 and said fuck it.

OB, as the Obeachians call it, has old hippie shops where you can buy crystals and that shit, bars that still do black-light effects, and used-record stores that sell actual records, including ones by a staggering variety of obscure reggae bands. The only thing that ever roused the Obeachians from their usual "Peace, dude," torpor was when Starbucks wanted to move into the neighborhood.

Then there was civil insurrection, or the Obeachian version of it anyway.

"The Frisbees will be flying tomorrow," Johnny Banzai had correctly predicted, and, indeed, there was a mass Frisbee demonstration, a marathon Hacky Sack show of force, and a sit-in along Newport Avenue, which didn't really work because a bunch of people sitting on the sidewalk doing nothing looked pretty much like any other day. So corporate culture, in the personification of Starbucks, won out, but it's really there for tourists because the Obeachians won't go near the place. Neither will Boone.

"I respect all local taboos," he says.

And you have to love a community that named one of its major streets after Voltaire, and that Voltaire Street leads to a beach set aside for dogs. Dog Beach occupies a prime piece of real estate that curls around from the floodway onto the open ocean, and you can see some of the best quadrupedal Frisbee athletes in the world there. Of course, they can't throw the disk, but they can sure as hell run and catch it, doing sometimes spectacular leaps and spins to bring it down. You also have surfing dogs at Dog Beach. Some of them ride in tandem in front of their masters, but others actually ride on their own, their masters setting them on the board just in front of the white water.

All of which inspired a conversation the day The Dawn Patrol went down to check out the Frisbee demonstration, got bored, and walked over to watch dogs surf.

"Have you ever pulled a dog out of the water?" Boone asked Dave.

"No. Dogs are generally smarter than people."

"Plus, they have better traction," Johnny observed. "Lower center of gravity and four feet on the board instead of two."

"Paws," Sunny said.

"Huh?"

"Not feet," Sunny said. "Paws."

"Right."

"But they can't paddle," Hang Twelve said, maybe a little jealous because prior to this conversation he held the "most toes on a board" honors.

"Dogs can't paddle?" High Tide asked.

"No," Hang said.

"You ever heard of the 'dog paddle'?" Tide said.

"That thing little kids do in swimming pools?" Hang asked.

"Yeah."

"Yeah, I've heard of it."

"Where did they get the name?" Tide asked.

Hang thought about this for a few seconds, then said, "But dogs can't paddle *boards;* that's what I meant. Dogs weren't meant to surf."

"That thing that runs from the board to your ankle," Tide said. "What's it called?"

"The leash," Hang replied.

"End of story," said Tide.

They eventually resolved that if dogs *could* paddle boards, they'd be the world champion surfers every year, because dogs *never* fall. They jump off at the end of the ride, shake the water out of their fur, and wait to go back out again.

"Kind of like you," Dave said to Tide. "You jump off, shake your fur, and go back out again."

Because Tide is one hairy guy.

"They've been looking for Bigfoot all over those remote forests," Johnny chimed in. "They should have just come out to PB and looked into the water."

"Surfing Sasquatch," Sunny said. "Film at eleven."

Anyway, they hung out for a while, watched dogs surf and chase Frisbees, then went back to Newport Street, to find that the protestors had gotten bored sitting around there and had gone to find another place to sit around and maybe get some coffee.

You gotta love Ocean Beach.

Now Boone turns inland onto Brighton Avenue, pulls up in front of Angela Hart's four-story apartment building, and tells Petra to—

"I know," she says. "'Wait in the van.'"

"You're an officer of the court," Boone says, digging around the back of the van for his burglary tools. "Do you really want to witness breaking and entering? Stay here, be a lookout."

He finds the thin metal jimmy.

"What should I do if I see something?" Petra asks.

"Warn me." He gets out of the van.

"How?"

"Honk?"

"How many—"

"Just freaking *honk,* okay?"

He goes into the building and walks up to the third floor, ready to slip the lock, but someone already has. Boone listens for a few seconds but doesn't hear anyone moving around. Unless, he thinks, whoever's in there heard me coming up the stairs and is staying still, waiting behind the door to blast me when I come in.

Boone opens the door a little, then quickly shuts it again. Doesn't hear anything, so he kicks the door wide open and goes in hard, hands up and ready.

Nothing.

Whoever was here came and went. Which is really bad news, because whoever was here might have taken Tammy with him.

Boone has a sickening thought.

Killers usually kill the same way. They don't mix it up. A guy who fucked up and tossed the wrong woman off a balcony would probably try to redeem himself by tossing the right woman off a balcony.

Boone sees the slider that opens off the small living room. The slider is open; a slight breeze blows the curtain back.

He walks across the room, steps out onto the balcony, and looks down.

Nothing but the little garden.

No woman's body, splayed and broken.

Boone takes a deep breath and steps back inside. It's your typical one-bedroom San Diego apartment—a living room with a small kitchenette attached, separated by a breakfast bar. Furniture from Ikea. There are, as Boone might have noted in his cop days, no signs of a struggle. Everything looks tidy—magazines neatly arranged on the coffee table, no drag marks on the blue carpet.

If someone took her, she went without a fight. Which she would have done, Boone thinks, if they had a gun pointed at her.

The bad news is that whoever broke in didn't toss the place. Wasn't looking for clues to Tammy's whereabouts, maybe because he already had her.

He steps into the kitchenette. Most of a pot of coffee sits in the white Krups automatic maker. The little red light shows it's still on. A half-full cup sits on the counter. Cute little mug with smiling hippos holding red balloons. Coffee with milk in it. A half piece of wheat toast, no butter, on a small orange plate.

And a small jar of nail polish.

The lid on, but not tight.

She left, willingly or not, in a hurry.

He goes into the bedroom.

The bed's unmade.

And smells like a woman.

What is it Johnny B. calls me when he wants to bust my chops? "Sheet sniffer"? It's true. And the bed does smell like a woman slept in it recently. One woman, alone. It's a double bed, but the covers are only pulled back on the left side.

The room is very feminine. Frilly, girlie, pink. A teddy bear with a red ribbon around its neck sits on the right side of the bed, up against the headboard. Strippers, Boone thinks, and their stuffed animals.

He checks out the framed photos on top of the chest of drawers. Angela and what looks to be her mother. Angela and a sister. Angela and Tammy. It's weird, sad, to look at these pictures of a smiling woman with her family and friends and think of the body lying by the pool, her head in a halo of blood.

Boone studies the picture of Tammy—long red hair, a chiseled face with a long nose that totally works for her, thin lips.

But it's her eyes that get to you.

Cat-shaped green eyes that glow out of the photo.

Like a big dangerous cat staring at you from out of the dark. A lot of strength in those eyes, a lot of power. It surprises him. Her MySpace photo that he'd had Hang pull up had showed the typical dumb stripper. This picture shows something else, and he's not sure what that is.

She's smiling in this picture, her arms around Angela's shoulders. The picture looks like it was taken on some sort of outing—biking, maybe. Angela has a white ball cap jammed on her head, her red ponytail sticking out through the back. She's laughing, happy—Boone can understand why she framed this picture. A good memory of good times. He'd bet that he'd find the same picture at Tammy's place.

He opens the closet and flips through the clothes. They're all in Angela's size, not Tammy's, who's a good couple of inches taller, and also a little thinner. So if Tammy was here, she brought an overnight bag, didn't unpack it, and left with it. Which is a good sign, because kidnappers don't usually let their victim take along luggage. Unless they played her, told her she was just going on a vacation until things blew over, let her take her bag to reassure her.

Boone goes into the bathroom.

Opens the shower curtain. It's still wet on the inside, as are the shower walls. The toothbrush on the sink is still moist. So is the cap on the tube of facial cleanser.

She slept alone, Boone thinks, got up late, showered, cleaned up, made toast and coffee, and sat down on a stool at the kitchen counter to do her nails while she ate.

But she didn't finish.

Neither her nails nor the meal.

He opens the medicine cabinet. The usual array of girl stuff on the shelves. Only one prescription bottle for Biaxin, written for Angela—an antibiotic that she didn't finish taking. Some Tylenol, aspirin, makeup bottles . . . no birth-control pills, which he would have expected to find.

He walks out of the bedroom and heads out, stopping to take the bottle of nail polish and put it in his pocket. He also shuts the slider door.

Even in San Diego, you never know when it might rain.

# 32

"Well?" Petra asks when he gets back to the van.

"You're sort of a woman," Boone says. "Do you remember what kind of scent Tammy wears?"

"CK," Petra replies, ignoring the insult. "Why?"

He pulls out the bottle of nail polish and shows it to her.

"That's what she wore to our meeting."

"She was just there," Boone says, slamming his hand into the wheel. "She was *just there*."

Petra is a bit surprised, and pleased, to see him display a little frustration. My God, she thinks, could it be a sign of some drive in the man? She's also amused, and a little intrigued, that he has a knowledge of women's perfumes.

"They might have her," Boone says. He explains what he saw in Angela's apartment.

"What do we do?" she asks.

"We cruise the neighborhood," he says, "in case she's still around, not knowing what to do or where to go next. If we don't see her, you take a taxi back to your office while I canvass the neighborhood."

He would have just said "while I hang out and talk to people," but he thought she'd like "canvass the neighborhood" better. Besides, it might distract her from the "back to your office" part.

It doesn't.

"Why is my absence required?" she asks.

"Because no one will talk to you," Boone says. "And they won't talk to me if I'm with you."

"I'm some sort of social leper?"

"Yes."

*Sort of a woman*, she thinks. *Social leper.* Then she says, "Men will talk to me."

Pleased by his lack of response, she adds, "Hang Twelve talked to me. Cheerful talked to me. They gave you up to me in a heartbeat."

They did, Boone thinks. In less than a heartbeat.

"Okay," he says. "You can hang."

Lovely, she thinks. I can hang.

# 33

Yeah, she hangs, but that doesn't produce Tammy Roddick.

If Tammy is walking the streets of Ocean Beach, she's disguised as a wino, an old hippie, a middle-aged hippie, a young retro hippie, a white rasta dude with blond dreads, an emaciated vegan, a retired guy, or one of the dozen or so surfers waiting for the big swell to go off at Rockslide.

Petra talks to all of them.

Having established the point that she can talk to men, she feels obligated to do just that, and she gets a lot of useful information.

The wino (for two dollars) tells her that she has a lovely smile; the old hippie informs her that rain is nature's way of moistening the earth; the middle-aged hippie hasn't seen Tammy but knows a wonderful place for green tea; the young retro hippie hasn't seen Tammy, either, but offers to give Petra a Reiki massage to ease her obvious tension (and his). The white rasta guy knows exactly where Tammy is and will take Petra there for the price of a cigar, except that he describes Tammy as a five-foot-four blonde, while the vegan informs her that his clean diet makes his natural essences taste sweet, and the retired guy hasn't seen Tammy but offers to spend the rest of his life helping Petra look for her.

The surfers tell her to come back after the big swell.

"Guys will definitely talk to you," Boone says when Petra tells him about her conversations. "No question."

"And I suppose you, on the other hand, have produced a definite lead."

Nope.

Nobody's seen anybody who looks like Tammy. Nobody on the street saw her leaving Angela's building. Nobody saw nothing.

"So now what do we do?" Petra asks.

"We go to her place of employment," Boone says.

"I hardly think she's at work," Petra snaps.

"I hardly think so, either," Boone says. "But someone there might know something?"

"Oh," Petra says. She looks at her watch. "But it's only two in the afternoon. Don't we want to wait until evening?"

"Strip clubs are open twenty-four/seven."

"They are?" Petra says. Then: "Of course, I suppose you'd know."

"Believe it or not," Boone says as he gets back into the Boonemobile, "I really don't spend that much time in strip clubs. As a matter of fact, I rarely go to them at all."

"Sure you don't."

Boone shrugs. "Believe what you want."

But it's the truth, he thinks. Strip clubs are interesting for about five minutes. After that, they're about as erotic as wallpaper. Besides which, the music is terrible and the food is worse. You'd have to be basically mentally ill to eat in a strip club anyway, "naked asses" and "buffet line" being two phrases that should never, ever, be matched in the same sentence. Guys who are coming off a prison hunger strike won't eat at a strip club unless they're actually brain-damaged.

Speaking of which, Hang Twelve had eaten like a starved baboon when they took him to Silver Dan's for his birthday. The kid scarfed the buffet like a vacuum cleaner, from one end of the table to the other.

"It's amazing," said High Tide, no stranger to the sin of gluttony himself, watching him. "It's almost admirable, in a disgusting kind of way."

"I feel like I'm watching something on the Nature Channel," Dave said as Hang stacked a handful of luncheon meats on a Kaiser roll, spread a huge glob of mayonnaise over the meat, and started to eat with one hand while dipping a spear of broccoli into a tub of onion dip with the other.

"Animal Planet?" Tide asked.

"Yeah."

"At least he's eating his vegetables," Johnny said. "That's good."

"Yeah?" Dave asked. "I wonder if he saw the guy that just had his hand on his package get to the broccoli first."

"Over the jeans or under?" Johnny asked.

"Under."

"God." Then Johnny said, "He's going for the shrimp, guys. Guys, he's going for the *shrimp*."

"I'll just dial 9-1-1 now," Boone said. "That extra second could save his life."

Hang came back to the table and set the heaping plate of food down. His goatee was festooned with crumbs, mayonnaise, onion dip, and some substance that nobody even wanted to try to identify. "Shrimp, anybody?"

They all passed. Hang consumed a couple of dozen shrimp, two huge sandwiches, some unidentifiable hors d'oeuvres that nobody even bothered to make the obvious pun about, twenty miniature pigs in a blanket (ditto), a pile of cottage fries, three helpings of Silver Dan's "pasta medley," and some strawberry Jell-O with grapes (and God knows what else) floating around in it.

Then he wiped his chin and said, "I'm going back."

"Go for it," Boone said. "It's your birthday."

"His *last*," Johnny said as they watched Hang work his way down the table again like a piece of machinery on a mass-production line.

"Over/under on the number of hairs he's swallowed?" Dave asked.

"Scalp or pubic?" asked Johnny.

"Forget it," Dave said.

Hang came back to the table with a plate of food that would have dismayed a Roman orgiast. "Good thing I went back," he said. "They put out fresh cheese."

Boone looked at the fresh cheese. It was sweating.

"I need a little air," he said.

But he hung in, staring at Hang Twelve with a mixture of awe and horror. The kid never came up to breathe; he just kept robotically shoveling food into his mouth as his eyes never left the stage. Hang's wholehearted devotion to free food and naked women was almost touching in its religiosity.

"We could get him a lap dance," Dave suggested.

"Could kill him," Tide said.

"But quickly," Johnny said.

But none of the girls—any one of whom would have cheerfully ground her ass on Adolf Eichmann's crotch for twenty bucks—would go anywhere near Hang's lap.

"He's going to puke," Tawny said.

"Puke?" Heather said. "He's going to *erupt*."

"Do you know there's a whole magazine devoted to that?" Dave said. "People who vomit to express their love? It's a whatchamacallit. . . ."

"Mental illness," Boone said.

"Fetish," Johnny said. "And, Dave? Shut up."

"I'm not going to puke," Hang said through a mouthful of penne carbonara.

"What did he say?" Johnny asked.

"He said he's not going to puke," Boone said.

"The fuck he isn't," said a guy from the next table.

Tide instantly took up for Hang. "The fuck he is."

"Here we go," Boone said.

"Oh, yeah," said Dave. "It's on."

Yeah, it was. Ten minutes later, The Dawn Patrol (sans Sunny, who had adamantly refused to come and bought Hang an ice-cream cake instead) had five hundred and change on the table that Hang could consume another plate of food and keep it down for a period—established after a tough and bitter negotiation—of forty-five minutes. A number of side bets bypassed that issue altogether and focused on which would come up first, the shrimp, the penne, or the cheese.

"I have fifty on the cheese," Johnny confided to Boone as Hang was devouring his third plate of buffet food.

"You have seventy-five that he's not going to throw up at all," Boone said.

Johnny said, "I'm trying to make some of it back."

"You think he's going to yank?"

"You *don't*?"

Well, yes, but you have to take up for your guy.

The next hour made its way into San Diego strip club lore as everyone in the entire club—horny guys, plain degenerates, sailors, marines, bartenders, waitresses, bouncers, and naked women—stopped what they were doing to observe a twenty-one-year-old soul surfer struggle to keep the contents of his bloated stomach right there in his stomach. Even Dan Silver took a break from counting money in his office to check out the scene.

Boone watched as Hang's face turned a little green and beads of sweat popped out on his forehead. Hang shifted in his chair; he reached down and touched his toes. He took deep breaths—at Johnny's suggestion, based on two trips to the labor room with his wife—he panted like a dog. At one point, he let out an enormous belch. . . .

"No vomit, no vomit," High Tide quickly said as several of the official judges looked closely at the front of Hang's JERRY GARCIA IS GOD T-shirt.

Hang managed to, well, hang.

The crowd counted down the entire last minute. It was a triumph, a ticker-tape parade, New Year's Eve in Times Square with Dick Clark as half of the onlookers counted the numbers and the other half chanted, "Hang Twelve, Hang Twelve, Hang Twelve. . . ."

Hang's face shone with victory.

Never before in his life had he been the object of this much attention; he had never won anything, certainly never won a lot of money for himself or other people. He had never been the hero, and now he was. He was *glowing,* accepting the pats on the back, the congratulations, and the shouts of "Speech, speech, speech."

Hang smiled modestly, opened his mouth to speak, and spewed trajectory vomit all over the innocent bystanders.

Johnny won his initial bet, plus the fifty on the cheese.

It was the only even *semi*-fun time that Boone had ever spent in a strip club.

But if Tammy were a nurse, he thinks, we'd be going to the hospital; if she were a secretary, we'd be going to an office building. But she's a stripper, so . . .

"You don't have to come," he tells Petra, praying she'll take him up on the bailout offer.

"No, I want to."

"Really, it's pretty sleazy," Boone says, "especially in the daytime."

If a strip club at night is tedious, in the daytime it's the birth of the blues—third-string strippers grinding halfhearted "dances" to a mostly empty room scarcely populated with lonely alcoholics coming off graveyard shifts, or horny losers figuring (wrongly) they have a shot with the C-team girls.

It's horrible, and, annoyed as he is with Petra's type A bullshit, he still wants to spare her the full hideousness.

She's having none of it.

"I'm going with you," she insists.

"There won't be any male strippers," he says.

"I know," she says. "I still want to go."

"Oh."

"What do you mean, 'Oh'?" she asks.

"Look," Boone says, "there's nothing wrong with it. Personally, I think that—"

Petra's eyes widen.

Totally striking. Amazing.

"Oh, 'Oh,'" she says. "I understand. Just because I'm immune to your Neanderthal anticharm, you jump to the conclusion that I therefore just have to be—"

"You're the one who wants to go to a—"

"On business!"

"I don't know why you're getting so worked up," Boone says. "I thought you were this politically correct—"

"I am."

"Look, around here it's all good," Boone says. "I'll bet half the women I know . . . well, not half, okay, a tenth anyway . . . of the women I know play for the other—"

"I do not play for . . ." Petra says. "It's none of your business whom I play for."

"For whom I play," Boone says, correcting her. "Dangling . . . uh . . ."

"Preposition," she says.

Otherwise, she doesn't talk to him the whole way to the strip club.

Which makes him wish he'd thought up the lesbian thing a lot sooner.

# 34

Petra's quiet for the whole drive.

Which is a relatively long one, because the club, TNG, is all the way up in Mira Mesa, in North County.

Boone takes the 8 east, then turns north on the 163, through the broad flatland of strip malls, fast-food joints, and wholesale outlets. He turns onto Aero Drive, just south of the Marine Corps air-training base, and pulls into the parking lot of TNG.

TNG is the name of the club, and the stripper cognoscenti know that the initials stand for "Totally nude girls"—as opposed, Boone thinks as he parks the van, to partially nude girls, or sort-of nude girls. No, the owners of TNG wanted to make sure that prospective customers knew that the girls were completely, absolutely, totally nude.

"It's not too late for you to wait in the van," he tells Petra.

"And potentially miss meeting my Alice B. Toklas?" she asks as she gets out. "No way."

"Is she a friend of Tammy's or something?" Boone asks.

"Never mind."

They go in.

All strip clubs are the same.

You can dress them up all you want, create any dumb gimmick you can think of, go for the down-low sleazy or the "gentlemen's club" faux sophistication, but at the end of the day it all amounts to a girl on a stage with a pole.

Or, in this case, one totally nude girl on a pole and another totally nude girl unenthusiastically writhing on the stage without the benefit of a pole.

TNG has no pretense at sophistication. TNG is a bare-bones, stripped-down (as it were) stroke joint (same) where guys come to look at naked women, maybe get a lap dance, or, if they're feeling fat, go with a dancer behind a beaded curtain into the VIP Room to get a "deluxe lap dance."

The club is pretty empty at this time of the day. This is a working guy's hang, and most of the working guys are working. Two marines, judging by their haircuts, sit on stools at the stage-side bar. A depressed-looking sales-man type, playing hooky from his calls, sits alone, one hand on a dollar bill, the other on his lap. Other than that, it's just the bartender, the bouncer, and a totally nude waitress serving her apprenticeship on the floor before she can make the giant leap to the stage.

The bouncer makes Boone right away.

Boone sees the flicker of recognition, and then he sees the guy move away a little bit and make a cell phone call. So we're working on a clock, Boone thinks as he steers Petra away from the stage-side stool and into a booth along the back wall.

The waitress comes over and stands expectantly.

"What would you like?" Boone asks Petra.

"A wet wipe?" she asks.

"I meant like a drink."

"Yes, hemlock with an arsenic twist, please."

"The lady will have a ginger ale," Boone says, "and I'll have a Coke."

The waitress nods and walks away.

Petra looks at the stage.

"I thought you said this was a strip club," she says.

"I did. It is."

"But don't you have to have some clothing on," she asks, "in order to strip it off?"

"I guess so."

"But they're already nude."

"Totally."

"So they just stand there," Petra says, "and sort of dance, and that's all they do?"

No, that's not all they do, Boone thinks. But he really doesn't want to get into that, and he's relieved when the waitress comes with their drinks. Petra reaches into her bag, comes out with a linen handkerchief, with which she carefully wipes the rim of her glass, then uses the handkerchief to hold the glass.

Well, we all have our own brand of paranoia, Boone thinks. Hers is catching a venereal disease from a glass; mine is getting knocked into tomorrow by a date-rape drug that the bouncer told the bartender to slip into my drink. Except the purpose wouldn't be to take sexual advantage of me; it would be to drag me out in the alley and beat me half to death.

Because clearly the bouncer got a "Be on the lookout for Boone Daniels" notice and he's called Dan Silver to get his instructions.

That's the bad news.

The good news is, if they're protecting something here, it means that there's something to protect.

He thinks about sharing that gem with Petra, then thinks better of it.

Anyway, she's staring at the girls on the stage.

"Either of them do anything for you?" Boone asks.

"It's fascinating," Petra says. "Sort of the car crash phenomenon—you don't want to look, but you can't look away."

Yeah, you can, Boone thinks, feeling his thirty-second curiosity clock running down.

The girl twisted on the pole is your stereotypical blond knockout with big hair and bigger boobs. She's too attractive for the day shift and she knows it. But she must have done something to piss the manager off—shorted him on his kickback, refused to give him a blow job, or maybe she was just getting uppity and talking about moving to a better club downtown—and now she's being punished by having to slog it out for the low-money losers in the afternoons. Now she's working the salesman hard, hoping that he's drunk enough to spring a hundred for a trip to the VIP Room so she can start earning her way back to nights.

The other girl is strictly day shift. She's petite, her face really isn't pretty, and she's small-chested. Her best feature is her long brown hair, and she's working it hard to make up for her other deficiencies. She has that look of a girl who's been told by everyone everywhere that she just isn't good enough, so she works her ass off making up for it. She works harder at being a better lay; she gets up early to make her latest boyfriend his breakfast; she bails him out of jail after he's beaten her up. She's the kind of girl who'll end up doing bottom-of-the-barrel porn videos because some producer tells her she's pretty.

She's looking down at the stage, in her own world, grinding her hips to the music—but in reality, she's moving to a private sound track of her own. She glances up and sees Boone, then looks right back down again as she turns, flinging her long hair across her back like a flogger, then looks over her shoulder at him again.

Sure enough, when the song ends and a new one begins, she dances off the stage, down onto the floor, and over to his booth.

"I'm Amber," she says. "Would you like a lap dance?"

"Would you like a lap dance?" Boone asks Petra, aware that she probably thinks a lap dance is something they do in Lapland.

Amber turns her attention to Petra. "I find girls so sensual," she says. It's a rehearsed line and comes off that way.

"No, thank you," Petra says, and Boone can tell she's actually trying not to hurt the girl's feelings.

Which is nice, Boone thinks.

"How about you?" Amber asks Boone. "Would you like a lap dance?

Or, for a hundred, we can go into the VIP Room. Wouldn't you like to have some private time with me?"

"Yeah, I would," Boone says.

"You *what*?" says Petra.

"I'll make you happy," Amber says.

"Give me two hundred," Boone says to Petra.

"I beg your pardon."

"Give me two hundred dollars," Boone repeats. "I want to go into the VIP Room."

*"Twice?"*

"Just shut up and give me the money."

Amber doesn't react to any of this. She totally gets digging into her purse and giving her boyfriend money.

"It's going on your expense account," Petra says, slapping two bills into Boone's outstretched palm. "*You* can explain to Alan Burke why you—"

"No worries."

He takes the two hundred and follows Amber through the beaded curtain into the VIP Room.

# 35

The VIP Room has a line of easy chairs against one wall, kind of like an old shoe-shine shop.

Amber sits Boone down in one of them as the waitress comes in with a glass of cheap champagne. She hands it to Amber, who, in turn, hands it to Boone as she says, "You can feel my tits, but no kissing, and no touching below the belt."

The belt? Boone wonders.

She starts to climb on his lap.

"You feel *good*," she says.

Boone lifts her up by the arms and puts her back on the floor.

"Forget about the dance," he says. "I want to ask you some questions."

She rolls her eyes. "No, I wasn't molested as a child. No, I'm not a victim of incest. No, I'm not putting myself through college. No, I don't—"

"Do you know Tammy Roddick?"

Amber says, "I'm not supposed to talk about her."

"Who told you that?"

"I don't want to get in trouble," she says. "Look, I *need* this job. I have a kid at home. . . ."

Of course you do, Boone thinks. Of fucking course.

"A hundred for the dance," Boone says. "Another hundred for anything you can tell me."

"I can't tell you anything."

"Can't or won't?"

"Both." She glances through the curtain to see if the bouncer is there. He isn't.

"Did you know Angela Hart?"

"What do you mean, 'did'?"

"She's dead," Boone says. "They threw her off a motel balcony. It'll be on the news tonight."

"Oh my God."

"They'll do the same to Tammy," Boone says. "I'm trying to find her before they do. If you know anything that can help me, you'll be helping her."

He keeps an eye on the curtain and an eye on her while she tries to make up her mind. Then she says, "I don't want the money. Angela used to watch my kid sometimes when I couldn't find a sitter."

"What's your kid look like?"

"What's it to you?"

"It might help."

"He's—"

"Never mind."

"All I know about Tammy," she says, "is that she has a boyfriend."

"Who?"

"His name is Mick," Amber says. "He hangs out here a lot."

"Does Mick have a last name?"

"Penner?"

"Are you asking me or telling me?"

"I'm pretty sure," Amber says.

Boone asks, "Has he been in today?"

"I haven't seen him in a while," Amber says; then she looks over Boone's shoulder.

Boone turns and recognizes Tweety.

He's a PB local, hanging around the gym, the GNC store, the bars. Tweety is a juiced-up roid freak with a head even bigger than his huge body. Big flat face with small blue eyes. And he's gigantic—six-six and large-framed already, and whatever shit he's shooting into himself, it's working. He wears a Gold's Gym muscle shirt on the "if you got it, flaunt it" fashion theory. Gray sweatpants over Doc Martens. Tweety sports short-cropped yellow hair: not blond—bright yellow.

Hence the "Tweety" tag.

"Out," he says to Boone.

"I didn't kiss her or touch her below the figurative belt," Boone says.

"Out. Now."

Boone hands Amber a hundred-dollar bill. "Thanks for nothing, bitch. Way to help your friend."

"Fuck you, asshole."

Tweety grabs Boone by the elbow. "You don't understand 'out'?"

"Yeah, I do," Boone says. "For example, are you *out* of the closet yet? Is your skull going to pop *out* of your skin? Has your dick shrunk *out* of sight yet? Oh, here's another one: Have you thrown a girl *out* of a building lately?"

Tweety would be the perfect candidate for the job. He could easily have "pressed" Angela and heaved her off the balcony.

Tweety's face turns red.

Guilt, roid rage, or both? Boone wonders.

"Well, have you," Boone asks, adding, "Tweety?"

Tweety pops a beautiful right cross, plenty of leverage in the hips, weight balanced and coming forward.

Boone isn't there to take it.

He steps to the left, feels the air whoosh by his nose as the heavy fist comes through, then smashes the blade of his foot down into the side of Tweety's kneecap, which dislocates with a sickening *pop*. Tweety crashes to the floor, rolls into a fetal position, grabs his knee, and howls in pain.

Boone's not exactly eaten up with sympathy. He reaches down, gets his middle and index fingers into Tweety's nostrils, and pulls, because:

1. There are no weights you can pump to strengthen your nose.
2. Steroids might make your head big, but they don't make your nostrils any stronger.
3. It hurts like crazy.
4. And where the nose goes, the head and neck are bound to follow; however, if they don't, your nose is coming off.

So basically, Boone tries to rip Tweety's nose off his face, presenting him with a choice—suffer rhinoplasty or talk.

"Do you have her?"

"Who?"

"You know who, Tweety," Boone says. "I'm going to ask you one more time. Do you have Tammy Roddick?"

"No!"

Boone lets him go.

Tweety makes a valiant effort to get up. It works okay on the one leg, but when he tries to put weight on the dislocated knee, it gives out under him and he falls forward onto the floor.

But Boone backs up, just in case.

He's tempted to give Tweety another kick in the knee, but it would probably be bad karma, something Sunny's always talking about since deciding to become a Buddhist. Boone doesn't totally get the whole karma thing, but he decides that kicking a guy in his dislocated knee would probably compel Sunny to chant a few thousand more mantras, another concept he's not totally with.

"You should have a mantra," Sunny told him.

"I have one," Boone replied.

"'Everything tastes better on a tortilla'?" Sunny said. "It's a start."

Anyway, Boone doesn't kick Tweety in the knee and further decides he should get out of there before the bouncer decides to check out what's happening in the old VIP Room.

But Tweety says, "Daniels? I'll be seeing you again. And when I do—"

Boone comes back and kicks him in the knee.

What Sunny doesn't know . . .

Boone walks out of the VIP Room.

"That was quick," Petra says. "Sated?"

"Our absence has been requested," Boone explains.

"I've been thrown out of better places," Petra says.

She follows him out the door.

# 36

Dave the Love God looks out at the burgeoning ocean and thinks about George Freeth.

George freaking Freeth.

Freeth was a legend. A god. "The Hawaiian Wonder" was the father of San Diego surfing and the first-ever San Diego lifeguard.

If you don't know about Freeth, Dave thinks, you don't know your own heritage, where you came from. You don't know about Freeth, you can't sit in this lifeguard tower and pretend to know who you even are.

It goes back to Jack London.

At the turn of the last century, London was in Honolulu, trying to surf, and he saw this "brown-skinned god" go flying past him. Turned out it was Freeth, son of an English father and a Hawaiian mother. He taught London to surf. London talked Freeth into coming to California.

Around the same time, Henry Huntington built a pier at his eponymous beach and was trying to promote it, so he hired Freeth to come give surfing demonstrations. He billed Freeth as "The Man Who Can Walk On Water." Thousands of people went down to the pier to see him do just that. It was a smash, and pretty soon Freeth was going up and down the coast, teaching young guys how to ride a wave.

He was a prophet, a missionary, making the reverse journey from Hawaii.

The Man Who Could Walk On Water.

Hell, Freeth could do anything in or on the water. One day in 1908, a Japanese fishing skiff capsized in heavy surf off Santa Monica Bay. Freeth swam out there, righted the skiff, and, standing up in it, *surfed* it back to shore, saving the seven Japanese on board. Congress gave him a Medal of Honor.

It was the only gold medal he'd receive, though. He tried to get into the Olympics but couldn't because he had taken Huntington's money to walk on water. Buster Crabbe went, became a movie star, and got rich. Not George Freeth. He was quiet, shy, unassuming. He just did his thing and kept his mouth shut about it.

People in California were really starting to get into the ocean. But there was a problem with that: They were also starting to drown in the ocean. Freeth had some of the answers. He created the crawl stroke, which life-guards still use; he invented the torpedo-shaped life float that they still use.

Eventually, he migrated down to San Diego and became the swim coach of the San Diego Rowing Club. Then, one day in May of 1918, thirteen swimmers drowned in a single riptide off Ocean Beach. Freeth started the San Diego lifeguard corps.

He lived less than a year after that. In April of 1919, after rescuing another group off Ocean Beach, Freeth got a respiratory infection and died in a flophouse in the Gaslamp District.

Broke.

He had saved seventy-eight people from drowning.

So now Dave's thinking about George Freeth. In his thirties now, Dave is wondering if he's headed for the same fate.

Alone and broke.

It's all good when you're in your twenties—hanging out, picking up tourist chicks, slamming beers at The Sundowner, jerking people out of the soup. The summer days are long and you think you're going to live forever.

Then suddenly you're in your thirties and you realize that you aren't immortal, and you also realize that you have nothing. No money in the bank, no house, no wife, no real girlfriend, no family.

And every day, you're out there rescuing people who have all that.

So that time back at Red Eddie's hilarious housewarming party, Eddie made the offer. A little night work. "Use your skills," Eddie said, "to make yourself some money, some real money, brah."

Easy money, easy work. Just drive a Zodiac out there, pick up the product, bring it in. Or go down to Rosarito, bring a boat back up. Where's the harm? What's the bad? Not like it's heroin, or meth, or coke.

"I dunno, Eddie," Dave said.

"Nothin' to know or not to know," Eddie replied. "When you're ready, just say the word."

Just say the word.

Later that same week, he went out into a riptide to pull in a *turista* who'd let herself get sucked out. The woman, not small, was so hysterical that she damned near pulled Dave under with her. She grabbed on to his neck and wouldn't let go, and he damned near had to knock her out to get her under control and onto the sled.

When he got her back to the beach, all she could say was, "He hit me."

He watched her and her indignant hubby get into their Mercedes and drive away. No thank you, just "He hit me."

Dave thought about George Freeth.

Brought surfing to California.

Saved seventy-eight lives.

Died broke at thirty-five.

Dave called Eddie and said the word.

# 37

There are thousands of Mick Penners.

A stripper's boyfriend who hangs around strip clubs is not exactly a unique profile. He's a definite type, this guy, and you can see him every-where. He's that weird dude who gets his rocks off watching his girlfriend take her clothes off for a roomful of guys, and he's alternately turned on and repulsed by it. On the one hand, he thinks he's a stud because he has a hot chick that other guys want; on the other hand, he's jealous that other guys want her. So when the girl comes home—and a Mick Penner usually lives with her while she pays the rent—he works out his ambivalence by slapping her around and then taking her to bed.

You can see a Mick Penner hovering in the back of any strip club, keeping an eye on his girl, chatting up the other dancers, bothering the bar-tender, generally being a pain in the ass. The more benign Mick Penners leave it at that; the worse ones mooch off the girl, taking her tip money as soon as she makes it. The worse ones yet use her to get to other girls. The very worst pimp her out.

The Mick Penners of the world always have something cooking, always have something on the stove, always are running some scam or the other. And it's always the next big thing, financed by the stripper girlfriend until the ship comes in. A real estate investment, a start-up tech company waiting for the bust-out IPO, a screenplay that Spielberg's people have expressed interest in, a Web site. It's always going to bring in a million bucks and it never does. Something always happens somewhere along the way to the big payoff, but no worries—by that time, a Mick Penner is on to the next big thing.

"How do we find this Mick Penner?" Petra asks.

"You're in luck," Boone says. "I know the dude."

"You do?"

"Yup," Boone says.

On the way to the Hotel Milano, he tells her how he knows Mick Penner.

# 38

Mick Penner parks cars.

This is how Boone knows him. If you're a private investigator in a resort town like San Diego, you know the parking valets at the major hotels and restaurants. If you're a more financially successful private investigator than Boone Daniels, you go around at Christmastime handing out twenty-dollar bills to the parking valets at the major hotels and restaurants.

Not that Boone hasn't handed out a few bills in his day. He has, lots of times, and more than once to Mick Penner, who is a daytime valet at the Hotel Milano in La Jolla.

You do this because nobody in California goes anywhere except in their cars. You want to track somebody in Cali, you track their vehicle, and vehicles have to park somewhere. And when they park at a hotel, you have a good idea about what they're doing there.

You want to know who's having lunch with whom, who's laying out big bucks for a dinner party to make a deal, who's banging somebody they shouldn't be, you stroke the parking valet. You want to stake out someone at a hotel and you don't want to be seen, you lay off a couple of blocks and let the valet call you when the person rings for his car. You need video of a husband, wife, boyfriend, girlfriend getting in or out of a car in a hotel parking lot, you pay one of the valets to let you park in there. You're looking for some high-rolling scam artist, you want a parking valet to give you a jingle when your guy checks into his hotel.

Parking valets, concierges, desk clerks, room-service waiters—their base salaries are just that, a base; the smart ones make their real money from tips and tip-*offs*.

And Mick Penner is one of the smart ones.

Mick is a good-looking guy. Slim but built, about six-one, with black hair, deep blue eyes, and white teeth. He has what you might call movie star good looks.

He'd better have.

Mick parks cars and fucks trophy wives.

This is why he works the day shift. See, you'd think a parking valet would want nights, when the tips are bigger, but Mick does matinees, when he can flash that smile at the ladies who lunch.

It's a numbers game.

Mick smiles at a lot of ladies who lunch, and enough of them are going to have lunch and then have Mick. And enough of them are going to tell their friends that Mick spends some of his afternoons up in the rooms sharing the unique joy that is Mick.

The ladies don't give him cash—that would make him a prostitute, and Mick doesn't see himself that way. They give him gifts—clothes, jewelry, watches—but that's not where the money is.

The money is in their homes.

When Mick gets tired of banging a woman, or she gets tired of him, or the gifts get thin, Mick cashes out. He's very careful about which women he picks to give him his severance pay—they have to be married, have to have signed a prenup, have to have a real, rooting interest in keeping their marriages intact.

But if a woman qualifies, then Mick puts in a call to a friend who does high-level house burglaries. Mick has her keys, right? He gets them copied, and he knows for a fact when she's not going to be in the house. So the woman is snuggled up with Mick in bed in a room overlooking the ocean while Mick's pal is in her house, taking the jewelry she decided not to wear that day. And maybe her silverware, crystal, artworks, loose cash, anything portable.

Even if the woman figures out that sweet Mick fucked her over, she isn't going to tell the cops where she was; she's not going to tell them who might have access and knowledge. She's going to keep her mouth shut, because, at the end of the day, it's the insurance company's problem.

It's not that Mick does this a lot, just enough to help finance the next big thing.

Mick's a screenwriter. He hasn't written a word in about three months, but he has an idea that's drawn some attention from the assistant to a senior VP at Paramount. It's a sure thing, just a matter of time, just a matter of sitting down and doing it.

But Mick's been too busy.

Boone pulls the van up to the valet stand at the Milano, an exclusive, bucks-up hotel in the heart of La Jolla Village.

Calling La Jolla Village a village is like calling the *Queen Mary* a rowboat.

Boone's always thought of a village as a place with grass huts and chickens running around, or a quiet row of thatch-roofed cottages in one of those English movies that a girl made him go to.

So he's always been amused at the folksy pretentiousness of calling some of the most expensive real estate on earth a village. The Village occupies a bluff overlooking the ocean, with a magnificent sweep of a view, a cove that features some of the best diving in California, and a small but tasty reef break. There are no grass huts, running chickens, or thatch-roofed cottages. No, this village features platinum-card boutiques, exclusive hotels, art galleries, and froufrou restaurants that cater to the beautiful people.

The Boonemobile looks distinctly out of place in the Village, among the Rollses, Mercedeses, BMWs, Porsches, and Lexuses. Boone thinks that the locals might figure that he's a cleaner or something, but the housecleaners in the Village drive better cars than the Boonemobile.

Anyway, he pulls it up to the valet stand at the Milano. A valet ambles over, ready to tell whoever this is that he has the wrong address. Boone thinks he might have the wrong place, too. Several parking valets are standing around, none of them Mick.

Boone rolls down his window. "Hey."

"Hey, it's you," the valet says. He and Boone touch fists. "What brings?"

"Alex, right?"

"Right."

"Mick around?"

"It's his day off," Alex says.

"His day off?" Boone asks. "Or he just didn't show?"

"Okay, door number two," Alex says, glancing at Petra. He lowers his voice and adds, "You need a room, I can probably hook you up."

Boone shakes his head. "I'm good."

Alex shrugs. "Dude didn't show today, didn't show yesterday. He's gonna lose the gig, he doesn't straighten up."

"D'you cover for him?"

"I made up some bullshit story. I dunno, the flu."

Boone asks, "Where does he lay his head these days?"

"He was crashing with this stripper chick," Alex says. "In PB."

"I tried," Boone says. "He's not there."

"Oh, you know her."

"Yeah."

"Fucking Mick, huh?" Alex says with a smile of envious admiration.

"Fucking Mick," Boone agrees. "Anyway, you have his phone number, right?"

"It's in the shack. I can get it."

"It would be a help, man. I'd appreciate it."

"Be right back."

Alex trots away.

"She's with this Mick person," Petra says.

"That's how I read it," Boone says.

"Do you think they're still in town?"

"Not if they're smart."

If they're smart, they're two days' drive away, maybe up the coast in Oregon or even Washington. Or they drove out to Vegas, where Tammy could get work easily. Hell, they could be anywhere.

Alex comes back and hands Boone a slip of paper with Mick's number on it.

"Thanks, bro."

"No worries."

"Mick still drive that little silver BMW?" Boone asks.

"Oh yeah. He loves that car."

"Well, late, man."

He slips Alex a ten.

"Late."

Parking valets driving Beemers, Boone thinks. The trophy-wife business must be booming.

He backs out into the street and drives down to the cove and finds a parking spot overlooking the beach where the seals gather. A couple of big males are lying out on the rocks, with tourists standing above them snapping pictures.

"So we think that Mick and Tammy have disguised themselves as sea lions?" Petra asks.

Boone ignores her. He grabs his cell phone.

"What are you doing?" Petra asks.

"I'm calling Mick to tell him we're on our way over."

"You're kidding."

"Yeah."

"Yo. I mean, Pacific Surf," Hang says when he picks up.

"Hang?"

*"Boone?"*

"Get off whatever porn site you're on and run a reverse for me," Boone says. He gives him Mick's phone number.

"That's a cell phone, Boone."

"I know."

"Gonna take a minute."

Boone knows this, too. Hang will use the number to go on the service provider's Web site, get a new password for the one he "lost," then access the billing record to get a home address.

It's going to take at least five minutes.

Hang's back on in three.

"Two-seven-eight-two Vista del Playa. Apartment B."

"Down in Shores?" Boone asks.

"Hold on a sec."

Boone hears him tapping at some keys, then Hang says, "Yup. You take—"

"No, I got it, thanks."

Boone pulls out of the slot and heads back up to the Village, then heads north for La Jolla Shores. Mick's place is only ten minutes away, and Boone already knows what he's going to find there.

No Mick.

No Mick's Beemer.

No Tammy.

Dan Silver is already irritable.

And concerned.

What had Eddie said? "Open mike night at Ha Ha's is over, big man. It's time you got serious, you feel me?"

Yeah, Dan felt him. Felt him like a rock lodged in his belly. Felt what Red Eddie was telling him, too. Clean up your mess. And what a fucking mess it is. That dumb goddamn roid case Tweety going out and killing the wrong gash.

Amber is scared. She looks small and pale and weak next to him, which she is, all of those three things. He has her sitting in a plain wooden-back chair in the VIP Room and he stands over her, staring down.

"I didn't tell him anything," Amber says.

"Didn't say you did," Dan says in his best calming voice. "What I'm asking you is, where is Tammy?"

"I don't know."

"Do you like working here?" Dan asks.

"Yes."

"They treat you good, don't they?"

Amber nods. "Uh-huh."

"So you don't want to get fired."

"I need this job."

"I know," Dan says. "You have a kid, right?"

"Yeah," Amber says. "And, you know, food, rent, day care . . ."

"I feel you," Dan says. He slowly walks behind her, then hauls off and hits her with a lazy punch to the kidneys. Lazy for him, but with his strength, it's enough to knock her off the chair and send her sprawling on the floor, gasping in pain. "Now you feel *me*."

He picks her up with one hand and sets her back down again, very gently. Squatting in front of her, he says, "If I hit you in the kidneys one more time, you don't dance for a month or two. It hurts you just to try to get up off the couch, don't even think about going to the bathroom."

Amber drops her face into her hands and starts to cry. "She baby-sat my kid for me so I could go to a movie sometimes."

"That's nice." He walks behind her and raises his fist.

"All I know is that she has a boyfriend," Amber says quickly. "His name is Mick Penner."

"Where does he live?"

"I don't know," Amber says. "I swear."

"I believe you, Amber," Dan says. He takes a roll of bills out of his jeans pocket, hands her a hundred-dollar bill, and says, "You buy something nice for that kid of yours."

"Let's go get Tweety taken care of," Dan says back in the main room.

# 40

Boone makes the short drive down to La Jolla Shores.

It might be the prettiest beach in San Diego, Boone thinks. A gentle two-mile curve from the bluffs of beautiful-people La Jolla Village to the south all the way to the Scripps Pier in the north, with the pale sienna cliffs of Torrey Pines in the background.

Just off to his left, to the south, are the twin hotels—the La Jolla Shores and the La Jolla Tennis and Beach Club—that sit right on the beach. And the Tennis and Beach Club houses the famous Marine Room restaurant, where on a stormy night you can sit and eat shrimp and lobster with the waves hitting right against the window.

Boone likes Shores, as the locals simply call it, even though the surf usually isn't very challenging, because it's calm and pretty and people always seem to be having a good time there, whether they're in the water, playing on the sand, strolling the boardwalk, or having a cookout in the little park that edges the beach. At night, people come down and make bonfires and sit and talk, or play guitars, or dance to the radio, and you can hear all kinds of music down here at night, from rasta to retro folk to the exotic, twisting chants that the groups of Muslim students like.

Boone likes to come down here for that reason, because he thinks it's what a beach is supposed to be—a lot of different kinds of people just hanging out having a good time.

He thinks that's what life's supposed to be, too.

Mick's car is parked in the narrow alley behind his building.

A silver Beemer with the hopeful vanity plate that reads SCRNRITR.

"I'll be a son of a gun," Boone says.

"They're here?" Petra asks, her voice a little high and excited.

"Well, his *car's* here," Boone says, trying to lower her expectations. But the truth is, he's pretty hopeful that they're in there, too.

"Wait in the van," he says.

"No way."

"Way," Boone says. "If I go in the front, they might come out the back?"

"Oh. All right, then."

It's total bullshit, Boone thinks as he gets out of the van, but it will keep her out of my way. He walks up the stairs to Mick's door and listens.

Faint voices.

Coming from the television.

Other than that, nothing.

Boone tries the door.

It's locked.

There are two windows on this side of the apartment. The venetian blinds are closed on both, but even through the glass, Boone can smell the dope. Mick and Tammy must be having a hell of a party.

Boone raps on the door. "Mick?"

Nothing.

"Yo, *Mick.*"

No response.

So either they're in there hiding or in the bedroom, stoned, and can't hear anything. Well, Boone thinks, if they can't hear anything . . . He kicks the glass in, reaches through the hole, unlocks the window, and slides it open. Then he climbs through.

Mick Penner is asleep on the sofa.

Passed out is more like it. He's lying facedown, one arm dangling to the floor, his right hand still holding a bottle of Grey Goose.

Boone walks right past him into the bedroom.

No Tammy.

He opens the bathroom door.

No Tammy.

He looks at the back door. Still locked from the inside.

Tammy isn't here and she didn't just go out the back. There are no women's clothes, no makeup in the bathroom, no smell of perfume, moisturizer, hair spray, nail polish, nail polish remover.

It smells like a guy's place.

A guy on a steep downhill slide.

Stale sweat, old beer, unchanged linens, garbage, a trace of eau de vomit. Mick himself reeks. When Boone steps back into the living room, it's instantly apparent that the guy hasn't hauled himself into a shower for a few days.

Mick isn't cute or pretty right now. If his trophy wives could see him passed out on this couch—his dirty hair disheveled, his teeth green with grime, dried grunge caked around his lips—they wouldn't be slipping between the clean, crisp sheets of the Milano with him. If they were in a good mood, they might, *might,* drop a quarter into his hand and keep moving.

"Mick." Boone gently slaps him across the face. "Mick."

He slaps him again, a little harder.

Mick opens one jaundiced eye. "What?"

"It's Boone. Boone Daniels. Wake up."

Mick closes his eye.

"I need you to wake up, dude." Boone grabs him by the shoulders and sits him up.

"The fuck you doing here?" Mick asks.

"You want some coffee?"

"Yeah."

"You got any?"

Boone walks into the kitchen area.

Dirty dishes are piled in the sink or strewn over the counter. Empty boxes of microwave meals overflow the garbage can or have just been tossed on the floor. Boone opens the fridge and finds an opened bag of Starbucks espresso on the door shelf. He dumps the grounds out of the filter in the coffeemaker, washes the carafe, finds a new filter, puts the coffee on, and scrubs out a cup while he listens to Mick puking in the bathroom.

Mick emerges, his face dripping with water where he splashed it on himself.

"Fuck, dude," Mick says.

"You've been slamming it," Boone says.

"Hard." Mick sniffs his armpits. "God, I stink."

"I noticed."

"Sorry."

"No worries." Boone hands Mick a cup of coffee.

"Thanks."

"It's hot, bro. Don't toss it."

Mick nods and takes a sip of coffee.

Boone sees his hand quiver.

"Tammy Roddick."

"Doesn't ring a bell," Mick says.

Something in Mick's face—a little tension along the jawline, the blue eyes going hard. The look is unmistakable—it's the look of a guy who's in love with a woman who's dumped him.

"Does *this* ring a bell?" Boone asks. "A burglary at the home of a Mr. and Mrs. Hedigan in Torrey Pines about three months ago. Maybe I should go over and ring the Hedigans' bell, ask them if *your* name—"

"Nice, Boone. Real nice," Mick says. "I thought we were friends."

"Not really," Boone says. I don't slip my friends twenties to answer questions. My friends aren't sleazy matinee call boys. "Have you seen Tammy lately? Like today, for instance?"

Mick shakes his head. "I *wish* I had."

Yeah, Boone thinks. So much for the unrung bell. "What do you mean?"

Mick's face gets all soft and serious. "I loved her, Boone. I mean, I loved that fucking bitch. Really *loved* her, you know?"

He met her at Silver Dan's. Watched her dance and was, like, mesmerized. Got a lap dance from her and asked her out, like on a real date. To his surprise, she accepted. He met her at Denny's after her shift and bought her breakfast. Then they went to her place.

"I thought I knew what good sex was," Mick says. "Not even close."

He loved just being with her, just looking at her. She had these green cat eyes, man, that you couldn't take your own eyes off of. They were hanging out watching TV one night. They had the Animal Channel on, and it was a documentary about leopards, and Mick looked at her and said, "Those are *your* eyes, babe. You have leopard eyes."

Yeah, but it wasn't just the sex, and it wasn't just her eyes—he loved just being with her, man. All that corny, romantic, chick-flick bullshit he never believed in? Mick started doing it, man. Walks on the freaking beach, breakfast in bed, holding hands, talking.

"She was smart, man," Mick says. "She was funny. She was . . ."

Mick actually looks like he's going to cry. He looks down into his coffee cup like it has memories at the bottom.

"So what happened?"

"She dumped me."

"When?"

"Three months ago?" Mick says. "At first, I was all like, you know, fuck the bitch, but then it really started to eat at me, you know? I even fucking called her, man, left messages on her machine. She never called me back."

"When did you last see her?"

"I tried to go see her at her new club," Mick says. "She had the bouncers toss me. I'm PNG at TNG."

"When was that?"

"Three, four days ago?" Mick says. "I dunno. How long have I been drinking?"

"What happened?" Boone asks.

"What do you mean?"

"I mean, if you guys were so in love and everything," Boone says. "What happened?"

He's not ready for the answer that Mick gives him.

"Teddy D-Cup."

Teddy D-Cup is what happened.

# 41

Teddy D-Cup.

Aka Teddy Cole.

Dr. Theodore Cole, M.D., board-certified cosmetic surgeon.

Teddy D-Cup does boobs.

Yeah, well, he does noses and chins, too, liposuctions, face-lifts, and tummy tucks, but boobs are Teddy's profit center, hence the moniker.

Teddy is the Michelangelo of bosoms. His work is displayed at society functions, beaches, runways, movies, television shows, and, of course, strip clubs, wherever finer breasts are seen. They are status symbols, prestige items. It's gotten to the point where women actually boast that their "tits are by Teddy."

Strippers will work for years to save up the cash to get a pair by Teddy, although the word is that good Dr. Cole does have a scholarship program for girls he considers especially . . . uh . . . promising.

Like Tammy, according to Mick.

"She wanted a bigger rack," Mick says. "I told her she didn't need one, that she was gorgeous, but you know chicks."

Not really, Boone thinks, but he goes along with it.

"I told her if she was going to do it, she had to go to the best," Mick says.

"Teddy D-Cup."

"Sure," Mick says. "I knew all about him from the hotel. Believe me, I know Teddy's work, up close and personal. Women who go to the Milano can afford Teddy."

"But Tammy couldn't."

"She saved up," Mick says. "You don't know her—she's single-minded, man. Once she sets her sights on something. I mean, it was like work, work, work. Money, money, money."

"So?"

Mick shakes his head. "I drove her to him, bro. I literally drove her to the first consultation. She comes out, we're in the car, we're not two blocks away, and she tells me maybe we should stop seeing each other. Do you believe that? She traded me in for a new set of tits."

"So she's seeing Teddy now."

"She's with him all the fucking time, man."

"How do you know that?"

"I've followed them," Mick says. "Is that pathetic, or what? I've banged half the hot rich babes in this town, and I'm sneaking around following this fucking mercenary cunt stripper, sitting in my car like some doof— That cheap fuck takes her to this little motel up around Oceanside—do you believe that, a guy with his kind of money?"

Boone gets this sinking feeling. "Hey, Mick?"

"What?"

"You didn't do anything to her, did you?"

"No," Mick says. "I *thought* about it."

Then he asks, "Is she okay, Boone? Is she in some kind of trouble? Why are you looking for her?"

"She ever talk about Dan Silver?" Boone asks. "The fire at his warehouse?"

"She mentioned it happened." He's alarmed now. All geeked. "Is she okay? Is she hooked up with Dan again?"

"I don't know," Boone says, "but as your *friend,* I'm going to strongly suggest you get out of town for a while. Some people are looking for her who are going to be looking for you. You don't want them to find you. They're going to ask the same questions I did, but they may not believe your first answers."

"She's in trouble," Mick says.

"Throw some shit in a bag," Boone says. "Put some serious distance between you and here."

"I have to find her. I have to help her."

"You gonna rescue her?" Boone asks. "Then she'll take you back?"

"I just want her to be okay," Mick says. "Is that fucked up, or what?"

Actually, Boone thinks, it might be the least fucked-up thing he's heard all day. He warns Mick to get out of town again, and then he leaves to go see Dr. Theodore Cole.

# 42

Tweety sits in the office of TNG, looking at his swollen knee. It looks bad; it looks like it's going to keep him out of the weight room for a while.

"We better get you to the hospital," Dan says.

Tweety looks sad. "I don't have health insurance."

"Not a problem," Dan says. "I got you covered. Come on."

Dan and the bouncer lift Tweety to his feet—well, *foot*-carry him outside—and squeeze him into the front seat of a Ford Explorer. The bouncer gets behind the wheel. Dan gently swings Tweety's legs in, then gets in the backseat.

Tweety says, "I'm gonna kill that fucking Daniels."

"We'll do it for you," Dan says. He tells the bouncer to head south on the 15, down to Sharp Hospital, the nearest urgent-care facility.

"Oh, man," Tweety says, "anybody got any Vike or Oxy or something? I need *something* to kill the pain."

Dan sticks a .22 pistol in the back of Tweety's head and pulls the trigger twice.

"Oughta do it," he says.

You roid-shooting, wrong woman–killing, stupid son of a bitch.

# 43

"Did you take a nap?" Petra asks when Boone gets back to the van.

"I call them 'siestas,'" Boone says. "It sounds better."

He fills her in on his conversation with Mick.

"So now we think that Tammy's with this Teddy person?" Petra asks.

"Or at least he knows where she is," Boone says. Not that this is necessarily good news. If Tammy went to Teddy and asked him for help, he could have bought her a first-class ticket to Tahiti. For all they know, she's sitting on a beach with a mai tai resting on her new chest.

Laughing at everybody.

"Where's this doctor's office?" Petra asks.

"Right back in La Jolla Village," Boone replies. Within sight of the Milano. It's been that kind of back-and-forth day. "But first, we're going to fuel up."

She leans over and looks at the fuel gauge. "The tank is three-quarters full."

"I meant me," Boone says. "You, too, if you want."

It's just a couple of blocks to Jeff's Burger. It's a matter of near-religious devotion to Boone never to enter the vicinity of Jeff's Burger without having one of his burgers. Luckily, there's a parking spot right out front. Boone pulls the van in, turns off the engine, and asks, "You want something?"

"Actually, a Caesar salad with dressing on the side would be nice."

"You got it."

He goes in and orders two cheeseburgers with everything. When the burgers arrive, he dissects one, puts the meat into his own burger, then scrapes the lettuce, tomato, and onions into the lid of the plastic go-plate and goes back to the van.

"What's this?" Petra asks when he hands her the plate.

"Caesar salad, dressing on the side."

"In what country, may I ask?"

"Mine," Boone says. "If you don't want it, the seagulls will."

She closes the plate and tosses it over her shoulder into the back of the van. He shrugs and eats as he drives back up to La Jolla Village. The burger tastes great and makes the drive back there go quickly. As they pull into the parking lot of Teddy's building, Boone calls information and gets Teddy's number.

"You're phoning?" Petra asks.

"Hard to put one over on you, Pete."

"Why not just march in there and demand to speak with him?"

The receptionist has the perfect cultured voice, and Boone guesses that she has the perfect chiseled face to match. As the first face you'd see when you walk into a cosmetic surgeon's office, she has to be perfect.

"May I help you?"

"I'd like to speak to Dr. Cole," Boone says.

"Do you have an appointment for a telephone consultation?"

"No," Boone says.

"Are you a patient? Is this an emergency?"

"I'm not a patient, but I'd really like to talk to him."

"Let me see . . . Dr. Cole had a cancellation in May. I could perhaps squeeze you in."

Boone says, "I was thinking more like now."

"Now?" she asks incredulously.

"Now," Boone says.

"That would be impossible."

"Tell Teddy that Tammy Roddick wants to talk to him."

"Dr. Cole is in a consultation," the receptionist says. "I am not going to interrupt him."

"Yeah, you are," Boone says. "Because if you don't, I'll call Teddy's house and see if *Mrs.* Dr. Cole would like to talk with Tammy. So unless you want to make the current Mrs. Cole the next ex–Mrs. Cole, with all the hassle and alimony that entails, not to mention the potentially deleterious effect on your next Christmas bonus, I suggest you get Teddy on the horn and interrupt his consultation. I'm betting he'll thank you."

There's a long, stony silence.

She breaks first. "I'll see if he wants to be interrupted."

"Thanks."

She comes back on a second later with a voice edged in aggravation. "Can you hold for Dr. Cole?"

"Oh, you bet."

A few seconds later, Teddy comes on the line. "This is Dr. Cole."

"My name is Boone Daniels," Boone says. "I'm a private investigator representing the law firm of Burke, Spitz and Culver. We have reason to believe that you might have information as to the whereabouts of Tammy Roddick."

"I don't think I know a Tammy Roddick," Teddy says smoothly and without hesitation. He's used to denying knowledge of women, not only to the gossip media but also to his wives and girlfriends.

"Think some more," Boone says. He describes Tammy, then continues: "A guy named Mick Penner says she dumped him for you. It's credible information, Doc—everyone knows you have a thing for strippers."

"Boone Daniels . . ." Teddy says. "You have a friend who's a prodigious eater."

"Hang Twelve."

Teddy says, "I was there that night. I lost two hundred bucks."

"Can we quit paddling around, Doc?" Boone asks. "It's important we find Tammy Roddick. There's good reason to believe she's in serious trouble."

Silence while Teddy thinks about this. And silence isn't the response you'd expect, Boone thinks. Usually if you tell a guy something like this, he instantly asks, "Trouble? What kind of trouble?" So maybe Teddy already knows.

"In any case," Teddy says. "I don't have to talk to you."

"No, you don't," Boone says, "but you should. Look, if *I* figured you out, the cops are going to be about a half step behind me. And there are other parties. . . ."

"What other parties?"

"I think you know Dan Silver."

Another silence, then:

"Jesus Christ," Teddy says. "Strippers are always trouble. If it's not one thing, it's another. If they don't want a free boob job, then it's a nose job. Or they're knocked up, or they want to go into therapy. Or they want to get married, or they threaten to call your wife. . . ."

"What are you going to do?" Boone asks.

"Right?"

"No," Boone says. "I mean, what are you going to do? Look, Teddy, of the possible choices of people you can talk to, I'm the least worst option. The cops will charge you with impeding an investigation, and you don't even want to *know* what Dan might do. He's sort of a cosmetic surgeon himself."

"I see what you mean."

"You're in the deep water," Boone says. "I can pull you out. You *and* Tammy."

More thinking.

"Can I get back to you on this?" Teddy asks.

"*Right* back?"

"Five minutes."

"Sure," Boone says. "I'm in my office. Use this number."

He gives Teddy his cell number.

"Five minutes," Teddy says before he gets off the phone.

"You don't think he's actually going to ring you back?" Petra asks. "I told you we should have just marched right in there."

She starts to open the door.

"Don't do that," Boone says.

"Why not?"

"Because we're not looking for Teddy," Boone says. "We're looking for Tammy."

"Symmetrical and yet cryptic," Petra says. "But what do you mean?"

"I mean, sit tight."

She shuts the door, then asks, "'Deleterious'?"

"Means having a negative or destructive effect," Boone says.

"You've been holding out on me, ape man."

"You don't know the half."

Teddy D-Cup comes out of the building and strides toward his car.


# 44


Teddy Cole is a beautiful man.

Literally.

Teddy is a living testament to the reciprocal professional courtesy that exists among top-line plastic surgeons. Teddy's been chin-sculpted, Botoxed, nose-jobbed, skin-peeled, hair transplanted, eye-tightened, face-lifted, tummy-tucked, dental-worked, lasered, and tanned.

A walking advertisement of his own trade.

He's about five-ten, slim, his skin glowing with artificial health, the muscles under his black Calvin Klein silk shirt showing hours at the gym. His hair is blond with ash tips, his eyes blue, his teeth perfectly white.

Teddy has to be in his late fifties, but he looks like he's in his early thirties, except that his face has been lifted so tight and high that his eyes have a slightly Asian look to them. Boone's afraid that if Teddy smiles too wide, he might actually break. But no cause for concern right now, because the good doctor isn't smiling. His face is set in fierce concentration as he heads for his Mercedes.

"You're actually smarter than you look," Petra says to Boone.

"Low bar to jump," Boone says. He waits for Teddy to pull out of the lot, then starts the van and follows.

"Can you tail him without him seeing us?" Petra asks.

"'Tail' him?"

"Well, can you?"

"If I don't screw it up," Boone says.

"Well, don't."

"Okay. Thanks."

It's one of your slower chases, as chases go. Lots of brake lights and waits at traffic signals as they follow Teddy up Prospect Avenue and then north on Torrey Pines Road. Teddy takes a left onto La Jolla Shores Road and they follow him through the beach community, then up the steep hill onto the campus of the University of California at San Diego, where they meander through the narrow, winding road past classroom buildings, dorms, and graduate-student apartments.

Boone drops a couple of cars back and follows Teddy up to Torrey Pines, past the Salk Institute and the whole complex of medical research buildings that define the area. Then it's through Torrey Pines State Reserve, up to the top of the hill, where there's this great, sudden view of the ocean stretching out in front of them, from Torrey Pines Beach all the way up to the bluffs at Del Mar.

Highway 101.

# 45

U.S. Highway 101.

The Pacific Coast Highway.

The PCH.

The Boulevard of Unbroken Dreams.

The Yellow Brick Road.

You may get your kicks on Route 66, but you get your fun on Highway 101. You may take 66 to find America, but you won't find The American *Dream* until you hit the PCH. Sixty-six is the route, but 101 is the destination. You travel 66, you *arrive* at 101. It's the end of the road, the beginning of the ride.

Back in the back-in-the, those early surfers lugged their heavy wooden boards up and down what was then a virtually empty highway. They had the joint pretty much to themselves, a small wandering band of George Freeth disciples searching for the promised wave. And they found it, breaking all up and down 101. They could just pull off the road and hit the beach, and they did, from Ocean Beach to Santa Cruz.

Then World War II came along, and America discovered the California coast. Hundreds of thousands of soldiers, sailors, and marines were stationed in San Diego and Los Angeles on their way to the Pacific, and when they came back, *if* they came back, a lot of them settled in the sun and the fun. Like, how are you going to keep them down on the farm after they've seen Laguna?

While their counterparts were reengaging with American society by creating suburbia and making a religion of conformity, *these* cats wanted to get away from all that.

They wanted the beach.

They wanted to surf.

This was the genesis of the "surf bum," the image of surfing as not only a culture but as a *counter*culture. For the first time, surfers defined themselves in *contrast* to the dominant culture. Not for them the nine-to-five job, the gray flannel suit, the tract home, two kids, manicured lawn, swing set, and driveway. Surfing was freedom from all of that. Surfing was sun, sand, and water; it was beer and maybe a little grass. It was timeless time, because surfing obeys the rhythms of nature, not the corporate time clock.

It was the antithesis of mainstream America at the time, and there came into existence little surfing communities—call them "colonies" or even "communes" if you have to—up and down Highway 101.

And a lot of these surfers were *beat,* man; they were the West Coast beatniks, Southern California Division, who, instead of hitting the streets of San Francisco—North Beach coffeehouses and poetry readings—took their bongos to the real beach and found their dharma in a wave. These guys had seen "civilization" on the battlefields and in the bombed-out cities of Europe and Asia and didn't like it, and they came to Pacific Beach, San Onofre, Doheny, and Malibu to create their own culture. They camped on the beaches, collected cans to buy food for the cookouts, played guitars and ukuleles, drank beer and wine, screwed beach bunnies, and *surfed.*

The little surf towns that sat on the 101 like knots on a string grew up around them. Fast-food stands sold quick, cheap burgers and tacos to surfers with didn't have a lot of jangle in their pockets and were in a hurry to get back and catch the next set. Beachside bars served guys in huaraches and damp board trunks, and it was no shirt, no shoes, no problem in those joints. Movie theaters in those little towns on the 101 started to show the first, primitive surfing movies to packed houses, party to follow.

The surf bums were so far out of mainstream America and yet so *very* American at the same time in their belief in technology, because some of these boys were your Tom Edison, Wright brothers, gee-whiz, *can-do* Americans, who just couldn't help but try to build a better surfboard. They took all that technology that came out of World War II—aerodynamics, hydraulics, and especially the new materials that had emerged and revolutionized the sport. Bob Simmons in La Jolla and Hobie Alter in Dana Point invented the first practical, lightweight board out of a new material—polyurethane. With the advent of the foam board, *anyone* could surf. You didn't need to be a Greek god like George Freeth. Anyone could now carry a board down the beach and into the water.

And these lightweight boards could do maneuvers that the heavy old wood boards just couldn't do. Instead of riding straight down the face of the wave, now the surfer could cut across its face, change directions, cut back. . . .

It was the golden age of surfing, the 1950s, there along the 101.

So many goddamn legends were out there challenging the waves, testing the limits, cruising that highway with their classic woodies, looking for the next great break, the sweet new ride, the secret spot that the newcomers hadn't found. Miki Dora—aka "Da Cat"—and Greg Noll—aka "Da Bull"—and Phil Edwards—aka "the Guayule Kid"—they rode waves nobody had ridden and in ways nobody had ridden them. Edwards was fifteen, *fifteen freaking years old,* when he paddled out into the wave known as Killer Dana and rode it. Then he stayed on the beach all summer with his girlfriend, cooking potatoes over an open fire.

Living to surf, surfing to live.

Along the 101.

It must have been heaven then, Boone thinks as the road plunges down toward the ocean like some kind of water slide, like it's going to dump you right into the water, but then at the last second it veers right and hugs the coastline. Paradise, Boone thinks—long, lonely stretches of beach with legends walking on water. He knows his surf history; he knows all the stories, knows about Da Cat, Da Bull, the Guayule Kid, and dozens of others. You can't *not* know them and be a real surfer; you can't not *see* their stories every time you drive this road, because that history is all around you.

You drive right past Hobie's old shop, right past the break where Bob Simmons died in a wave back in '54, past San O, where Dora and Edwards went out together and combined their styles and created modern surfing.

In that golden age.

Like all golden ages, Boone thinks as he veers right again, crosses the railroad track, and climbs up to the famous old beach town of Del Mar, it had to end.

The golden age was done in by its own success.

As the culture of Highway 101 became the culture of America itself.

*Gidget* hit the screens in 1959, creating a new kind of sex symbol—the

"California girl." Fresh-faced, sun-tanned, bikini-clad, sassy, healthy, and happy, Gidget ("It's a girl." "No, it's a midget." "It's a *gidget.*") became a role model for girls all across America. Girls in Kansas and Nebraska wanted to be Gidget, to wear bikinis and cruise the strips of the 101 beach towns.

*Gidget* begat a slew of beach movies, which would be forgettable except for lingering images of Annette Funicello, previously of the Mickey Mouse Club, who swapped her mouse ears for a bikini. These movies featured handsome guys like Frankie Avalon and bodacious babes like Annette and had just a suggestion of sex about them—*Beach Blanket Bingo* in 1965 never revealed what was happening on or under the blanket. And they usually had a "beatnik," replete with beret and goatee, wander on playing the bongos, and they always featured the "kids" dancing on the beach to music.

Surf music.

It also came right out of technology.

In 1962, Fender guitar developed a "reverb" unit, which produced the big, hollow, "wet" sound that became the trademark of surf music. In the same year, the immortal Dick Dale and the Del-Tones used the reverb on "Misirlou," featuring the classic Dick Dale guitar run that sounded like a wave about to break. The Chantays responded the same year with "Pipeline."

In 1963, the Surfaris released the first breakout, national surf hit— "Wipe Out," with the sarcastic laugh, then the famous percussion riff that every teenage drummer in America tried to copy, and the surf music craze was *on.* Boone inherited all this music from his old man, all those old surf bands like the Pyraminds, the Marketts, The Sandals, the Astronauts, Eddie & the Showmen.

Yeah, yeah, yeah, and The Beach Boys.

They just *blew it up.*

The Beach Boys had kids all across the *world* singing "Surfin' Safari," "Surfin' U.S.A," and "Surfer Girl," mimicking a lifestyle they'd never lived, mouthing the names of places they'd never been: Del Mar, Ventura County Line, Santa Cruz, Trestles, all over Manhattan and down Doheny way . . . Swami's, Pacific Palisades, San Onofre, Sunset, Redondo Beach, all over La Jolla. . . .

All along Highway 101.

Boone doesn't know the answer to that old Ethics 101 question from his freshman year in college—if, knowing what you know now, you had a chance to strangle little Adolf Hitler in the cradle—but he's clear about the answer for Brian Wilson. You'd splatter his baby brains all over the bassinet before you'd let him make it to the recording studio to turn the 101 into a parking lot.

By the mid-sixties, every kook with a record player or a transistor radio was hitting the surf, crowding the breaks, jamming the waves. People who never wanted to surf wanted the *lifestyle.* (There's a messed-up, inbred mongrel of a nonword, Boone thinks. Lifestyle—trying to be both and ending up neither. Life*style*—like *pseudo*life, a bad imitation of something worth living. Like you don't want the life, just the *style.*) So they headed out to sunny Southern California and fucked it up.

What was it the Eagles sang—"You call some place paradise, / kiss it goodbye"? Well, pucker up for Highway 101. So many people moved to the SoCal coast, it's surprising it didn't just tilt into the ocean. It sort of did; the developers threw up quick-and-dirty condo complexes on the bluffs above the ocean, and now they're sliding into the sea like toboggans. Those little beach towns swelled into big beach towns, with suburbs and school systems, endless strip malls with the same shit in each of them.

You had traffic jams—*traffic jams*—on the 101.

Not people trying to go surfing—although it can be hard to find a parking space at some of the more popular surf spots nowadays—but commuters on their way back and forth from *work.*

So Boone missed the golden age of surfing. He figures maybe he got in on the bronze age, but to him, the 101 is still the Highway to Heaven. "I never saw the golden age," he explained to his dad one time. "I only see the age I'm in."

There are still some golden days along the 101—particularly during the week, when the road is relatively free and the beaches aren't crowded. And the truth is, you can still find an empty beach some days; you can still have a break all to yourself.

And there are days when that drive along the 101 is so beautiful, it will break your fucking heart. When you look out the window and the sun is painting masterpieces on the water, and the waves are breaking in a single white line from Cardiff to Carlsbad, and the sky is an impossible blue, and people are playing volleyball, and your brother and sister surfers are out there just having a good time, just trying to catch a wave, and you realize you are living in the dream.

Or drive it at dusk, when the ocean *is* golden, and the sun an orange fireball, with dolphins dancing in the break. Then the sun flames red, and it slips quietly over the horizon and the ocean slides to gray and then to black and you feel a little sad because this day is over, but you know it will begin again tomorrow.

Life on Highway 101.

This is the road that Boone takes, following Teddy north along the coast.

# 46

Boone needs to be on his game going through Del Mar, because there are plenty of side streets for Teddy to turn onto, but the doctor doesn't turn off toward the beach or up into the hills; he stays on the main drag and heads north, across the old bridge over the San Dieguito River, on past the famous old racetrack, then up through Eden Gardens and Solana Beach.

Now the road, old Highway 101, parallels the railroad track on its right, through the town of Solana Beach, and then onto the narrow open stretch of coastline at Cardiff, which is one of Boone's favorite places in the world, where the highway edges the beach and you feel like you could reach out the car window and touch the water. The whitecaps are already peaking, tall, but nothing to what they'll be this time tomorrow. Even from the van, he can hear the ocean getting ready to go off, the big swell starting to build, a heavy heartbeat that matches his own.

The big swell.

Sunny's shot.

*One* wave, one macker, and it changes her life.

One great photo and she makes the net, the magazines. She gets the sponsorship she's been working for and it's her takeoff. She'll be all over the world, making the tournaments and the big wave contests. She'll surf Hawaii, Oz, Indo, you name it.

"Where did you just go?" Petra asks.

"Huh?"

"Where were you? You looked like you were a million miles away just now."

"Nope. On the job."

But aware that they're fast coming up on the funky old surf town of Encinitas and the great right break called Shrink's, arguably the best wave in SoCal, maybe the place to be when the swell rolls in.

If he weren't on the job, he'd turn in at the small parking lot on the bluff and take a look at how it's building out there. But I can't, he thinks, because I have to follow Dr. D-Cup to locate a stripper.

Teddy drives up through Leucadia, where the big eucalyptus trees line the road on the inland side and cheap motels, drive-thru burger/taco stands, and little shops take the ocean side.

Ocean side, Boone thinks . . . Oceanside. Isn't that where Mick Penner said that Teddy takes Tammy for their little matinees? Well, he thinks as he follows Teddy through Leucadia and across the bridge that spans the Batiquitos Lagoon into Carlsbad, we're on our way to Oceanside.

The road drops back down again and flanks the long stretch of open beach, with its promenade along the breakwater, then takes a right jog into the faux-Tudor village of Carlsbad, with its English shingled roofs. There's a store here where you can buy all kinds of English food, and Boone thinks of mentioning this to her, but then he figures that she probably already knows about it, so he keeps his mouth shut.

The route curves right again, then crosses Buena Vista Lagoon and takes them into Oceanside.

Heads up, Boone thinks.

Teddy takes a right, turning east onto Highway 76, drives all the way through town and out into the suburbs and developments that house a lot of the marines from Camp Pendleton, then takes a left into the countryside.

Where the hell is he going? Boone wonders. Boone drops back a ways because the traffic has thinned out so much.

Then Teddy takes a right and heads inland.

What the hell? Boone thinks.

There's not much out here now. It's one of the few even semi-rural spaces left in metro San Diego County, out here by the old Sakagawa strawberry fields.

# 47

They cling to the landscape, these pieces of old farms.

They dot the local map like small, shrinking atolls in a roiling sea of real estate development.

In housing-hungry San Diego, buildings are going up everywhere. Housing developments, condo complexes, and high-rise apartment buildings are taking the place of the old fields of flowers, tomatoes, and strawberries. With the residential developments come the strip malls, the high-end shopping complexes, the Starbucks, Java Juices, and Rubio's, the Vons, Albertsons, and Stater Bros.

Once a steady but slow tide, the building boom became a tsunami flooding the little islands of agricultural land. They're still there, but harder to find, especially this close to the coast. Farther inland along Highway 76 are the avocado orchards of Fallbrook, then the vast orange groves among the hillsides and canyons. Farther south, in the flatlands of Carmel Valley and Rancho Peñasquitos, small fields fight a slow, losing war against development, surrounded now by new million-dollar "spec" homes built on the plateaus between the wooded canyons where the illegal workers live in camps of jerry-rigged tents and tin-roofed shacks.

Up here in Oceanside, along the banks of the San Luis River, some of the old strawberry fields stubbornly hold out. Drought, insect infestations, depression, racism, voracious development—it doesn't matter, the farmers hang on. They could easily sell the land for far more than they make farming it, but that doesn't matter, either.

It's a way of life.

Not that you could find a single Japanese-American, a Nisei, actually working these strawberry fields. They're two generations removed from that, the kids and grandkids having moved into the city and the suburbs, where they're now doctors, lawyers, accountants, entrepreneurs, and even cops.

The old man who owns these particular fields wouldn't have had it any other way. Upward mobility was always the idea, and now a different generation of immigrants, field hands from Mexico, Guatemala, and El Salvador work his fields, and the kids come to visit for an "afternoon in the country."

Old man Sakagawa loves seeing his great-grandchildren. He knows that he'll be leaving this world soon, and he knows that when he passes, this world, these fields, this way of life will pass with him. It makes him sad, but he also believes what the Buddha said, that the only constant is change.

But it does make him wistful, that the Sakagawa fields will fade like morning mist under a blazing dawn.

Now Boone follows Teddy east along North River Road, past a gas station and a food mart, then past an old church, and then . . .

Son of a bitch, Boone thinks.

Fucked-up, lovesick Mick Penner was right.

The motel is one of those old 1940s places with an office and a line of little cottages in the back. Someone has tried to freshen the place up—the cottages have recently been painted a bright canary yellow, with royal blue trim—one of those attempts to make it so retro that it's hip.

Teddy pulls into the gravel parking lot and gets out. He doesn't stop at the office but goes right toward the third cottage, like he knows just where he's going.

"We got her," Boone says.

"You think so?"

"Yeah, I do."

He pulls into the parking lot and parks on the other end from Teddy's car. "You have your subpoena?"

"Of course."

"Then let's deliver it," Boone says.

Then I'll call Johnny Banzai and let him know that we have a potentially important witness for him in his fresh murder case. Then I'll go home, catch some sleep, and be fresh and ready when the big waves hit.

He's thinking these happy thoughts when Teddy suddenly walks back from the cabin, carrying a small black bag. He walks right past his car;

then he crosses the road and walks up about fifty yards to a thick bed of reeds that stands between the San Luis River and the western edge of the old Sakagawa fields.

"What's he doing?" Petra asks.

"I don't know," Boone says. He reaches behind and grabs a pair of binoculars and trains them on Teddy as the doctor walks to the edge of the reeds.

Teddy looks around, then steps into the reeds. Inside of two seconds, he disappears from sight.

Boone sets the binoculars down and jumps out of the van.

"Go look in the cabin, see if she's there," he says to Petra, and then he crosses the road and jogs down to the edge of the reeds. Foot traffic has trampled down the front edge of the reed bed, and narrow paths cut into the standing reeds like tunnels. Soda cans, beer bottles, and fast-food wrappers lie among small white plastic garbage bags. Boone picks up one of the bags, unties the top, and then gags, fighting back the vomit.

The bag is full of used condoms.

He drops the bag and steps into one of the tunnels that lead through the reeds. It's like being in another world—dark, narrow, and claustrophobic. The late-afternoon sunlight barely penetrates the tall reeds, and Boone can't see five feet in front of him.

So he doesn't see the shotgun.

# 48

The curtains on the cabin windows are open, and Petra can see into the small front room, which has a sofa, a couple of chairs, a kitchenette area and a table.

But no Tammy.

Petra walks around to the side, where another window offers a view of the small bedroom, where there is likewise no Tammy.

Maybe she's in the bathroom, Petra thinks.

She walks around to that side, puts her head against the thin wall, and listens. No sound of running water. She waits for a minute, hoping to hear the toilet flush, or the taps running, or anything, but it's perfectly still.

For one of the few times in her life, Petra doesn't know what to do. Should she wait here, in case Tammy is inside? Should she go back to the van and wait, in case Tammy just hasn't shown up yet but is on her way?

And how does she know it's even going to be Tammy, and not some other bimbo that Teddy is shagging in his Bang for Boobs program. And where was Teddy going? What could he possibly be doing in a bed of reeds, looking for the baby Moses, for God's sake? And what, if anything, has Boone found? Should I follow him? she wonders.

She decides to go back to the van and wait.

Except waiting isn't her best thing.

She gives it a shot, she does, but it isn't going to happen. What she really wants to do is go see what Boone is finding out. She makes it about three minutes, then bails.

# 49

Mick Penner should have.

Bailed, that is.

Should have taken Boone's advice, thrown his shit into a bag, gotten into his beloved BMW, and hit the highway.

He doesn't, though.

He intended to. One of those "road to hell" deals. He meant to get moving, but then he decided that one beer and a quick toke would help him get his shit together. He's on his third Corona when the door comes in.

Dan Silver's first punch goes into Mick's liver and crumples him. Mick's on his knees, hunched over in agony, sucking for air, when the kick comes into his solar plexus and makes breathing an impossibility.

Mick flops on the floor like a fish on the dock.

Then they're kicking him, shoes and boots smashing into his thighs, his shins, his ankles, his ribs. He rolls over on one side and pulls his arms over his head and manages to blurt out, "Not my face. Please, not my face."

His face is his living, and he knows it. Knows now in one of those stark moments of clarity that he's never going to be "SCRNRITR," no matter what his license plate reads, that the best he can hope for is a few more years of being a parking valet/male whore.

But he doesn't even get that if they fuck up his face.

They pick him up and set him down on the sofa.

"You don't want your pretty face messed up?" Dan asks. "You better tell me what I want to know."

"Anything, man."

Except what he wants to know is how to find Tammy.

Love is a powerful thing.

Elusive, ephemeral, enigmatic—love can make you do some fucked-up shit. It can drive you to depths you never thought you'd go; it can lift you to heights you never knew you could climb. It will show you the worst and the best in yourself. Love can strip you down to bare shame; love can reveal pure nobility.

Mick holds out a long time.

He loves her, he knows that these guys want to hurt her, will hurt, maybe kill her, and he loves her. In the end, he gives them everything they want, but it takes them a while to get it. He gives them Teddy, gives them the motel in Oceanside, gives them Boone.

He gives up everything and hates himself for it.

Dan leaves almost admiring the dumb shit.

Had to fuck him up real bad before he caved.

# 50

When he comes to, they start beating him, kicking him, cursing him.

Barely conscious, Boone rolls into a fetal position and covers up his head as the boots, fists, and the shotgun butt rain down on him.

And the words:

*Pendejo, lambioso, picaflor.*

A shotgun butt slams into his ankle. A few more of these, Boone thinks, and I'm never walking out of here. He opens his eyes, sees a pair of feet, grabs them, and lifts. The feet go flying, and Boone pushes himself up and topples over on the man. Boone's real lucky, because this turns out to be the guy holding the shotgun, who doesn't really know what he's doing because the safety is still on, so Boone is able to rip the gun out of his hands.

Boone rolls onto his back, points the shotgun up, and flips off the safety. It's only a little .410, the kind farmworkers use to shoot crows, but at this range it would do the job.

There are three men—campesinos—Mexican farmworkers.

The man who was holding the shotgun looks about forty, maybe a little younger. Deep brown weather-worn face and a black mustache already flecked with silver. His black eyes glare at Boone as if to say, Go ahead and pull the trigger, *pendejo*. I've seen worse.

The kid standing beside him looks scared. Eyes wide, long black hair stuffed under an old Yankees cap. Dirty long-sleeved T-shirt, jeans, and ancient, torn New Balance sneakers. He's holding a machete, wondering what to do with it.

The old man has his machete ready to strike, poised beside his white straw hat. He wears the old-style campesino shirt under overalls. And old cowboy boots—Boone felt the sharp pointed toes digging into his ribs.

If they wanted to kill me, I'd be dead, Boone thinks as he struggles to his feet, holding the shotgun on them. They could have blown my head off, or chopped me to pieces with the machetes. But they didn't. What they wanted to do was to give me a good beating, which they sure as hell did.

Teach me a lesson.

But what?

Boone thrusts the shotgun out a little, like, I will shoot you, and backs his way to the clearing in front of the reed caves. A little girl sits there, her arms wrapped around her knees, rocking herself. Her legs are dirty under her cheap cotton dress. Her hair is long and stringy. She looks terrified, and fingers a small crucifix that hangs around her neck from a thin chain.

"It's okay," Boone says.

She scoots back deeper into the cave.

"Don't be scared," Boone says. Fucking moron, he tells himself. You really think she's not going to be scared by a *güero* holding a shotgun? He reaches his hand down for her.

The teenage boy rushes in with the machete.

I don't want to shoot you, Boone thinks, backing off. But the boy keeps coming, the blade of the machete gleaming gold in the light of dusk. Boone takes another step back and raises the gun, then, at the last second, ducks under the blade and swings the gun butt into the boy's stomach.

The boy collapses onto his knees. Boone sees that the boy is sobbing, more in frustration than pain. He kicks the machete away from the kid's hand, hauls the boy up, wraps a forearm lock around his throat, and sticks the shotgun barrel into the side of his head. "I'm leaving now. Take one step toward me, I'll paint the air with him."

He turns around, puts the boy's body between him and the two campesinos and backs out of the reeds. When he gets to the clearing, he shoves the boy away. The boy turns and stares at him. A look of pure hatred. The kid spits on the ground, then turns and walks back through the reeds. Boone watches him for a second.

When he turns around, Petra is standing there.

# 51

"My God," she says, "what happened?"

Blood drips from the corner of his mouth and from his nose, and he looks like he's been rolled in the dirt.

"You're supposed to be watching the motel," he says.

"I was concerned about you," she replies. "Apparently for good reason. Where did you get a shotgun?"

"Someone gave it to me."

"Voluntarily?"

"Sort of."

He walks back up the road to the motel.

Teddy's car is still there.

"Did you find Teddy?" Petra asks.

"No," he says.

"We should get you to a hospital."

"Not necessary."

He opens the side door of the van and digs around until he finds a small first-aid kit. He gets into the front seat, twists the rearview mirror, and looks into it as he cleans the cuts and scratches on his face, swabbing them with pads and then rubbing in antiseptic. Then he places a Band-Aid on the cut over his left eye.

"Can I help?" Petra says.

"I asked you for help," Boone says. "You were supposed to be watching the motel."

"I already apologized for that."

He finishes applying the Band-Aid, then grabs a vial of pills, shakes one out, and swallows it.

"What—"

"Vicodin," he says. "Karate candy. I didn't find Teddy or Tammy. All I found was a *mojado* camp."

"A . . ."

*"Mojados,"* Boone repeats. "'Wetbacks.' Illegals. They work the fields; some of them live in camps. Usually, the camps are tucked up in the canyons; this one was in the reeds along the river. I wasn't exactly welcome."

But it's weird, he thinks, that the *mojados* were so aggressive. Usually, they'll do anything to avoid attention. The last thing in the world they want is trouble, and beating up a white guy is definitely trouble.

Boone leans forward and rubs the back of his neck, annoyed at the ache but grateful that the shotgun hadn't snapped a vertebra.

And what was Teddy doing in there? Boone asks himself. There aren't a lot of cosmetic surgery candidates in the *mojado* camps, not any that could afford Teddy anyway. And why did Teddy apparently get a pass while I got a shotgun butt to the neck? Or maybe Teddy didn't get a free ticket; maybe he's lying in a heap somewhere. Maybe worse. But what the *hell* was Teddy doing there in the first place?

Well, the only thing to do is wait and ask him. Boone grabs a beanie from the back and pulls it over his head. Then he slides down in his seat, rests his neck against the back of it, and closes his eyes.

"What are you doing?" Petra asks.

"Grabbing a few z's," he says, "until Teddy gets back from doing whatever he's doing."

"But what if you fall asleep?"

"I *am* going to fall asleep," Boone says. "That's the idea."

Besides, it's Rule number four.

These are Boone's four basic rules about stakeouts:

1. If you have a chance to eat, eat.
2. If there's a place to go to the bathroom, go.
3. If there's a space to lie down, lie down.
4. If you can sleep, sleep.

Because you never know when you're going to have a chance to do any or all of the four things again.

"But aren't you worried about being asleep when Teddy comes back?" Petra asks.

"No," Boone says, "because you're going to wake me up."

"What if I fall asleep?"

Boone laughs.

"And what if—"

"You should give up those what-ifs," Boone says. "They're gonna kill you."

He slides farther down in the seat, pulls the beanie over his eyes, and falls asleep.

# 52

Sunny spreads the mat out on the polished floor of her little house in Pacific Beach and lies down.

The old bungalow is just a half block from the beach. It was her grandparents' house; they bought it back in the twenties, when average people could afford something like that. Her grandfather died a long time ago; her grandmother passed just a few years back, after a long, sad struggle with Alzheimer's.

Eleanor Day had been quite a woman. Sunny holds on to the memories of long walks on the beach with her, and building sand castles, and how her grandmother bought Sunny her first surfboard and called her "Gidget," like the TV show. Sunny loved to stay with Grandma at the beach. It was her favorite place in the world.

Sunny visited her a lot in the home. Some days, Eleanor would know who Sunny was; other days, she'd get her confused with her daughter, or her sister, or an old friend from college. It made Sunny sad, but it didn't stop her from visiting.

She knew who Eleanor was.

Sunny was living in a small apartment when she got the word that her grandmother was gone. The Dawn Patrol came to the funeral, and no one was more surprised than Sunny when the lawyer told her that she had inherited the old two-bedroom bungalow near the beach.

Her grandmother had wanted Sunny to have it because she knew that she would appreciate it.

She does, of course.

It holds a lot of memories, a lot of love.

Now she takes a few deep breaths, then launches into the rigorous Pilates exercises that make up her daily routine. She goes at it hard for an hour—stretching, twisting, moving into heavy aerobic drills, then stretching it down.

Then she moves over to the old surfboard that she stretched across two cinder blocks. She lies down on the board, jumps to her knees, then instantly up to her feet; then she lies back down again. She does this a hundred times, until the movement is as smooth, powerful, and automatic as it can be. Her heart pounding, a fine sheen of sweat coating her skin, she moves to the free weights and lifts, first working her upper body and arms. She wants the arm and shoulder strength for paddling and for that sudden burst of speed and energy needed to get into a big wave. Then she works the trapezium and neck muscles, which will help keep her neck from getting snapped in the worst-case scenario of going over the falls headfirst.

After that, she straps weights to her ankles and does leg lifts, then picks up a bar and does toe lifts and deep squats, strengthening her quads, calves, and thighs, which will help keep her on the board in the big waves. While her long legs are an advantage in swimming, they work against her in staying on the board, so she has to make sure that they're like steel.

Sunny is a finely honed athlete, five-eleven, big-boned, with a swimmer's broad shoulders, negligible body fat, and those long legs.

"You're a gazelle," Dave the Love God once said to her as he watched her walk in from the water.

"She's not the gazelle," Boone said correcting him. "She's the lioness."

Sunny's always loved Boone for saying that. Well, for a lot of things, but his saying that was enough to love him.

And she keeps her body in superb shape with running, swimming, lifting, stretching. Truth be told, it's not the ideal surfer's body. Most of the best woman surfers have smaller, more compact frames—easier for balance and for the lightning-quick turns and shifts that win competitions.

But Sunny plans to turn her size to her advantage.

A big body, she thinks, for the big waves.

So far, big-wave riding has been pretty much a male preserve. There are a few women starting to ride them, but still plenty of room for a female surfer to stand out in a male lineup. She knows she has the size, weight, and strength to handle the thunder crushers.

Up to now, she's been caught in a vicious circle: You need money to travel to the big waves in Hawaii and Tahiti, but without sponsorship, she doesn't have the money, but she can't get a sponsorship until she rides the big waves, but in order to ride the big waves, she has to travel. . . .

But now the big waves are coming to her. Almost literally to her back door, and all she has to do is walk outside, paddle out, and catch one of the big mackers. The beaches and bluffs will be lined with photographers and video guys, and all she needs is one ride, one monster ride, with her tawny hair waving like her personal flag against the black wave, and she knows that her picture will be on the front cover of the mags.

And the sponsorship will follow.

So lift, she tells herself. Push past the pain; it's only pain. Every fiber-ripping lift will help you stay up in that wave. This is what you've been training for for months, for years, all your life. So do one more, one more, one more. . . .

The lifting done, she goes back on the mat and stretches some more, then lies back, breathes, and imagines herself riding the big wave.

It's not mere fantasizing; she carefully breaks it down, moment by moment, from the paddle in to the drop to the heavy right break, into the tube, then out again with the blast of spray. She imagines it again and again, each time in more detail, and in each repetition she does it stronger and better. She never imagines missing the wave, or wiping out, or getting sucked over the falls.

Sunny keeps it rigorously positive.

The sound of her moment coming to her.

She gets up, wipes herself down with a towel, and sits and listens to the ocean.

# 53

Petra watches Boone sleep.

It's a somewhat edifying experience, in that she's never actually watched a man sleep before.

Not that there haven't been men in her bed, but she has typically fallen asleep before they have, or, preferably, they have gotten up and left after the sexual act and a decent period of "cuddling," although, truth be told, she could do without the latter. It seems to be expected, however, even though she suspects that the man could dispense with it as well.

If she's in the man's bed, she gets up and leaves after the polite interval, because she prefers to sleep alone, and, especially, wake up alone. She's hardly decent—physically, emotionally, or psychologically—until she's had that first cup of Lapsang souchong, and besides, the last thing she wants to be doing in the morning is looking after a man's needs, feigning cheerfulness as she makes him coffee, eggs, sausages, and the like.

That's what restaurants are for.

Now she watches Boone Daniels sleep and she's fascinated.

One moment the man was totally, utterly awake and one second later he was just as totally, utterly asleep, as if he didn't have the proverbial care in the world. As if he weren't financially bereft, as if he didn't have a crucial witness to locate, as if an apparently violent gangster wasn't out to harm him, as if . . .

I weren't even here, she admits to herself.

Is that what's bothering you? she asks herself. That this man can simply ignore you to the extent of actual *unconsciousness*?

Ridiculous, she tells herself. Why would you care if this . . . primitive doesn't find you as fascinating as, let's face it, most men do? It's not as if you have any interest in him, not as if you've made the slightest effort to attract him.

Of course, you never make the slightest effort, she thinks. Be truthful, woman, you're very lazy when it comes to that. Lazy because you *can* be, because a frank assessment in the mirror tells you so, and because men tell you so.

They act like idiots and they're ridiculously easy to bring into your bed, if that's what you want.

Not that there have been that many.

A few well-selected, well-heeled, polite, appropriate sexual partners, one or two of whom she had considered as potential husbands and who, she supposes, have evaluated her as a potential wife.

But they are all much too career-oriented and, face it, selfish for marriage. At least at this point in her life, in any case. Perhaps after she makes partner, she might seek out a more serious relationship, perhaps find a man who might be a suitable husband. In the meantime, she's content to find the occasional young lawyer or banker who's appropriate to take to company dinners and, even more occasionally, to bed.

Or am I, she wonders, so content?

You are lonely, she admits to herself. It isn't a sudden revelation, an epiphany of sorts, but more of a creeping realization that she's been missing something, something she never thought she wanted—a close emotional connection with another person. The realization shocks her. She's always been, as long as she can remember, totally self-sufficient.

Which is the way she likes it.

But now she's beginning to feel that she needs somebody, and she doesn't like the feeling.

At all.

She regards Boone again.

How can the man sleep at a time like this?

She briefly considers waking him up but then rejects the idea.

Maybe I'm just jealous she thinks, envious at this ability to sleep so easily.

She doesn't fall asleep easily or sleep particularly well. Instead, she lies awake thinking about cases, about things she needs to do, second-guessing herself about decisions she's made, worrying about them, worrying about how she's perceived at the firm, whether she's working hard, whether she's working too hard and arousing dangerous jealousies. She worries about her wardrobe, her hair. She worries about worrying. Half the time, she can't sleep because she's worrying about not getting enough sleep.

If it weren't for Ambien, she might not sleep at all.

But this waterlogged Cro-Magnon with a PI license, she thinks, *he* sleeps like a baby. It must be true, then: Ignorance *is* bliss.

Her mind turns to the girl at the restaurant that morning. The tall, athletic creature with the tawny hair. Clearly, he's sleeping with her, and who could blame him? She's gorgeous. But what on earth could she see in him? She could have any man she wanted, so why does she choose *this*? Could he be *that* good in bed? Worth having to wake up to? Certainly not.

It's a mystery.

She's working it through when she sees Teddy walking up the road.

# 54

"Ouch."

Boone's awake even before he feels Petra's elbow dig into his ribs.

You develop a sixth sense on stakeouts after a while. You can be asleep, but there's an internal alarm clock that will wake you up when something's going down.

Boone pulls his beanie up and sees Petra pointing down the road at Teddy.

He has a little girl with him.

The girl from the reeds.

# 55

"Stay in the van."

"But—"

"I said, stay in the fucking van," Boone snaps in a voice that even Petra doesn't question. He gets out of the van and walks toward the cabin.

It has a central front door with a small window on either side. A front sitting room leads into a back bedroom and a bath. The curtain is open on one of the windows and Boone sees Teddy sitting on the bed next to the girl, shaking some pills from a vial into his hand.

Boone feels like kicking the motel door in, then beating the uncouth piss out of Teddy until the good doctor needs a cosmetic surgeon for himself.

Because Teddy D-Cup, with access to literally hundreds of beautiful women, is feeding roofies to a little girl in a motel room preparatory to raping her. And now Boone knows what the good Dr. Cole was doing in the strawberry fields—shopping for a family so fucking desperate, they'd sell their daughter to him. And the *mojados* who worked Boone over in the reeds were taking his back.

It's a beautiful world.

Boone throws his shoulder into the door, which splinters around the bolt lock and opens. He's into the bedroom in three long strides and has Teddy by the shirtfront on the fourth. He lifts Teddy up and holds him in the air.

The girl screams and runs out the door.

"This isn't what it looks like," Teddy says.

Christ, Boone thinks, does every fucking child molester have to say that every fucking time? No, dude, it's *always* what it looks like. Boone pivots and slams Teddy into the wall. Pulls him in toward his own chest and then slams him again.

Teddy yells, "I'm helping her!"

Yeah, I'll bet you are, Boone thinks. He takes his right hand off Teddy's shirt, clenches it into a tight fist, and cocks his arm, ready to blast Teddy's face into oatmeal. Except suddenly it isn't Teddy's face; it's Russ Rasmussen's. Boone's world goes red. Tilting crazily, like a bad wipeout.

"Boone!"

Through the red haze, he hears Petra, gets that she disapproves, but he doesn't care.

*"Boone!"*

He turns around to tell her to butt out.

Dan Silver is holding a gun to her head. Two of his boys stand behind him.

"Let him go, Boone," Dan says.

The world comes level again, back into focus. Boone says, "He's a short eyes."

"We'll take care of him," Dan says. "Let him go now or I'll put two in her pretty head before I do you."

Boone looks at Petra. Her pale skin is absolutely white, her eyes are big and full of tears, and her legs quiver. She's scared to death. Boone lowers his clenched fist but then jams his palm into Teddy's ribs before releasing his grip on the man.

Teddy slides to the floor.

"Good thing for you I showed up," Dan says to him, "before this barbarian beat the shit out of you. I feel like the cavalry riding in. Nick of time and all that happy bullshit. You're coming with me voluntarily, aren't you, Dr. Cole?"

"Yes, I am."

"Help him up."

Dan's boys take Teddy by the arms and walk him out the door.

"This isn't over, Teddy," says Boone.

Dan gestures at Petra. "You banging this, Daniels?"

Boone doesn't answer.

"No, you ain't," Dan says. "She's *much* too juicy for you."

He turns to Petra. "You get tired of slummin', you want a *real* man, you come see me, honey. I'll take good care of you."

She hears herself say, "I'd rather fuck a pig."

Dan smiles, but his face turns red. "Maybe we can work that out for you, bitch."

"Enough," Boone says.

"You're in no position to—"

"I said, 'Enough,'" Boone repeats. Something in his voice tells Dan to back off before he has to shoot this guy. And this guy is Eddie's asshole buddy, something about him pulling Eddie's brat out of the drink or something. And the last thing in the world Dan needs right now is more problems with Red Eddie.

"Stay in here for a few minutes," Dan says. "You come out, 'Friend Of Eddie' or not, I'll smoke you. Her, too."

He takes a moment to leer at Petra and then walks out.

"You okay?" Boone asks Petra.

She sits down heavily on the bed and puts her head in her hands. Boone understands it. You get a gun pointed at your head, it changes you. It makes you realize how quickly you could not exist anymore. In that second, all you want is your life—desperately, fervently—and you'd give almost anything for it. And that moment of realization changes you as a person. You're never quite the same after you realize you'd do almost anything to live.

But talk about guts. "I'd rather fuck a pig"? To a guy who has a gun pointed at your head! That's a crazy, sick kind of courage. He walks over and puts his hand on her head, strokes her hair a little, and says, "It's all right. You're okay."

"I was so afraid," she says.

Then Boone realizes that she's crying. "You were amazing," he says. "Really brave."

A second later, they hear two shots.

*Pop.*

*Pop.*

What they call "execution-style."

# 56

The girl runs back into the reeds, because she doesn't have anywhere else to go.

Her name is Luce.

She doesn't find anyone in the reeds. They're all gone now, so she crawls into one of the little caves, huddles there, and says the Rosary as she rubs the little crucifix. It will be a cold night, she knows, but the other girls will be back at dawn.

She wraps her arms around her knees and waits for the sun to rise again.

# 57

Dan Silver sits beside Teddy Cole in the backseat of the Explorer.

He grabs Teddy's right index finger and says, "Your hands are your life, aren't they, Doc?"

Teddy's chin-sculpted, Botoxed, nose-jobbed, skin-peeled, hair-transplanted, eye-tightened, face-lifted, tummy-tucked, dental-worked, lasered, and tanned face turns absolutely white with fear. He tries to speak, but the words get jammed in his throat. All he can manage is a weak, shaky nod.

"Hands of a surgeon, right?" Dan asks. "That's what you are, cosmetic surgeon to the stars? *Nip/Tuck*? So, what if I start breaking your fingers, one by one, starting with your thumbs? It's going to hurt like you wouldn't believe, Doc, and, afterward, no more strippers, starlets, and trophy wives for you."

Teddy tries to hold out.

For Luce's sake, for Tammy's sake, for the sake of his own soul—if that isn't a hopeless, antiquated concept. He holds out until Dan starts counting down from ten.

He makes it to six.

"I'm only going to ask you once," Dan says, "and I'm really hoping I don't have to ask you ten times. Where is Tammy Roddick?"

# 58

The Boonemobile rests on its front bumper, like a wounded bull on its front knees, exhausted in the ring.

Its front right tire is flat.

Boone looks at the van. "God*damn*it."

"I thought they shot Teddy," Petra says. She goes into the front seat and roots around in her purse. "They took my phone."

"Mine, too," Boone says. "It's a good thing I took Teddy's."

He pulls Teddy's RAZR out of his pants pocket and scrolls through Teddy's call history. Seventeen calls in the past two days made to the same number. He punches it in.

Tammy picks it up right away, like she's been waiting for the call.

"Teddy?" Tammy asks.

Her voice sounds anxious, worried, scared.

"Where are you, Tammy?"

"Who is this?"

"Wherever you are," Boone says, "get out now."

"What are you—"

"Teddy is on his way," Boone says, "with Dan and some of his thugs. He gave you up, Tammy."

"He wouldn't do that."

"He wouldn't *want* to," Boone says, "but I guarantee you, if he hasn't already, he will. Get out. Let me meet you somewhere. I can help you."

"Who are you?"

"Petra Hall is here with me."

"Oh, fuck."

"You want to talk with her?"

"No," Tammy says.

"Look," Boone says, "you have no reason to trust me, but you have to get out. *Now.*"

"I don't know."

"Let me meet you somewhere," Boone says. "I'll pick you up, take you somewhere safe."

She clicks off.

"Damn it!" Boone says. He gets on the horn to Hang Twelve while he goes into the back of the van, pulls out a spare tire and a jack, then goes to work on the car.

"I could do that for you," Petra says.

"I'll bet you could," Boone says, fitting the tire on. "But I don't want you to wreck your clothes."

Boone gets the tire on, tightens down the lugs, and releases the jack. He's putting it back into the van when Hang calls back.

He has the number traced.

# 59

The Institute of Self Awareness was founded back in the 1960s.

Of course.

If there was any single word that typified that decade, it was *self.*

Some shrink came down from Esalen with a head full of acid and a trust fund and bought the old Episcopalian retreat that had been founded on a bluff above one of the best right breaks on the entire West Coast.

The shrink didn't surf but didn't mind those who did using the stairs on the south side of his property to go out and hit that marvelous break. To honor that generous man, and because The Institute of Self Awareness was too cumbersome to pronounce all the time, the beach below the retreat simply became known as "Shrink's."

The Institute of Self Awareness became first a hippie, and later a New Age retreat where people could check into a room, eat vegetarian meals, take meditation seminars, yoga classes, and otherwise become aware of themselves.

"What does that mean?" Dave the Love God asked Boone one day while they were sitting in the lineup at Shrink's waiting for the next set and looking up at the retreat's cottages.

"It has nothing to do with masturbation," Sunny told Hang Twelve.

"I don't know," Boone said. "I guess you just do it."

"Yeah, but do *what*?" Dave asked.

"Whatever it is."

Then the set came in and they forgot about the question.

Boone had only been vaguely aware that the place was even called The Institute of Self Awareness anyway. He had always known it as Shrink's, had carried his board down those wooden steps probably hundreds of times, and there was no way he was ever going to check into a room, eat vegetarian meals, take meditation seminars, yoga classes, and otherwise become self-aware.

For one thing, he couldn't afford the steep room rate. For another thing, he wasn't introspectively inclined. For a third and final thing, he was already pretty aware of who he was.

"If there is one thing that can be said about Boone," Sunny Day proclaimed during a reasonably drunken session at The Sundowner after closing time, "it is that he knows who he is."

"That's true," Boone said. "I surf, I eat, I sleep, I work—"

"Sometimes," High Tide said.

"Sometimes," Boone said, "and, every now and then—more then than now—I make love. And that's about it."

But now he wishes that he had gone to the place at least once, so he'd know the lay of the land, because now he's pretty sure that's where Tammy is.

The Institute of Self Awareness has developed a specialized and lucrative clientele.

To wit, people—especially famous people—who have become aware that their real selves might need a little cosmetic surgery, need a place where they can hide from the prying eyes of the public while the swelling goes down, the black eyes fade, and time passes before they reemerge into the world with their new noses, breasts, faces, lips, stomachs, butts, or all of the above. So the ISA now makes a lot of its income by providing a cocoon in which celebrities can hide until they fully morph into their new selves.

And the institute zealously guards its clientele against the paparazzi, the tabloids, and the just plain curious. The founding shrink may not have thrown up any fences against the surfers, but the new management has built high walls to shield its guests against even the longest lenses of the paparazzi. The walls are topped with strands of barbed wire and motion sensors, lest anyone should try to climb in. Beefy security guards patrol the perimeter and man the front gate of the reception room, barring entrance to everyone but expected visitors and attending physicians.

So while tourists and local visitors can walk around the gardens all they want, to get into the private part of the retreat itself is akin to entering the gates of Troy.

Teddy can walk right in.

Theodore Cole, M.D., is a cash cow for The Institute of Self Awareness. Teddy not only has strippers in there recovering from boob jobs; he has Hollywood stars and starlets, Orange County trophy wives who want a little distance from their home turf, and San Diego society matrons from La Jolla who have coincidentally discovered their need for spirituality along with their face-lifts.

So if Teddy wants to store a girlfriend inside the walls for a night or two, the welcome mat is out. And if Teddy says that no one is going to get in there to look for her, then no one is going to get in there to look for her.

# 60

When the Explorer pulls into the parking lot of The Institute of Self Awareness, the driver rolls down the window and Teddy, now in the front passenger seat, leans across and waves to the guard.

"Good evening, Dr. Cole," the guard says, giving a slight stink eye to the car full of guys who don't look like they're seeking any kind of awareness, self or otherwise.

"I'm just going in to check on a client," Teddy says, feeling Dan's pistol jammed into the back of the seat against his spine.

"Should I call ahead?" the guard asks.

"No," Dan murmurs.

"No," Teddy says.

The gate swings open, the Explorer goes through, and the gate swings shut behind it. Teddy directs the driver to a small parking lot.

"Now take us to where she is," Dan says. "And, Doc, if you mess with me, I'm going to put one in your spine."

Teddy leads them along the curving walkways lit by the little solar-powered lamps. Most of the guests are in their cottages, but a few are out taking a stroll around the grounds. One in particular, a tall redheaded woman in a white terry-cloth robe, attracts Dan's attention.

"Hey, is that . . ." Dan says, then names a famous movie actress.

"Could be," Teddy says.

"What's she getting, a boob job?"

"Nose," Teddy says. She wanted her nose shaved down. A tuck around the eyes. A little something to hold off the day when she has to play the bitch mother or the eccentric aunt. But Teddy's mind isn't really on that. He's thinking about some way that he can tip Tammy off, get her out of there before . . . He doesn't even want to think about what happens after the "before."

As they approach Tammy's cottage, he can see lights on through the curtain of the front window.

"You got a key?" Dan asks him.

"Well, it's a card."

"What the fuck ever," Dan says. "You let yourself in, you leave the door open behind you. Got it, Doc?"

"Yeah."

"Doc?"

"What?"

"If you're thinking about trying to be a hero," Dan says, "stop thinking. You may be boss hog in the operating room, but this ain't your world, hoss. It will just get you in the wheelchair basketball league. Tell me you understand."

"I understand."

"Good. Open the door."

Teddy walks up to the Lotus Cottage. It's always been one of his favorites, redolent with memories. Teddy has put some serious talent in the Lotus Cottage and has gotten some head in there that you wouldn't believe. Hand shaking, he fumbles with the card and eventually manages to insert it into the lock. The little green light comes on, followed by the soft click of the lock opening. Teddy gently pushes the door open a crack and says, "Tammy? It's me."

Dan shoves him out of the way and steps into the cottage.

The living room is all done in white. Bone white walls, with black-and-white photographs of lotuses in silver frames and a flat-screen plasma television set. A white sofa, white chairs. The wood floor is painted black, but the carpet's white.

Tammy isn't in the living room.

Dan moves toward the closed bedroom door. He nudges it open with the toe of his boot and then steps through, pistol up and ready to shoot.

She's not in the bedroom, which is similarly decorated. White walls, black-and-white photos, white bedspread on the double bed, and a flat-screen television, smaller than the one in the living room. The guests must watch a fuck of a lot of TV while they're self-actualizing, Dan thinks as he moves to the bathroom door and listens.

The shower is running.

One of them fancy new "rain showers" by the sound of it.

He leans into the bathroom door.

It's locked.

Women always lock the door when they're taking a shower, Dan thinks. He blames it on *Psycho*.

Dan leans back and launches a kick into the door. The jamb splinters with a crash. Dan steps into the bathroom and points the gun to his left, toward the shower.

But she ain't in it.

And the window is open.

# 61

A steep set of stairs runs down to the beach from the back of Shrink's.

It cuts through a berm of red clay planted with succulent ankle-high ground cover that blossoms red in the spring but now looks silver and glossy under motion-activated lamps set in the ground every twenty feet.

Dan negotiates the stairs with surprising grace for a big man. He holds the pistol in one hand; the other glides along the pipe railing as he calls, "Tammy? I just want to talk with you, baby!"

If she's out there, she doesn't answer.

The night fog is coming in fast, already obscuring the water and the beach. Dan pauses on a landing and listens.

"Tammy!" Dan yells. "There's nothing to be afraid of! We can work this out, girl!"

He waits for an answer, the pistol poised to shoot in the direction of a voice. No response comes, but then he hears footsteps, running down the stairs below him.

Dan chases her down the stairs.

Onto the beach, into the fog.

# 62

Boone and Petra run down the stairs at Sea Cliff Park, just south of Shrink's, Boone trying to hear Tammy as she whispers into her phone, "He's coming. I can hear him."

"Keep coming this way," Boone says. "We're almost there."

He makes it down to the beach and looks north, the direction Tammy should be coming from. But it's tough to see anything—the fog has moved in and set up housekeeping for the night, and the moon hasn't thought about getting up yet.

"Tammy?" Boone says. "Can you see me?"

"No."

Boone peers into the fog.

Then he sees her.

Dressed only in a white robe, she looks like a ghost. Or maybe an escapee from a mental hospital, her long red hair disheveled and wild in the moist night air. She's running, as much as she can run in the heavy sand, her long legs working against her, struggling for balance. She's not even sure what she's running toward, just a voice on the other end of a telephone, saying he was going to help her. At first, she didn't believe him, but there was something in the voice that changed her mind.

She sees him and tries to run faster.

Boone trots toward her, grabs her as she falls into his arms, gasping for breath.

"He's behind me," she says.

"Dan?"

She nods and gulps some air. Petra comes up and helps Boone lift Tammy to her feet. Tammy looks at her. "I'll testify. I'll do anything you want."

"Good. Thank you."

"Let's get you out of here," Boone says.

The shot comes out of the fog.

# 63

Johnny Banzai hears the shot.

You don't hear a lot of gunshots in Encinitas, especially not west of the PCH, and certainly not in the proximity of The Institute of Self Awareness, where people do not tend to "find themselves" at the wrong end of a gun. No, the guns around Shrink's tend to be surfboards, not firearms.

Gunshots are going to grab any cop's attention, but these shots really reach out and grab Johnny's head, because they're coming from the direction of his destination, the aforementioned ISA, and Johnny's aware that he's getting there in the wake of Boone Daniels.

Boone caught this wave first and Johnny jumped in, and now they're both pumping it to get to the real Tammy Roddick first. Johnny has some very pointed questions to ask her, he has some equally sharp queries for Boone, and he wants to know from both of them what they have to do with the Jane Doe lying beside the motel pool.

It didn't take all that long to find out that the Jane Doe wasn't Tammy. Then he went to Roddick's place of employment, Totally Nude Girls, and found out that (a) Tammy's boyfriend had been Mick Penner; (b) she dumped him for Teddy D-Cup; and (c) Boone was a step ahead of him. A quick visit to Teddy's La Jolla office and the flash of a badge got Teddy's receptionist to give up that the good doctor was on his way to make a house call at Shrink's after getting a phone call from a man who claimed that he was Tammy Roddick.

Classic Boone.

Goddamn him.

Except now Johnny hears shots, and he hopes to hell that he gets to arrest Boone and not do an investigation on his killing.

He opens his window, attaches the flasher unit to the roof of the car, and hits the siren. Then he gets on the radio and calls for uniformed backup. "Shots fired. Plainclothes officer approaching the scene." It's dark and rainy out and he doesn't want to be standing there with a gun in his hand when nervous uniforms show up. They might see the gun before they see the badge.

Then he pushes the pedal to the floor.

Banzai.

# 64

Chess with guns in the night and fog.

Cool game in theory, scarier than shit in practice.

Adrenaline-pumping, ass-clenching, heart-racing scary. A paintball freak's wet dream, but these bullets aren't loaded with paint; they're lead. And if you fuck up, you're not going to get splattered; you're going to get *splattered.*

Boone tries to move himself and the two women through the muted fireworks display without getting shot. Which isn't easy because the beach is narrow at high tide, and Dan and his two boys keep closing off the space. Boone can't make a break toward the bluffs because they have that covered, and he can't get them up or down the beach because they have that sealed off.

Dan shoots and makes his target move, shoots and makes them move again—and each time they move, he directs his guys and closes off the space. Just like in the ring, he's patiently walking them down, working them into the corner for the kill.

Boone hears sirens in the distance. Cops are coming, but are they going to come in time? In the dark and fog, the shooters will take more chances than they otherwise would, knowing they can probably get away in the mist and confusion.

So the question, he thinks as he pushes Petra and Tammy to the sand and lies on top of them, is whether or not he has time to wait for the cavalry to ride in. A spray of bullets zipping just over his head makes up his mind. The police are going to get there in time to find their bodies. So they have to make a move.

There's only one place left to go.

# 65

High Tide sits in The Sundowner enjoying an End of the Workday Beer. The End of the Workday Beer is the best beer there is, with the possible exception of the occasional Weekend Morning Breakfast Beer or the Post Surf Session on a Hot Afternoon Beer.

But High Tide likes the End of the Workday Beer best because, as a supervisor for the San Diego Public Works Department, he puts in a hard, long workday. Josiah Pamavatuu, aka High Tide, is a busy man when weather like this pulls in. He'll have crews out 24/7 for the next few days, and he'll have to keep track of them all, making sure that they're getting the job done, keeping the water flowing smoothly underneath the city.

It's a lot of responsibility.

That's okay—High Tide is up to it. He's enjoying his brew when Red Eddie comes in and sits down on the stool beside him.

"Howzit, brah?" Eddie asks.

"Howzit."

"Buy you a beer?"

Tide shakes his head. "Driving, brah. Just one before home to the kids."

"Good man."

"What you want, Eddie?" Tide asks.

"*Bruddah* can't have a beer wid a *bruddah* he don't want somethin'?" Eddie asks. He raises a finger, points it at Tide's beer, and the bartender brings him one of the same.

"You're about da business, Eddie," Tide says.

"Okay, business," Eddie says. "Your buddy Boone."

"What about him?"

"He's on a wave he shouldn't be on."

"I don't tell Boone what he can ride."

"If you're his friend, you would," Eddie says.

"You threatening him?" Tide asks. His fist tightens on the beer mug.

"D'opposite," Eddie says. "I'm trying to toss him a line, pull him in. He's looking for some *wahine;* she's causing a lot of aggro. If certain peoples was to locate the chick first, Boone's out of the impact zone, you know what I mean."

"Boone can take care of himself," Tide says. But he's worried why Eddie's approaching him about this. He waits for the other sandal to fall.

Doesn't take long.

"You have a cuz in Waikiki," Eddie says. "Zeke."

It's true. Like a lot of Samoans, Zeke moved to Hawaii five years ago to try to make some money. It didn't work out that way. "What about him?"

"He's an icehead."

"Tell me something I don't know." The whole family's been worried sick about Zeke. His mother can't sleep, can't eat her dinner. She begged Tide to go over, straighten him out, and Tide took some sick days, flew to Honolulu, sat down and tried to talk some sense into Zeke. Got him into rehab. Zeke was out three days, went back to the pipe. Last time Tide heard, Zeke was sleeping rough out in Waimalu Park. Only a matter of time before he ODs, or some other icehead takes him out for a dime.

Ice is the devil.

"What you saying?" Tide asks.

"I'm saying I can get the word out," Eddie says. "Zeke is taboo. You help Boone see things right, deliver this girl to the proper address, no dealer in the islands will sell Zeke a taste."

Tide knows it's a serious offer. Red Eddie has that kind of reach. All he has to do is put out the word, and no dealer in his right mind would even be seen talking to Zeke. They'd run away from him like he had leprosy. Zeke would have to straighten out.

"Don't say yes, don't say no." Eddie finishes half his beer, lays a twenty on the bar, and gets up. "Don't say nothin'. I'll know by your actions what your answer is. I just think, brah, we island guys have to stick together. We're the *ohana,* eh? *Aiga.*"

Eddie heads for the door. One of his *moke* boys opens it for him and he walks out, flashing Tide the *shaka* sign as he goes.

The devil comes in many forms.

The serpent to Eve.

Ice to a tweeker.

This time, it's a rumor that wafts through The Sundowner like warm air under the ceiling fans.

The Boonemobile is parked by Shrink's. Daniels must be checking out Shrink's. If Daniels is there, he must be scoping it out for the big swell. It's going to peak at Shrink's.

Tide finishes his beer, walks out to his truck, and heads north.

Family is family.

# 66

Johnny Banzai rolls up to the security shack at the Institute of Self Awareness and stops in front of the gate.

"I'm sorry, sir," the guard says. "This is private property. You can't come in here."

"Actually, I think I can." He shows the guard his badge.

The guard tries to hang. "Do you have a warrant, Detective?"

"Yeah," Johnny says. "My warrant is, if you don't open that fucking gate like two seconds ago, I'm going to drive through it anyway. Then, first thing in the morning, a battalion of health inspectors is going to arrive for a close look at the sushi and the celebrities. Then the fire inspectors are going to—"

The gate opens.

Johnny drives through.

# 67

Navy SEALs do it in training, but they're freaking Navy SEALs.

Lie in the ocean in winter at night, that is, not moving as frigid water washes over them, drops their body temps toward hypothermia, makes them shake uncontrollably, their bones and flesh aching with cold.

But that's what Boone, Petra, and Tammy do as Danny and his boys hunt the beach for them. Boone wraps an arm around each woman and holds her as hard as he can, feels them shiver as he tries to relax his own body. It's the only way to survive psychologically—force yourself to relax, not tighten up.

Cold and wet are a deadly combo. You can survive cold, you can tolerate wet, but the two of them together can kill you, send your body into shock, or force you out of the water into lethal gunfire.

Boone knows they don't have a lot of time left. He looks over at Petra. Her face is set in grim determination. Stiff upper lip and all that happy crap, but the woman is holding on; she's a lot tougher than she looks.

Tammy's eyes are shut tight, her lips clamped together, her jaw muscles locked. She's holding on.

Boone tightens his grip on both of them.

Dan is puzzled.

He had Daniels and the two *broads* in a box, and they're gone.

Just *gone.*

Like the fog wrapped them up and took them.

He looks out toward the surf. No way, he thinks. No fucking *way.* That's suicidal. The cop sirens come closer and Dan hears footsteps running down the stairs. Turns to see those big cop flashlights piercing the fog.

Time to boogie.

# 68

High Tide turns into the parking lot at Sea Cliff Park and pulls up next to the Boonemobile.

Boone ain't in it.

What the hell, Tide wonders, is Boone doing up here on the bluff over the south end of Shrink's at night? Checking out the surf? Really, *bruddah*?

Tide heads down the stairs toward the beach. Hurts his knee, walking down stairs, but what are you going to do? He has to have a word with Boone, and down the stairs is where Boone is apparently at.

Except he ain't.

When Tide gets down on the sand, he doesn't see Boone standing there checking out the waves.

All he sees is fog.

Then he spots something in the shallow white water. At first he thinks it's a dolphin, but a dolphin wouldn't be in the trench in this weather and he sees only one, and dolphins travel in groups. Must be driftwood, something came in with the tide.

The driftwood stands up.

"BOONE!" High Tide yells. *"HAMO!"*

Brother.

High Tide walks into the water and grabs Boone, then sees that there are two women with him. Boone grabs one of them, Tide the other, and they stagger onto the beach.

Boone mumbles, "Tide . . ."

"Easy, bro."

"Are they—"

"They're okay." Tide takes off his jacket and wraps it around the smaller woman, who's shivering uncontrollably. Then he takes off his wool beanie and puts it on the head of the tall redheaded woman. It's not enough, but it will help for the time being.

Boone says, "How did you . . ."

"Beach-bongo telegraph," High Tide says. "Word's all along the coast you're here."

"We gotta get off this beach," Boone says. He hefts the smaller woman into a fireman's carry.

Petra starts to say, "I can—"

"I know you can."

He carries her anyway. Tide easily sweeps up the redheaded woman and holds her close to his chest as they climb the steps back up to the parking lot. When they get there, Tide grabs two blankets and some towels from the back of his truck as Boone starts to undress Petra.

"What are you doing?" she murmurs.

"Have to get you out of these," Boone says. "Hypothermia. Give me a hand, *hamo*?"

Boone, his fingers trembling with cold, strips Petra down to her underwear, wraps her tightly in the blanket, then vigorously rubs her hair dry while Tide does the same with Tammy.

"How about you?" Tide asks.

"I'm okay," Boone says.

They get the women into the cab of Tide's truck, then Tide starts the engine and cranks the heater on full blast. Boone goes to the back of his van, strips down, towels off, and changes into a pair of jeans and a sweatshirt.

Tide climbs into the van.

"S'up, brah?"

"It's complicated, Tide," Boone says. "Can you give me a hand? I need to buy some time."

"What you got in mind?"

When Boone tells him, High Tide objects. "It's the *Boonemobile,* man."

But Boone puts the van in neutral, and he and Tide push it to the edge of the bluff, then take a running start and shove it through the thin wooden guardrail.

"Good-bye," Boone says.

The van launches off the edge, stays upright for a second, then somersaults down onto the beach. A second later, a muffled explosion goes off; then a small tower of flame rises up through the fog.

Hell of a bonfire on the beach tonight.

A Viking funeral for the Boonemobile.

# 69

The devil doesn't give you easy choices.

If he did, he wouldn't be the devil, just some gyppo piker wannabe masquerading as the real deal.

The real devil doesn't ask you to choose between good and evil. For most people, that's too easy. Most people, even when faced with temptations beyond their previous imaginings, will choose to do good.

So the real devil asks you to choose between bad and worse. Let a family member die of a horrible addiction, or betray a friend. That's why he's the devil, man. And when he's really on his game, he doesn't make you choose between heaven and hell; he gives you a choice between hell and hell.

Josiah Pamavatuu is a good man, no doubt about it. Now he drives his truck with two wet and shivering women at his side and his best friend in the back, a man who is like family to him.

But *like* ain't *is*.

Is is is.

# 70

Johnny Banzai finds a shaken Teddy D-Cup drinking an "organic martini" in the Lotus Cottage.

"Where's Tammy Roddick?" Johnny asks him.

Teddy points his thumb in the general direction of the beach.

From whence comes an explosion and a ball of flame.

# 71

Hang Twelve runs.

Pushing off on all twelve toes, he hoofs it as hard as he can toward Sunny's house. Like he's trying to pump the fear through his bloodstream and out of his body.

It ain't working.

Hang is terrified.

Word traveled down to Pacific Beach with the speed of rumor itself. The Boonemobile went off the bluff at Sea Cliff Park and burst into flames. Boone Daniels hasn't been found. The firemen are there now. There's already talk of a paddle-out and a memorial service after the big swell is over.

Hang doesn't know what to do with his fear, so he takes it to Sunny.

You gotta understand where he's coming from.

Where he came from.

Father a tweeker, mother a drunk, Brian Brousseau's home life, if you want to call it that, was a bad dream during a nightmare. Brian got about as much care and attention as the cat, and you don't want to see the cat. He was about eight when he started picking up the leftover roaches lying around the crappy little house.

Brian liked the feeling he got from smoking the roaches. It eased his fear, muffled the fights between his mom and dad, helped him get to sleep. By the time he was in junior high, he was toking up every day, before and after school. When school was finally over, he'd wander down to the beach, smoke up, and watch the surfers. One day, he was sitting in the sand, just toasted, when this surfer came out of the water, walked up to him, and said, "I see you here every day, grom."

Brian said, "Uh-huh."

"How come you just watch?" Boone asked. "How come you don't surf?"

"Don't know how," Brian said. "Don't have a board."

Boone nodded, thought about it a second, looked down at the skinny little kid, and said, "You want to learn? I'll show you."

Brian wasn't so sure. "You a fag, man?"

"You want to ride or not, dude?"

Brian wanted.

Scared as shit, but he wanted.

"I can't swim," he said.

"Then don't fall off," Boone said. He looked down at Brian's feet. "Dude. Do you have six toes?"

"Twelve."

Boone chuckled. "That's your new name, gremmie—'Hang Twelve.'"

"Okay."

"Stand with your feet about shoulder width," Boone said.

Hang got up. Boone shoved him in the chest. Hang stepped back with his right foot to keep his balance. "What—"

"You're a goofy-foot," Boone said. "Left-footed. Lie down on the board."

Hang did.

"On your *stomach,*" Boone said. "Jesus."

Hang turned over.

"Now, jump up on your knees," Boone said. "Good. Now into a squat. Good. Now stand."

Boone made him do it twenty times. By the time Hang finished, he was sweating and breathing hard—it was the most exercise he'd done maybe in his life—but he was totally into it. "This is fun, dude!"

"It's even more fun in the water," Boone said. He led Hang out to where some small waves were coming in shallow, had him lie down on the board, and pushed him into a wave. Hang rode it in like a boogie board.

Insta-love.

Hang kept Boone out there all frigging afternoon, until the sun set and after. On his third ride, he tried to stand. He fell off on that wave and the next thirty-seven. The sun was a bright orange ball on the horizon when Hang stood up on the board and rode it all the way to shore.

First thing he'd ever achieved.

The next day was Saturday, and Hang was out there first thing in the morning, standing on the beach and staring out at The Dawn Patrol.

"Who's the grem?" Dave asked from the lineup.

"A stoner kid," Boone said. "I dunno, he looked lost, so I took him out."

"A stray puppy?" Sunny said.

"I guess," Boone said. "He took to it, though."

"Grems are a pain in the ass," Dave warned.

"We were all grems once," Sunny said.

"Not me," Dave said. "I was born cool."

Anyway, it was tacit permission to go bring the kid in. Boone got off the board on his next ride and went up to Hang. "You wanna surf?"

Hang nodded.

"Yeah, okay," Boone said. "I have an old stick in my quiver over there. It's a piece of shit, a log basically, but it will ride. Get it out, wax it; then I'll show you how to paddle out. You stay close to me, out of other people's way, try not to be a total kook, okay?"

"Okay."

Hang waxed the board, paddled out, and got in everyone's way. But that's what grems do—it's their job. The Dawn Patrol ran interference for him, both with the ocean and the other surfers. No one messed with the kid because it was clear that he was under The Dawn Patrol's collective wing.

Hang took the board home that night.

Leaned it against the wall next to his bed.

Hang might have been invisible at home, he might have been a nothing at school, but now he had an identity.

He was surfer.

He was Dawn Patrol.

Now he runs toward Sunny's house, gets to her door, and pounds on it. A few minutes later, a sleepy Sunny comes to the door.

"Hang, what—"

"It's Boone."

He tells her about Boone.

# 72

Cheerful sits at the hovel that is Boone's desk, trying to balance the books.

Boone Daniels is a perpetual pain in the ass. Immature, irresponsible, a hopeless businessman.

But what were you, Cheerful asks himself, before Boone came into your life?

A lonely old man.

Boone once saved him several million dollars in alimony when the businessman uncharacteristically fell head over heels in love with a twenty-five-year-old Hooters waitress, for whom he bought a new rack and fuller lips to heighten her low self-esteem. Her self-image lifted, she promptly felt herself attractive enough to screw a twenty-five-year-old wannabe rock star and begin a television career that she intended to finance with California community property.

Boone felt bad for the lovesick old guy and took the case, took the pix, made the video, and never showed either of them to Cheerful. He did show them to the soon-to-be ex–Mrs. Cheerful and told her to take her big tits, full lips, guitar-stroking boyfriend, and a $100K alimony settlement, get out of San Dog, and leave Cheerful the hell alone.

"Why should I?" she asked.

"Because he's a nice old man and you fucked him over."

"He got his money's worth," she said. Then she looked at him with an expression of lust she no doubt learned from porn videos and asked, "You want proof?"

"Look," Boone replied, "you're hotter than hell, and I'm sure you're the whole barrel of monkeys in bed, but, one, I like your husband; two, I'd cut my junk off with a jagged, shit-encrusted tin can lid before I'd ever stick it anywhere near you; and three, I'll not only take your home movies and photo album into court, but I'll put them on the Net, and then we'll see what that does for your television career."

She took the walk-away deal.

And made it big on TV playing the second lead, the sassy best friend, on a sitcom that's been draining viewer IQs for years.

"What do I owe you?" Cheerful asked him afterward.

"Just my hourly."

"But that's a few hundred," Cheerful said. "You saved me millions. You should take a percentage. I'm offering."

"Just my hourly," Boone said. "That was the deal."

Cheerful decided that Boone Daniels was a man of honor but a crap businessman, and therefore he made it his hobby to try to get Boone on some sort of sound financial footing, which is something like trying to balance a three-legged elephant on a greased golf ball, but Cheerful persists anyway.


You had money, sure, he tells himself now, but nothing else. You'd do your books, count your money, and sit around your condo eating microwave meals, watching television, cussing out the Padres' middle relief, and thinking about how miserable you were.

Ben Carruthers—multimillionaire, real estate genius, total personal failure. No wife, no kids, no grandkids, no friends.

Boone opened up the windows, let some air and sunshine in.

The Dawn Patrol brought youth into your life. Hell, it brought *life* into your life. Much as you grouse about them—watching these kids, getting to be a part of their lives, sticking your beak into Boone's cases, playing the curmudgeon—they make it worth getting up in the morning.

Boone, Dave, Johnny, High Tide, Sunny, even Hang Twelve—they're precious to you, admit it. You can't imagine life without them.

Without Boone.

The kid Hang Twelve sits staring at the phone, willing it to ring.

Cheerful thinks he needs to say something to the kid. "He's okay."

"I know."

But he doesn't.

Neither of them do.

"You hungry?" he asks Hang.

"No."

"You have to eat," Cheerful says. He takes a twenty from his wallet, hands it to Hang. "Go over to The Sundowner, get us a couple of burgers, bring them back."

"I don't really feel like it," Hang says.

"Did I ask you what you felt like?" Cheerful says. "Go on, now. Do what I tell you."

Hang takes the money and leaves.

Cheerful goes to the Yellow Pages, gets the number of Silver Dan's, and calls it. "Let me speak to Dan Silver," he says. "Tell him Ben Carruthers is on the line."

He waits impatiently for Silver to get to the phone.

# 73

Dan takes his time getting to the phone.

He's a little uneasy about what Ben Carruthers might have to say to him. The real estate mogul is asshole buddies with Boone Daniels.

Or the late Boone Daniels, if the word on the street is right.

Dan had sent one of his guys over to The Sundowner to keep his eyes and ears open, to find out if anyone had seen or heard from Daniels after he did his Houdini on the beach. Daniels is a major fucking pain in the ass, and now he has Tammy Roddick. Except, the word came in that Daniels drove his piece of shit vehicle off the cliff and went out in flames.

So Dan has constructed a hopeful scenario: He hit Daniels with one of his shots. The dumb fuck made it up to his van somehow, but, weak with loss of blood, put the car in drive instead of reverse and went airborne.

Crash and burn.

The even more optimistic version is that Tammy Roddick and her big fucking mouth went over the cliff with him and the fire guys are going to scrape out two crispy critters instead of one. And then there's the mouthy British broad, the one that would rather fuck a pig. Well, maybe her stuck-up twat is melted to the seat springs, too.

Now this old man is calling. What's up with that?

He picks up the phone.

"Dan Silver?"

"Yeah?"

"You know who I am," Carruthers says. "I'm going to give you my accountant's number; he'll tell you exactly how much I'm worth. I'll pay off your debt to Red Eddie. Cash, interest, I'll put it to bed."

"Why would you do that?"

"So you call the dogs off Boone Daniels," Carruthers says.

The fuck? Dan asks himself. Is Daniels *alive*? He decides to check it out. "I heard he had an accident."

"I heard that, too," Carruthers says. "That's the other reason I want you to know how much I'm worth. It's in the eight figures somewhere, and, Dan Silver, if Boone is dead, I'll spend every cent of it to have you tracked down and killed."

Dial tone.

# 74

Cheerful had bought the Crystal Pier back in the day when it was pretty run-down. He renovated it and flipped it, with the proviso that he retain the last cottage on the north side of the pier.

He gave the cottage to Boone.

Boone didn't want to take it.

"It's too much, Cheerful," he said. "Way too much."

"You saved me *millions* from that gold-digging little bitch," Cheerful responded. "Take the cottage. Then you'll always have a place to live."

Boone didn't take the cottage, not ownership anyway. What he took was a long-term lease at a lower-than-market rent.

So Boone became a permanent resident of the Crystal Pier Hotel. He lives literally over the ocean. He can, and does, hang a fishing pole outside his bedroom window, right into the water. The cottage itself is made up of a small living room with a kitchenette, a bedroom off to one side, and a bathroom off to the other.

Now High Tide drives up to the gate at the base of the pier, kills his headlights, and punches in the code he knows by heart. The gate slides open and High Tide drives the van down the pier all the way to the end, and into a little parking spot, now vacated by the late Boonemobile, next to Boone's cottage.

Boone has been lying down in the back. He gets up, quickly slips over the side, and walks around to the driver's door as the women slide out the passenger side.

"Thanks, bro."

Tide shakes his head and touches his fist to Boone's.

"Dawn Patrol."

Tide turns the truck around and drives off the pier. Turns left and parks the truck just behind the new lifeguard station that Dave rules like a feudal warlord. He sits and juggles the phone in his hand, thinking about what he needs to do.

Then he does it.

"Boone wasn't in the van," he says into the phone. "He's at his place."

Then Josiah Pamavatuu—former gang banger, football star, surfing stud—lays his head on the steering wheel and sobs.

# 75

Boone lowers all the window shades and turns on one lamp by the side of the sofa. Then he goes into his bedroom, opens the drawer of his night-stand, and takes out the .38 that he's saving to shoot Russ Rasmussen.

"You guys need to take hot showers," he says. Then he runs water into a kettle and puts it on the stovetop. "I'll make something hot to drink."

Petra is surprised that the place is so neat and clean.

Everything stored in its place—the efficiency of small spaces. A sur-prisingly good collection of pots and pans hangs from a rack above a small but good-quality butcher's block, on which two expensive Global knives are set on magnetized strips.

The man likes to cook, Petra thinks.

Who would know?

Unsurprisingly, the white walls of the living room are decorated with framed photos of waves, which give Petra an involuntary shudder after what they've just been through. She can't know it, but the pictures are of local breaks—Black's, Shores, D Street, Bird Rock, and Shrink's.

"I'll get you guys something to change into," Boone says, walking into his bedroom.

Tammy jumps when a big wave goes off like a cannon, sounding like it's crashed right on the cottage.

"Are you all right?" Petra asks.

"I want to talk to Teddy."

"I'm not sure that's a good idea," Petra says.

Boone emerges from the bedroom carrying a stack of sweatshirts, sweatpants, and socks. "They'll be big for you," he says, "but they'll keep you warm anyway."

"Warm is good," Tammy says. She takes a blue hooded La Jolla Surf Systems sweatshirt and a pair of black sweatpants and goes into the bathroom. Boone and Petra hear the shower running.

"God, that sounds good," Petra says.

"Yeah, it does."

"I still have salt water running from my nose," she says. "I must look a fright."

"You look nice," Boone says, meaning it. "Listen . . . you did good out there. In the water. I mean, you were great. You didn't panic."

"Thanks," she says.

Boone says, "Would you like some tea?"

"That would be lovely."

"I have herbal or Earl Grey."

"Earl Grey is perfect."

"Just plain, right?" Boone asks. "No milk or sugar."

"Actually, lots of both, please," she says. "Perhaps it's the near-death experience, but I feel greedy."

"Nothing like almost dying to let you know how good life is," Boone says.

Yeah. How good life is, with her full lips and warm neck and sea gray eyes there for the reaching out and her looking in his eyes, her mouth already tasting his, and then the pot whistles like an alarm and their lips don't touch.

"Life imitating bad art," she says.

"Yeah." Boone pours the water into a mug and hands it to her.

"Thanks."

"You're welcome."

"How about you?" she asks.

"I'll make some coffee."

Tammy comes out of the bedroom.

It's the first time Boone has really seen her.

She's tall. Not Sunny tall, but tall, with long, lean legs. Her face has clean, strong, natural lines and her eyes, although they look smaller without makeup, are still catlike. But it's a different breed of cat—wild, feral, but somehow calm. She's a striking woman, and it's easy to see why Mick Penner and Teddy fell hard for her. She sits down on the small couch in the middle of the living room and puts her feet up on the coffee table.

Boone says, "Have something hot to drink first. Warm you up inside."

"Go change," Petra says. "I can take care of her."

"She can take care of herself," Tammy says, getting up. She goes into the kitchen, chooses the herbal tea, and makes a cup. "Go get some dry clothes on, Tarzan. I'll make the coffee."

Boone goes into his room to change.

"I need to talk with Teddy," Tammy says.

Petra's gobsmacked. Certainly Tammy realizes that Teddy revealed her hiding place to Dan Silver—in fact, served her up on a plate to save himself. She says, "I'm sure Dr. Cole is fine."

After all, he did what Dan wanted.

"I want to talk with him."

"Let's check with Boone about that," Petra says.

"You're going to do him," Tammy says to Petra.

"I beg your pardon."

"If I wasn't here? You'd jump him in the shower."

"We have a professional relationship."

"Uh-huh."

"He's a barbarian."

"Whatever."

Whatever, Petra thinks. But is it possible? Am I really feeling something for Daniels? Is it some sort of animal attraction, or perhaps just a residue of the gratitude I'm feeling for him for not letting me die on the beach? Of course, he put me on the beach in the first place. The incompetent boob.

But he was pretty damn competent when the bullets were flying, wasn't he? He was pretty damn competent in the freezing water in the dark, wasn't he?

Boone comes back into the room.

"I'll think I'll have that shower," she says.

"Yeah, get warm," Boone says.

She takes some clothes from the stack and goes into the bathroom.

# 76

First words out of Tammy's mouth?

"I want to talk to Teddy."

"Your boyfriend is a pedophile," Boone says. He tells her about what he saw at the motel up near the strawberry fields. Her face doesn't register any of the possible reactions—shock, anger, indignation, disgust, betrayal . . .

"I want to talk to Teddy," she says. "I *need* to talk to Teddy."

Boone sighs and runs it down for her. First, they don't know where Teddy is. Second, Teddy already gave her up once; if she calls him now, he'll give her up again. Third, at least for a little while, Dan and the rest of the world have good reason to believe that she's dead, and if she talks to Teddy, they'll have good reason to believe she's alive and try to do something about it.

She's real impressed by the argument. "Where's my phone?"

"Soaked in cold salt water," Boone says. "I don't think you're going to get a lot of bars."

"Let me use yours."

"I was in the water beside you."

"You don't have a phone in your house?" she asks.

"No."

"What if people want to get hold of you?"

"That's why I don't have a phone in my house," Boone says. He doesn't tell her about the three other cellies he has in a kitchen drawer. He's blown away. The woman hasn't said one word or asked one question about her friend Angela, who took her rap for her. All she cares about is a slick boob butcher who likes to do little migrant girls. A guy who gave her up in a heartbeat to save his own worthless ass.

Nice.

"Do you think he's all right?" she asks.

"Couldn't care less."

"I want to see him."

"You're not going anywhere."

"You can't keep me here against my will," she says.

He's had it. "That's true. Go out there, Tammy. Go find Dr. Short Eyes, see what happens. But don't expect me to come to your funeral."

"Fuck you," Tammy says. "I'm a payday to you, that's all. You need me alive so you can pick up your check. It doesn't give you the right to moral judgments, cowboy."

"You're right."

"And I don't need you to tell me that," Tammy says. "I know what you think of me. I'm a stripper—a dumb piece of meat. Either I have a drug problem or I'm fucked up because my daddy didn't pay me enough attention, or else I'm just too lazy to get a real job. I'm a skank. But it doesn't stop you from coming in with your dollar bills, does it?"

True, Boone thinks. And it doesn't stop me wanting to keep you alive. Or is it that I just need to deliver you to the courtroom?

"Stay away from the windows," Boone says. "Keep your head down. In fact, you might be better off in the bedroom."

"You think you're the first guy to tell me that?" she asks, eyes hard as emeralds.

"I'll make you a deal," Boone says. "I don't judge you and you don't judge you."

"Easier said than done."

"Yeah."

She sneers. "What would you know about it, surfer dude?"

"You don't have a monopoly on regrets, Tammy."

Boone can feel the ocean swell, literally under his feet. The waves push against the pilings, wash through, and then pull on their way out. The big swell is coming, and when it goes out again, it will take with it the life he knew. He can feel it, and it scares the hell out of him. He wants to hold on, but he knows there's no holding on against the sea.

When a tsunami comes in, it hits with incredibly destructive force, crushing lives and homes. But it's almost worse when it recedes, dragging lives out into the endless sea that is the irredeemable past.

# 77

Petra gets out of the shower, then wanders into Boone's bedroom, telling herself she's going to catch a quick nap, but really to snoop.

No, not snoop, she thinks.

Simply to find out a little more about the man.

Like the rest of the place, the bedroom is neat and clean. Nothing remarkable about it, save for the fishing pole sticking out of the window, except . . .

Books.

Used paperbacks on a bedside table and in a small bookcase in the corner. Some stacked by the bed. And not just the sports books or crime novels that she might have expected if she thought that he actually read, but genuine literature—Dostoyevsky, Turgenev, Gorky. Over in the corner is a stack of—Can it be? she thinks—Trollope. Our oceangoing nature boy is a crypto–Phineas Finn?

She thinks of all the little jibes she's given him all day about being an uneducated philistine, then thinks about the books that are stacked on her bedside table—trashy romance novels and bodice rippers that she doesn't have to read anyway. And he's been having me on all day, his private little joke.

Bastard.

She keeps snooping.

There's a small desk in the corner, with a computer and terminal on it. Guiltily, she slides the desk drawer open and sees photographs of a little girl.

A darling, almost a stereotype of your classic California girl—blond hair, big blue eyes, a spray of freckles across her cheeks. She's looking directly into the camera without a trace of self-consciousness. A happy little girl.

Petra picks up the photo and sees the little nameplate at the edge of the frame.

RAIN.

The girl's name.

*Bastard,* Petra thinks. He never told me he had a daughter. He never even mentioned that he'd been married. Maybe he wasn't. Maybe the girl is a love child and Boone never married her mother. Still, he might have mentioned it. Be fair, she tells herself. He had no obligation to tell you.

She digs deeper.

More pictures of the girl. Carefully preserved in plastic sleeves. Photos of her playing, at a birthday party, opening presents in front of a Christmas tree. Oddly, not a single photo of Rain with Boone. Not a single daddy-daughter shot that one would expect.

And the pictures seem to stop when the girl is around the age of five or six.

So Boone Daniels has a six-year-old daughter, Petra thinks. Whom he clearly adores but doesn't talk about.

Disregarding the better angels of her nature, Petra digs under the photos and finds a file folder. She opens it, to see some pencil sketches, "artist's renderings" some would call them, of a girl as she would look as she got older.

Her name is Rain.

"Rain at seven," "Rain at eight," "Rain at nine" . . .

Is Boone not allowed to see his daughter anymore? Petra wonders. They're so sad, these sketches—all he has of his little girl.

There are other files in the drawer, all labeled "Rasmussen." Must be another case he's working on, Petra thinks, although Boone hardly seems to be the type to bring work home.

You are full of surprises, Mr. Daniels, she thinks.

Feeling ashamed, she quickly puts everything back in order and goes into the living room.

"I've been told I belong in the bedroom," Tammy says. She gets up from the couch, goes into the bedroom, and shuts the door behind her.

"She wants to talk with Teddy," Petra says, sitting down on the couch.

"She mentioned that," Boone replies.

The sweatshirt—a black Sundowner—is huge on her, and she's had to roll the legs of the sweatpants way up. But Boone thinks she looks prettier than hell.

"You look good," he says.

"You're a liar," she says. "But thank you."

"No," he says. "You should go with that look."

"Hardly lawyerly."

"Maybe that's it."

The doorbell rings.

# 78

Boone takes the .38, moves to the side of the door, nudges the curtain aside, and looks out.

Sunny stands at the door.

Her blond hair, shiny in the moist night air, peeks out from under the hood of a dark blue sweatshirt. Arms folded inside the waist pouch, she hops up and down with chill and anxiety.

Boone opens the door, yanks her inside, and shuts it behind her.

"Boone, Tide told me—"

She sees Petra sitting on the couch.

In Boone's sweats.

Which she used to wear herself, in happier times, after long mornings in the water and afternoon lovemaking.

"Excuse me," Sunny says, her voice colder than the water. "I didn't realize—"

"It's not—"

"What it looks like?" She glares at Boone for a second, then slaps him hard across the face. "I thought you were *dead,* Boone! You let me think you were dead."

"I'm sorry."

She shakes her head. "I'll tell Cheerful and Hang. They were worried about you."

"You have to get out of here, Sunny," Boone says.

"No kidding."

"I meant—"

"I know what you meant."

It's not safe, Boone thinks, is what I meant.

But she's already walking away. He looks out the window and sees her taking long strides down the pier, into his past, out of his life.

# 79

"I'm sorry," Petra says a moment after the door slams.

"Not your fault," Boone says.

"I'll talk to her if you'd like," Petra says. "Explain the misunderstanding."

Boone shakes his head. "It's been over with us for a long time. Maybe it's good this happened."

"Clean break sort of thing."

"Yeah."

Petra feels bad, but not as bad as she thinks she should. A door has been opened, and she wonders if she should step through it. Not immediately— that would be inappropriate and tawdry, to say the least. But the door is open, and she has this feeling it will stay open for a while.

But she does take a small, tentative step forward. "Is Sunny the mother?"

"What?"

"Rain's mother?"

The door slams shut.

"Try to get a little sleep," Boone says. "In the morning, you can go out and get Tammy some decent clothes. We'll take her to court; she can testify and we'll be done with this shit."

He pulls a chair up near the door, his back to her, and sits with the .38 on his lap.

# 80

"No bodies," the fireman says to Johnny Banzai.

"You're sure," Johnny says.

The fireman gives him a hard, sarcastic look. He's real thrilled to be out on the beach on a cold, damp night with the surf spitting spray into his face. To put out a fire on a piece-of-crap van that some clown apparently pushed off the bluff for shits and giggles. He says, "I'm going to send this joker a hell of a bill."

"Do it," Johnny says.

He leaves the scene and walks back up the stairs to Shrink's, where Teddy D-Cup is still sitting in the Lotus Cottage. Johnny has no real reason to hold Teddy, but he didn't tell him that, and the doctor seems to be in a cowed and obedient frame of mind. He's also about half shit-faced, which makes Johnny wonder what's in an organic martini that makes it organic.

Johnny sits down across from Teddy.

The plasma television has a Lakers game on, the purple and gold of their uniforms as vivid as a Mardi Gras parade.

"So?" Johnny asks.

It's a standard opening of his. Never start by asking a witness a closed-ended question. Just get them talking and they'll tell you the first thing on their minds.

Doesn't work with Teddy. He looks blankly at Johnny and repeats, "'So?'"

"So what are you doing here?" Johnny asks.

"Visiting a patient."

"Would that patient be Tammy Roddick?" Johnny asks. In the background, Kobe totally *works* a defender, blows around him, and slams the ball home.

"What if it is?" Teddy says.

"Where is she?" Johnny asks.

He sees a different look come over Teddy's face. An expression that looks like . . . is it relief?

"I don't know," Teddy says. "She wasn't here when I got here."

"How *did* you get here?"

"Huh?"

"How did you get here?" Johnny asks. "Your car isn't in the lot."

"That's a good question," Teddy says.

"That's why I asked it," Johnny says. Kobe has the ball again and he's dribbling around. Will not pass it. Typical, Johnny thinks. "Doctor?"

Teddy looks serious and thoughtful. He looks Johnny in the eye and says, "I don't really have an answer to that question."

"Why?"

"Why what?"

"Why don't you have an answer?"

There's a long silence; then Teddy says, "I don't really have an answer to *that* question, either."

"Look, asshole," Johnny says. "I have a dead woman in the morgue who was carrying the ID of a stripper you're probably banging. Now the real Tammy Roddick is missing, Boone's vehicle is Iraq war footage, and I find you in Tammy's room, which you certainly arranged for. Now you can answer my questions in this civilized setting, or I can take you down to the precinct, leave you in a smelly interview room for a few hours, and then see if you can get your thoughts collected."

It sobers Teddy up a little.

Which turns out not to be a good thing, because it seems as if he suddenly remembers that he's a high-priced surgeon with connections. He looks at Johnny and calmly says, "It's not illegal for a doctor to visit a patient, and I can't control the fact that she wasn't here. As for exploding vans—"

"How did you know it was a van?"

"I have no idea about it," Teddy says. "As I will explain to the beautiful wife of your chief when I see her. She has a beautiful smile, don't you think? And those eyes . . ."

"I've never met her."

"I'd be happy to introduce you."

The banzai part of Johnny would like to whip the cuffs on Teddy, take him to the house, and show him the other side of life in San Diego, but his more rational side knows that it would be futile and self-defeating. Teddy will have a high-priced lawyer there in five minutes, who will make the correct point that Johnny has no reason to hold his client, no reason at all. So Johnny swallows the smarmy power play about the chief's wife, along with the hard facts about being a cop in a city where great wealth lives alongside great poverty.

Johnny Banzai is neither naïve nor idealistic. He generally takes life as he finds it and doesn't waste his time or energy tilting at windmills. But sometimes it gets to him, the knowledge that if Teddy, for instance, was Mexican, black, Filipino, Samoan, or just plain old white trash, he'd be in the back of Johnny's car already. But Teddy is rich and white, with a good address in La Jolla—substitute Del Mar, Rancho Santa Fe, or Torrey Pines if you want—so he skates.

An obvious fact of life, Johnny thinks—the next time a rich white guy gets worked by the cops will be the first time. So get over it. But sometimes he'd like to take the badge, wing it into the ocean, and join Boone on the beach, rather than take any more shit from any of the beautiful people.

Now he says, "Dr. Cole, I have reason to believe that Tammy Roddick's life is in immediate danger. I'm trying to find her before the bad guys do. If you have any knowledge that would help me do that, you should give it to me right now."

"I really don't," Teddy says.

"Can you get home all right?" Johnny asks.

"They have a courtesy car," Teddy says.

"With a driver?" Johnny asks, jutting his chin at the martini.

"Of course."

Of course, Johnny thinks.

# 81

Boone gets up to make another cup of coffee.

He's trashed, aching from the beating he got back by the strawberry fields, and the adrenaline surge from the beach is long gone. His body screams for sleep, but it's just going to have to wait until he delivers Tammy to the courtroom, so he goes for more caffeine.

Petra's out.

Sound asleep on the sofa, snoring softly.

Boone tries to work up some righteous indignation over Sunny's false, unspoken accusation, but he can't. The truth is that he does feel some attraction to Pete, and if Sunny hadn't come to the door when she did, he might have done something about it.

He looks over at Pete.

Angelic when she sleeps.

But he's pissed off at her for snooping in his room. Looking at his books, digging up the stuff about Rain. Women, he thinks—it's always a mistake letting them into your space, because they prowl it like cats, check it out to see if they can make it their own.

So he's pissed at her but attracted to her at the same time. What *is* that? he wonders. Is it that "opposites attract" thing? He always thought that was some cheesy Paula Abdul song attached to some cartoon, but here it is. If you had to pick a woman who's totally wrong for him, out of every woman in the entire world, you'd choose Pete: ambitious, elitist, snobbish, career-oriented, fashion-conscious, argumentative, belligerent, sarcastic, ball-busting, high-maintenance, nosy. . . .

But there it is.

Fuck.

Too complicated for me, he thinks.

Just get this case over, deliver Tammy Roddick to court, get back in time to get into the big swell. The ocean is simple—not easy, but simple—and a wave is something you know how to handle.

Just stay in the water, never come out.

But it isn't that simple, is it?

A woman's been killed, a pedophile is out there, and somebody has to do something about both those things. Dan Silver has to go down for Angela Hart's murder—Johnny will be on that until he gets it done—and Teddy D-Cup has to get squared for his little trips to *Mister Roger's Neighborhood.*

First things first, though, Boone tells himself as the water starts to boil. He takes the kettle off the heat before it whistles and wakes Pete up. First get through the night, then get Tammy to testify, then clean your head out in the big waves.

Then see to Dan and Teddy.

Yeah, except . . .

He sees movement through the edge of the kitchen window.

Out on the pier.

He pulls the curtain back for a better view and sees them out there, moving like cats hunting in the night. One of them is edging along the pier railing on the near side; another one takes the opposite side. Boone thinks he can make out two more on the base of the pier, but he's not sure.

And now a Hummer rolls slowly past in the street.

It's hard to really see them in the dark and the mist, but just by the way they move, Boone can see they're Hawaiians.

He touches Petra's arm and wakes her up.

She looks around the room, not knowing where she is.

"Go into the bedroom," Boone says. "Shut and lock the door behind you, lie down on the floor."

"What—"

"Just listen," Boone says, and to her surprise, she does. "If you hear shooting, take Tammy and go out the window. You can swim into shore easily."

"All right," she says. "Will you—"

"I'll be fine," he says. "Go."

He waits until she goes into the bedroom and he hears the lock click.

Then he walks over to the cottage door, checks that he has a round chambered, and waits.

Tide, he thinks, what did Eddie offer you?

# 82

Love's a funny goddamn thing.

Makes you do shit you'd never thought you'd do.

Then suddenly you're doing it.

In Teddy Cole's case, it makes him take the chauffeured ride home, go to his garage instead of the house, take one of his other Mercedeses and head straight for the strawberry fields. He knows he's not going to find her there at night—she's never there at night—but it's the best shot he has, so that's what he does.

Love is a funny goddamn thing.

# 83

Red Eddie sits in the back of the Hummer and watches the guys move up the pier toward Boone's cottage. He checks out the two others lingering around the base of the pier and knows that for every one he sees, there are probably two he can't.

Large respect for the Samoans guarding Boone Dawg from harm. They're good at what they do.

Respect to Josiah Pamavatuu also.

The guy went the other way. Bad for his icehead cousin, to be sure, but good for him. Gonna be rough on the big man, though; Samoans are huge on family.

And Boone Daniels is a cockroach—you just can't kill the *kanaka*.

Eddie had actually been very relieved when he got the word that Boone wasn't charcoal. It's a blessing. What is a curse is Dan Silver, who is *gripping*.

"She testifies tomorrow," Dan says. "She saw everything—she'll kill us."

Red Eddie draws the herb smoke deep into his lungs, holds it for the count of three, then exhales. He passes the blunt to Dan as he sings, "Oh, Danny Boy, the lights, the lights are shining. . . . Relax, Daniel Spaniel."

"You relax," Dan snaps, shaking his head to refuse the smoke.

Red Eddie shrugs. "I will."

Relax and think.

Relaxation, Red Eddie knows, is the prerequisite for efficient thought. No sense in getting all geeked up—you just cut off the flow of blood to your brain exactly when you need it the most. So he takes another hit of the weed to boost his intellectual capability, and then comes to a conclusion.

Eddie turns to Dan Silver and says, "Sorry, chief. You're out of luck."

Danny doesn't want to accept it. "You telling me your guys can't take a bunch of Sammy gang bangers?"

The Hummer is full of very *moke hui* boys and another car, also packed with muscle, waits just a block away. Doubtless they could do some serious damage to the Sammies and blow their way into Boone Dawg's crib, Eddie knows, but that's the problem—the last thing in the world Eddie wants is to trigger a transoceanic war.

And that's what it would be, too. Let one of these Sammy guys get scratched, it would start a blood feud, with obligations for revenge. So the Sammies would crack a Hawaiian, then Eddie would have to crack back, and it would never end. And not just here, either; it would speed back to Honolulu in a heartbeat, and there'd be aggro there and in freaking Pago Pago, too. It would get out of freaking control, cause a lot of heartache, and interfere with business.

And Eddie's all about the business.

No, the High Tide dude was smart, Eddie thinks. He figured all this out and put a screen around his boy Boone. A screen of *ohana* that he knew I would never attack.

Round to you, Tide.

"Sorry," he says to Dan. "It just ain't on, man."

"That cunt's going to testify in the morning," Dan says. "God knows what's going to come out of her stupid fucking mouth."

"You better hope," Eddie says, "she confines her remarks to the little pig roast at your dumb-ass warehouse."

Because Dan has dumped him in the shit, letting this *wahine* see things she shouldn't have seen. And the timing couldn't be worse—he has a shipment due to come in tomorrow night, and he doesn't want Dan's sloppy business practices shining a spotlight on that part of his business.

"That's why I'm saying," Dan says. "Let's go in and take her now."

Eddie shakes his head. Ain't gonna happen. Not only are the Samoans standing in the way, but there's Boone to consider. No way is Boone going to stand aside and let Danny cancel that girl's reservation. Eddie's already told his boys: If they have a clean shot at the *wahine,* take it, but nothing, *nothing,* better happen to Boone Daniels.

Now nothing's going to happen at all.

Not right now anyway.

"So what am I supposed to do?" Dan asks.

"Try using your head for a change," Eddie says. His cellie goes off. "What?"

"Five-oh rolling up," one of his guys in the other car says. "One cop, a Jap."

"Time to take the party someplace other," Eddie says.

The Hummer rolls out.

# 84

Johnny makes the Samoan gang bangers right away.

O'side—Samoan Lords—Tide's old crew.

Which is interesting, what the hell High Tide has to do with all this. Johnny fronts one of the kids. "Call your *matai.* Tell him Johnny B. wants to go through and he's not in the mood to take any shit." The kid gets on the phone, talks in Samoan for a second, looks at Johnny with undisguised hostility, and says, "It's cool."

"Thanks so much."

Johnny walks down the pier, goes to Boone's cottage, and bangs on the door. "Boone, open the damn door! It's Johnny!"

Boone opens the door.

"You're a dick," Johnny says.

"No argument."

"You had a lot of people worried, Boone," Johnny says. "I thought I was going to have to organize a paddle-out for you. You could have called your friends, let them know you're okay."

"I'm okay."

"Does Sunny know?" Johnny asks. "That she doesn't have to grieve for you?"

"She knows."

"I guess Tide must have told her, huh?" Johnny says, gesturing generally to the gang bangers, who seem to have melted into the landscape.

"What do you mean?"

"The Samoan Lord bodyguards," Johnny says.

"I thought they were Hawaiians," Boone says, feeling stupid and ungrateful for thinking that Tide had sold him out.

"They all look alike to me, too," Johnny says. "Can I come in, Boone? Or are you going to keep all your friends out in the cold?"

"You have a warrant?"

"Not yet," Johnny says.

"Then I guess I'll stand out in the cold with you."

"So you have Tammy Roddick," Johnny says.

Boone doesn't answer.

"How did we end on different teams on this thing, B?" Johnny asks. "I don't think we have divergent interests here. You want Roddick to testify against Dan Silver in a civil suit tomorrow morning. The SDPD could care less. We just want to talk to her about Angela Hart's death. Hell, I'll walk her to the courtroom myself."

"If she was still alive."

"What's that supposed to mean?"

Boone hesitates.

"You got something on your mind," says Johnny, "say it."

"Dan Silver got the word pretty fast that it was Angela and not Tammy dead at the motel, Johnny," Boone says. "I'm worried he got it from cops."

"Fuck you, Boone."

"I didn't say it was *you,* Johnny."

"Fuck you, Boone," Johnny says.

"Okay, fuck me."

"You think it was Harrington?" asks Johnny. "He's a lot of things, but he's not dirty."

Boone shrugs.

"Sanctimonious asshole," Johnny says. "Only Boone Daniels knows the truth, because he walks on water."

"Jesus, Johnny."

"So to speak."

"Can you protect her?" Boone asks.

"Can *you*?" Johnny asks. "I mean, you can in the short run, but what about *after* she testifies? Have you thought of that? You think Dan Silver's just going to forget she just cost him a pile of money? You're going to devote your life to protecting this girl?"

Boone's thought about it. It's a problem.

"It's an insurance company, Boone," Johnny says. "They've got lots of jangle; they can afford to take a hit. Roddick was right to run. I only wish she'd run farther, because the company doesn't give a shit what happens to her *after* she lays it down for them, do they? Her only chance is if I put Dan in the hole, and that isn't going to happen on the arson charge. But if she's a witness on a capital case, I can protect her."

"We each have jobs to do, Johnny."

"So fuck Angela Hart, right?" Johnny says. "Tag it a suicide. Just another dead stripper. 'No humans involved.'"

"She's not my job."

"No, she's mine," Johnny says. "Put your hands behind your back."

"Really, Johnny?" Boone says.

"I have reason to believe that you are interfering with an ongoing investigation," Johnny says. "I have reason to believe that you have knowledge material to at least one homicide investigation. I'll get the warrant to search your place, but in the meantime, I'm taking you in on a vandalism charge."

"Vandalism?"

"Pushing your van through a municipal guardrail," Johnny says. "Causing a fire on a public beach."

Boone turns around and puts his hands behind his back. Johnny gets his handcuffs out.

"Cuffs, John?"

"Hey, you want to *act* like a skell . . ."

*"Is there a problem, Officer?"*

A woman comes to the door. Dressed, sort of, in Boone's clothes. Her hair is damp, as if she just came out of the shower. Johnny recognizes her as the woman Boone was with when he arrived at the Crest Motel, the woman who went over and looked at the body. Her accent is clearly English.

"Who are you?" Johnny asks.

"Petra Hall, attorney-at-law."

Johnny laughs. "Boone's *lawyer*?"

"Among other things, yes."

From the looks of her, Johnny has a good idea about what the "other things" are. It's unlike Boone to sleep with clients, but it's hard to blame him in this case. The woman is a stunner, and the voice and the accent are . . . Well, it's hard to blame him.

"Sorry, Boone," she says now, "but I couldn't help but overhear a bit of your conversation. I don't know what you think you saw, Officer—"

"Detective," Johnny says.

"Sorry, *Detective*," Petra says, "but I can assure you that Mr. Daniels was not on any beach tonight. I can . . . quite personally . . . vouch for the fact that he's been snug and warm right here all evening. As for removing Mr. Daniels in handcuffs, I can also assure you that my client will have nothing further to say, that, based on my representations, you no longer have a justification for detaining him, and that, if you do so, I will have a writ of habeas corpus awaiting you when you arrive at what I believe you refer to, somewhat quaintly, as 'the house.' Release my client, Detective, immediately."

Johnny lowers the handcuffs and clips them back on his belt. "Hiding behind women, now, B?"

Boone turns around to look at him. "I've evolved."

"Apparently," Johnny says. He looks at Petra. "Tell your 'client' that I'll be back with the appropriate paper. Advise him not to go anywhere,

*Counselor,* and I suggest you further advise him that he's risking his PI card with this bullshit. And on the topic of 'cards,' I'm sure you know that any attorney, as an officer of the court, who lies to the police in the course of an ongoing investigation—"

"I know the law, Detective."

"So do I, *Counselor,*" Johnny says. He looks at Boone, "I'll be back with a warrant."

"You do what you have to do, Johnny."

"Don't worry about that," Johnny says. "I'm glad you're alive, Boone. But you're riding this one all wrong, selling out for an insurance company. It's turning you into a real jerk."

He turns and walks down the pier.

Boone watches him go.

Wondering if he'll have *any* friends when this is over. This case is tearing The Dawn Patrol apart, Boone thinks, and he doesn't know if they'll ever be able to put it back together again.

# 85

Teddy D-Cup stumbles through the reeds.

Trips, falls, picks himself up, and pushes toward the light of a small campfire in the clearing in front of the little caves.

He's greeted with a shotgun. A teenage boy grabs a machete and gets up. The old man just sits by the fire and looks up at him. Then the man with the shotgun sees Teddy's face and lowers the barrel. "Doctor . . ."

"*¿Tomas, dónde está Luce?*" Teddy asks.

"Gone. With the others," Tomas says.

"*¿Dónde la encuentro?*" Teddy asks. Where do I find her? He's learned a little Spanglish in his days in the reeds.

"You don't." The guy learned a little English from *his* days in the reeds.

Teddy sits down heavily in the dirt and puts his head in his hands.

"*A madrugada,*" Tomas says.

Wait until dawn.

# 86

Boone stands with one foot on the railing and looks out at the ocean.

Might as well be out in the open. There's no real danger now—Tide's crew has the pier covered. Red Eddie would never try to go through them, and he wouldn't let Dan Silver do it, either.

Johnny B. has gone to try to find a judge in the middle of the night— good luck with that—but has called a black-and-white, which is parked at the end of the pier. Maybe Johnny was right, Boone thinks. Maybe I am becoming an asshole. Just look at what I thought about Tide, that he sold me out to Red Eddie.

A total asshole thing to think.

Johnny was right about something else: Tammy Roddick is a dead woman if she testifies. If they can't kill her to prevent it, they'll kill her to avenge it. And I should have thought of that. *Would* have thought of it if I wasn't so busy proving to Pete what a hotshot PI I am.

Asshole.

He stares out at the ocean, the whitecaps barely visible in the fog and faint moonlight. The ocean is ripping, getting itself geared up for the big party.

Petra comes up behind him.

"Am I intruding?" she asks. "I mean, any more than usual?"

"No, no more than usual."

She stands next to him. "Is your swell coming in?"

"Yup."

"You'll be able to catch it now."

"Yup."

"I thought that would make you happy," she says.

"I thought it would, too," Boone replies. "You know what the best thing is about a wave?"

"No."

"A wave," Boone says, "puts you in your exact place in the universe. Say you're just all full of yourself, you think you're the king of the world, and you go out, and then this wave just slams you—picks you up, throws you down, rolls you, scrapes you along the bottom, and holds you there for a while. Like it's God saying, 'Listen, speck, when I let you back up, take a gulp of air, and step away from yourself a little bit.' Or say you're really low; you go out and you're feeling like crap, like's there's not a place for you in the world. You go out there, and the ocean gives you this sweet ride, like it's all just for you, you know? And that's God saying, 'Welcome, son, it's for you and it's all good.' A wave always gives you what you need."

It's cold out. She leans into him. He doesn't move away. A few seconds later, he puts his arm around her shoulders and pulls her tighter.

"I've been thinking about it," she says.

"About what?"

"About what your detective friend said," Petra says, "about not being able to protect Tammy. We should let her go, help her disappear, and God bless."

Boone's shocked. This isn't the ambitious, career-oriented, ruthless lawyer talking.

"What about your case?" he asks. "Making partner?"

"It's not worth another life," Petra says. "Not hers, not yours. Let it go."

He loves her for saying it, thinks a whole lot more of her that she made the offer. A totally cool, compassionate thing to do. But he says, "I can't."

"Why not?"

"It's too late," Boone says. "A woman's been killed, and someone has to do something about that. And . . ."

"What?"

"There's something else," Boone says. "Something that's not making sense. Something's really wrong here and I can't figure it out. I just know I can't let it go until I do."

"Boone—"

"Let it go, Pete," he says. "We have to ride this wave out."

"Do we?"

"Yeah."

Boone leans down and kisses her. Her lips are a surprise, soft and fluttering under his. Nice, more passionate than he would have thought.

He breaks off the kiss.

"What?" she asks.

"I have to go see someone."

"Now?"

"Yeah," Boone says. "Right now. You'll be safe. Tide's guys are all over it and there's a cop over there. Just lie low and I'll be back."

He starts to go, then comes back and says, "Uh, Pete. I liked the kiss."

So did I, she thinks as Boone disappears into the mist. Actually, I wanted more. But whom could he be going to see at this time of night?

# 87

"Daniels is *here*?" Danny asks.

"Make yourself gone," Red Eddie says.

Shouldn't be a problem—Eddie's house has, like, eight bedrooms. But Danny doesn't move. Instead, he says, "Do him."

"Did you just give me an order?" Eddie asks.

"No," Danny says. "It was more of a . . . suggestion."

"Well I 'suggestion' you get your fat ass somewhere else," Eddie says, "before I remember how much aggro you've caused me and turn you into a supersize dog biscuit, you dumb, wrong woman–killing fuck."

Eddie's a little irritable.

Danny withdraws.

"Let him in," Eddie says to the *hui* guy. "Don't keep him waiting."

Boone comes in, steps down into the sunken living room. The air reeks of dope—very rich, expensive dope. Eddie is wearing an imperial purple silk robe, black sweatpants, and a black beanie.

"Boone Dawg!" he hollers. "What brings you to my crib?"

"Sorry it's so late."

"The aloha mat is always out for you," Eddie says, proffering a joint. "A taste?"

"I'm good."

"I *am* surprised to see you, Boone Dawg," Eddie says. He lights the joint again and takes a hit.

"You mean you're surprised to see me *alive,*" Boone says.

"If I wanted you dead," Eddie says, "you'd be dead. In fact, I laid down very specific rules of engagement to our friend Danny; to wit, Boone Daniels is to be considered a civilian, a big red cross flying over his head, not to be touched."

"I was shot at," Boone says.

"And missed," Eddie replies. "You want some Cap'n Crunch?"

"Yeah."

"Crunch!" Eddie yells. "Two bowls! And open some fresh fucking milk!"

He looks at Boone and shakes his head. "Entourages these days, you have to tell them *every*thing."

He gestures for Boone to sit down in a chair shaped like a palm frond in front of an enormous flat-screen plasma TV showing *The Searchers.* A minute later, a *hui* guy comes in with two bowls of cereal and hands one to Boone. Eddie digs in like he hasn't eaten since he was in seventh grade.

"This is good," Boone says.

"It's Crunch," Eddie says, putting the DVD on pause. "So, Boone-ba-ba-doone, what do you want?"

"Anything in this world."

"That's a little vague, *bruddah.*"

"'Anything in this world,'" Boone repeats. "Remember?"

*"Riiiiight,"* Eddie says. He sets the bowl in his lap and opens his hands wide. "Anything in this world. What is it you want?"

"Tammy Roddick's life."

"Oh, Boone."

"She testifies and she walks," Boone says. He has a spoonful of the cereal, then wipes his mouth with his sleeve. "She gets a lifetime pass."

"I take you to Cartier," Eddie says, "and you choose a Timex. I offer you any car on the lot, you pick out a Hyundai. I sit you down at Lutèce, you order a burger and fries. You're selling yourself cheap, Dawgie Boo, cashing in this chip for a stripper."

"It's my chip," Boone says.

"It is, it is," Eddie says. "You sure about this, bro?"

Boone nods.

"Because you are my friend, Boone," Eddie says. "You gave me back the most precious thing in my life and you are my *friend*. I'd give you anything. You want the house next door? Yours. You want *this* house? I move out to*night;* you move in. So as your friend, Boone, I'm begging you, don't waste this gift. Please, brah, don't throw my generosity away on some cheap gash."

"It's what I want."

Eddie shrugs. "Done. I won't lay a hand on the bitch."

"Thank you," Boone says. *"Mahalo."*

"You know this is going to cost me."

"I know," Boone says.

"And it means I'm throwing Danny to the sharks."

"You leave him to his own karma," Boone says.

"One way of looking at it."

Boone asks, "Did you have that woman killed, Eddie?"

"No."

"Truth?"

Eddie looks him square in the eye. "On the life of my son."

"Okay."

"We good?"

"We're good."

"More Crunch?"

"No, I'd better get going," Boone says. Then: "I dunno, what the hell, why not."

*"More Crunch!"* Eddie yells. "You ever see *The Searchers* in high-def?"

"No."

"Me, neither," Eddie says. "I mean, I've never seen it all."

Eddie hits some buttons on the remote and the DVD comes back on. The image is so good, it almost feels like John Wayne is real.

# 88

Danny comes back into the room when Boone leaves.

"You sold me out?" he asks Eddie.

Eddie shakes his head. "Mo bettuh you *think* for once before you open your poi hole," Eddie says. "What did I promise him? I promised him that the bitch gets to waste more air. So fucking what?"

"So she'll testify," Danny says. "She'll tell what she saw, what she knows—"

"Then we had better provide her with some motivation to the contrary," Eddie says. "What does she want?"

Two years at Wharton, you can sum up what he learned in four words:
Everybody
Has
A
Price.

# 89

The girl Luce lies on a bare, dirty mattress.

She's sad and scared, but somewhat comforted by the presence of the other girls, who lie around her like a litter of puppies. She can feel the warmth of their skin, hear their breathing, smell their bodies, the sour but familiar smell of sweat and dirt.

In the background, a shower nozzle drips with the steady rhythm of a heartbeat.

Luce tries to sleep, but when she closes her eyes, she sees the same thing—a man's feet as seen from under the hotel bed. She hears Angela's muffled cry, sees her feet being lifted. Feels again her own terror and shame as she cowered under the bed as the feet walked out again. Remembers lying there in an agony of indecision—to stay hidden or run. Recalls the nerve it took to get up, go to the balcony, and look over the edge. Sees again the hideous sight—Angela's broken body. Like a doll tossed on a trash pile back in Guanajuato.

Now she hears footsteps again. She pulls the thin blanket tightly over her shoulders and clamps her eyes shut—if she cannot see, perhaps she cannot be seen.

Then she hears a man's rough voice.

"Which one is she?"

Heavy footsteps as men walk around the mattresses, stop, and walk again. She pulls the blanket tighter, squeezes her eyes shut until they hurt. But it does no good. She feels the feet stop above her, then hears a man say:

"This one."

She doesn't open her eyes when she feels the big hand on her shoulder. She risks moving her hand to grab the cross on her neck and squeeze it, as if it could prevent what she knows is going to happen. Hears the man say, "It's all right, *nena*. No one is going to hurt you."

Then she feels herself being lifted.

Dawn comes to Pacific Beach.

A pale yellow light that infiltrates the morning fog like a faint, unsteady glimpse of hope.

A lone surfer sits on his board on the burgeoning sea.

It isn't Boone Daniels.

Nor is it Dave the Love God, or Sunny Day, or High Tide, or Johnny Banzai.

Only Hang Twelve has come out this morning. Now he sits alone, waiting for people who are not going to show up.

The Dawn Patrol is missing.

# 91

The girls emerge from the tree line that edges the strawberry fields.

Walk like soldiers on patrol toward the bed of reeds.

Teddy Cole watches them come.

He's slept rough in the reeds, his body aches with cold, and he shivers as he tries to focus on the girls' forms, peers through the mist, trying to make out individual faces. He smells the acrid smoke of a cook fire behind him, tortillas heating on a flat pan set on the open flame.

Teddy watches as the girls become distinct forms and now he sees the subtle differences in their stature and gait. He knows each of these girls—their arms and legs, the texture of their skin, their shy smiles. His heart starts to pound with anxiety and hope as distinct faces come into focus.

But hers is not one of them.

He looks again, fighting against disappointment and an ineffable sense of loss, but she isn't there.

Luce is gone from The Dawn Patrol.

# 92

Sunny sits at her computer with her herbal tea and checks on the swell.

Not that she needs a sophisticated computer program to tell her that the big swell is coming like Christmas, tomorrow morning. She can *feel* it burgeoning out there. A heavy, pregnant sea. She can feel her heartbeat matching the intensity of the coming waves—a heavy bass drumbeat in her chest.

Sunny goes back to the computer, checking for wind and current to see where the best spot will be to grab the wave, *her* wave. She checks the surf cams, but it's still too dark to really see anything. But the imagery on the computer—the current, the wind—it's unmistakable: Her wave is headed right for Pacific Beach Point.

Restless, she gets up again, goes to the window, and looks out at the actual ocean. It's dark and foggy, but the sun is starting to penetrate the marine layer and it feels odd to her, unhappy and strange, not to be out on the water with The Dawn Patrol. It's the first morning in years that she hasn't shown up.

She thought about going but just couldn't make herself do it. It seemed impossible to be there with Boone. It's ridiculous, she thinks now. Silly. She knows Boone has been with other women since they split up. She's been with other men. But there was something about seeing it—seeing that woman in *her* clothes, looking so comfortable and at home—that felt like a terrible betrayal. And Boone letting me think that he'd been killed, when he was doing her . . .

So she'd skipped The Dawn Patrol.

Maybe it's a good thing, she thinks. Time to move on. Catch my wave tomorrow and ride it into my new life.

She goes to get dressed. It will be busy at The Sundowner with all the surfers coming in, and Chuck could probably use the extra help.

So she decides to go in early.

# 93

High Tide thinks about going to The Sundowner, too.

He's hungry and cold, and a cup of hot coffee and a stack of banana pancakes soaked in maple syrup sound pretty damn good.

It's been a long night, sitting in his car, a half block south of Boone's crib, directing his old troops like a general who's come out of retirement to fight a war. And it felt good, in a weird way, to know that he could issue the battle cry and the boys would respond as if no time had passed. But it felt bad, too, bringing back the old days that he had left behind.

That bad feeling was nothing compared with the heartache that came with letting his cousin down. But life is full of tough choices, and he chose one family over the other.

Done.

But now he looks out at the ocean and sees that the family he chose isn't together. He didn't go out this morning because he was busy guarding Boone, and God knows where *he* is now. Johnny's not out there because he's probably well and truly pissed off at Boone and working the murder case. And Sunny's mad—hurt and betrayed.

Only Hang Twelve is out there, sitting like a latchkey kid waiting for Mom or Dad to come home.

He's thinking this when someone taps on his window.

Boone's standing there.

Tide rolls down the window.

"It's over," Boone says.

"That's good."

"There's still time for you to hit the water," Boone says.

"You?"

Boone shakes his head, then looks up at his cottage. "Stuff to take care of."

"Yeah, I think I'll give it a pass this morning," Tide says. "Get me some breakfast instead."

"Sounds good," Boone says. "And Tide? Thanks, huh."

"No worries, brah."

You're *aiga.*

# 94

Johnny Banzai grabs a few hours of sleep, gets up, and picks a shirt, slacks, sports jacket, and tie from his closet. Then he rejects all of it in favor of a charcoal gray suit. He has to be in court today, maybe in front of a judge, and he's found that the extra touch of formality is usually worth it.

It feels odd, going to work from the house instead of the beach, changing clothes in his bedroom instead of his car. He's missed sessions of The Dawn Patrol before, because of work or family obligations, but this feels different.

Like the end of something.

The start of something else.

Phases and stages, I guess, Johnny thinks as he knots a bloodred knit tie and checks it in the mirror. At a certain time in your life, you think you'll never get married; then you are. Then you think you'll never have kids, and then suddenly you have two. And you've always said that you'd never leave The Dawn Patrol, but maybe now . . .

That stunt Boone pulled.

Not the thing with the Boonemobile—that was classic Boone, although it's hard to see him sacrifice the old van that held so many memories for all of them. So many road trips up and down the coast. The waves, the beer, the music, the girls. Hard to see that all go up in flames, but maybe it was necessary.

No, it was the stunt with the lady lawyer, the Brit. Maybe it was the accent that pissed Johnny off, but more probably it was Boone pulling the shit that Johnny expected from the La Jolla beautiful people, the rich and influential, and not a lifelong surfing buddy.

Face it, he tells himself as he looks down at his wife, Beth, sleeping in bed. You never thought you'd see Boone go for the money, never thought you'd see him go for that kind of woman. The whole ambitious professional thing.

Well, never say never.

Johnny kisses his wife and receives a murmured "Morning," then stops off at each of his kids' rooms to check in on them. His son, Brian, is sound asleep, clad in Spider-Man pajamas, stretched out in the bottom bed of the set of bunks he'd wanted so that he could have friends for sleepovers. Abbie is likewise, curled into her Wonder Woman blanket, the lightest sheen of sweat on her upper lip. And thank God, Johnny thinks, that she takes after her mother.

He looks at her lying there so peaceful and innocent, and, hopefully, so safe, and it makes him think of the little girl's toothbrush in the room at the Crest Motel. Who was the girl? What was she doing there? Where is she now?

Johnny walks over, kisses his daughter softly on the cheek, and heads out the door.

It's going to be a tough day. Dan Silver's civil trial starts at nine and Tammy Roddick is scheduled to take the stand shortly afterward, and Johnny is going to be in the gallery when she does. So he'll have to get into a judge's chamber early to get a warrant written for both Boone and Roddick. She'll probably be on the stand for a couple of hours or more; then Johnny intends to pick them both up and get some answers about Angela Hart's death.

Sorry, B, he thinks.

I'm invoking the jump-in rule.

# 95

Boone stands on the pier and watches Hang Twelve sit out in the water by himself.

Kid's not even bothering to catch any of the good waves that are coming in like a machine's cranking them out. Just sits beyond the break and lets them roll under him like he's catatonic or something.

Boone waves his arms and yells, "Hang!"

Hang Twelve looks over, sees Boone, and then looks away.

A few seconds later, he paddles in. Boone watches him pick up his board, walk up the beach, and head up the street.

# 96

Petra's sitting at the kitchen table when Boone comes in. Her hands are wrapped around a mug of tea.

"Look, it's all good," he says. "It's over. It's taken care of."

"What do you mean?" she asks.

"You're good to go," Boone says. "Tammy can testify about the arson, tell the cops whatever she knows about Angela's murder. Danny's not going to do a thing."

"Why not?"

"Because he wants to live," Boone says. "I can't tell you any more."

Can't tell them that he made a deal that, in effect, cuts Danny off from Red Eddie. And Danny would take a fall on the lawsuit, even the murder, before he'd hurt Tammy, because she's now under Eddie's protection. And violating Red Eddie's protection is a capital offense, no appeals, no last-minute calls from the governor.

"You want to go to The Sundowner?" Boone asks. "Grab some breakfast?"

"What did you trade?" Petra asks.

"Huh?"

"You obviously made a deal with Red Eddie," Petra says. "What I'm asking is, what did you give in return?"

"Not so much," he says. When he sees her skeptical look, he adds, "I did him a solid once. I cashed in the chip."

"Must have been quite a chip."

"Sort of."

She's touched. "You did that for me?"

"I did it for Tammy," Boone says. "And for you. *And* me."

"We can't have breakfast in The Sundowner," Petra says.

"Why not?"

"Because it would be too awkward," Petra says. "It would be rubbing it in her face."

"Sunny doesn't care," Boone says.

Men are idiots, Petra thinks. "She's still in love with you."

"No, she's not," Boone says.

Yes, she is, Petra thinks. The question is, are you still in love with her? I don't think so, because you have too good a heart to be in love with her and kissing me. But you might still be in love with her, Boone, and not know it. Just as you might be falling in love with me and not know it.

"We don't have to go to The Sundowner," Boone says.

# 97

Yeah, but a lot of people do.

With the swell headed toward PB Point, maybe half the big-wave surfing world is jammed in The Sundowner, macking down, talking about what's going to happen tomorrow.

Sunny's in hyperdrive, pouring coffee, taking orders, and running trays to the surfers, the Jet Ski drivers, the clothing and gear execs, the photographers and filmmakers, magazine editors, and plain old hangers-on who've gathered for the big event—the first monster wave to hit the SoCal coast in years. Everybody's been waiting for this for so long—for the golden age to come home.

It's going to be big. Not just the waves but the moment.

It's a media event; it's going to be splashed all over the mags, the videos and DVDs, the clothing catalogs. Reps are going to get made or ruined, rivalries fought out like these waters are the plains of Troy, huge egos fighting for waves, fighting for rides, fighting for the glory, fame, endorsement contracts, sponsorships.

Someone's going to be in the big picture.

The cover shot.

Someone is going to be the star of the movie and the rest aren't, and the knife hasn't been made, the steel not forged, that could cut the tension, the vibe in The Sundowner this morning.

Or the testosterone, Sunny thinks.

It's all about the boys today.

Talking trash, acting all cool, being guys together. She's *invisible* to them, except she's the waitress who brings them their food.

"Getting to you?" Dave asks, sitting at the counter, not talking to anybody, reading his newspaper. The most famous surfers in the world are all around him and it's nothing to him. Tomorrow, he might have to haul some of these guys out of the soup, out of the white water, and then they'll have his total attention. This morning, he doesn't give a damn.

"A little," Sunny says.

"They'll know who you are tomorrow," Dave says.

"I don't know."

That's an understatement. She hates to admit it, but she is intimidated. It's the Hall of Fame in here: Laird and Kalama and the whole "Strapped" crew in from Maui; the Irons brothers with the Kauai Wolf Pack; Mick and Robby and the boys from Oz; Flea and Malloys down from Santa Cruz; and the SoCal locals—Machado and Gerhardt and Mike Parsons, who rode that monster wave out on the Cortes Bank. These are the established guys with nothing to prove and they're all pretty cool and laid-back because of it.

But the younger ones, the up-and-comers, they're a different breed of cat. For example:

Tim Mackie, "Breakout Surfer of 06," holds his mug in the air like a trophy and points at it. Handsome as well, sculpted, cocky—the whole world is going his way, so why shouldn't he expect an instant refill? It's good being Tim Mackie.

"Pour it on his crotch," Dave says.

"No."

She goes over, pours him a fresh cup—no thanks, no eye contact—and then comes back to the counter to pick up her order for the table of Billabong execs.

"I'll tow you in if you want," Dave says.

She knows where he's going with this. Most of the surfers here are tow-in guys—their Jet Ski partners will put them into the big waves, and the surfers who simply paddle in will be at a huge disadvantage. It might be worse than that—the waves might simply be *too* big, and therefore too fast, for her to catch without a ski.

"Thanks," she says. But she's never done the tow-in thing, and it takes technique and training. Besides, she's not equipped for it—her big boards are shaped for paddle-in surfing. "I think I'll just stick to what I know."

"Usually a good idea," Dave says.

But he's worried about her.

She could get shut out, by the other surfers or by the waves themselves. And, even if she catches one, she needs someone to look after her, to pull her out of the impact zone if something goes wrong.

Boone will be out there, so that will be good.

Sunny takes off with a shoulder full of western omelets, and Dave goes back to his paper. She hustles back to the sound of the bell announcing her next pickup. This is for tomorrow, she thinks, my big chance.

Either I do it or this is my life.

Humping coffee and eggs.

Tim Mackie holds up his mug again and points.

Sunny holds up her middle finger.

# 98

Tammy comes out of the bedroom into the kitchen.

Boone gives her the good news.

Her response is underwhelming.

But predictable.

"I want to talk to Teddy."

"Once again," Petra says, "I don't think that's such a good—"

"Either I talk to Teddy," Tammy says, "or I don't testify. You think it over, let me know what you decide."

She walks back into the bedroom.

"Succinct," Boone says.

# 99

They reach Teddy at his home number.

Wife must be out of town, Boone thinks.

He hands the phone to Tammy.

"Teddy?" she asks. "Are you alone?"

That's all she asks. That's it. After all the "I want to talk to Teddy" OCD, she asks that one question, apparently gets her answer, and punches off.

Then says, "Okay, I'll testify."

# 100

Downtown San Diego is surprisingly small.

You can easily walk around it in the better part of an hour, and it might be the only major city in the country where a healthy person can walk from the airport to downtown with no problem.

That walk would take you along the bay that borders downtown on the west and south, and created the city. Mexican explorers stopped in San Diego back in the 1500s for its excellent harbor and left behind the usual mixture of soldiers and missionaries that defined most of Southern California until the Anglos took it in 1843. By the 1850s, a fleet of Chinese junks fished for tuna from the harbor, but were later moved out by Anglo and Italian fishermen.

Downtown was pretty sleepy until the big real estate boom of the

1880s, when town fathers like the Hortons, Crosswhites, and Marstons built up a legitimate downtown with office buildings, stores, banks, and restaurants. The seedy Stingaree District, with its bars, gambling joints, and brothels thrived between downtown and the southern harbor, and madams like Ida Bailey and gamblers and procurers like Wyatt Earp and his wife made fortunes and gave San Diego the risqué reputation that still clings to it today down in what is now known as the Gaslamp District.

But it was the U.S. Navy that really defined downtown San Diego and still does. From virtually anywhere you stand in downtown, you can see a navy base or a ship. Take that walk from the airport and you'll see aircraft carriers docked in the harbor, navy planes landing at their base on North Island. Sometimes you'll see a submarine pop up from underwater right in the bay and glide into port.

San Diego is a navy town.

Back in 1915, the good city fathers chased all the brothels out of the Gaslamp, but then they had to invite them back when the navy threatened to stop its ships from calling in port, an embargo that would have bankrupted the city.

And it's more than symbolic that downtown's major street, Broadway, ends on a pier.

A few blocks east on Broadway sits the courthouse.

Petra, with Boone in the passenger seat and Tammy in the back, pulls into the parking structure of her office building and finds her designated spot.

Tammy looks great cleaned up in a cream-colored blouse over a black skirt that Petra bought for her in the ladies' department at Nordstrom, which is really no surprise. What did surprise Petra was how good Boone could look.

She didn't think he owned a sports jacket, never mind the tailored black suit with a crisp white shirt and a sedate blue tie.

"Wow," she said. "I had no idea."

"I have two suits," Boone replied. "A summer wedding and funeral suit and a winter wedding and funeral suit. This is the winter wedding and funeral suit, which doubles as a going-to-court suit."

"Do you go to court a lot?"

"No." Nor to very many weddings, Boone thinks, and, even more fortunate, to fewer funerals.

They walk out of the parking structure and walk the two blocks to the courthouse.

The courtroom is small and modern. On the third floor of the Superior Court Building here in the downtown area, the room is painted in those institutional blue tones that are meant to soothe and don't. The two counsel tables are uncomfortably close together, and the witness stand is close to the jury.

The gallery holds only about twenty people, but that's ample space for this morning. An insurance bad-faith case isn't sexy and rarely attracts much of a crowd. A few of the courthouse regulars, trial junkies, mostly retired people who have nothing more exciting to do, are sitting in the gallery, looking bored and vaguely disappointed. An insurance company representative, conspicuous in his gray suit, sits in the front row taking notes.

Johnny and Harrington are there.

Semi–pissed off, because they couldn't find a judge who'd let them take Tammy in before she testified in the civil case. *Semi,* because they really want to talk to her about the Angela Hart case, but on the other hand, if she's here to fuck Danny Silver, that can't be a bad thing. Let her get deeper into the shit with Silver, so she has no place else to go except to them.

Petra sits at the defense table.

You couldn't tell from her looks, Boone thinks as he slips in and sits down in the back row, that she's been up for more than twenty-four hours, almost shot, and nearly frozen. She looks fresh and focused in a pinstriped charcoal gray suit, her hair pinned up, subtle makeup on her eyes.

Very professional.

Maximum cool.

She turns and favors him with a smile as subtle as her makeup before she turns around to watch Alan Burke, who is just starting his examination of Tammy Roddick.

She looks good. Just enough like a stripper to believe that she was with Silver Dan the night his warehouse burned down, not enough like a stripper to lose credibility. She's wearing a lot less eye makeup, but those green cat eyes still jump out at you. And she's calm.

Ice.

Alan Burke always looks good. Hair combed straight back like a blond

Pat Riley, his skin tanned from surfing but glowing from the SPF lotion he uses religiously. Alan may be the last guy left in the Western world who still looks good in a double-breasted suit, and this morning he has on a navy blue Armani, a white shirt, and a canary yellow tie.

He's smiling.

Alan is always smiling, even when things are going bad, but especially when he's shredding an opposing witness. But he has a friendly witness now, one who's about to kill his opponent for him.

Dan Silver sits beside his lawyer at the plaintiff's table, giving Tammy the stink eye. Dan is one of those guys who never look good no matter what you dress them in. If it's true that the clothes make the man, then nothing can make Dan Silver. He's forsaken the cowboy rig this morning for an ill-fitting suit, tight across the shoulders but baggy against his trunk. The suit is a greenish gray, which does nothing to help Dan's sallow skin, bad complexion, and heavy jowls. His hair is in an old-fashioned pompadour with a little ducktail, a statement that things were better in the 1950s. Now he sits at the plaintiff's table and glares at Tammy.

Silver's lawyer is the infamous Todd "the Rod" Eckhardt, a plaintiffs' lawyer known around the greater San Diego Bar community for his shameless willingness to sue anybody for anything. Todd has sued for all those reasons that make the general public loathe and despise lawyers—the hot coffee spilled on the lap of a driver doing seventy in a thirty-five-mph zone; the "food product" that came out of a microwave hot; and, Boone's personal favorite, a lady of the evening who sued a blessed-by-nature john for neck injuries that would prevent her from ever effectively again carrying out her trade and earning a living.

So Todd the Rod is a millionaire many times over and doesn't try to disguise the fact. He comes into depositions and hearings with a valet—yes, a valet—who looks like he came out of some 1940s British black-and-white film about exploring the Irrawaddy or something, carries Todd's briefcases and Red Files, and helps him off with his coat. Todd leaves him at home for trials, however, lest it provoke jealousy from the jurors. At the trial level, Todd is strictly a man of the people.

His only saving grace as far as Boone is concerned—and Todd has tried to hire Boone on several occasions—is that Todd is perhaps the homeliest human being ever to waddle into a courtroom. Todd would have to approach obese from the upside—looking at Todd, it's hard to believe that he has a skeletal structure, more like he's a single-cell—well, a *fat* single cell—organism with a shock of white hair, bug eyes, and a very large brain. If you propped Todd up beside Dave the Love God, you could only come to the conclusion that extraterrestrials do roam the earth, because these two specimens could not possibly spring from the same species. Todd doesn't sit down; he sort of oozes into a chair and assumes a slouching posture that makes you think he's Play-Doh that some negligent child left out in the rain. Greasy sweat runs out of his pores like an oil leak. He's disgusting.

Todd the Rod got his sobriquet back in the nineties when a lot of San Diego beachside houses were collapsing. Todd would stick a metal rod into the dirt of the building pad, pronounce it "improperly compacted," file suit against the contractor, the city engineers, the building inspector, and the insurance company, and usually win.

Alan has a different version of how Todd got his name. "Don't let his prehuman appearance fool you," Alan told Boone before a trial against Todd a couple of years ago. "If you give him the slightest opening, he'll jam a rod so far up your ass, it will come out your mouth."

So Alan has no intention of giving Todd the Rod an opening. In fact, he's getting ready to counterjam the rod. He asks Tammy the usual warm-up questions—name, address—and then gets right into it.

"And where were you employed at that time?" Alan is asking.

"Silver Dan's," Tammy replies.

"What did you do there?" Alan asks.

"I was a dancer," Tammy says, looking calmly at the jury.

"A dancer."

"A *stripper,*" Tammy says.

"Objection," Todd mumbles.

The judge, Justice Hammond, is a former federal prosecutor, a by-the-book, no-nonsense hard-ass not known for his patience with courtroom antics or his sense of humor. Like most members of the human race, he despises Todd the Rod, but he's keeping his emotions very much in check.

"Overruled," Hammond says.

Alan continues: "And were you at Silver Dan's the night of October 17, 2006?"

"Yes," Tammy says.

"And were you there after closing?" Alan asks.

"Yes, I was."

"Why?"

"I was dating Dan at the time," Tammy says. "We were going to go out to breakfast."

"And did you go out to breakfast?"

"Not directly," Tammy says, looking at Dan.

"Where did you go?"

"Dan said he had an errand to do," Tammy says, "at a warehouse he owned."

"And did you go to the warehouse?" Alan asks, closing in. He spots Boone in the gallery and gives him a quick wink before turning back to Tammy.

"We did," Tammy says.

Alan turns his back to her to look at the jury, then at Dan, then at Todd—just to stick it in a little—then back at the jury. He walks over to the jury box and asks, with the immaculate timing of a really good stand-up comic, "When you went there, did you get out of the car?"

"Yes."

"Then what did you do?"

"I went inside."

"And . . ." Alan pauses to signal the jury that something important is coming up. ". . . did you see anything unusual?"

Here it comes, Boone thinks. A few more words out of her mouth and we're done. We can all get on with our lives, and I can try to find a little peace inside a giant wave.

Tammy looks straight at Dan, who pulls a little silver cross on a chain out of his pocket and fingers it nervously. Yeah, Boone thinks as he watches this, like Jesus is going to jump in on your side, pull you out of the deep water.

"No," Tammy says.

Shit, Boone thinks.

Alan keeps the smile on his face, but it definitely tightens up. This wasn't the answer he was expecting. Boone can see Petra's back stiffen, her head straighten up.

Dan Silver just smiles.

Alan moves away from the jury and walks up to the witness stand. "I'm sorry, Ms. Roddick. Perhaps I wasn't being clear. When you went into the warehouse that night, did you see Mr. Silver there?"

"Yes."

"And was he doing something?"

"Yes."

"What?"

"He was just looking around, checking the back door, that kind of thing," Tammy says. "Then we went to Denny's."

She looks at the jurors with an expression of total innocence.

"Ms. Roddick," Alan asks, his voice edging toward threat, "didn't you tell me that you saw Mr. Silver pouring kerosene on the floor in the basement?"

"No," Tammy says.

"You didn't tell me," Burke says, "that you saw him run a twisted sheet into that kerosene?"

"Objection."

"No."

"Or hold his cigarette lighter to that sheet and set it on fire?" Burke asks.

"Objection . . ."

"No."

"Ob—"

"I have your sworn deposition here," Burke says. "I can show it to you, if you'd like."

"—jection!"

Boone sees Petra start hammering on her laptop, bringing up Tammy's deposition transcript. The jurors are literally leaning forward in their seats, totally awake now; the case has suddenly become really interesting, like they see on *Law & Order.*

"Yeah, okay. I told you those things," Tammy says.

"Thank you," Alan says. But he's not happy. Torching your own witness, as it were, is never a good thing, because the other side gets to stand up and confront her with the conflict in her own testimony. But it's better than nothing.

Except—

Tammy says, "Because you promised me money to say it."

That's not good, Boone thinks.

The jurors gasp. The trial junkies in the gallery sit up with ears pricked. Petra turns in her chair and looks at Boone. Then she shakes her head sadly and goes back to her computer.

Todd the Rod morphs into a semi-vertical position that could be mistaken for an actual human being standing up. "Move for a directed verdict, Your Honor. Not to mention sanctions for gross misconduct."

Alan says, "Mistrial, Your Honor."

"I'll see you both in chambers," Hammond says. "Now."

Fucked, Boone thinks as he watches Todd the Rod ooze toward the judge's chambers.

Epic macking fucked.

# 101

Boone intercepts Tammy as she walks out of the courtroom.

"They got to you, didn't they?" Boone asks.

She just shakes her head and pushes past him into the hallway. He follows her, just a few steps ahead of Johnny and Harrington.

"What did they offer you," Boone says, taking her by the elbow, "that's worth more than your friend's life?"

She turns those green eyes on him. "If you'd seen what I've seen—"

"What have you seen?"

Tammy jerks her arm away, hesitates for a second, then says, "There's a world out there you know nothing about."

"Educate me."

But Johnny steps between them. He shows his badge and says, "Sergeant Kodani, SDPD. Ms. Roddick, we have some questions for you regarding the death of Angela Hart."

"I don't know anything about that."

"You might know more than you think," Johnny says. "In any case, we'd appreciate your coming down to the station to discuss it with us. It won't take long."

"Am I under arrest?" she asks.

"Not yet," Harrington says, pushing in. "Would you like to be?"

"I have things I have to—"

"What," Harrington says, "you're late for the pole?"

"Just come with us, Ms. Roddick," Johnny says. He guides her toward the door.

Harrington looks at Boone. "Another stellar performance from you, Daniels. Congratulations. At least this time, you got a grown-up killed. Maybe next time, it'll be an old lady."

Boone punches him.

# 102

Tammy Roddick is stone.

That's what Johnny Banzai thinks.

"Angela had your credit cards," he says. "Why?"

Tammy shrugs.

"Did you give them to her?"

She stares at the wall.

"Or did you check into the motel *with* her?" Johnny asks.

She checks her fingernails.

The interview room is nice. Small but clean, with the walls painted in a soothing light yellow. A metal table and two metal chairs. The classic one-way mirror. A video camera with microphone bolted to the ceiling.

So, as much as Harrington would like to bust into the room, call her a stupid fucking twat, and bounce her off the walls, he can't do it without making a guest appearance on *America's Worst Police Videos*. All he can do is watch, through a swollen eye, as Johnny takes another tack.

"Hey, Tammy," Johnny says, "you *saw* her get killed, didn't you? You were there. You got away. You could give us the guy who did it."

She finds an interesting stain on the table, wets her finger, and rubs it out.

"That's the good-parts version," Johnny says. "You want to hear the bad version?"

She goes back to the shrug.

"The bad version," Johnny says, "is that you set her up. You both saw Danny set the fire, but you made a deal and she wouldn't, so you got her in that room to be killed. Try to follow along here, Tammy, because I'm presenting you with a very important choice. It's a one-time offer. It goes off the table in five seconds, but right now you get to choose which you want to be—witness or suspect. We're talking first-degree homicide, premeditated, and I'll bet I can get 'special circumstances' tossed in. So you'd be looking at . . . I don't know. Let me get my calculator."

"I want a lawyer," Tammy says.

Which is some sort of progress, Johnny thinks. At least we've gone verbal now. The problem is, she's verbalized the magic words that will stop the interview.

"Are you sure about that?" Johnny says, playing the standard card because he's not holding any better ones. "Because once you ask for a lawyer, you choose suspect."

"Twice," she says.

"Excuse me?"

"This is twice I'm asking for a lawyer," she says.

Johnny pushes his luck. "Who was the kid, Tammy?"

"What kid? I want a lawyer."

"The kid in the room with Angela, a little girl, pink toothbrush?"

"I don't know. I want a lawyer."

But she knows. Johnny sees it in her eyes. Dead as stone until he mentioned the kid, and then there was something in there.

Fear.

You're a cop for more than a few weeks, you know fear when you see it. He leans over the table and says real quietly, "For the kid's sake, Tammy, tell me the truth. I can help. Let me help you. Let me help *her*."

She's at the tipping point.

Again, he knows it when he sees it. She could go either way. She's going toward Johnny's when—

There's a commotion in the hall.

*"I'm her attorney! I demand access!"*

"Get out of here," Harrington says.

*"Has she asked for a lawyer? She has, hasn't she?"*

Tammy sets her jaw and looks at the ceiling. Johnny gets up, opens the door, and sees Todd the Rod standing in the hallway. The lawyer looks over his shoulder at Tammy.

"It's okay now," he says. "I'm here. Not . . . one . . . more . . . word."

He has her out of there in thirty minutes.

# 103

Boone's in a lot longer.

After all, he hit a cop.

A detective, no less.

In a courthouse hallway.

And Boone didn't just punch Harrington once. He went off on him—big heavy hands and muscles hard from years of surfing slamming punch after punch into Harrington's face, ribs, and stomach until Johnny Banzai managed to get some kind of judo hold on him and choke him out.

Now Boone lies on a metal bench in the cell and nobody fucks with him. He shares the cell with mostly blacks, Mexicans, and some white-trash drunks, bikers, and tweekers and nobody fucks with him.

He hit a cop.

A detective, no less.

In a courthouse hallway.

Boone could run for president of the cell and win by acclamation. They love him in there. Guys are offering him their bologna sandwiches.

He's not hungry.

Too fucking miserable to eat.

It's over, he thinks. I took Harrington's bait like the chump fish I am, and now I'm looking at a felonious assault rap on a law enforcement officer. That means certain jail time, and my PI card is gonzo.

Half The Dawn Patrol's pissed at me and the other half must think I'm a total barney, and they're totally correct in that. I let this Roddick babe play me like a fish, make me chase her like she didn't want to be caught, and then, bang, she turns around and rams a hole in the boat.

And we're all going down with it.

Roddick set us up. She was never going to testify against Danny. She sold the insurance company a story so it would deny Silver's claim. Then he could sue for the big bucks when she changed her story. The whole chase thing was to make us want her more. And it worked.

Judge Hammond will deny Alan's motion for a mistrial and grant Todd's motion for a directed verdict. When court reconvenes in the morning, he'll instruct the jury that the insurance company has already been found guilty and that all they need to decide is how much to award in punitive damages.

Which will be in the millions.

And Alan will be referred to the State Bar Association for ethics charges, not to mention the district attorney's office for suborning perjury. So will Pete.

Her career is fucked. She'll be lucky if she keeps her Bar card, never mind make partner. If she does manage to stay in the law biz, she'll be doing fender benders and slip-and-falls until her hair is gray.

A skinny white tweeker approaches Boone and shoves a couple of pieces of stale bread at him. "You want my sammich?"

"No, thanks."

The tweeker hesitates, his shrunken meth-reduced mouth trembling with anxiety. "You want a blow job?"

"Get away from me."

The tweeker sidles off.

But this is what life's going to be, Boone thinks. Stale "sammiches," tweekers for friends, and offers of jailhouse love.

He rolls over and faces the wall, his back to the cell.

No one's going to fuck with him.

# 104

Petra sits on a plastic chair bolted to the wall of the receiving station at the downtown jail.

She's glad to be there, though, glad to be anywhere that isn't in the proximity of Alan Burke, who'd gone off on her like a pit bull on crank.

"Good job," he'd said, storming down the street outside the courthouse.

"I didn't know," she said, working hard to keep up with him.

He stopped and whirled on her. "It's your *job* to know! It's your *job* to get witnesses ready to testify! For *our* side, Petra! Not the *other* side! It's my fault for not having mentioned that earlier, I guess!"

"You're right, of course."

"I'm *right*?" he yelled, holding his arms out like Christ crucified, spinning in a 360 and yelling to everybody on Broadway, "Hey, I'm right! Did you hear that? The associate attorney who's never tried a case in her fucking life tells me I'm right! Does it get any better? Does life get any happier than this?"

People walked by them, chuckling.

"I'm sorry," Petra said.

"Sorry's not good enough."

"My resignation will be on your desk by the end of the business day," Petra said.

"No, no, no, no," Alan said. "Too easy. You're not walking away from this. No. You're going to stay for the whole long, miserable march to death, humiliation, and destruction. Right by my side."

"All right. Certainly. Yes."

"Are you sleeping with him?" Alan asked.

"With whom?"

"With Todd the Rod!" Alan yelled. "Boone! Who did you think I meant?"

Petra turned beet red and stared at him, mouth agape. Then she said, "I don't think that's an appropriate question for an employer to ask an employee."

"Sue me," Alan said, and walked away. Then he turned around, came back, and said, "Look, we fell for a trick older than dirt. It's not your fault, I should have spotted it. They set us up. Burned a cheap building down, produced a phony arson witness, then had her flip on us in court to get a punitive damages award. They win; we lose. It happens. Now go bail Boone out. We don't shoot our wounded."

So now Petra sits on the plastic chair waiting for the desk sergeant to process paperwork. He seems to be working at glacial speed.

# 105

It's a *Beauty and the Beast* scene.

Tammy Roddick walking down Broadway in the company of Todd the Rod. Draws smirks from passersby whose sole thought is that the ugly fat man has maxed out an AmEx black card for a matinee at the Westgate Hotel.

They go to the Westgate, all right, but not up to a room.

Todd the Rod walks her into the parking structure, right to a gold Humvee, where Red Eddie sits in the backseat eating a fish taco smothered in salsa. He stops chewing long enough to say, "Get in, pretty lady."

Tammy balks.

Todd the Rod is already sleazing his way toward the elevator.

"No worries, sistuh," Eddie says. "No one going to touch a hair on your head. On the life of my child."

She gets into the backseat with him.

"Where is she?" she asks.

He holds up a white paper bag. "Taco?"

"Where is she?"

"She's safe."

"I want to see her," Tammy says.

"Not yet."

"Right fucking now."

"You're a real *tita,* huh?" Eddie says. "You know *tita,* Hawaiian for 'tough girl'? I like that. We got some time to kill, *tita,* maybe we can kill it together. Oooh, look at them green cat eyes, getting so angry. Gets me hot, *tita,* gives me wood."

"I held up my end of the deal," Tammy says.

"And we'll hold up ours," Eddie replies. "Just not yet. You have to develop a little patience, *tita.* It's a virtue."

"When?"

"When what?" Eddie asks, taking a huge bite of the taco. The salsa drips from the side of his mouth.

"When do you hold up your end of the deal?"

"Some things have to happen first," Eddie says. "Things go as planned, you *keep* that sexy mouth shut . . . tomorrow morning."

"Where?"

Eddie smiles, wipes the salsa from his lips, and sings, "'Let me take you down, cos I'm going to . . .'"

# 106

Boone can't let go of Teddy D-Cup.

Lying there on the metal bench, his mind keeps going back to Teddy in the motel room with the little *mojada* girl. Natch you can't let go of it, he tells himself. Face it, you have a serious jones going for pedophiles. Don't let it twist your thinking on this.

Yeah, but it's not, Boone thinks. There's something there, something about the Teddy-Tammy connection that doesn't jive.

Work through it.

Tammy leaves Mick Penner for Teddy. No surprise there—she's trading up, except most of Teddy's strippers work him for some cosmetic work, and Tammy hasn't had a stitch of plastic surgery. Okay, maybe she just didn't want any or they haven't gotten around to it yet.

Mick knows his girl is doing Teddy because he followed them to the cheap motel up near the strawberry fields. Which doesn't make any sense, because Teddy could do his matinees at any upscale hotel in La Jolla, or even at Shrink's, and a girl like Tammy would expect—in fact, insist on—a little luxury.

So why does he take her to the cheap joint all the way up in O'side?

Because it's near the strawberry field where he picks up a little *mojada* girl. But that doesn't make any sense. You'd think that's the last place he'd take Tammy; you'd think the good doctor would want to keep that little assignation *way* deep on the down low.

It doesn't make sense on another level: Pedophiles are pedophiles because they like little girls, not grown women. But Teddy is notorious for banging fully grown strippers and got his nickname for giving them big, fully grown, triple-X adult boobs.

Teddy D-Cup likes women.

Yeah, except, you saw him in the room with the child, so . . .

A guy's staring at him from across the cell. Big guy who looks like he hits the weight room pretty regularly.

"What?" Boone asks.

"You remember me?"

The whole cell is quiet, watching this develop, hoping for a little relief from the mind-numbing monotony of jail.

"No," Boone says. "Should I?"

"You tossed me out of The Sundowner once."

"Okay." Like, big freaking deal, Boone thinks. I've thrown a lot of idiots out of The Sundowner.

The guy gets up and stands over Boone. "But you ain't got your big Samoan buddy or that other guy with you now, do you?"

Boone sort of remembers him now. East County guy who got a *turista* drunk and was going to take her somewhere for a gang bang. He makes a point of looking around the cell, then says, "No, I don't see either of them here. So?"

"So, I'm going to beat the shit out of you."

"I don't want any trouble."

The guy sneers. "I don't give a fuck what you want."

A biker sitting against the wall asks Boone, "You want us to take care of this?"

"No, but thanks," Boone says. He's had a bad day, a *really* bad day that's not going to get any better. He hasn't had any sleep, he's aching and tired and irritable, and now this pumped-up kook is trying to make his day even worse.

"Get up," the guy says.

"I don't want to."

"Pussy."

"Okay, I'm a pussy," Boone says.

"You're my bitch."

"If you say so," Boone says, folding his arms across his chest and closing his eyes. He feels the guy reach out to grab him, flicks his hands out to separate the guy's arms, then knife-edges both his own hands into the guy's neck.

The guy is done now; he just doesn't know it yet. Stunned from the double strike to the carotids, he can't react quickly enough as Boone slides his hands around the back of his neck, holds his head, and brings his knee up three times into his chin. Boone lets go, pushes, and the guy slides to the floor unconscious, blood trickling from his mouth.

Boone lies back down.

There's a short pause; then the tweeker who had offered Boone a bologna sandwich and a blow job scoots over to rob the unconscious man. He reaches inside his shirt and yanks out a small chain with a little crucifix on it, holds it up to Boone, and asks, "You want this?"

Because jailhouse law says it belongs to Boone by right of conquest.

Boone shakes his head.

Thinking, You're an idiot, Daniels.

A total barney.

He gets up from the bench, steps over a few guys to get to the bars, and calls out to the jailer. "Yo, bro! Any word on me getting out of here?"

# 107

Yeah, as a matter of fact.

Ten minutes later he walks out of the building with Petra. She tries to put a brave face on things. "At least now," she says, "you can catch your 'big swell.'"

"Doesn't matter," Boone says.

It doesn't? Petra thinks. Because it certainly seemed to matter a great deal just a day ago. My God, could it have been just a day?

Boone asks, "Can I borrow your car?"

To go to the beach? she wonders. She starts to ask, but there's an energy to him that makes her stop. It's a man she hasn't seen before— intense, focused. It's admirable, but also a little frightening.

"You're not going to push it off a cliff, are you?" she asks.

"Not planning on it."

She digs into her purse and hands him the keys.

"Thanks," Boone says. "I'll get it back to you."

"I'm taking that to mean," Petra says, "that you don't want me to go with you."

He looks at her with seriousness that, again, she hasn't seen in him before, and again, that simultaneously scares and excites her.

"Look," he says, "there are some things you have to do alone. Can you dig that?"

"I can."

"I'm going to make this all right."

"I know you are."

He leans down and kisses her lightly on the cheek, then turns and walks away with a stride that she can only describe to herself as "purposeful."

She gets it.

Thinks, You have a few things to make right, yourself.

Petra calls a cab and tells the driver to take her to The Sundowner.

# 108

Boone drives to Tammy's place.

She won't be home—Danny will have whisked her away somewhere by now. He parks Petra's car right out front, takes the stairs up to Tammy's place, and picks the lock.

The apartment's the usual usual. He heads right for the bedroom because that's where people keep their secrets, there or in the bathroom. Tammy's bedroom looks a lot like Angela's, right down to the same framed picture of the two of them on top of the bureau.

And you're an idiot, Boone thinks. You look at her in those pictures, she hasn't changed a bit. Teddy didn't do any work on her, so what's up between them?

He goes into the bathroom and opens the medicine cabinet. Nothing on the shelves of any interest, but a small wallet-size photo is carefully wedged into the seam between the glass and the frame on the lower left corner of the inside of the cabinet door.

It's a face shot of a young girl. The picture was taken outdoors, but the background is indistinct due to low light and the close-up on the face, but—

The girl from the strawberry fields, the reeds.

The girl in the motel room with Teddy.

Probably Latina, judging from the brown skin, long, straight black hair, and dark eyes. But she could be Native American, hard to tell. What she definitely is, is a very pretty, sweet-looking little girl with a shy, hesitant smile, wearing a cross on a thin silver chain.

The same cross and chain that Dan Silver took out of his pocket just before Tammy flipped on her testimony.

So it was no setup, Boone thinks, at least not on Tammy's part. She was responding to a threat. Silver has the girl, whoever she is, and he was letting Tammy know that the right words had better come out of her mouth.

Boone takes the picture out and looks on the back. A child's handwriting.

Te amo,
Luce

Well, at least we have a name now, Boone thinks. At least the kid has a name.

But who is she? Boone wonders. And why is her picture on the inside of a medicine cabinet door? Why do you hide a picture but want to be reminded of it every day? How does a stripper meet a *mojada* girl? And why does she care?

Think, think, he tells himself, trying to fight through the fatigue that's smacking at him as the adrenaline drains. Tammy left Mick and went to Teddy. Why?

Go back to your cop days, he thinks. Chronology. Do the time line. Tammy leaves Mick just after the fire at Danny's warehouse. She becomes obsessed with making money; she spends her time with Angela; she goes to Teddy.

Teddy and she start going up to Oceanside. But if they're not having sex, what are they doing? Teddy knew right where to go to find the girl. Right down into the reeds by the old Sakagawa strawberry fields. Obviously, he'd been there before . . . with Tammy.

And not just once, but lots of times between the fire and . . . the arson trial.

At which Tammy does a 180.

*If you'd seen what I've seen.*

What, Tammy, what did you see?

# 109

Sunny takes a moment to watch the sun go down.

A bright red ball today, painting the sea a carmine red. Beautiful, dramatic, but somehow a little ominous. Tonight is the last night of your old life sort of thing. Indeed, the ocean's kicking it up. Getting it into gear. She can feel it in the air, in her blood. It makes her heart pound.

She watches it for a few moments and then starts to walk to her house. Chuck wanted her to work a double, but she wants to go home and get some rest before the big day tomorrow. She's walking home along the boardwalk when Petra catches up with her.

"Could I have a word with you?"

"Depends on the word," Sunny says without stopping or even slowing down. Petra has to struggle to keep up with her long-legged stride.

"Please?"

"That always worked when I was a kid," Sunny says. She stops and turns to look at Petra. "What do you want?"

Her subtext is clear to Petra: What do you want now? You already have the man I love. Sunny Day is a beautiful woman, Petra thinks, even more beautiful in the soft dusk that casts a glow on her face. Even clad in old jeans and a thick sweatshirt, and not wearing a bit of makeup, the woman is simply lovely.

"I just wanted to tell you," Petra says, "that what you saw at Boone's cottage wasn't truly indicative of the reality of the situation."

"In English?"

"Boone and I haven't been together. Sexually."

"Well, yippee for you, Girl Scout," Sunny says. "But don't let me stop you."

She starts to walk away again.

Petra reaches out and grabs her elbow.

"If you want to keep that hand . . ." Sunny says.

"Oh, stop it."

"Stop what?"

"The tough-girl act."

"You're going to find out it's no act," Sunny says, "if you don't let go of my arm."

Petra gives up. She drops her hand and says, "I just came to tell you something about Boone."

She turns away. She's a few steps down the boardwalk when she hears Sunny call after her, "Hey, flatland babe? You don't have anything to tell me about Boone."

"No, I suppose not," Petra says. "My apologies."

Sunny blows out a stream of air, then says, "Look, I've been slinging plates to a restaurant full of testosterone cases all day. I guess I'm a little aggro."

"Aggravated."

"Right," Sunny says. "So what did you want to say about Boone?"

Petra tells her about Boone attacking Harrington.

"I'm not surprised," Sunny says. "That's where it all started."

"Where what all started?"

"Boone's . . ." She searches for words. "Boone going adrift, I guess."

Petra asks, "What is his story, anyway?"

"What's his *story*?"

"I mean, I don't understand him," Petra says. "Why he's so . . . under-employed . . . beneath his abilities. Why he left the police department . . ."

Sunny says, "It didn't work out."

"What happened?"

Sunny gives a long sigh, thinks about it, and says, "Rain."

"His daughter."

"What?" Sunny says.

"Doesn't Boone have a daughter named Rain?" Petra asks. "I mean, I thought he had her with *you,* actually."

"Where did you get *that*?" Sunny asks.

"I saw some pictures at his place."

Sunny tells her the story of Rain Sweeny.

"I understand," Petra says.

"No, you don't," Sunny replies. "Boone still works that case. He never stops trying to find her. It eats him up."

"But surely the poor girl is dead."

"Yes, but Boone won't let it go."

"Closure," Petra says.

"Well," Sunny replies, "Boone wouldn't know that word, or he'd *pre-tend* not to. But between you and me? Yeah, I guess 'closure' gets it done. Anyway, that's Boone's 'story.' As for you and him . . . Boone and me? We don't own each other. Now, if you don't mind, I have a wave to catch."

Petra watches her walk away.

A golden girl on a golden beach.

Wonders how, and if, Boone could ever let her go.

# 110

Sunny wonders the same thing.

She gets back to her place, peels off her sweatshirt, and flings it against the wall. Is it really *over* over with Boone and me? Can he just let me go like this?

I guess so, she thinks, recalling the image of the little Brit curled up on Boone's couch. Even if what she said about not having sex with Boone was true, it's only a matter of time. The woman is pretty, Sunny thinks. A total betty. Of course Boone would want her.

Yeah, but it's more than sex, isn't it? Sunny thinks as she goes to her computer to log on to the surf report. She's so different, this chick, and maybe that's the point. Maybe Boone wants something totally different for his life, and that's fair.

So do I.

And it's coming. She sees it on the screen. A big whirling splash of red spinning its way toward her, bringing the hope of a different life.

The hope and the *threat,* she thinks.

Am I ready for this?

Ready for change?

I guess that's what Boone wants.

Is it what *I* want?

She sits down in front of her little statue of Kuan Yin—the female personification of the Buddha and the Chinese goddess of compassion—and tries to meditate, clear all this relationship shit out of her head. There's no room for it right now. The big swell is coming, it will be here tonight, and she'll be in the water at first light and will need every ounce of concentration and focus she possesses to ride those waves.

So breathe, girl, she tells herself.

Push out the confusion.

Breathe in the clarity.

It's coming.

# 111

Dave the Love God tries to tell Red Eddie the same thing.

He sits on the deck of the new lifeguard station at PB, looking out at an ocean that is getting sketchier by the second, and tries to tell Eddie that, basically, it's not a fit night for man or beast, or boatloads of boo.

Eddie's not buying it. He thinks it's shaping up to be a *perfect* night to do this—black, foggy, and the Coast Guard sticking close to shore. "You are Dave the motherfucking Love God!" he says. "You're a freaking legend. If anyone can do this . . ."

Dave's not so sure. Freaking legend or no, he's going to have all he can handle tomorrow, and more. The water is going to be a freaking zoo, with every big-name surfer and a few dozen wannabes out there in surf that should be black-flagged anyway, trying to ride waves that are genuinely dangerous. People are going to go into the trough, get trapped in the impact zone under the crushing weight of the big waves, and someone is going to have to go in there and pull them out, and that someone is probably going to be Dave. So being out all night and then coming into a situation where he needs to be absolutely on top of his game is not a good idea.

He doesn't want to lose anyone tomorrow.

Dave the Love God lives his life by the proposition that you can save everybody. He couldn't get up in the morning if he didn't think that, all evidence and personal experience notwithstanding.

The truth is that he has lost people, has dragged their blue and swollen bodies in from the ocean and stood watching the EMTs trying to bring them back, knowing that their best efforts will be futile. That sometimes the ocean takes and doesn't give back.

He doesn't sleep those nights. Despite what he teaches his young charges—that you do your best and then let it go—Dave doesn't let it go. Maybe it's ego, maybe it's his sense of omnipotence in the water, but Dave feels in his heart that he should save everybody, get there in time every time, that he can always snatch a victim out of the ocean's clutches, never mind what the *moana* wants.

He's lost four people in his career: a teenager who got sucked out on a boogie board and panicked; an old man who had a heart attack outside the break and went under; a young woman distance swimmer who was doing her daily swim from Shores over to La Jolla Cove and just got tired; a child.

The child, a little boy, was the worst.

Of course he was.

The screaming mother, the stoic father.

At the funeral, the mother thanked Dave for finding her son's body.

Dave remembered diving for him, grabbing him, knowing the instant he touched the limp arm that the boy was never going home. Remembered carrying him to shore, seeing the mother's hopeful face, watching the hope dissolve into heartbreak.

The night of the funeral, Boone came by with a bottle of vodka and they got good and drunk. Boone just sat there and poured as Dave cried. Boone put him to bed that night, slept on the floor beside him, made coffee in the morning before they went to The Sundowner for breakfast.

Never talked about it again.

Never forgot it, either.

Some things you don't forget.

You just wish you could.

And the chances of losing another one tomorrow are very real, Dave thinks, running through his mind the list of highly skilled, experienced surfers who have died in recent years trying to ride big waves. There were lifeguards out there those days, too, great watermen who did everything they could, but everything wasn't enough.

What the ocean wants, it takes.

So now he interrupts Eddie's stream-of-consciousness, polyglot rap and says, "Sorry, bro, it's not on for tonight."

"Gots to be tonight," Eddie says.

"Get someone else, then."

"I want *you.*"

He mentions the price—three months of Dave's salary for plucking people out of the current. Three freaking months of sitting on the tower looking out for other people who go home to their houses, their families, their bank accounts, their trust funds.

Then he says, "You take a walk on me tonight, David, you keep walking. You retire on a lifeguard's pension, take a job delivering the mail or flipping burgers, *bruddah.*"

Fuck it, Dave thinks.

I ain't no George Freeth.

# 112

*There's a world out there you know nothing about.*

Boone's thinking about this as he leaves Tammy's apartment, gets back in the BMW, and starts to drive. It's getting dark and the streetlights are coming on; the ocean is going slate gray and headed toward black.

What were you trying to say, Tammy? Boone thinks.

Okay, back it up again.

Tammy has a picture of a girl named Luce in her apartment. Teddy goes into the reed beds by the strawberry fields and, protected by a bunch of armed *mojados,* comes out a little while later with the same girl. He takes her to a motel room, feeds her drugs, and is about to rape her, when you bust in. You put Teddy into the wall.

The girl runs, Danny's muscle comes in. They grab Teddy and he leads them right to where he's stored Tammy at Shrink's. You get there first. They try to shoot her, but it doesn't work. You get her back to your place, tell her about Angela, and . . .

She's not surprised.

Tammy knew already.

She didn't send Angela to the Crest Motel to switch places; she went *with* her. She was in the motel the night Angela was murdered. Was it a jealousy thing? Did Tammy set Angela up? Did she kill her herself? Tammy's a big, strong girl; *she* could have pitched Angela off that balcony.

That would be crazy, because when she left the motel, she went to Angela's place. She took a shower; she lay down. Made coffee she didn't drink, toast she didn't eat. Then she called Teddy, who hid her out at Shrink's. You put some heat on him and he ran, not to Tammy but to . . .

The strawberry fields, looking for the girl.

And Teddy knew right where to look for her because he'd been there before. He drove right to the strawberry fields, and when I tried to follow him, I got the shit beat out of me by a trio of very angry *mojados* kicking and punching me and calling me a—

*Pendejo, lambioso . . .*

Bastard, ass-licker . . .

*. . . picaflor.*

Child molester.

So they were used to guys coming to the reeds to look for little girls. That's what they thought I was doing there, so that must be a place where pedophiles go. And the guy with the shotgun, the kid with the machete, the old man, they were fed up with it. They saw a chance to do something about it and they did it, except . . .

It was okay for *Teddy* to go to the strawberry fields to find a little girl, but not me. They let him through, but they stopped me, so . . . You're a moron, Daniels, he tells himself. The *mojados* weren't selling the kid; they were protecting her. But they let Teddy take her to the motel room.

He pulls onto Crystal Pier, gets out of the car, and goes into his place. Walks into the bedroom, goes to the desk, and opens the drawer.

Rain Sweeny looks up at him.

She has a silver chain with a cross around her neck.

"Talk to me," Boone says. "Please, honey, talk to me."

*There's a world out there you know nothing about. . . .*

*. . . If you'd seen what I've seen.*

Boone sets the picture of Rain down and gets the pistol from his nightstand. Sticks it in the waistband of his jeans and heads back out.

He's going to make this right, but he has one place to stop first.

Make that right, too.

# 113

Sunny goes over to the wall to inspect her quiver of boards.

Her quiver is her toolbox, her fortune, her biggest investment. Every spare dollar left after food and rent has gone into boards—short boards, long ones of different shapes and designs for different kinds of surf. Now she selects her big gun, pulls it off the rack, takes it from its bag, and lays it on the floor.

It's a real rhino chaser—ten feet long, custom-shaped for her, it cost twelve hundred dollars, a lot of tips at The Sundowner. She examines it for nicks or hairline cracks; then, finding none, she checks the fins to make sure they're in solidly. She'll wait until morning to wax it, so she puts it back in its bag and up on the rack. Then she takes down her other big gun, a spare, because waves like this could easily snap a board in half and, if that happens, she wants to have another ready to go so she can get right back out there.

Then she checks her leash, the five-foot cord that attaches at one end to the board, on the other end to a Velcro strap around her ankle. The invention of the leash made it possible to ride big waves, because the surfer could retrieve the board before it crashed into the rocks.

But it's a double-edged sword, the leash. On the one hand, it helps potential rescuers find a surfer trapped underwater in the impact zone, because the board will pop to the surface and "headstone," and divers can follow the leash down to the surfer. On the other hand, though, the cord can get tangled on rocks or coral reefs and trap the surfer under the water.

Hence the Velcro "easy release" strap, and now Sunny practices her release. She straps the leash to her ankle and lies flat on the floor, then bends all the way forward and rips the Velcro off, removing the leash. She does this ten times from a lying-flat position, then rolls onto her side and does it ten more times each from the right and left side. Then she puts her feet up on the back of her couch, lies on the floor, and pulls herself up to rip the Velcro off. The routine builds the abdominal strength that could one day save her life if she's trapped underwater and has to do one of these "sit-ups" against a strong current of water pushing her back. It's a mental discipline, too, practicing in the calm, dry apartment so that the move will become so automatic that she can do it underwater, with her lungs burning and the ocean exploding over her.

Satisfied with the maneuver, she gets up, goes into the narrow kitchen, and makes herself a cup of green tea. She takes the tea to the table, turns on her laptop computer, and logs on to www.surfshot.com to check the progress of the big swell.

It's a swirling red blotch on the electronic map of the Pacific, building now up around Ventura County. The crews up there will be in the water in the morning, getting their big rides, making the mags.

But the swell is clearly moving south.

She stays on the site and checks buoy reports, water temperatures, weather reports, wind directions. It takes the perfect combination to produce the really big swell. All the kite strings have to come together at the same moment; a failure of any single element could destroy the whole thing. If the water gets too warm, or too cold, if the wind changes from offshore to onshore, if . . .

She leaves the table and sits in front of the little shrine, made of a pine plank over cinder blocks. The plank supports a statue of Kuan Yin, a small bust of the Buddha, a photo of a smiling Dalai Lama, and a small incense burner. She lights the incense and prays.

Please, Kuan Yin, please, don't let it stall out there, blow itself out in the sweeping curve of the South Bay. Please, compassionate Lord Buddha, let it come rolling to me. Please don't let it lose its anger and its force, its life-changing potential, before it gets to me.

I've been patient, I've been persistent, I've been disciplined.

It's my turn.

*Om mani padme hum.*

The jewel is in the lotus.

Life is going to change, she thinks, whatever happens tomorrow.

If I get a sponsorship, go out on the pro circuit—no, she corrects herself, not if—*when* I get my sponsorship, go out on the pro circuit, I'll be traveling a lot, all over the world. I won't be at The Sundowner, I won't be at The Dawn Patrol.

And Boone?

Boone will never leave Pacific Beach.

He'll say he will, we'll promise that we'll make time for each other, we'll talk about him coming out to where I am, but it won't happen.

We'll drift, literally, apart.

And we both know it.

To be fair to Boone, he's been supportive.

She remembers the conversation they had two years ago, when she was struggling with the decision of where to go with her life. They were in bed together, the sun just creeping through the blinds. He had slept, as always, like a rock; she had tossed and turned.

"Am I good enough?" she asked him out of the blue.

But he knew just what she was talking about. "Totally good enough."

"I think so, too," she said. "I've been thinking I need to get serious. Really get ready to take my shot."

"You should," he said. "Because you could be great."

I could, she thinks now.

I can.

I will.

There's a knock on the door.

She opens it and sees Boone standing there.

# 114

Dave the Love God launches the Zodiac into Batiquitos Lagoon.

This is freaking crazy, he thinks, and he's absolutely right. Heavy surf warnings are out, the Coast Guard has issued a small craft advisory, and if anything qualifies as a small craft, it's a freaking Zodiac.

He steers the Zodiac out of the lagoon toward the open ocean. It's near to being closed out; it's going to be tough busting out through the break. But Red Eddie is right: Dave knows these waters; he knows the breaks, the current, the sweet spots. If he can get out on a board, he can get out in a boat.

He does.

Takes an angle, drives through the shoulder between two breaks, gets outside, and points the Zodiac south. He decides to hug pretty close to the coast until he gets far enough south to turn seaward, toward the coordinates that Eddie had given him to meet the boat that's coming up from Mexico with the cargo.

# 115

"I was just thinking about you," Sunny says.

"Bad stuff?"

"No."

Sunny lets Boone in and he sits down on the couch. She offers him a cup of tea, but he doesn't want anything. Well, he doesn't want anything to drink, but he seems to want to say something and can't seem to get there.

She helps him out. "What happened to us, Boone?"

"I don't know."

"We used to be great together," she says.

"Maybe it's the big swell," Boone says. "It seems to be bringing something in with it."

She sits down beside him. "I've been feeling it, too. It's like how a big swell washes in and sweeps things away with it, and it's never the same again. It's not necessarily better or worse; it's just different."

"And there's nothing you can do about it," Boone says.

Sunny nods. "So this other chick . . ."

"Petra."

"Okay. Are you and she . . ."

"No," Boone says. "I mean, I don't think so."

"You don't *think* so?"

"I don't know, Sunny," Boone says. "I don't know what it is. I don't know what I used to know. All I know is that things are changing, and I don't like it."

"The Buddha said that change is the only constant," Sunny says.

"Good for him," Boone says. Old dude with a beer belly and a stoned smile, Boone thinks, sticking his nose between me and Sunny. "Change is the only constant"—New Age, retro-hippie, Birkenstock bullshit. Except it's sort of true. You look at the ocean, for instance; it's always changing. It's always a different ocean, but it's still the ocean. Like me and Sunny—our relationship might change, but we're always going to love each other.

"You look tired," Sunny says.

"I'm trashed."

"Can you get a little sleep?" she asks.

"Not yet," he says. "How about you? You need your rest—big day coming."

"I've been hitting the chat rooms," she says. "All the big boys are going to be there. A lot of tow-in crews. I'm going to give it a shot anyway, but . . ."

"You'll *shred* it," he says. "You'll kill them."

"I hope so."

"I *know* so."

God, she loves him for that. Whatever else Boone is or isn't, he's a friend, and he's always believed in her, and that means the world to her. She gets up and says, "I really should be getting to bed."

"Yeah." He gets up.

They stand close for a few painful, silent moments; then she says, "You're invited."

He wraps his arms around her. After today, after she rides her big wave, everything is going to be different. She's going to be different; they're going to be different.

"I have something I have to do," Boone says. "Tonight."

"Okay." She squeezes him tightly for a second, feels the pistol. "Hey, Boone, there's a few dozen bad punch lines here, but . . ."

"It's okay."

She squeezes him tighter for a second, then let go. Holding on, the Buddha says, is the source of all suffering. "You'd better go, before we both change our minds."

"I love you, Sunny."

"Love you, too, Boone."

And that's a constant that will never change.

# 116

The small boat pitches and rolls in the heavy swell.

Waves smashing over the bow, the boat slides into the trench and then climbs out again, threatening to tip over backward before it can crest the top of the next wave.

Out of control.

The crew has experienced rough seas before, but nothing like this. Juan Carlos and Esteban have seen *The Perfect Storm,* but they never thought they'd be *in* the fucking thing. They don't know what the hell to do, and there might be nothing they *can* do—the ocean just might decide to do them.

Esteban prays to San Andrés, the patron saint of fishermen. A fisherman's son who found life in their small village too boring, Esteban went to the city in search of excitement. Now he fervently wishes that he'd listened to his father and stayed in Loreto. If he ever gets off this boat, he's going back, and never take his boat out of the sight of land.

"Radio in a distress call!" Esteban yells to Juan Carlos.

"With what we've got down below?" Juan Carlos replies. They have thirty-to-life in the hold. So they keep banging north against the tough southern current, trying to make the rendezvous point, where they can turn over their cargo.

The cargo is down below.

Terrified.

Crying, whimpering, vomiting.

Up on top, Juan Carlos says to Esteban, "This thing's going under!"

He might be right, Esteban thinks. The boat is a dog, a bottom-heavy tub built for calm seas and sunny days, not for sledding down the face of mountains. It's bound to capsize. They'd be better off in the lifeboat.

Which is what Juan Carlos is thinking. Esteban can see it in the older man's eyes. Juan Carlos is in his forties but looks older. His face is lined with more than the sea and the sun; his eyes show that he's seen some things in his life. Esteban is just a teenager—he's seen nothing—but he knows he doesn't want to carry this memory on the inside of his eyelids for the rest of his life.

"What about them?" Esteban yells, pointing below.

Juan Carlos shrugs. There isn't room in the life raft for them. It's a shame, but a lot of things in life are a shame.

"I'm not doing it," Esteban says, shaking his head. "I'm not just leaving them out here."

"You'll do what I tell you!"

Esteban plays the trump card. "What would Danny say? He'd kill us, man!"

"Fuck Danny! He's not out here, is he?" Juan Carlos replies. "You'd better worry about not dying out here; then you can worry what Danny's going to do!"

Esteban looks down at the children below.

It's wrong.

"I'm not doing it."

"The fuck you're not," Juan Carlos says. He whips the knife out from beneath his rain slicker and thrusts it toward Esteban's throat. Two will have a much better chance handling the lifeboat in these seas than one.

"Okay, okay," Esteban says. He helps Juan Carlos unlash the lifeboat and swing it over the side. It takes a while because they have to wait several times as the boat slides and then crests, almost tipping over. He and Juan Carlos have to grip the rails with all their strength just to hang on and not be pitched into the sea.

They swing the boat out, but they can't climb into it because the boat rolls in that direction, almost lying flat on the water, the sea just inches from the gunwales. Juan Carlos slides toward the water but catches himself on the rail, his strong hands gripping for his life.

Esteban kicks at the older man's hands.

Holding on himself, he kicks again and again as Juan Carlos screams at him. But Esteban keeps kicking him. Juan Carlos never breaks his grip, but Esteban's feet break his fingers and the older man loses his hold and slips into the ocean. He tries to grab Esteban's leg and take the boy with him, but his hands are too smashed to hold on and the ocean takes him.

Juan Carlos can't swim.

Esteban watches him struggle for a moment and then go under.

When the boat rights itself again, Esteban hauls himself up, staggers to the wheel, and turns the boat back into the oncoming wave. With his other hand, he unties his rope belt, then uses it to fasten himself to the column of the wheel.

And prays.

San Andrés, I have fallen so far into evil that I would sell children. But I would not kill them, so I beg you for mercy. Have mercy on us all.

The sea rises up in front of him.

# 117

Dave can't believe what he's looking at.

He crests the top of a wave and sees the boat sitting in the trench, sideways to the oncoming wave, dangerously low in the water, sitting like a log to be rolled. The lifeboat dangles to the starboard side on its davits, as if the "Abandon ship" order had been given but not executed.

Where the hell is the captain? Dave wonders. What's he thinking?

Dave surfs the Zodiac down the wave, racing the break to the boat. He gets there seconds before, enough time to jump on, tie on, and hold on as the wave smashes into the side and knocks the boat on its side.

Miraculously, it bobs back up again, and Dave makes his way to the wheelhouse.

The pilot's unconscious, lying on the deck, next to the wheel, blood running from a cut on his head. Dave recognizes young Esteban from several of these pickups, but what the fuck is the boy doing tied to the wheel? And where is Juan Carlos?

Dave turns the boat back into the surf, locks the wheel on that setting, and kneels down beside Esteban. The kid's eyes open, and he smiles.

"San Andrés . . ."

Saint Andrew, my ass, Dave thinks.

Then he hears voices.

It's a night for weird voices. It could be the wind playing tricks, but these voices seem to be coming from below.

He walks around and opens the hatch.

Can't fucking believe what he sees:

Six, maybe seven young girls huddled together.

# 118

Dave gags.

Even standing on deck in the sea air, the bottom reeks of vomit, urine, and shit, and Dave has to fight not to gag. Dave the Love God is seriously shaken up, maybe for the first time in his entire life. "Stay there," he yells, shoving his palms out to make his point. "Just stay there!"

He strides back to the wheelhouse. Esteban is picking himself up off the deck. Dave grabs him by the front of the shirt and shoves him against the wheel.

"What the *fuck*?" Dave yells.

Esteban just shakes his head.

"I didn't sign up for *this*!" Dave hollers. "Nobody told me about *this*!"

"I'm sorry!"

"Where's Juan Carlos?"

Esteban points to the water. "He fell over."

Good, Dave thinks. Adi-fucking-os. He'd just as soon toss Esteban over the side, too, but he needs him to help get these kids off the sinking boat and into the Zodiac.

It isn't easy.

The girls are sick, dizzy, and scared to death, reluctant to leave what little safety they have on the boat for the pitching sea. It takes all of Dave's lifeguard demeanor to calm them down and get them into his boat. He gets in first and stretches up his arms while Esteban hands them down one by one. He settles them into the Zodiac, carefully arranging them to balance the weight.

The boat is going to be too heavy and sit too low in the water to be really safe, but there isn't really a choice. He either leaves them out here or he does his best to get them all in. He's not so worried about the open sea—the storm is calming down and he can negotiate the swells. The critical moment is going to be busting through the shore break, where the overloaded boat could easily flip or swamp. He doubts any of these kids are strong swimmers. If he doesn't bring the boat in upright, most of them will probably drown in the heavy white water that comes with the big swell.

Esteban hands the last girl down and then starts to climb in.

Dave stops him.

"You're not on the list, *pacheco.*"

"What am I supposed to do?"

"Turn the boat around and take it back to Mexico," Dave says. "What do you usually do?"

"I can't go back," Esteban says.

"Why not?"

Esteban hesitates, then says, "I killed Juan Carlos. He was going to leave them out here."

"Get in."

Dave works his way to the aft of the boat.

There's no place for him to sit down, so he stands.

# 119

Boone pulls into Teddy's driveway and gets out of the car.

The night air is wet, somewhere between mist and gentle rain. The light coming from Teddy's living room window looks soft and warm.

Boone can see them through the window. Teddy's at the bar, fixing a stiff and dirty martini. Tammy paces the room. He tries to give her the drink, but she won't take it, so Teddy sips it himself.

He looks startled when Boone rings the doorbell.

Looks to Tammy, who looks back at him and shrugs.

Boone waits as Teddy opens the door a crack, the chain link left on. Boone shoves the pistol through the crack and says, "Hi. Can I come in?"

# 120

Yeah, he can.

A gun is its own invitation.

Teddy unhooks the chain lock and opens the door.

Boone goes in and kicks it shut behind him.

Teddy's house is as beautiful as he'd expected. Huge living room with a vaulted ceiling. Expensive custom paint with faux brush techniques. Expensive modern paintings and sculpture, a grand piano.

The center of the room is taken up with a floor-to-ceiling column that's a saltwater aquarium. A startlingly bright panoply of tropical fish circle serenely around the column. Tall green undersea plants stretch up toward the surface and wave like thin fingers in the mild, motor-driven current. At the back of the room, a slider gives a view of a huge spotlighted deck and, beyond that, the open ocean.

"Nice," Boone says.

"Thanks."

"Hi, Tammy."

She glares at him. "What do you want?"

"Just the truth."

"Trust me, you don't want it."

"There's a little girl involved," Boone says. "Now you're going to tell me the truth or, I swear, I'll splatter both of you all over this pretty room."

Teddy walks back toward the bar. "Would you like a drink?" he asks. "You're going to need one."

"Just the story, thanks."

"Suit yourself," Teddy says, "but I'm sitting down. It's been an exhausting couple of days, as you know."

He sits down in the large leather easy chair and looks at the fish in his tank. "Tell him, Tammy. It's almost over now anyway."

Tammy tells her story.

# 121

Tammy grew up in El Cajon, out in East County.

The usual stereotypical stripper back story: Her dad wasn't around a lot; her mom made an unsteady living as a waitress in a local restaurant and usually stayed for a few beers after her shift was over.

She was a lonely little girl. A latchkey kid who made herself instant macaroni and cheese, which she ate while watching celebrity shows on television and dreaming about becoming one of the actresses on the red carpet. It didn't seem likely then—she was skinny and gangly and had red hair, which the boys made fun of.

They stopped making jokes around the time she turned fourteen. Tammy didn't blossom—she *exploded* into a sexuality that seemed to happen overnight and was scary and confusing to her. Suddenly, boys wanted her, and she saw the way that grown men looked at her when she'd go to the restaurant to say hello to her mom. She wanted to say to them, I'm fourteen years old; I'm a kid. But she was afraid to speak to or even look back at them.

A good thing. Men would see the intensity in those incredible green eyes and mistake it for something else.

Okay, she learned to use it, she admits it freely. Why not? High school was a nightmare. She was never good at school—there were diagnoses of dyslexia and ADD—so being an actress wasn't going to happen. She couldn't read a script out loud and never got cast in the Drama Club productions. She thought about being a model, but you don't exactly bump into Eileen Ford in El Cajon, and she couldn't afford the money for photographers to create a portfolio. She did a little modeling for a local "sportswear" catalog and made a couple hundred dollars, but that was about it.

Tammy graduated from high school with a C-minus average, and it looked like waiting tables was her future. She did it for a year or so, enduring the crappy tips, the leers, the comments, and the offers, and then one day when she was twenty, she was walking home in the hundred-plus heat along the flat sunbaked sidewalk and decided that she had to do something, anything, to get out of there. So she took her red hair, amazing green eyes, and long legs, got on a bus to Mira Mesa, walked into a strip club, and auditioned.

She thought it would be hard, but it wasn't so hard, taking her clothes off. Okay, so it wasn't the red carpet; it was a platform and a pole. And yes, it was a cliché. But Tammy learned quickly that if she paused in her dance and cast those eyes out over the front row, she would get tips; if she picked out one guy and trained those cat eyes on him, she could easily get him into the Champagne Room, or the VIP Room, or whatever the hell room where the bigger money got made.

A year or so later, she found her way to Silver Dan's.

A couple of weeks after that, Dan Silver found his way to her.

Of course he did.

The owner of a strip club—in this case, a chain of strip clubs—has a sort of droit du seigneur when it comes to the girls. They don't have to date him, and if they do date him, they don't have to sleep with him, but it's a good professional move if they do.

You sleep with the boss, you don't have to blow the night manager to get a good shift. The bartenders pour your drinks without coming on to you or wanting a cut. The other girls find space for you in front of the mirror. The really creepy customers pick up on the vibe and keep their distance.

Tammy had been around long enough to know that, and even if she hadn't, Angela would have told her. Angela was her best friend at Silver Dan's. They hit it off right away—similar background, similar outlook, same tough attitude. It was Angela who told her that if the boss came calling, she'd better open the gates, or life could get impossible for her at the club.

So she dated Dan.

Yeah, but it was more than that, wasn't it, if she really wants to look at the truth of herself. Dan wasn't just a convenient lay or a good dinner— like most pimps, he was a daddy. He was that fucking father figure she'd been missing. Cliché, cliché, stereotype, and cliché but there it was. He treated her like a daughter and a fuck, incest sans the DNA and felony concerns, made her obey him and wear the clothes he picked out, made her call him "Daddy" as he did her from behind and pulled her hair like you'd jerk on the reins of a recalcitrant filly. She hated it and she loved it.

She started sleeping with Mick Penner as rebellion. He was the opposite of a daddy—a boy-child lady-killer who fucked up and fell in love with her. She'd still come when Dan beckoned—and God knows how many other women he was doing on the side—but she'd go bang Mick and play house with him, and Mick treated her gently and with consideration, and she couldn't get too much of that.

She *was* with Danny the night of the fire. He told her to wait in the car, but she got bored and impatient. She stood outside and smoked a cigarette, but when that was done, she thought, Fuck Danny, and went inside.

What she saw changed her world.

Dirty mattresses on a concrete floor, an old showerhead surrounded by a torn plastic curtain strung on a clothesline, an open toilet in the corner. Random blankets, no sheets, some stained pillows without covers.

The girls were like zombies.

Later, Tammy would learn that these behaviors were symptomatic of severe and repetitive trauma, but that night Tammy just saw a group of young girls looking at her with dead eyes.

Except one.

One little girl came over, threw her arms around Tammy's legs, pressed her head against her thighs, and held on tight.

That was, of course, Luce.

Tammy didn't know what to do. Didn't know how to handle this girl, didn't know who these children were. She guessed at their ages—the oldest seemed to be a young teenager; the youngest couldn't have been more than eight. The girl clutching her legs was probably eleven or twelve. All the girls had brown skin, black hair, dark eyes. They wore cheap clothes that looked like they'd come from the Salvation Army or an AM VETS store. Most were holding some vestiges of childhood or family—a stuffed dog, a plastic flower, a book.

Luce wore a silver chain with a small cross.

Tammy stroked the girl's hair. It was greasy and dirty, but Tammy didn't mind. She stroked the girl's hair and made soft cooing sounds.

Dan didn't.

Dan blew fucking up.

He came down the hallway, saw Tammy in the room, and yelled, "What the fuck are you doing in here? I told you to wait outside!"

Most of the girls threw themselves facedown on their mattresses and did their best to cover their heads with blankets. Luce held tighter to Tammy and pressed her face harder against her legs.

Tammy didn't back down.

"What the fuck am I doing here!" she yelled back. "What the fuck is *this,* Dan?"

Dan grabbed her by the arm and started to haul her out, Luce still clinging to Tammy's legs. Dan stopped and grabbed the girl, trying to peel her off, but Tammy shoved and hit out at him and Dan had to let go of Luce to grab Tammy by the wrists.

"You leave her alone!" Tammy yelled. "Or I'll—"

"You'll what?" Danny asked. "You'll fucking *what?*"

She brought a knee up into Danny's balls.

That was fucking what.

Dan keeled over.

Luce regained her grip on Tammy. One of Dan's bouncers came out of a back room, hoisted Tammy away from the crying girl, hauled her out of the building, and forced her into Dan's car. As he was pushing her out the door, she heard the little girl yelling, *"¡Los campos fresas! ¡Los campos fresas!"*

Dan came out a couple of minutes later and got into the driver's seat. Slapped her across the face. "You *cunt.*"

"You bastard," Tammy said. "Who were those girls? What are you doing with them?"

"They're illegals, all right?" Dan said. "I get them jobs as maids."

"Bull-fucking-*shit,*" Tammy said. "I know what business you're in, Dan."

"That's right," Dan said. "I'm in the sex business, Tammy. I sell sex. You can't handle that?"

"They're *children*!"

"In Mexico? Half of them would be married by now. They'd be churning out babies already."

"Keep telling yourself that, you sick motherfucker."

"They'd be starving back home," Dan said.

"Yeah, they look like they're doing great here," Tammy said. "Fuck you, Dan, I'm calling the cops."

He clamped his hand around her throat, pulled her face close to his, and said, "If you do that, you stupid twat, I'll kill you. And just in case you don't care about your own useless life, think about the kids. Their families owe money to the guys who bring them in. If they don't produce, the snakeheads take it out on their families. *Capisce?*"

She nodded, but he didn't let her go for a few seconds, just to make a point. To make the point further, he unzipped his fly and forced her head down. "You open your mouth, it's for *this*." When he let her up, she could see, through watery eyes, the bouncer loading the girls into an old van.

A few seconds later, flames blew out the windows.

Dan drove her home.

She didn't go to the cops. She went to the insurance company and told them that she saw him set the fire, that she could put him at the scene. It was a mistake, she'd tell Teddy later. She wanted to get back at Dan Silver, and she wanted them to look harder at the fire. Maybe they'd find something that would put them onto what was really happening there.

She did something else.

She looked for Luce.

Tammy went out to the strawberry fields, *los campos fresas,* and looked for the girl. Her first few trips, all she saw were the workers in the fields, and then one day, she left the new strip club she was working at and went straight out to the fields, arriving there shortly before dawn.

She saw a bunch of men leave the fields and walk down to the side of the river, where a stand of tall reeds hid the men from view. She drove down the road to the other side, parked her car, and walked in a little ways.

Tammy waited until all the field-workers had gone away and then went in. A Mexican man with a shotgun went to stop her, but Tammy ignored him and he let her pass. She found Luce on a "bed" of stamped-down reeds. Tammy took some hand wipes out of her bag and helped the girl clean herself off.

Speaking broken Spanish and English, she and the girl talked, but mostly she held the girl and stroked her hair. The man with the shotgun told her she'd have to go, that the pimps would come very soon to take the girls back to where they lived.

"Where do they live?" Tammy asked.

"All over the place. The men move them around," he told her. "They go to different fields all day, or to hidden 'factories,' sometimes to the *mojado* camps at night. But they always bring them to this place, the strawberry fields, at sunrise every day." The local pedophiles had a cute name for it. They called it "The Dawn Patrol."

The man with the shotgun told Tammy again that she had to go.

"Tell her I'll be back," Tammy said. "What's her name?"

The man, Pablo, asked the girl her name.

"Luce."

"Luce, I'm Tammy. I'll come back to see you, okay?"

Tammy did go back, three or four times a week. Pablo always escorted her in, and even the pimps who brought the girls in the van came to tolerate her when they saw that she wasn't going to go to the police. She took Luce—and all the girls—food, clothing, cold medication, books. She took them condoms. She took them female love and affection.

It wasn't enough.

Tammy confided in Angela. Told her all about Luce and the strawberry fields.

"They need medical care," Tammy said. "They need a doctor."

Angela took her to see Teddy. He had done Angela's boobs—she had done him to get the insider discount.

Teddy didn't believe her at first, thought she was a psycho. He felt sorry for her, figured she had been an abused child who had twisted her trauma into delusion. He was going to recommend a good psychiatrist, but Tammy challenged him to go and see for himself.

So Teddy rode up one day with her. He wanted to call the police. Tammy begged him not to, told him why. What she needed, what the girls needed, was a doctor.

"I'm hoping that's you," she said.

It was.

He went back again and again. At first, Pablo was hesitant, and the van drivers absolutely forbade it. But Teddy overcame their resistance with wads of cash and assurances of silence, and the men weren't total animals.

They had *some* compassion, and Teddy convinced them that it was in their interest to have the girls checked for venereal disease, that it was just good business.

"The girls are raped multiple time a day, six days a week," Teddy tells Boone now. "They give them Sundays off. The men pay five to ten dollars to have sex with them. It doesn't sound like this would add up to a lot of money, but multiply it by several locations a day, all over California. Hell, all over the country, more and more. Now you're talking serious money. The variety of potential and actual STDs is *staggering*. No matter what we do, a third of these girls are going to become HIV-positive. And then there's vaginal trauma . . . anal tears. Not to mention the day-to-day garden-variety colds, flu, respiratory infections, hygiene issues. You could set up a clinic there and staff it twenty-four/seven and you'd still be overwhelmed."

But Teddy did what he could.

He did set up a clinic. He rented a full-time room at the motel and stocked it with antibiotics and other drugs, hiding them in locked cabinets, as otherwise the room would be broken into and the drugs stolen. He went up there two, three, five times a week as his schedule allowed, usually with Tammy.

The pimps tolerated them.

As long as they got the girls in and out, as long as the girls met their schedule, as long as nobody breathed a word, it was okay. Just. There was always the threat that the operation would be shut down, and Teddy, no matter how hard he tried to argue, no matter what kind of cash he threw at them, was never, *ever* allowed anywhere near the "safe houses" where the girls lived.

"'Safe houses,'" he says to Boone. "There's a tasty irony. More like petri dishes, fecund hothouses for bacteria. If I could get to them and institute just some basic hygienic procedures, we could eliminate at least half of the chronic diseases they suffer from."

But it was no good. They could never find out where the girls were housed, and they were afraid to push it. And the girls themselves changed all the time. They were shuffled around, disappearing, sometimes returning, new girls arriving every few weeks.

It made Tammy crazy with fear.

Once, Luce went missing for two weeks and Teddy had to sedate

Tammy. When the girl returned, Tammy swore that she couldn't go through that again, that they had to do something.

"She loved the girl," Teddy says. "Do you have kids?"

Boone shakes his head.

"I have three," Teddy says. "By a couple of different wives. You fall in love with them, you know? And the thought of anything happening to them . . ."

She decided to take Luce.

Tammy and Angela decided that they would take the girl and raise her themselves. They knew they just couldn't take her—that would endanger Luce's family back in Guanajuato—so they decided to *buy* her.

What kind of life could Luce have otherwise? *If* she survived the chronic rape, the STDs, the trauma, the exposure, the beatings, the malnutrition, psychological abuse, emotional deprivation, if she lived through her teenage years, then into her twenties, what could she expect? To be moved to an actual brothel? To a sweatshop? If she went through all of that without going to crack or getting hooked on meth, even then, what kind of life would she have?

What's the price of a twelve-year-old girl?

Twenty thousand dollars.

Because they not only had to pay for the price of a lucrative working girl; they also had to pay the always-accruing interest on her debt, the money she owed the smugglers for getting her into the country, and the interest on the debt she owed for room and board.

Twenty large, growing every day.

So Tammy and Angela ramped it up. They worked extra shifts. They used every trick they knew to manipulate men into taking them into the VIP Room. Once inside, they turned on all their charms to make the men fork over big tips.

Every dance, every slide down the pole, every lap they ground themselves on went into the purchase price for Luce.

It wasn't enough.

Teddy gave them the rest of the money.

Tammy went to Danny and *bought* Luce.

Cash on the barrel.

It was good, it was done, and then—

"The lawyers came knocking," Boone says.

Teddy nods.

Danny went ballistic; he was terrified about what might come out in court, never mind just the arson suit; he made all kinds of threats. He told Tammy she could forget about Luce. The women decided to run and take the girl with them. They left their apartments and checked into the Crest Motel, intending to get a train out of town the next morning.

They never made it.

Luce had an sick stomach—she was upset and nervous. The vending machine at the motel was broken, so Tammy walked down to a convenience store to get a soda to try to settle Luce's stomach.

When she got back, Angela was dead and Luce was gone.

Tammy panicked. She was afraid to go to her place, so she went to Angela's, got scared there, too, and called Teddy. He picked her up and took her to Shrink's, then volunteered to go and try to find Luce.

Which he did.

The girl had gone back to the only familiar place she could find.

The strawberry fields.

Where Boone found them.

The rest of the story he knows.

Boone saved Tammy from Dan at the beach below Shrink's and then took her home. He made his deal with Red Eddie that she wouldn't be touched. But Dan figured out something that was worth more to her than her own life, worth more than revenge or even justice for Angela's killing.

Luce.

# 122

"Do you have her now?" Boone asks.

Thinking, you're a total fucking idiot, Daniels. You read both these people so wrong, it's pathetic. You're not looking at a dumb, dishonest stripper and a pervert plastic surgeon. You're looking at two heroes. And the late Angela Hart was a third.

Tammy drops her face into her hands and starts to cry.

Teddy says, "No, they said if everything went well, they'd call late tonight or early tomorrow morning and turn Luce over to us. The deal is that Tammy takes Luce and never comes back."

Dan gets away with having Angela killed, but what's more important? Justice, or a girl's life? If we could talk to Angela, she'd tell us to make that trade. We can't save them all—hell, we can't save *most* of them. But we can save one. One girl gets a life.

What's the life of one little girl worth? Boone asks himself.

A lot.

Everything.

"I can call John Kodani," Boone says. "He'll understand. He'll—"

"No cops," Tammy says through splayed fingers.

"Silver said that if he as much as smells the police," Teddy says, "he'll kill Luce."

He'll kill the three of you anyway, Boone thinks. A man that evil won't keep his word, not to you, not even to Red Eddie. A man who sinks that far into darkness fears nothing, no one, not even God or eternity.

Tammy lifts her head and looks right at Boone. Her emerald eyes are wet with tears, swollen, and rimmed with red. She's been crying a lot since Boone last saw her. *What I've seen.* "I'm begging you," she says. "I'm *begging* you. Leave it alone. Let the girl have a shot at a life."

"He's going to kill you."

"I'll take the chance," Tammy says.

Boone says, "I'll go with you."

"No," Tammy says. "He said just me. Not even Teddy."

"He's setting you up, Tammy."

She shrugs. Then says, "Promise me."

"Promise you what?" Boone asks.

"Promise me you won't call the police," she says. "Promise me you won't interfere."

"Okay."

*"Promise."*

"I promise."

Boone starts to leave. He stops at the door, looks back, and says, "I'm sorry. For what I thought about you both. I was wrong and I'm sorry."

Teddy lifts the martini glass and smiles.

Tammy nods.

Boone looks back through the window at them as he walks to the car. Teddy stands behind the chair with his hands on Tammy's shoulders. They look like worried parents in a hospital waiting room.

Below the house, the ocean smashes against the bluffs in a fit of rage.

# 123

Dave hears the breakers from about two hundred yards away.

He can't see them in the dark, but the sound is unmistakable.

Rhythmic, steady.

Real bombs.

"Esteban!" he yells. "Tell these kids to hold on!"

What was it Boone always said, Dave thinks, that I could surf these waters blindfolded? Well, I hope he was right. You feel surfing more than you see it, but that's on a board, not a glorified rubber raft overloaded with helpless kids.

Doesn't matter, he tells himself.

That's what you have to do.

Surf this boat in.

He guns the engine to get as much speed as he can and prays that it's going to be enough. The last thing he wants to do is get into one of the mackers late, because he'd go over the top for sure and flip the boat. And he has to keep the boat straight, its bow perpendicular to the wave, because if he gets it even a little sideways, it will roll.

So he has to get into the wave right, angle the boat into the left break, and keep it moving when it crashes on the bottom or it will get swamped in the white water.

He feels the wave swelling under the boat, picking it up, and pushing it forward.

It's just another fucking wave, he tells himself. Nothing to it.

"Esteban!"

"Yes?"

"Who's that fucking saint you pray to?"

"San Andrés!"

"Well, hook us up!"

The wave lifts and takes them over the top.

The kids scream.

He's in time. Now he tilts the rudder to break left and move diagonally down the face of the wave. He can feel the water rising behind him, then curling over him, and then they're out of the tube and the boat crashes heavily into the white water.

It bounces hard, and for a second he's afraid he's going to lose it, let it slip out from under him and turn sideways and get rolled, but he manages to keep it straight and it settles into the wash and glides into the mouth of the lagoon.

Dave says a quick prayer of thanks.

To San George Freeth.

"Esteban, take the rudder," Dave says. When the kid, visibly shaken but grinning like a fool, takes over, Dave digs in his pocket for his cell phone.

SOP.

Let the guys know the delivery is on the way.

# 124

Boone drives up the Pacific Coast Highway.

Through all the beach towns, past all the great breaks.

Thinks about all the waves, the rides, the wipeouts. The long leisurely hours in the lineups, or hanging out on the beach, talking story. The cook-outs, grilling fish for tacos, watching the sun go down. The bonfires at night, sitting close to the flame to get warm, watching the stars come out, listening to someone play the guitar or the uke.

Doing things you love, in a place you love, with people you love . . . that's what life *is,* what it *should* be anyway. If you spend your life that way—and I have, Boone thinks—then you should have no regrets when it's over. Maybe just a little sorrow knowing that you're riding your last wave.

If you even know it's your last.

*What I've seen.*

What I've seen, Boone thinks. I've seen the world from the inside of a wave, the universe in a single drop of water.

*There's a world out there you know nothing about.*

The sun will come up soon, The Dawn Patrol will be out, shooting for the big waves, Sunny will be taking her shot. He'd like to be out there with them, would like to be out there forever. But there are some sunrises you have to see alone.

Boone turns inland from the ocean and heads for the strawberry fields. He's on The Dawn Patrol.

# 125

Johnny Banzai and Steve Harrington sit in their car and wait.

Below them, an old van makes its way down the narrow dirt road to a clearing at the edge of Batiquitos Lagoon.

"You think that's them?" Harrington asks.

Johnny shrugs.

Since Dave's call, Johnny doesn't know what is what. He doesn't know anything about anything anymore. The call was surreal. "It's Dave. I'm coming into Batiquitos Lagoon with a load of wetbacks. Johnny, they're *kids.*"

But he bets it's them. It's four o'clock in the morning; there's not a lot of reason to be driving a van down to the lagoon. Unless you're picking up something you're not supposed to be picking up.

He lifts the night scope and scans the lagoon.

A few minutes later, he sees the boat.

"Jesus God," he murmurs, handing the scope to Harrington.

"They're kids," Harrington says. "Little girls."

Johnny takes the glasses back and counts seven little girls, a young male Hispanic, and Dave.

"You want to take them here?" Harrington asks.

"Fuck no."

"What if we lose them?"

"Then I'll commit ritual seppuku," Johnny says.

"What's that?" Harrington asks. "Some sort of Jap thing?"

"You should read a book every once in a while," Johnny replies. He turns the glasses onto the van and can make out the license plate. He calls it and a description of the van into the Sex Crimes Unit waiting on the 5.

Then he turns back to the boat, which is making a gentle, perfect landing onshore.

# 126

Dave hops out of the Zodiac.

The ground feels funny under his feet.

"I thought I was delivering herb," he says to the guy who gets out of the van, a cute little shit named Marco.

"You thought wrong," Marco says. "You got a problem?"

"No problem," Dave says, because the guy is holding a wicked-looking little machine gun under one arm. "Just tell Eddie I'm out."

"*You* tell him," Marco says. He reaches into his pocket, pulls out a fat envelope, and hands it Dave. "Help me get the merchandise into the van."

"Do it yourself," Dave says, stuffing the envelope into his jacket. "I'm done."

"Whatever, bro."

Another guy gets out of the van and starts herding the girls into it. They go obediently, passively, like they're used to being moved around.

"Jesus, they stink!" Marco says. "What'd you do with them?"

"Seasick," Dave says. "It was a little rough out there, bro. And you might have let me know I was driving people. I would have been better prepared. You know, life jackets, shit like that?"

"If I had told you," Marco says, "would you have gone?"

"No."

"So?"

"What do they do now?" Dave asks. "They're like maids or something like that?"

"Yeah," Marco says. "Okay, something like that. Look, much as I'd like to stand around and shoot the shit . . ."

"Yeah," Dave says.

He goes back to the Zodiac, praying that Johnny got his call. He casually opens his cell phone and sees the text message: "Back-paddle." Dave starts the engine, then takes the boat to the other side of the lagoon, where he left his truck. When he lands the boat, he says to Esteban, "Disappear, dude."

"What?"

"*Va te,*" Dave says. "*Pinta le.* Get the fuck out of here."

Esteban looks at him for a second, then gets off the boat and disappears into the reeds.

Dave kneels, bends over the edge of the boat, and throws up.


# 127


They follow the van out to the 5, then north to the 78, and east to the town of Vista, where the van pulls up to a nondescript house in a lower-middle-class neighborhood.

Nothing special, just your basic suburban cul-de-sac.

A garage door opens and the van pulls in.

Johnny gets on the radio.

The Sex Crimes Unit is there in five minutes, with a SWAT team. The SCU lieutenant is a woman named Terry Gilman, who used to work homicide and then jumped from the frying pan into the shit fire. She walks up to Johnny's car.

"Where'd you get this, Johnny?" she asks.

"You're looking good, Terry."

She straps a vest on, checks the load in her .9mm, and says, "If we don't find evidence, will your source testify?"

"Let's find the evidence," Johnny says as he gets out of the car.

"Sounds good to me." Terry Gilman is *pissed.* She hates snakeheads in general and snakeheads who run children in particular. She's almost hoping this thing goes south so she can use the nine on one of them.

They hit the front door like Normandy.

A SWAT guy swings the heavy ram and the door cracks open. Johnny is the first guy through. He ignores the adults scrambling to get away— SWAT will wrap them up. He just keeps pushing through until he comes to a door that opens to a basement stairway.

Pistol in front of him, he goes down the stairs.

It's a dormitory, a barracks of sorts.

Dirty mattresses are set side by side on the concrete slab. A rough open shower in one corner, an open toilet in the other. Blankets everywhere. A few dirty, stained pillows. An old TV set hooked up to a video player.

Kids' movies.

A few children's books in Spanish.

The girls from the boat have jammed themselves into one corner. They stand there holding one another, staring at him in sheer terror.

"It's all right," Johnny says to them, lowering his pistol. "It's all going to be all right now."

Maybe it is, he thinks.

I have *these* kids.

But where are the children who *were* living here?

# 128

Boone drives past the reed bed and keeps going until he finds a place where he can turn off and see the fields and the road.

Now he sits and looks at the fields, silver and dewy as the sun starts to rise behind the hills to the east. On the far side of the fields, where they dip to meet the river, the reed bed stands like a wall, sealing the fields off from the rest of the world, blending into a line of trees that old man Sakagawa planted as a windbreak so many years ago.

On the other side of the fields, on a small rise near its eastern edge, old Sakagawa's house sits in a small grove of lemon and walnut trees. The old man will be getting up soon, Boone thinks, if he isn't already, sitting at his table with his tea and his rice with pickled vegetables.

The workers are already coming out, filing onto the fields with their tools over their shoulders, like the rifles of soldiers moving out on a early-morning mission. An army of phantoms, they come from nowhere. They hide at night in the creases and folds of the San Diego landscape, emerge in the soft light of the early dawn, coming into the open to work, and then disappear again at dusk into the wrinkles and seams, the last unwanted places.

They're the invisible, the people we don't see or choose *not* to see, even in the bright light of day. They're the unspoken truth, the unseen reality behind the California dream. There before we wake up, gone before we fall asleep again.

Boone settles back and watches them start to work. They fan out in well-organized lines, practiced, almost ritualistic, silent. They work with their backs bent and their heads down. They work slowly, in a methodic rhythm. There's no hurry to get done. The field will be here all day, was here yesterday, will be here tomorrow.

But not for many tomorrows, Boone thinks. He wonders if these men know that someday soon they will not be out here. It will be the bulldozers and road graders that will come out at dawn, machines, not men who work like a collective machine. Exhaust fumes instead of sweat.

In place of the fields, there will be luxury homes and condominiums. A shopping plaza or a mall. In place of the workers, there will be residents and shoppers and diners. And these men will have disappeared to some other netherworld.

Boone feels a bit of welcome warmth come through the car window.

The sun has crested the mountains.

# 129

Johnny goes back upstairs.

Lieutenant Gilman is standing beside the prisoners, who are sitting on the floor, their arms cuffed behind them. Three men, two women.

"Whoever they had here," Johnny whispers to her, "they're gone."

She looks to him and Harrington. "Do what you need to do."

Harrington steps over to one of the skells, who made the mistake of making eye contact. He lifts him to his feet. "What's your name?"

"Marco."

"Let's you and I go have a little chat, Marco," Harrington says. He walks him down the hall, toward the bedrooms. "You don't have to come, Johnny."

"No, I'm in," Johnny says.

He follows Harrington down the hallway, into one of the bedrooms, and closes the door behind him. Harrington bounces Marco off the wall, catches him on the rebound, and knees him in the balls. He lifts his head and says, "I am *not* fucking with you, asswipe. You're going to tell me where those kids are, or you're going to pull a gun on me and I'm going to have to paint the wall with your brains. And that's my *second* shot. My first goes into your gut. ¿*Comprende, amigo?*"

"I speak English," Marco says.

"Well you'd better *start* speaking it," Harrington says. He pulls his pistol and jams it into Marco's stomach.

"They just left," Marco says.

"Left for *where*?"

"The fields."

"*What* fields?"

"The strawberry fields."

Johnny feels his skin go cold. "*What? What* did you say?"

"The strawberry fields," Marco says. "The old Sakagawa strawberry fields."

Johnny feels dizzy, like the room is spinning. Shame flows through his blood. He lurches to the door and shoves it open. Staggers down the hall, through the living room, and out the door. He leans on the car and bends over to catch his breath.

It's coming on dawn.

# 130

The first faint rays of sunlight hit Pacific Beach, warming, if only psychologically, the crowd of photographers, magazine people, surf company execs, lookie-loos, and hard-core surfers who stand shivering on Pacific Beach Point in the cold morning, waiting for the light.

The bluff they're standing on is historic ground. Surfers have been riding that reef break almost since George Freeth, and it was way back in the 1930s, when this was still a Japanese strawberry field, that Baker and Paskowitz and some of the other San Diego legends built a shack on this bluff and stored their boards here and proudly adopted the name that the farmers gave them—"the Vandals."

Just off to the north, the big swell is pounding the reef. Sunny stands at the edge of the crowd, her board beside her like a crusader's shield, and watches the sunlight turn the indistinct gray shapes into definitive waves.

Big waves.

The biggest she's ever seen.

Mackers.

Thunder crushers.

Dreams.

She glances around her. Half the big-wave riders in the world are here, most of them professionals with fat sponsorships and double-digit mag covers behind them. Worse, most of them have Jet Skis with them. Jet Skis with trained partners who will pull them into the waves. Sunny doesn't have the cash for that. She's one of the few paddle-in surfers out here.

And the only woman.

"Thank you, Kuan Yin," she says softly. She isn't going to bitch about what she lacks; she's going to be grateful about what makes her unique. The only woman, and a woman who's going to paddle into the big waves.

She picks up her board and heads down toward the water.

# 131

Dave's out there already.

He sits out behind the massive break on a Jet Ski, ready to pull people out if they need it. It's his sacrifice, his penance, not riding the big waves. He hasn't slept—he's exhausted—but somehow he felt that he had to be here, but not surf.

There was just something that felt wrong about it, going out there and having the time of his life when he's seriously questioning what his life has even become. He can't shake the image of the girls huddled in the hold of the boat—who they were, where they were headed, whether or not Johnny managed to intercept them.

And then there's all that. Johnny's going to want some questions answered, and the answers are going to blow up life as they know it.

Which maybe isn't such a bad thing, Dave thinks as he checks his equipment—mask, snorkel, fins—things he might need if he has to get off the ski and dive into the soup.

Maybe this life needs a little blowing up.

A change.

Even if Johnny doesn't ask the questions, Boone will.

But where the fuck is Boone? He should be out here with me and Tide and Sunny, should at least be here for Sunny, backing her up, helping her deal with the big-name Jet Ski crews that will try to block her out.

Boone should be here for her.

# 132

The girls look like ghosts.

Boone spots them coming out of the trees. The last of the morning mist hugs their legs and mutes their footsteps. They don't talk to one another, walk side by side, or chat and laugh like girls going to school. Instead, they walk single file, almost in lockstep, and they look straight ahead or down at the ground.

They look like prisoners.

They are. Now Boone sees two men walking behind them. They're not carrying guns—at least Boone doesn't see any—but they're clearly herding the girls along. It doesn't take much effort, as the girls seem to know where they're going. And the men are behind the girls, not in front of them.

It's a drill, a routine.

The men in the fields look up as the girls come out of the tree line. Some of the workers stop their work and stare; others lower their heads quickly and go back to work, as if they've seen something shameful.

Then Boone spots her.

Thinks he does anyway. It's hard to tell, but it sure looks like Luce. She wears a thin blue vinyl jacket with a hood she hasn't bothered to pull up. Her long black hair glistens in the mist. Her jeans are torn at the knees and she wears old rubber beach sandals. She moves like a zombie, shuffling steadily ahead.

Then she turns.

All the girls do—as if on a conveyor belt, they turn away from the strawberry fields and toward the bed of reeds.

Boone gets out of the car, stays as low as he can, and runs toward the trees.

I know I promised you, Tammy, he thinks. But there are some promises you can't keep, some promises you shouldn't.

He picks up his pace.

# 133

Old men don't sleep much.

Sakagawa is already awake and now sits at the small wooden table in his kitchen and impatiently waits for first light. There is much work to be done, and the endless battle against the birds and insects to be fought. It is a daily battle, but if Sakagawa were to be honest with himself, he would admit that he actually enjoys it, that it is one thing that keeps him going.

So he sits, sips his tea, and watches the light flow onto his fields like a slow flood of water. From his vantage point, he can just make out some of the workers, the Mexicans who come just as the Nikkei had come so many years ago, to work the land that the white man didn't think he wanted, coated as it was with salt spray and blasted by the sea winds. But the Nikkei were used to salt and wind from the home islands; they knew how to farm "worthless" land along the sea. And from the salted soil, the old man thinks now, we grew strawberries . . . and doctors and lawyers and businessmen. And judges and politicians.

Maybe *these* workers will do the same.

He bends over slowly to pull on his rubber boots, which keep his old feet dry in the damp early-morning fields. When he straightens up again, his grandson is standing there.

"Grandfather, it's Johnny. John Kodani."

"Of course. I know you."

Johnny bows deeply. His grandfather returns the gesture with a short, stiff bow, as much as his ninety-year-old body can muster. Then Johnny pulls out one of the old wooden chairs that have been in this kitchen for as long as he can remember and sits down across from the old man.

"Would you like tea?" Sakagawa asks.

Johnny wouldn't, but to refuse would be brutally rude, and with what he has to tell the old man, he wants to exercise every gentle kindness. "That would be nice."

The old man nods. "It's a cold morning."

"It is."

The old man takes a second cup and pours the strong green tea into it, then slides it to Johnny. "You're a lawyer."

"A policeman, Grandfather."

"Yes, I remember." Perhaps, he thinks, it is good that the Nikkei are now police.

"This is very good tea," Johnny says.

"It's garbage," the old man says, even though he has it specially imported from Japan every month. "What brings you? I am always happy to see you, but . . ."

*I haven't been here for months*, Johnny thinks. *I've been "too busy" to stop by for a drink of tea, or to bring his great-grandchildren for him to see. Now I come by at five in the morning with news that will break his heart.*

"Grandfather . . ." Johnny begins. Then he chokes on his own words.

"Has someone died?" the old man asks. "Your family, are they well?"

"They're fine, Grandfather," Johnny says. "Grandfather, down by the old creek, where we used to play when we were kids . . . Have you been down there lately?"

The old man shakes his head.

"It's very far to walk," he says. "A bunch of old reeds. I tell the men to clean up the garbage people toss from the road." He shakes his head again. *It is hard to understand the disrespect of some people.* "Why do you ask?"

"I think people . . . your men . . . your foreman are doing something down there."

"Doing what?"

Johnny tells him. The old man has a hard time even understanding what his grandson is saying, and then he says, "That's impossible. Human beings do not do such things."

"I'm afraid they do, Grandfather."

"Here?" the old man says. "On my farm?"

Johnny nods. He looks down at the floor, unable to face his grandfather. When he looks up again, the old man's face is streaked with tears. They run down the creases in his face like small streams in narrow gullies.

"Did you come to stop them?" the old man asks.

"Yes, Grandfather."

"I will go with you." He starts to get up.

"No, Grandfather," Johnny says. "It's better you stay here."

"Those are my fields!" the old man yells. "I am responsible!"

"You're not, Grandfather," Johnny says, fighting back tears himself. "You're not responsible, and . . ."

"I'm too old?"

"It's my job, Grandfather."

The old man composes his face and looks Johnny in the eye. "Do your job."

Johnny gets up and bows.

Then he walks out of the kitchen and down into the fields.

# 134

The air smells like strawberries.

The acrid smell rushes through Boone's nose as he breathes heavily, sprinting toward the trees, hoping not to be seen. He makes it into the tree line, then turns west toward the reeds. He can run more upright now, in the cover of the trees, and he makes it quickly to where the tree line ends and the reeds begin.

The reeds are taller than he is. They loom over him, vaguely threatening, the tops blowing in the breeze as if waving him back. He pushes his way in and is soon lost in thick foliage. He can hear voices in front of him, though—men's voices, speaking in Spanish.

The last time you did this, he thinks, you got beaten half to death. He takes the pistol from his waistband and keeps it ready in his right hand. Pushing back reeds with his left, he plows ahead until he makes it to the creek.

He jumps in and wades toward the caves.

# 135

Sunny can't paddle into this surf.

The beach break is totally closed out. There isn't space enough between waves or sets to paddle out there, and the waves are too big to paddle over.

She comes out of the water and moves about two hundred yards south, between breaks, and paddles out onto the shoulder, then starts back north on the far side of the break. She's not alone in this maneuver—all the Jet Ski crews are out there making the same approach, buzzing around like giant, noisy water bugs. She paddles strong, smooth, and hard, her wide shoulders an advantage for a change.

The Jet Ski crews linger farther out, giving them room for the high-speed run-up into the wave.

The biggest wave Sunny's ever seen looms up behind her, with another after that. She paddles herself into perfect position for the next wave. It rolls toward her, a blue wall of water, its whitecaps snapping like cavalry guidons in the stiff offshore wind.

A beautiful wave.

*Her* wave.

She lies down on her board, takes a deep breath, and starts to paddle.

# 136

The shame is unbearable.

The Sakagawa family name is disgraced.

To think this was happening on my land, the old man thinks, in my fields, under my nose, and I am such a fool as not to have seen it.

It is intolerable.

There is only one way, the old man decides, to redeem the family's honor. He looks around the kitchen to find a suitable knife, then doubts that he has the physical strength to do what is necessary with a knife.

So he takes up the old shotgun, the one he uses against the birds.

It is not ideal, but it will have to do.

# 137

Boone crawls up the edge of the creek bed and looks over at the little clearing where he had his confrontation with the *mojados*.

Now Pablo's on guard, an ax handle in his fist, ushering about twenty field-workers into a ragged line in the clearing in front of the caves. One of the men who herded the girls walks up the line, collecting money. The workers pull dirty, wrinkled bills from their pockets, and don't look at the man as they give him the money. There are a couple of white guys in line. They don't look like farmworkers, just guys who like to do little girls.

The girls go into the little caves that have been chopped into the reeds. A couple of the girls sit down and just stare into nothingness; a couple of the others arrange their "beds." Boone crawls to the far edge of the clearing and sees Luce take off her thin blue jacket, carefully spread it out on the ground, then sit down, one leg crossed over the other—a young female Buddha—and wait.

For waves of men to fall on top of her and break inside her and then recede. And then the next wave comes in, and the next, every morning, inevitable as the tide. A perpetual cycle of rape, for as long as her short life lasts.

*There's a world out there you know nothing about.*

Tammy steps into the clearing.

She comes from the other side, from the road by the motel, the way Boone tried to come before Pablo laid him out.

Luce sees Tammy, springs up, and runs into her arms. Tammy holds her tightly. Then she slides down, squats in front of the girl, and looks her in the eye. "I've come to take you away," Tammy says. "Forever, this time."

Good, Boone thinks. Go, take the kid with you.

Give each other some kind of life.

Then Dan Silver comes into the clearing.

# 138

Dan says, "So we have a deal?"

"I just want Luce," Tammy says. "You'll never hear from me again."

"Sounds good," Dan says. He wears his trademark outfit—black shirt, black jeans, black cowboy boots. "Take her and go."

Tammy puts her arm around Luce's shoulder and leads her from the clearing, through the path trodden in the reeds, toward the road.

Boone loses sight of them as they go into the reeds.

What he does see is Dan wait a second, then walk into the reeds behind them.

# 139

Sunny takes off.

She paddles hard, two more strokes that take her onto the lip of the wave; then she shifts to her knees, then smoothly into her squat as she—

Goes over the edge.

She's strong in the wave, beautifully balanced; she's picked the exact line, then—

A Jet Ski zooms in and swings Tim Mackie into the wave.

If Mackie sees Sunny, he doesn't acknowledge it. He cuts right into her line.

Sunny has to pull up. She drops to her stomach on the board, but she's off-line and it's too late to paddle back over the crest of the wave. She tries to duck her nose up and under, but the wave won't let her and it takes her backward.

Over the falls.

Her board squirts into the air as she falls headfirst.

# 140

Boone crashes through the reeds.

Toward the sound of footsteps.

He can't really see them, just vague forms through the reeds. Then he gets a glimpse of Dan, who pulls his gun from the waistband of his jeans and looks around to pinpoint the sound of the footsteps coming at him.

"Run!" Boone yells.

Tammy pushes Luce in front of her, turns, and sees Dan. Then, with a dancer's grace, she whirls, her long leg snaps up, and she places a kick into the back of Dan's head.

It sends him reeling, but he stays on his feet.

"Run, Luce!" Tammy yells. "Run and don't stop running!"

But Luce doesn't run.

She won't leave Tammy, not again.

Dan recovers the grip on his pistol and aims it at Tammy, who puts herself between him and the girl.

Boone's almost there.

Tammy's too close for Boone to risk a shot, especially on the run in the confused tangle of the reeds, so he just dives at Dan, who turns the gun away from Tammy and on Boone and fires just as Tammy kicks his hand.

Boone plows into him waist-high and drives him backward. Dan can't get his hand turned to press the pistol into Boone, so he clubs him with the butt, slamming it into the back of Boone's head and neck, again and again.

Boone feels a searing, burning pain.

The world turns red and he feels like he's somersaulting.

A bad, bloody wipeout.

# 141

Remember when you were a kid in the swimming pool and you'd see how long you could hold your breath underwater?

This isn't that.

Getting caught in the impact zone is different from holding your breath in a swimming pool. For one thing, you can't come up; you're being rolled over the bottom—bounced, somersaulted, slammed, and twisted. The ocean is filling your nasal cavities and sinuses with freezing salt water. And it isn't a matter of how long you can hold your breath; it's a matter of *whether* you can hold your breath long enough for the wave to let you up, because if you can't—

You drown.

And that's just the beginning of your problems, because waves don't come to the party alone; they usually bring a crew. Waves tend to come in sets, usually three, but sometimes four, and a really fecund mother of a set might bring a litter of six.

So even if you make it through the first wave, you might have time to take a gasp of air before the next wave hits you, and the next, and so on and so forth until you drown.

The rule of thumb is that if you don't manage to extricate yourself from the impact zone by the third wave, your friends will be doing a paddle-out for you in the next week or so. They'll be out there in a circle on their boards, saying nice things about you, maybe singing a song or two, definitely tossing a flower lei out onto the wave, and it's very cool, but you won't be there to enjoy any of it because you'll be dead.

Sunny's in the Washing Machine, and it rolls her, tumbles her, somersaults her until she doesn't know up from down. Which is another one of the dangers of the impact zone: You lose track of which way is up and which way is down. So when the wave finally lets you up, you budget that last bit of air for the plunge to the sweet surface, only to hit rock or sand instead. Then, unless you're a really experienced waterman, you just give up and breathe in the water. Or there's already another wave on top of you.

Either way, you're pretty much screwed.

Keep your head, Sunny tells herself as she plummets. Keep your head and you live. You've trained for this moment all your life. You're a *waterman.*

All those mornings, those early evenings, training with Boone and Dave and High Tide and Johnny. Walking underwater, clutching big rocks. Diving down to lobster pots and holding on to the line until you felt your lungs were going to burst, then holding on a little longer. While those assholes grinned at you—waiting for the girlie to give up.

Except you didn't give up.

She feels a jerk upward and realizes that her board has popped to the surface.

"Headstoned," in surf jargon.

Dave will be out there already, watching for the board to pop up. He's on his way now. She forces herself to do a crunch, not to release the leash but so that if she does hit bottom, she'll take the blow on her shoulders and not on her head, snapping her neck.

She hits all right, hard, but on her shoulders. The wave somersaults her three or four times—she loses count—but then it lets go of her and she pushes up, punches to the surface, and takes a deep breath of beautiful air.

# 142

Boone gets his arms around Dan's arms and pins them to his side. Dan still has his gun in his hand, but he can't raise it to shoot.

Dan slams three hard knee strikes into Boone's ribs, driving the breath from Boone's body. Boone gasps but doesn't let go. To let go is to die, and he's not ready for that yet. He can feel his own blood, hot and sticky, running down his face.

He pivots on one hip, turning Dan around toward the river. Then he starts walking, holding tightly to Dan, pushing him toward the water. Dan tries to dig and fight, but Boone has the momentum. Dan rears his neck back, then slams it forward, head-butting Boone on the bridge of the nose.

Boone's nose breaks and blood gushes out.

But he holds on and pushes Dan toward the bank of the river. He plants his feet, pivots again, and crashes into the muddy water on top of Dan. Boone releases his grip, finds Dan's chest, and pushes him down. He can feel Dan's back hit the muddy bottom. Then Boone holds on and pushes. It's a matter now of who can hold his breath the longest, and he figures that's a contest he can win.

But he's losing blood fast, and with the blood, his strength.

He feels Dan wrap a leg around him and he tries to fight it, but Dan doesn't panic under the water and gets his leg locked around Boone's. Then Dan turns his own hips and spins. Boone's too weak to counter it, and Dan flips him under. Then Dan sits up, on top of Boone, grabs him around the throat, and pushes down hard.

Boone arches his back and tries to buck Dan off him, but he can't do it. He feels weak, and tired, and then very sleepy. His lungs scream at him to open his mouth and gasp. Take a nice deep breath of anything, even if it's water.

His brain tells him to give up. Go to sleep, end the pain.

In his mind, he's in the ocean.

A giant wave, a mountain, curls over his head.

Suspends in time for a second.

Hangs there, as if deciding.

Then it breaks on him.

Ka-boom.

# 143

Johnny Banzai charges into the clearing.

His badge is clipped to his jacket, his service revolver in his hand.

Harrington and the county people are right behind him, but Johnny has demanded he go in first.

Family fucking honor.

He goes in hard and fast, unconcerned with safety. He heard a gunshot in the distance and doesn't know what the hell is going on, but he hits the clearing ready for whatever it is.

Some of the men are already running. Others stand there looking startled and confused. Johnny doesn't care about the *mojados*—he sees three younger guys, better dressed, running away toward a line of trees, and young girls, looking around, milling in confusion.

Then he hears another gunshot.

It sounds like it's coming from the other side of the reeds, down along the river.

Johnny calls for an ambulance and sprints toward the sound.

# 144

Boone feels Dan's grip loosen, then let go; then Dan's body slides off him into the water. A slough of blood pillows around Boone's face. He pushes to the surface and sees, like a weird dream, an old Japanese man standing at the edge of the river.

A shotgun in his trembling hands.

In the distance, Boone hears yelling, sirens . . . but maybe it's his head playing games with him.

He crawls to the riverbank and pulls himself up.

Then he hears something else.

A woman crying.

A howl of ineffable pain.

# 145

Sunny looks up and sees that she's going to have to take another wave or two on her head, but it's okay, because she's in a good spot, close to the base of the waves, away from the point of maximum impact. But now she does release her leash, because the board is going to go in with the wave and she doesn't want to go with it.

She takes the two waves, then the set ends and Dave pulls her onto the Jet Ski.

"That kook," Dave says, "jumped in on you."

"I saw."

He takes her onto the shore.

People are running up the beach, including some lifeguards with medical equipment. She waves them off. "I'm okay. I'm good."

But Dave is already striding over to where Tim Mackie is running his pie hole to his entourage and some surf press.

"Yo, kook," Dave says. "Yeah, *you*. I'm talking to you."

"You got a problem, brah?" Mackie asks. He looks surprised. Like, People do not have problems with Tim Mackie.

"No, you have a problem," Dave says. "You could have killed her."

"Didn't see her, bro."

High Tide steps into it. "You should get your eyesight checked, then, *bruddah*."

"You don't do that shit on my beach," Dave says.

"This is your beach?"

"That's right," Dave says. He moves in, ready to separate Mackie's head from his body. But Tide steps in front of him. Sunny steps in front of both of them and pushes the boys aside.

"I can take care of myself. Thanks, but I don't need you to big-brother me."

"I'd do the same," Dave says, "if it was Boone or—"

"I can take care of myself."

Great, she thinks as the crowd stares at her. I wanted the wave of the day; instead, I got the wipeout of the day and a hassle with golden boy Tim Mackie.

"That wasn't cool," she says.

"Sorry," Mackie says. "My bad."

But he has this smirk on his face.

"A-hole," she says.

He laughs at her.

There's only one response to that. She picks up her board and starts back down the beach, to the point where she can paddle out again. She can hear the crowd murmuring words to that effect. "She's going out again. Do you believe it? After that? The chick's going back out there."

Damn right, she thinks, the chick is going back out there.

Going back out there to take the biggest wave.

# 146

Johnny Banzai runs.

It's tough going through the heavy reeds, which cut his face and slice at his arms as he tries to beat them back in front of him.

Then he hears, as if from a far distance, a woman's keening.

# 147

Luce lies in Tammy's lap.

Tammy strokes the little girl's hair and sobs. Her hands are hot and sticky with the girl's blood, which runs from the little hole in her neck.

"Stop it," Tammy says. "Stop it now."

Tammy presses her hand on Luce's neck, but the blood bubbles around it. She feels stupid, and weak, and dizzy and there's pain somewhere in her body, but she can't figure out where, and Luce's eyes are wide and she can't hear her breath and the bleeding just won't stop. She hears a man's voice saying, "I've got her."

She looks up and Daniels is there, trying to take Luce from her. Tammy holds her tighter.

"I've got her," Boone says.

"She's dead."

"No, she's not."

Not yet, Boone thinks. The girl is in really bad shape—she's bleeding out, going into shock—but she's still alive.

It's like a dream in the waking moments, part real, part illusion. Everything is still at a distance, as if from the wrong end of a telescope, and he feels as if he's wrapped in cotton, but he knows he has to keep moving if the girl is going to live.

The old Japanese man is already taking his jacket off.

Boone takes it and wraps it around Luce. Then he kneels beside her, runs his hand up her neck, finds the little entrance wound, and presses his thumb into it. He picks her up with the other arm, cradles her against his chest, and starts to move back through the reeds, toward the road, where an ambulance can reach them.

"Stay with us, Luce," he says. "Stay with us."

But the girl's eyes are glassy.

Her eyelids flutter.

# 148

Sunny wipes the spray from her eyes and looks again.

She saw what she saw.

About fifty yards out but coming fast.

Waves generally come in sets of three, and they've done the three. But every once in a while, a set has a fourth. This bonus wave is a freak—bigger, stronger, meaner.

A mutant.

Known among waterman as the "Oh My God Wave."

Which is what Sunny says as she sees it.

"Oh . . . my . . . God."

The wave of a lifetime.

*My* lifetime, Sunny thinks. My shot at the life I want, barreling right at me. I'm in the perfect spot at the perfect time. She rises up on her hips to look around and see what the Jet Ski crews are doing. They're lying out on the shoulder, waiting for the next set.

Well, the next set is here, boys, she thinks as she sees Mackie's Jet Ski start forward, easily fast enough to steal this wave from her. But then she sees High Tide paddle out between Mackie's ski and her. Golden boy Tim is going to have to go through him, and he *isn't* going to go through him. Not High Tide.

Normally, that would bother her, but she made her point on the beach and she's over it. It's only The Dawn Patrol looking out for one another and she accepts that.

This wave is mine, she thinks as she lies down on her board, turns it in, and points it toward shore. She starts paddling hard, looking once over her shoulder to see the big wave kick up behind her. She lowers her head as she feels the wave pick up the board, then lift it like a splinter, and then—

She's on top of the world.

She can see it all—the ocean, the beach, the city behind it, the green hills behind the city. She can see the crowd on the beach, see them watching her, see the photogs aiming the big cameras on their tripods. She can see a little boat moving in, photographers on board, getting close enough for shots but staying out of her line. Overhead, a helicopter zooms in and she knows the video guys are up there, ready to get her ride.

If I ride it, she thinks as she gets to her knees, ready to push up into her stance.

*If* hell.

No if about it.

Then she stops thinking.

The time for thought is over; now it has to be all instinct and action.

The nose of the board drops suddenly and she pushes up to her feet, planting them solidly, her calf muscles tensed. Time seems to stop as she's suspended for a second on the top of the wave. She thinks, I'm too late. I missed it. Then—

The board plunges down.

She leans right, just enough to catch the line, not enough to tip her into the wave and a horrible wipeout. She throws her arms out for balance, bends her knees for speed, and then she's off, down the face of this giant wave, her hair flying behind her like a personal pennant as she turns her feet right a little and cuts up higher into the wave, then plunges back down with incredible speed.

Too much speed.

The board bucks and bounces off the water and she's in the air for a second, the board a good foot beneath her. She lands on it, losing her balance, going sideways, headfirst toward the face of the wave.

The crowd on the beach groans.

It's going to be a bad one.

Sunny feels herself going, her shot getting away from her, and she cranks to the left, squats low, and rights herself as the wave crests over, and then—

She's in the green room, totally inside the wave. There is nothing else, just her and the wave, her in the wave, *her* wave, her life.

The watchers on the beach lose sight of her. They're holding their collective breath because all they can see is wave, the incredibly brave chick is in there somewhere, and it's an open question whether she'll come out.

Then a blast of white water shoots sideways out of the tube and the woman shoots out, still on her feet, her left hand touching the back of the wave, and the crowd breaks into a cheer. They're screaming for her, yelling for her as she cuts back up on the top of the wave again.

She's flying now and she uses the momentum to crest the top of the wave.

She's in the air, high over the wave, and as she jumps off the board, she does a full somersault before she hits the water on the far side of the wave. When she pops up, Dave is there on a Jet Ski. She grabs onto the sled, pulls herself on, pulls her board on, and lets him take her in.

The crowd on the beach is waiting for her.

She's mobbed by photographers, writers, surf company execs.

It was the ride of the day, they tell her.

No, she thinks.

It was the ride of a lifetime.

# 149

It's surreal.

What Johnny sees in the reeds.

Boone Daniels staggers toward him, a girl in his arms, his chest soaked with blood, more blood running down the side of his head.

"Boone!" Johnny yells.

Boone looks at Johnny with glassy-eyed, faint recognition and stumbles toward him, holding the girl out like a drowning man lifting a child up toward a lifeboat. Now Johnny can see Boone's thumb pressed deep into a wound on the child's neck.

Johnny takes the little girl from him, replacing his own thumb for Boone's. Boone looks at him, says, "Thanks, Johnny," and then crashes heavily, face-first, to the ground.

# 150

Waves.

Alpha waves, energy-transport phenomena, gentle vibrations run through Boone's jacked-up brain as Rain Sweeny paddles out through a gentle beach break, ducks under an incoming wave, and pops out the other side.

She shakes the water from her blond hair and smiles.

It's a beautiful day, the sky a cloudless blue, the water green as a spring meadow. Crystal Pier sparkles in the shimmering sunlight.

Rain looks up at the pier and waves.

Boone stands at the window of his cottage, smiles, and waves back, and then he's in the water, swimming toward her in smooth, easy strokes, the cool water sliding along his skin, a caress that eases the pain, which is swiftly becoming mere memory, a dream of a past life that seemed real but was only a dream.

Rain reaches out her hand and pulls him to her and then he's sitting on his own board next to her, rising and falling in the gentle swell. The Dawn Patrol sits off behind them, farther out on the shoulder. Sunny and Dave, Hang and Tide and Johnny. Even Cheerful is out this morning, and Pete, and Boone can hear them talking and laughing, and then a wave comes in.

It builds from far away, lifts and rises and rolls as it seems to take an eternity to crest, and then Rain smiles at him again, lies down, and starts to paddle, her arms and shoulders strong and graceful, and she moves into the wave with ease.

Boone paddles after her to catch the wave and ride it with her, all the way in to the beach, except, as he looks ahead, there is no shore, only an endless blue ocean and a wave that rolls forever.

He paddles hard, trying to catch her, desperate to catch her, but he can't. She's too strong, the wave is too fast, and he can make no headway. It makes no sense to him: He's Boone Daniels; there is no wave he cannot catch, but he can't catch this wave, and then he's crying, in rage and frustration, until his chest aches and big salty tears pour down his face to return to the sea and he gives up and lies on his board.

Exhausted, heartbroken.

Rain turns to him and smiles.

Says, This isn't your wave.

Her smile turns to sunshine and she's gone.

Over the break.

# 151

"Where did you go?" Johnny asks.

"I was just out surfing," Boone says. "I saw the girl . . . Did she . . ."

"She made it," Johnny says.

Boone smiles and lays his head back on the pillow. The pain in his melon is amazing, an evil combo plate of a vicious hangover and a board bounce off the skull.

"The doctors weren't so sure about you, B," Johnny says. "Whether you were going to come home from the Enchanted Forest. I thought I was going to have to do that paddle-out for you after all."

It had been a hell of a scene out there.

Boone out on the ground.

The little girl in shock.

Tammy Roddick bleeding from a bullet wound. She had saved the girl's life, absorbing most of the bullet's force before it passed through her into Luce. Now Tammy's in a bed down the hallway, not far from the little girl, and they're both going to be all right.

They weren't the only wounded. A couple of *mojados* went seriously John Woo on the snakeheads with a shotgun and a machete, though Terry Gilman didn't think she had enough evidence to make an arrest for that, and, in all the confusion, the *mojados* managed to drift away from the scene.

Also on the plus side, Dan Silver with a hole in his chest you could push your fist through. Which was a temptation, except he was already DOA.

Grandfather, Johnny thinks.

I should have known Grandfather wouldn't allow the family honor to be stained without doing something about it. And, boy, he did.

Harrington fixed the scene. Put the pistol in Dan Silver's hand and asked Grandfather questions that would elicit only answers that pointed to self-defense. Which, in a roundabout way, it was. You take an old man's honor, it's as good as killing him.

"Hey," Johnny says now.

"What?" Boone asks.

"Don't go back to sleep," Johnny says. "You have to stay awake."

Boone opens his eyes and looks around the room. It's crowded. Dave, Sunny, Hang, Tide, Cheerful. Pete's there, too. The nurses had objected, of course, tried to get them all out of there. But Tide had plopped himself down in a chair and asked, "You gonna move me?"

"Not without a derrick," the nurse said.

So the crew stayed. All through the long hours when it was touch-and-go, when Beth came in, took a look at Boone's chart, and told Johnny not to get his hopes up, and one of the other doctors took Cheerful aside and asked him if Boone had a living will.

"A living will?" Cheerful asked. "He doesn't have a checkbook."

Hang was inconsolable. Sat in a chair with his head down, staring at the floor. Dave squatted next to him and said, "Boone's too stupid to die from a few blows to the head. If Silver had clubbed his *ass,* then we'd have something to worry about."

"I was mad at him," Hang said. "He waved at me, but I blew him off."

"He knows you love him," Sunny said. "He loves you, too."

Hang put his face into her shoulder and sobbed.

A few seconds later, Tide said, "Hey, not so loud—you wanna wake him up?"

Which at least made them all laugh. At some point, Sunny had left the room to go out and get coffee for people, when she saw Petra in the hallway. Petra saw her, started to walk away, but Sunny caught up with her. "Where are you going?"

"I don't want to intrude."

"You're not," Sunny said. "Come on, I could use some help."

So the two of them went to the cafeteria, got some coffee and some junk food, and went back together to the room and waited together through the small hours, until Boone woke up and asked about the little girl.

Now he looks over at Sunny and asks, "You ride your wave?"

"You bet."

"You're a big star now."

"I am," Sunny says. "I'm surprised I'm even talking to you."

Boone sees Petra. "Hey."

"Hey."

She looks him in the eye for a second, then looks away, afraid she might start to cry, or show a sudden shyness she's never felt before.

Dave the Love God rescues her. He gets up, walks over to the bed, takes Boone's hand, and says, "Hey, bro."

"Hey."

"You look like hammered shit."

"That good?" Boone says. Then he adds something that convinces everyone but Dave that he still has one foot in the fun house. "Hey, Dave?"

"Yeah?"

"Eddie never saw *The Searchers.*"

# 152

Dave's still there that afternoon when Boone says, "I have to get up."

"You have to lie down," Petra says. "You have a major concussion.

They want you to stay here at least two more days for observation. They're going to run some tests, see if you have brain damage. Although, how'd they tell . . ."

"There's something I have to do," Boone says. He forces himself to sit up, then swings his legs out and puts his feet on the floor. It's sketchy, but he manages to get his legs underneath him and stand up.

"Boone . . ."

He's not listening. He gets dressed and walks down the hall toward the lobby. The nurses ignore him—they have their hands full with people who want help and have no time for people who don't. Johnny follows him in case he falls, but Boone doesn't.

Petra's out in the hallway. "Dave, don't let him be an idiot," she says. "Bring him back."

Dave opens the door for Boone and follows him out.

# 153

They drive south on the 101.

Boone sits in the passenger seat and looks out the window.

Beautiful, beautiful day.

Deep blue ocean.

Deep blue sky.

The big swell is almost over.

"So?" Boone asks.

They've been friends forever. They've ridden a thousand waves together. They're going to tell each other nothing but the truth. Dave tells him all about his work for Red Eddie.

"Did you know?" Boone asks. "About the kids?"

"Not until that night," Dave says. "I called Johnny. I didn't know what else to do."

Boone nods.

They both know what to do now.

# 154

Boone paddles out.

Eddie's on the line on the inside shore break.

"Yo, Boone Dawg!" Eddie yells. Then he sees Boone's head. "What happened to you, my *bruddah*?"

"A little aggro." Boone juts his chin to the outside reef. The waves aren't giant anymore, but they're big, and they're breaking outside. "Let's go outside, Eddie! You got the balls?"

"*Dangling,* brah!"

They paddle out, side by side, then pull up along the shoulder beside the break.

"We need to talk, Eddie."

"Talk."

"The girls," Boone said. "That was your operation."

"No, brah."

"Yeah, it was," Boone says. "The whole story about Dan owing you money was bullshit. You were just trying to cover your pathetic ass."

Eddie's not used to being talked to like that. His eyes get hard. "Watch yourself, Boone."

"You broke your word to me, Eddie," says Boone. "You told me you'd leave Tammy Roddick alone."

"Hey, that was Dan, not me," Eddie says. "I didn't promise anything about Dan."

"You're dirty," Boone says. "And you make everything and everyone around you dirty. I brought you into The Dawn Patrol and you made it ugly. You destroy everything around you, Eddie, just like you took those little kids and destroyed them. I'm sorry I met you. I'm sorry I pulled your son out of the water, if he grows up to be anything like you."

"*You* ever going to grow up, Boone?"

"Yeah," Boone says. "I am."

He shoots out his leg and kicks Eddie off his board.

Eddie falls into the water.

Boone wraps Eddie's leash around his own ankle and watches as Eddie tries to sit up and let himself loose. But Eddie can't reach the Velcro strap around his ankle. He turns and tries to swim, tries to bust to the surface, but Boone back-paddles like a cowboy on a pony with a calf on his rope.

Eddie flips over again and tries to reach Boone. He reaches up, desperately grabbing, first at Boone's foot, then at his own. But Boone just keeps pressing down on the leash, and looks into Eddie's widening eyes.

They say drowning is a peaceful death.

I hope they're wrong, Boone thinks.

He watches Eddie struggle. Watches him suffer.

Then he takes his foot off the leash. Not because he cares about Eddie's life, but because he cares about his own. Eddie grabs for his board, but Boone kicks his hand off. Choking and gasping for air, Eddie asks, "What the—"

"Here's the deal, Julius," says Boone. "I let you back on my board and tow you in to Johnny Banzai. He's already waiting with a warrant. You're looking at thirty to life. Or you go back in the water, and this time you don't come back up. And we'll throw a hell of a fucking party."

He starts to press down on the leash again. "Personally? I hope you take door number two."

But Eddie says, "Take me in."

Boone lets up on the leash and hauls the exhausted Eddie onto his board, then tows him to shore. Johnny's standing on the beach. Slaps the cuffs on Eddie, does the ritual reading of the rights, and shoves him into his car.

Eddie doesn't have one fucking thing to say.

"Are we good?" Dave asks Boone.

"We're good."

It's over.

# 155

Three weeks later.

Dusk on Pacific Beach.

It's cool, sweatshirt weather, as the mist is starting to move in as if the sun were pulling a curtain around its bed before going to sleep.

Boone stands in front of a grill, carefully turning pieces of yellowtail over the low fire. You have to be gentle with yellowtail. You have to cook it slowly or it dries out and loses its juice.

Johnny Banzai stands beside him, supervising.

Johnny lifts a Corona to his lips, takes a swallow, then says, "Harrington is really pissed he can't crank you on this thing."

Boone is too big a hero for anyone to mess with right now. The bust of the child-sex operation is all over the talk-radio stations. There's talk of medals, civic awards. Harrington mumbled to Johnny, "Tell that shitbag this doesn't change anything."

It doesn't, Boone thinks. Not really.

Angela Hart is dead.

And Rain Sweeny, if she's alive, is still in the wind.

"Anyway," Johnny says. "The DA arm-wrestled him into dropping the assault charges against you."

"That," Boone says, "makes the List of Things That Are Good."

"Yes," Johnny says. "But in what position?"

"The eternal question," Boone says.

"Fifth," Hang Twelve suggests.

"In front of free stuff?" High Tide asks. "You're *lolo*."

"Free stuff is very, *very* good," Dave says.

"You could use some free stuff," Cheerful says to Boone. "I've finished your books and free stuff would come in very handy."

"I have a paycheck coming in," Boone says. He gently removes the fish from the grill and sets the pieces on a plate. Then he lays some tortillas on the grill until they are just warm, but not burned.

"How's it coming?" he asks Petra, who sits on the sand with her legs crossed and a cutting board on her lap. She's just finishing slicing up the mango and red onion, and she's staring out at the sun just dipping on the horizon.

They'd talked after he got back from confronting Red Eddie.

"Right, I'll be the one to take the leap," Petra said. "Are we going to see each other again? I mean, outside of our professional relationship."

"Is that what we have?"

"So far."

"I dunno," Boone said. "What do you think?"

"I don't know, either," Petra said. "I mean, I don't know where it could go. We want such different things from life."

"Truth."

"But maybe that's not a *bad* thing," Petra said.

He knew what the smart thing would be. Walk away now. Because they *are* so different, because they *do* want different things from life. But there's something about those eyes you don't walk away from. And something about her.

A *lot* about her.

She's smart, tough, funny, hot, brave, cool.

She's a good person.

They decided to just take things as they come.

And Sunny?

Sunny's out there, he thinks as he watches the sun going down. What a future—all the places she'll go now, all the oceans she'll see, the waves she'll ride. It's her world now, all of it, and who knows if one of those waves will ever bring them together again.

"Here," Petra says. She gets up and hands him the cutting board. Boone slides the chopped mango and onion into a bowl, then adds some lime juice, a little jalapeño, and a handful of cilantro and mixes it all up.

Then he takes the tortillas off the grill, lays a piece of fish on each one, then spoons a generous dollop of the fresh mango salsa over the fish.

"Dinner's ready, guys!" he says.

He hands a taco to Petra.

"God, that's *won*derful," she says.

Boone serves the tacos, then takes a moment to look at the ocean, the setting sun, the long beach.

This is his beach, his world.

His friends.

His family.

"As I've always said . . ." he pronounces.

Everything tastes better on a tortilla.

•

A NOTE ABOUT THE AUTHOR

Don Winslow is a former private investigator and consultant. He lives in California. His previous novels include *The Winter of Frankie Machine, The Power of the Dog, California Fire and Life,* and *The Death and Life of Bobby Z.*

A NOTE ON THE TYPE

The text of this book was set in a typeface named Times New Roman, designed by Stanley Morison (1889–1967) for *The Times* (London) and first introduced by that newspaper in 1932.

Among typographers and designers of the twentieth century, Stanley Morison was a strong forming influence—as a typographical adviser to the Monotype Corporation, as a director of two distinguished publishing houses, and as a writer of sensibility, erudition, and keen practical sense.

Composed by Creative Graphics, Inc.,
Allentown, Pennsylvania
Printed and bound by Berryville Graphics,
Berryville, Virginia
Designed by Virginia Tan